THE TRANSIT OF VENUS

OTHER BOOKS BY
SHIRLEY HAZZARD

Cliffs of Fall

The Evening of the Holiday

People in Glass Houses

The Bay of Noon

*Defeat of an Ideal: A Study of the
Self-Destruction of the
United Nations*

THE TRANSIT OF VENUS

SHIRLEY HAZZARD

PLAYBOY
PAPERBACKS

The author wishes to thank the John Simon Guggenheim Memorial Foundation, and its president, Mr. Gordon Ray, for the generous award of a fellowship in connection with this work.

A portion of this book originally appeared in *The New Yorker.*

ACKNOWLEDGMENTS

Editions Gallimard: "Le Dernier Poème" from *Domaine Public* by Robert Desnos.

A. J. Gurr: From *The Maid's Tragedy* by Beaumont and Fletcher.

Macmillan Publishing Co., Inc., and A. P. Watt Ltd.: From "Meditations in Time of Civil War." Copyright 1928 by Macmillan Publishing Co., Inc., renewed 1956 by Georgie Yeats. From "Politics." Copyright 1940 by Georgie Yeats, renewed 1968 by Bertha Georgie Yeats, Michael Butler Yeats, and Anne Yeats. Both poems from *Collected Poems* by William Butler Yeats.

Macmillan Publishing Co., Inc.: "At Castle Boterel" from *Collected Poems* by Thomas Hardy (New York: Macmillan, 1953).

New Directions Publishing Corp.: From "Verso Sueltos" and "The Shuffled Deck," *Poems and Anti-Poems* by Nicanor Parra, translated by Miller Williams. Copyright © 1967 by Nicanor Parra.

THE TRANSIT OF VENUS

Published simultaneously in the United States and Canada by Playboy Paperbacks, New York, New York. Printed in the United States of America. Library of Congress Catalog Card Number: 81-80673. Reprinted by arrangement with The Viking Press.

Books are available at quantity discounts for promotional and industrial use. For further information, write to Premium Sales, Playboy Paperbacks, 1633 Broadway, New York, New York 10019.

ISBN: 0-872-16859-X

First Playboy Paperbacks printing August 1981.
Third printing August 1981.

Once more, for Francis

J'ai rêvé tellement fort de toi,
J'ai tellement marché, tellement parlé,
Tellement aimé ton ombre,
Qu'il ne me reste plus rien de toi.

—ROBERT DESNOS
"Le Dernier Poème"

Part I

THE
OLD WORLD

1

By nightfall the headlines would be reporting devastation. It was simply that the sky, on a shadeless day, suddenly lowered itself like an awning. Purple silence petrified the limbs of trees and stood crops upright in the fields like hair on end. Whatever there was of fresh white paint sprang out from downs or dunes, or lacerated a roadside with a streak of fencing. This occurred shortly after mid-day on a summer Monday in the south of England.

As late as the following morning, small paragraphs would even appear in newspapers having space to fill due to a hiatus in elections, fiendish crimes, and the Korean War—unroofed houses and stripped orchards being given in numbers and acreage; with only lastly, briefly, the mention of a body where a bridge was swept away.

That noon a man was walking slowly into a landscape under a branch of lightning. A frame of almost human expectancy defined this scene, which he entered from the left-hand corner. Every nerve—for even barns and wheelbarrows and things without tissue developed nerve in those moments—waited, fatalistic. Only he, kinetic, advanced against circumstances to a single destination.

Farmers moved methodically, leading animals or propelling machines to shelter. Beyond the horizon, provincial streets went frantic at the first drops. Wipers wagged on windshields, and people also charged and dodged to and fro, to and fro. Packages were bunged inside coat-fronts, newspapers upturned on new perms. A dog raced through a cathedral. Children ran in thrilling from playgrounds, windows thudded, doors slammed. Housewives were rush-

ing, and crying out, "My washing." And a sudden stripe
of light split earth from sky.

It was then that the walking man arrived at the path,
and stood. Above him, four old houses were set wide apart
on a high curve of hill: holding down, like placed weights,
the billowing land. He had been given their names in the
village—the names, not of masters but of dwellings. Brick
walls were threadbare, tawny; one showed a side of ivy,
green as an upturned lawn. The farthest and largest house
stood forward from a wood, claiming supremacy.

The man observed from a decisive turn of his own stillness, as if on some great clock he saw the hand fall to the
next stroke before his eyes. He turned off the road on the
first wave of rain and gale, put his suitcase down, took off
his soaked cap, beat it on his side, and stuffed it in a
pocket. His hair sprang up like the crops between the gusts
and, like them, was quickly, wetly flat. He climbed the hill
in the rain, steadily and with no air of wretchedness. Once
he paused to look back at the valley—or vale, it might be
sweetly, tamely called. Peal on peal of thunder swept it,
up and down, until the pliant crops themselves reverberated. On an opposing hill there was a castle—grey, tumid,
turreted, and not unsuited to the storm.

Approaching the farthest house, he paused again, looking
with as much plain interest as if the weather had been fine.
Water ran in his collar from his tilted head. The house
darkened, but stood firm. Through two or three centuries
of minor additions, Peverel had held to scale and con-
gruity like a principle; consistent except for one enlarged
high window—an intentional, frivolous defect like the
piercing of an ear for an ornament.

Mud was streaming over gravel and beaten clay. Ledges
of clipped privet were shaking all over. The man waded
up into the entrance of the house as if from the sea, and
pulled a bell. Quick footsteps were perhaps his own heart-
beats. The woman who opened the door was old, he
thought. Had he himself been a few years older, he might
have promoted her to middle age. Age was coiled in
smooth grey hair, was explicit in skin too delicate for
youth and in a tall if unmartial stance. She drew him in
over the paving of what had been a fine hall. Her eyes

were enlarged and faded with discovering what, by common human agreement, is better undivulged.

How calmly they exchanged names, ignoring the surf at his back and his saturated clothes. The cheap suitcase oozed orange on the black and white floor while Ted Tice took off his raincoat and hung it on a stand, as directed. A smell of wet wool, of socks and sweat was pungently released in the coldly soaped and well-waxed void.

All these slow matters had taken seconds, and in that time it could be seen, too, that the hall was circular, that a bowl of roses stood on a table beside a usual newspaper, beneath a dark picture framed in gold. Under the curve of a stair, a door was open on a corridor of Persian runner. And above, on the arc of stairs, there was a young woman, standing still.

Tice looked up to her. It would have been unnatural not to. He looked up from his wet shoes and his wet smell and his orange blotch of cheap luggage. And she looked down, high and dry. He had an impression of her body in its full dimensions—as if he had passed at her back and seen her strong spine, the black hair parting on the prominent cord of the nape, the fragile crease behind the knee. Her face was in shadow. In any case it would have been too pat, too perfect, if she had been seen to be beautiful.

"I was looking for Tom," she said, and went away.

Ted Tice took up his dissolving suitcase: a new arrival who must keep his counsel among initiates. Who would soon himself look for Tom, or know why others sought him.

"My husband," said Charmian Thrale, "is so much better, and will be down to lunch." Ted Tice was to work with Professor Sefton Thrale, who was so much better, for the months of July and August. In the meantime he was being led by Mrs. Thrale down the Persian carpet, past old photographs and a framed letter with a gold crest, and a series of engravings of the ports of Britain. Now Mrs. Thrale would say, "This is your room," and he would be alone.

She remained in the doorway as he crossed his new floor to put the suitcase where it would do least harm.

"Those double doors at the end of the passage, that is the room where we sit. If you wait in there when you're

ready, one of the girls will look in." As if he minded being
left when, at all times, he welcomed it.

She also mentioned the bathroom. She then said she
would go and set the table. Eventually he would learn this
too—to speak confidently and leave a room.

In the single low window there were blurred, divergent
shrubs and a glimpse of wet palings—all aslant, truncated in
the window frame, like an inept photograph. Scabs of
blackout paint remained on the glass. The bedroom was
plain, and might have done once for an upper servant.
Tice thought these words, "upper servant," without knowing
what they had signified in their time. He had been sent
here to help an eminent, elderly, ailing scientist write an
opinion on the site of a new telescope, and for all he knew
might be himself an upper servant. He was young and poor
and had the highest references—like a governess in an old
story, who marries into the noble family.

He spread crumpled clothes about the room and rum-
maged for a comb. Even his wet hair gave off an auburn
smell. On the table where he put his books there was an
inkstand made of brass and porcelain, and two wooden
pens. He hummed as he sat changing his shoes, occasionally substituting for the hum the words of an old song:

> *"Blow the wind southerly, southerly, southerly,*
> *Blow the wind south o'er the bonny blue sea."*

Then he put his fist to his mouth and thought, and
stared as if he would only slowly believe.

The room with double doors was as cold as the passage.
Chairs of ugly comfort, a rigid, delicate sofa, books elderly rather than old, more flowers. The wind shuddering in
a frozen chimney, the storm a waterfall on the bay window.
Ted Tice sat in one of the elephantine, shabby chairs and
rested his head on the stale extra piece of plush; rapt with
newness and impending newness. The room would have
been a study at one time, or a morning-room—the expression "morning-room" belonging to the same vague literary
category as upper servant. Somewhere there was a larger
room, blatantly unheatable, closed up for the duration.

The wartime phrase came readily, even in peace; even as you wondered, the duration of what.

In the fireplace, below the vacant grate, there was a row of aligned fragments, five or six of them, of toasted bread smeared with a dark paste and dusted with ashes.

He was used to cold and sat as much at his ease as if the room had been warm. He could not physically show such unconcern in the presence of others because the full-grown version of his body was not quite familiar to him; but was easy in his mind, swift and unhurried. From all indications, his body had expected some other inhabitant. He supposed the two would be reconciled in time—as he would know, in time, that the smeared toast was there to poison mice, and that Tom was the cat.

A book beside his chair was closed on a pencil that marked a place. He took it up and read the spine: *"Zanoni. A Novel By The Right Honourable Lord Lytton."* Such a book might well have appeared on the shelves of such a room. That it should be out, open, and read was more improbable.

For an instant he thought it was the same girl who now came in, the girl from the stairs. The reason for this was that they were sisters, although the present one was fair, and shorter.

She said, "I am Grace Bell."

The young man stood and again gave his hand and name. She had a very good new woollen dress, colour of roses. They both knew—it was impossible not to—that he saw her beautiful. But both, because of youth, feigned ignorance of this or any other beauty.

"You've been left in here a long time."

"I didn't realize." Though no fault on his part was involved.

"The lights have gone out. I was sent to bring you."

He had been sitting there in the dark because of the storm.

"It's this way." She spoke in brief announcements. Assurance showed she had been pretty since childhood. "What a lovely little girl"; and then: "Grace is turning into —turning out—quite a beauty." Beauty had turned inward, outward. There had also been classes in deportment.

He admired her ability to walk smoothly with him at her

heels. She was not at all plump but gave a soft impression, yielding. The dress was a rarity to him—the cloth, the cut. It was the first time Ted Tice had noticed the way a dress was made, though he had winced often enough for a brave showing in the clothes of the poor.

The rose-red dress had come from Canada by surface mail, having been posted by the son of this household, a government official to whom Grace Bell was engaged. He was bringing another dress to her when he returned to Britain from the Ottawa conference, and after that they would be married.

A little curled chrysanthemum of a dog was in heaven at her approach. "Grasper, Grasper." The dog jumped up and down, speechless. Someone was shaking a bell. Grace was opening a door. And the lights went up by themselves, as on a stage.

2

You could see the two sisters had passed through some unequivocal experience, which, though it might not interest others, had formed and indissolubly bound them. It was the gravity with which they sat, ate, talked and, you could practically say, laughed. It was whatever they exchanged, not looking at one another but making a pair. It was their eyes resting on you, or on the wall or table, weighing up the situation from a distance of events and feelings: their eyes, which had the same darkness if not the same distinction.

Because they were alike in feature, the contrast in colouring was remarkable. It was not only that one was dark and one fair, but that the one called Caro should have hair so very black, so straight, heavy and Oriental in coarse texture. Grace was for this reason seen to be fairer than she was—as she was judged the lighter, the easier, for the strength of Caro. People exaggerated the fairness, to make things neat: dark she, fair she.

Wearing a cardigan that had perhaps been blue, Caro was pouring water from a jug. You deferred to her future beauty, taking it on trust. In looks, Caro was as yet unfinished, lacking some revelation that might simply be her own awareness; unlike Grace, who was completed if not complete. Grace was smiling and handing corned beef and potatoes, innocently rehearsing a time when the meat and vegetables would be hers indeed. Ted Tice saw then that on her left hand she wore a ring set with diamonds. But had been loyal to Caro before he noticed this.

Caro did not necessarily belong here: Caro would decide at which table she belonged. She was young to have

grasped the need for this. Her other discovery of consequence was also not original: that the truth has a life of its
own. It was perhaps in such directions that her energies
had flowed, leaving her looks to follow as they might.

What she had read had evidently made her impatient
of the prime discrepancy—between man as he might be,
and as he was. She would impose her crude belief—that
there could be heroism, excellence—on herself and others,
until they, or she, gave in. Exceptions could arise, rare and
implausible, to suggest she might be right. To those exceptions she would give her whole devotion. It was apparently
for them she was reserving her humility.

Some of this might be read in her appearance. Having
not yet begun to act, she could indulge a theory. At the
same time, her lips were parted, tender, impressible, as
they might have been in sleep.

They had not yet addressed each other at table, the girls
and the young man. He, with impenetrable simplicity, was
listening to the old astronomer at the head of the table,
the eminent scientist. Your eminence: a jutting crag on
which a collar and tie, and spectacles, had been accurately
placed. Together, the youth and the old man were to read
the world's horoscope. Engrossed in listening, as was only
suitable, Ted Tice nevertheless quickly learned that the
two girls were from Australia, that Caro was staying here
while awaiting a government job in London, and that the
son at the Ottawa conference had the name of Christian.

Despite angina, the father had fast, definite gestures—
taking up his water-glass with a sort of efficiency and
setting it down with a hard little snap. Pressing a napkin
quickly to his sculpted mouth, not to waste time. Snap
snap, snap snap snap. He might have been at a desk rather
than a dining-table. He talked with abrupt velocity, also,
and had already reached the end of the world.

"Your generation will be the one to feel it. Some form
of social structure existed until now. Say what you like
about it. Now we're at the end of all that. You'll be the
ones to bear the brunt."

With rapid satisfaction he pointed out, to Ted and the
girls, their almost culpable bad luck. In the same way,
arrivals at a rainy resort will be told, "We've had fine
weather until today."

"There has been global order of a kind. Say what you like."

That of course they could not do.

When Sefton Thrale said the word "global" you felt the earth to be round as a smooth ball, or white and bland as an egg. And had to remind yourself of the healthy and dreadful shafts and outcroppings of this world. You had to think of the Alps, or the ocean, or a live volcano to set your mind at rest.

Professor Thrale did not much care for the fact that Grace came from Australia. Australia required apologies, and was almost a subject for ribaldry. Australia could only have been mitigated by an unabashed fortune from its newly minted sources—sheep, say, or sheep-dip. And no fabled property of so many thousand acres or square miles, no lucky dip, attached itself to Grace. On the contrary, Grace came encumbered with a sister; and even with a half-sister, happily absent on holiday at Gibraltar. Sefton Thrale would explain, "Christian has got himself engaged"—implying naïve bungling—"to an Australian girl." And with emphatic goodwill might add that Grace was a fine young woman and that he himself was delighted, "Actually."

The storm had drawn off for a breather. By daylight Ted Tice's face was seen speckled and flaked, artless as the face reflected in the salty mirror of a seaside kiosk in summer. His forehead was divided by a slight vertical groove. He had an injury to one eye—a brother had done it when they were children, playing in the yard with a stick: a light streak like the scratch of a fingernail on new paint.

"Mustard, Mr. Tice?" Professor Thrale was thinking it was downright fashionable these days to be a poor boy from a grimy town, a clever boy who got himself—the phrase implying contrivance this time—to a great university and made his impression there. Such persons went forward quickly, having nothing to relinquish; and might well attach themselves, as in this case, to new aspects of astronomy developed from radar techniques of the last war. It all hung together. Sefton Thrale recalled a paper, like a twinge of his illness, on which Ted Tice's precocious achievement was set out against all the odds; where willfulness was not disproved by aberrant undertakings—studies of radiation in postwar Japan, and an intention of spending the coming winter in Paris at work with a controversial physicist.

Sefton Thrale said to himself that Ted Tice would wind up in America: "That is where he will wind up"—a young man's ambition envisaged as a great winch on which abilities might be deftly and profitably coiled.

"The vegetables," said Mrs. Thrale, "are from our garden."

Over the braised celery Sefton Thrale indulged a rather reckless distaste for Ted Tice's clothes, curls, and accent, and for the fault in his eye. Tice's future ascendancy could not, like Caro's beauty, be taken on faith: some sign was needed as to whether he would win or fail—both possibilities being manifestly strong in him. Even if he were at last to carry all before him, it was hard to imagine him properly illustrious in age, like the Professor himself. It was hard to foresee that a name like Tice might carry weight, or that a streaked eye could become a distinction.

In fact Edmund Tice would take his own life before attaining the peak of his achievement. But that would occur in a northern city, and not for many years.

Sefton Thrale's own important work had been accomplished in youth, before the Great War. Later on he became a public figure by writing a small, lucid book that bridged, or claimed to bridge, a gulf or gap. He had stood with his unbudging foot on the fire-guard and his hand in his pocket, and talked of the future; and had kept this up so long and so publicly that persons of all kinds now recognized him at sight in the Sunday papers—"Still going strong, eh, you have to hand it to him." Unwieldy old geezer in a blazer of black-and-white vertical stripes. The blazer—pulled down at one side by his hand jammed in the pocket, gripping the presumed pipe—gave the effect of a sagging, half-timbered house.

He used outworn idiom: "Lombard Street to a china orange," "All round China to get to Charing Cross"; "The Old Lady"—even—"of Threadneedle Street": phrases outdated before his time, which he cultivated and kept going if not alive. Still spoke of Turkey as "the sick man of Europe," though the entire Continent was a casualty ward long since. His sympathies were with the manageable distances of the past rather than the extravagant reach of the future. The future had been something to talk about, one foot safely on the fender.

It was easy for youth to scent this out and condemn. Less easy to feel for what was human in it, let alone pitiful.

In the main Professor Thrale was allowed to hold forth, as now, in quick orations that supposed no disagreement. But, if challenged, lost his sure grip on pipe and future. A cloud of confused indignation would then rise from him, like dust from an old book whose covers have been banged together for cleaning. In private matters he had not been clever and had dissipated his wife's fortune, like his own potential, in naïve investments. A knighthood, now forthcoming, had been long delayed. But his name was public, and weighed in a public and political affair such as siting a telescope.

Ted Tice took mustard. It came out that he had been on holiday these past two weeks, walking in the West Country. He had an interest, furthermore, in prehistoric monuments, and had spent the solstice at an excavation near Avebury Circle. It was not difficult to imagine lofty stones as his companions.

Mrs. Thrale said they sometimes received, at Peverel, vibrations from the missile base near Stonehenge. Though considerately fired away from the monument, the rockets were not without local danger. A window had once shattered in a guest's bedroom, luckily causing no injury.

"Ah, yes," said Sefton Thrale. "But Paul Ivory carries his luck with him." Plucking the unknown guest out from the glass shards and flourishing him, in order to exclude Ted Tice; and, with this need to impress, offering Tice the advantage. "What news of Paul, by the way? Any news of Paul?"

Ted Tice was aware that men already hoped for his good opinion. And that, if balked of it, they might try condescension.

Palliating the Professor's misdemeanour, the three women quickly testified to an absence of news. And Ted Tice perceived that women's indulgence had been indispensable to Sefton Thrale's fame. As was expected of her, Mrs. Thrale made known that Paul Ivory was her godson, who would shortly come to stay. Ted might have heard of plays by Paul Ivory, in university productions; but had not. Well, in any case, a young person of promise who was soon to have a work produced on the London stage.

"Paul has all the qualities," said Sefton Thrale, and might have been making some contrast.

"Is he related to the poet?"

"In fact, the son."

Ted Tice could hardly know the subtle disturbance generated by his question—love for the Georgian poets being the remnant of Sefton Thrale's best self, which in turn derived, like his best work, from an earlier period. He would bring them in, forgotten or disparaged poets of his youth, with loyal calculation—the poignant quotation, the interviewer asking, "Now who said that?" and Thrale's retort: "A fine poet who died about the time you were born, young man" (the Professor having all the benign and practised public tricks); then the identification—of Bridges, Drinkwater, Shanks, or Humbert Wolfe; Thomas Sturge Moore; even Rupert Brooke on days when dander was up. Or Rex Ivory.

Mrs. Thrale remarked, "Rex Ivory was not a great poet. But he was a true poet." She felt it was an odd misconception that scientists had no taste for literature: "I have known many examples to the contrary."

Ted smiled. "I think we're permitted to be musical."

On occasion, Caroline Bell's eyes were as kind as her sister's. "They are also supposed to be taciturn."

"I may grow less articulate as I get older."

Charmian Thrale pointed out a photograph above the sideboard. Three young men in a garden, two of them seated in cane chairs, one standing with hands raised and spread. The standing figure, in open shirt and white trousers, declaimed to the others, who were conventionally dressed in their clothes of 1913. Heads of pale hair were helmets, were crowns or halos. A larger nimbus arched the garden, where trees were massed above larkspur and a long lawn was methodically streaked with rolling. It seemed to be near dusk. And the magical youths on the grass were doomed by coming war, even the survivors.

Charmian Thrale said, "Like an eve in a sinless world."

The remnant of the Sefton Thrale seated in that sinless photograph would have wished to make fellowship with

Edmund Tice because of his improbable inquiry. Again the women knew it, and sighed in their thoughts over the old man's curt answer: "In fact, the son."

The Professor proceeded to elaborate his preference, deftly aligning fork and knife. "Paul Ivory has already established some place for himself in literature. And is rising so swiftly that there is no telling where he may yet go."

Ted Tice grinned, by no means defenceless. "Like Heisenberg's Uncertainty Principle. Impossible to measure speed and position simultaneously."

It seemed that Caroline Bell could giggle like other girls.

"And is all but engaged"—the Professor was determined to prevail—"to the daughter of our neighbour at the castle."

Ted wondered what "all but engaged" might mean, and saw Caro smile with the selfsame thought. Whatever heresy had existed in this house had come from upper servants.

He recalled the castle, its grey walls discouraging even to lichens.

Seeing into their souls, the Professor told them, "It's a brave man these days who'll marry the daughter of a lord. With all you radicals around." This was meant for Ted and Caro, since Grace's way of quietly stacking plates exonerated her. Yet it was Grace who looked up and said, "Perhaps he loves her."

"Perfectly right. Young people should follow their fancy. Why not? Caro here would marry a mechanic if she was so minded."

They looked at Caro, who said, "I am not mechanically minded."

Sefton Thrale always felt worsted when there was laughter.

The girl went on, "It's true. I'm not only ignorant but have no affinity for mechanical things. Or for science either."

"You owe your existence to astronomy, young woman." Young man, young woman; yet they could not say, old man, old woman. The Professor was preparing to explain, when Caro said, "Do you mean, the transit of Venus?"

It was not the first time she had spoiled things.

He continued as if she had neither spoiled nor spoken. "Why did James Cook set sail in H.M.S. *Endeavour* for undiscovered Australia if not to observe, en route, at Tahiti, the planet Venus as it crossed the face of the sun on the third of June 1769 and thus to determine the distance of earth from sun?" He was teaching them a lesson.

Again they looked at Caro, established as a child of Venus.

Tice said, "The calculations were hopelessly out." Siding with the girl. "Calculations about Venus often are."

Sefton Thrale said, "There were distortions in the disc of Venus. A phenomenon of irradiation in the transit." It might have been his own expedition, or experience, he defended. "We call it the Black Drop."

The girl marvelled. "The years of preparation. And then, from one hour to the next, all over."

The young man explained that there were stages. He said, "There are the contacts, and the culmination."

They both blushed for the universe.

Professor Thrale said, "Now you are speaking of eclipse. Venus cannot blot out the sun." He flicked crumbs from his cuff. One could not relate in the presence of two virgins how, at Tahiti on that blazing day of June 1769, Venus had been busy in other matters. While their officers were engrossed with James Short's telescopes, the crew of the *Endeavour* had broken into the stores at Fort Venus to steal a heap of iron spike-nails—with which they procured for themselves the passing favours of Tahitian women; and the permanent infection of a venereal disease no subsequent floggings could cure.

Ted Tice said, "Another astronomer crossed the world to see that same transit, and was defeated." The inward tone in which men speak, casually, of what moves them. Tice could not teach a lesson, but would pay tribute. "A Frenchman had travelled to India years before to observe a previous transit, and was delayed on the way by wars and misadventure. Having lost his original opportunity, he waited eight years in the East for that next transit, of 1769. When the day came, the visibility was freakishly poor, there was nothing to be seen. There would not be another such transit for a century."

He was telling this to, and for, Caroline Bell. At that

moment he and she might have been the elders at the table, elegiac. She said, "Years for Venus."

"His story has such nobility you can scarcely call it unsuccessful." Ted Tice was honouring the faith, not the failure.

Professor Thrale had had enough of this. "And the poor devil returned to France, as I recall, to find himself declared dead in his absence, and his property dispersed." If that wasn't failure, nothing was.

The girl asked Ted Tice: "What was his name?"

"Legentil. Guillaume Legentil."

Mrs. Thrale had made custard. A mottled Irish maid brought dishes on a tray. Mrs. Thrale had been brought up to believe, on pain of losing her character, that her back must never touch the chair: never, never. This added to her air of endurance, and made it seem also that she looked you in the face more than is usual. It was she who had thought of the summer seaside in regard to the quality of Ted Tice—the speckled mirror dangling among the tags for deck-chairs and the keys for bath-houses, all vibrant with a warm padding of sandy feet. On the other hand, there were his nights spent among primitive stones.

Charmian Thrale's own reclusive self, by now quite free of yearnings, merely cherished a few pure secrets—she had once pulled a potato from a boiling pot because it showed a living sprout; and had turned back, on her way to an imperative appointment, to look up a line of Meredith. She did not choose to have many thoughts her husband could not divine, for fear she might come to despise him. Listening had been a large measure of her life: she listened closely—and, since people are accustomed to being half-heard, her attention troubled them, they felt the inadequacy of what they said. In this way she had a quieting effect on those about her, and stemmed gently the world's flow of unconsidered speech. Although she offered few opinions, her views were known in a way that is not true of persons who, continually passing judgment, keep none in reserve.

The girls' curved necks were intolerably exposed as they spooned their custard: you could practically feel the axe. Upright Mrs. Thrale could never be felled in the same way, at least not now. The young man and the girls remarked among themselves on the delayed season—"the late summer," as if it were already dead. They were like travellers managing an unfamiliar tongue, speaking in infinitives. Everything had the threat and promise of meaning. Later on, there would be more and more memories, less and less memorable. It would take a bombshell, later, to clear the mental space for such a scene as this.

Experience was banked up around the room, a huge wave about to break.

While the girls were clearing the table, the Professor led the young man to the windows, saying, "Let me show you." A rub of his dry, decisive hand on the damp glass only increased the blur, and he turned away, sulky: "Well, you cannot see it now." Not saying what new lesson would be taught on this blackboard.

Ted Tice knew it was the road he had come.

3

In the previous year Christian Thrale, who was then in his twenties, unexpectedly had an evening free from weekend work at a government office. In retrospect it seemed to have been an evening free, also, of himself. He did not often go alone to a concert or anything else of the cultural kind. On your own, you were at the mercy of your responses. Accompanied, on the other hand, you remained in control, made assertive sighs and imposed hypothetical requirements. You could also deliver your opinion, seldom quite favourable, while walking home.

As to pleasure, he was suspicious of anything that relieved his feelings.

The concert, on that particular evening, was furthermore too easy to get into. Yet, passing in light rain, he saw posters and bought a seat on the aisle.

He was scarcely in place when he had to stand again to let two women into the row. He lifted the folded mackintosh, the hat, and damp umbrella he had dumped on the empty seat alongside; and the younger woman, having stood back for the elder, now sat there. He had noticed her large-eyed good looks at once when she glanced up saying Sorry. But as the struggling out of coats went on, and the drawing off of stubborn gloves, he lost interest.

It was the other woman he next became aware of.

The older woman was small and dark and wore a red felt circlet on her head, trimmed with navy ribbon. Around her shoulders there was looped a swag of sharp little furs —the mouth of one fur fastened, peglike and with needle teeth, on the paw of the other. In her lap a handbag was crammed squat, and she dried this with rustling paper.

That she was in some way related to the girl, though not of an age to be her mother, was evident from their manner together.

It was hard to summarize, even in guesses, even in his mind, the relation of girl to woman. Until, as the musicians started to appear and more arrivals pushed along the rows, the phrase came to him: she is in her power.

The older woman had been coaxed for an outing, in the desperation of an interminable Sunday. That she expected nothing of the music was apparent from her turning this way and that, providing her own discordant tuning-up. "How people rig themselves out, will you just look at that one. I ask you." "They might've done the place up a bit by now. Wouldn't you think. They mean to use the war as an excuse forever." The girl sat quietly, an evasion she would not be allowed to get away with.

"You're cheery I must say. First you tell me I'm depressed, and then you don't have a solitary word to say for yourself."

Now that he knew the association was founded in fear, he still wondered whether they were cousins, perhaps, or aunt and niece. When she turned his way, the wide, high slope of the little woman's bright cheeks recalled the girl's.

"Not a breath of air in here." She flapped the furs on her breast, and the pronged fox-face snapped up and down. "That's the way you catch things. Remind me to gargle when we get home."

The lights lowered. Throughout the first work Christian was aware of the woman simmering there, a boiling turned low. The girl between them was impassive, hands lightly clasped, slim knees aligned under dark skirt. At the interval the little woman, murmuring to the girl, got up and went out to the ladies'.

She was no sooner down the aisle than Christian spoke. He had never done such a thing in his life, but knew there was no time to lose. They got swiftly through some piffle about Sibelius, and by the time the duenna returned Christian had written a phone number and suggested Saturday. All this, which should have seemed extraordinary to him, appeared inevitable and entirely right.

He got to his feet, and Grace said, "Dora, this is Mr. Thrale." He saw Dora's face flash with the realization they had stolen a march on her, and with an impulse to spoil things. Dora saw a sandy man, quite tall, who could easily present a threat. Christian had discovered they were half-sisters and from Australia. When the concert was over, he put them in a cab.

He did not, during that week, tell himself I must have been besotted, even though besotted was one of his words. He knew that something out of the ordinary had been set in motion. But did wonder if it would survive reunion with Grace, whose attraction could well decline at an address of furnished rooms. One would then be faced with the process of coming to one's senses. To do him justice, Christian Thrale feared rather than hoped for this.

On the Saturday he went to W. 11 by taxi, to take off the pall. The stairs were freshly painted white and had a scarlet carpet. There was a glass jar of yellow flowers on a landing.

It had not occurred to him, he himself might have brought.

As he went up he was shamed by a sense of adventure that delineated the reduced scale of his adventures. After the impetuous beginning, he would puzzle them by turning out staid and cautious. In a gilt mirror near the door he surprised himself, still young.

Grace's beauty was a vindication. He had relied on it, and it did not let him down. She was calm, as before, and smiled. There were the gold flowers again, on a table. Christian sat on a furnished-looking settee. No, no difficulty at all finding the address and knew the area quite well, actually, from once having had a dentist nearby. A kettle whistling in a kitchenette was swiftly muzzled by, he assumed, Dora.

Caro brought in the tray. My sister. A place was cleared for cups and plates. Christian sat again, and Caro opposite, with Grace bent between them: Is that too strong, these are from Fortnum's. With a silver blade she laid open a quadrant of cake. A little furrow of concentration between her eyes was beguiling as the grooved brow of a kitten. On the sofa Christian was a man on a river-bank, not so much gazing at the other side as aware of a current into which he must plunge. He saw Grace shining and rippling over afternoon stones. She leadeth me beside the still waters.

Opposite, Caro's still waters ran deep.

Unfortunately Dora has had to go to Wigmore Street to pick up her new glasses. Thank God. It was clear that Dora battened on the girls' occasions, might be absent from necessity but never from tact. As in the concert hall, it was evident they must make the most of the time before she returned, get things to a pitch where she could not reverse them. In relief at no Dora, Christian sat easy, had a second cup, and was pleased. Into the furnished staleness there came cool air from a window, and a scent of bath salts or cologne.

Against the light, Caro's head and shoulders were remarkable. Once or twice he made her laugh. But when he leaned for biscuits felt her eyes on him as if. As if, for instance, she knew about the sense of adventure on the stairs.

He found these women uncommonly self-possessed for their situation. They seemed scarcely conscious of being Australians in a furnished flat. He would have liked them to be more impressed by his having come, and instead caught himself living up to what he thought might be their standards and hoping they would not guess the effort incurred. Quickness came back to him like a neglected talent summoned in an emergency: as if he rose in trepidation to a platform and cleared his throat to sing.

The room itself appeared unawed by him—not from any disorder but from very naturalness. A room where there had been expectation would have conveyed the fact —by a tension of plumped cushions and placed magazines, a vacancy from unseemly objects bundled out of sight; by suspense slowly dwindling in the curtains. This room was quite without such anxiety. On its upholstery, the nap of the usual was undisturbed. No tribute of preparation had been paid him here, unless perhaps the flowers, which were fresh and which he himself if he had only thought.

It was a high room that Grace said had seen better days.

Christian said, "I can't imagine a better day than this."

A few objects, and the books, evidently their own. There was a warped picture of a woman's head painted on wood.

"Caro got it in Seville."

"It's an angel."

Caro had been three months in Spain for the language.

To do this she had gone as nursemaid to an English family, who had afterwards taken her to France and to Italy. Caro was now working—serving was what she said—in a bookshop while studying for a government examination.

It was even worse with Grace, who was in the Complaints Department at Harrods.

There could be no outcome to such activities but marriage. He knew all about Caro's examination and she would never pass it. It had only recently been opened to women, and he had never heard of a woman passing it. "It is stiff," he said. It did not even lead to prospects, you came in at the lower level, it was a way of having people with languages without giving them career service.

"An exploitation, if you like," he concluded.

Caro said, "I don't like," and took a cream wafer. "Peek Frean's," she read, before biting the lettering in half.

"I shall confine myself to saying," he began again, and stopped. He did not know where he got these expressions, I confine myself, I shall refrain from, I withhold comment upon—as if he had placed himself under house arrest. It might be from his father. He asked with whom had she dealt, where was she to present herself. And over the officials and bureaux of her answers assented with knowing confirmation—as a Greek will sagely nod at the mention of Hesiod or Pindar even if he has never read a line of them.

The situation of Grace was more pointed still, an abeyance. What could she possibly learn in a Complaints Department?

"I," said Grace Bell, "have learned that a soft answer does not turn away wrath." The girls fell to laughing together, their bodies slightly inclined each to each even across a tea-table.

Caro told him, "London is our achievement. Our career, for the time being." As if she read through his forehead like glass. "Having got here is an attainment, being here is an occupation."

Like a creature whose lair has been observed, he shifted to new cover. "Very sensible not to plan too far ahead."

They would talk about him afterwards, and Caro would adjudicate. He did not know if Grace would abide by the verdict or not. Caro would bite him in half like a biscuit.

He wondered how Caro stood up to Dora, and for a moment would have been curious to see them together. When Caro got to her feet, when she brought hot water or closed a window, she moved with consequence as if existence were not trivial.

When these girls were small their parents had drowned in a capsized ferry. Christian was to refer to this as "a boating accident" for the rest of his life.

"And do you then," to show his independence of their futures, "mean to try out life here, and return to—was it —Sydney?"

Caro laughed. "Life doesn't work that way."

As if she knew, and he did not.

A plate on which biscuits had lain was old, chipped, Italian, and had a border of rustic lettering. Caro had brought it from Palermo. Saying "May I?", Christian took it up and read aloud, turning the disc to decipher: *"Chi d'invidia campa, disperato muore.* Who lives—if I'm right? —in envy, dies in despair." He put it back on the table. The angel had been charming; the plate had a sharper edge.

How happy he was, all the same. Christian, who often feared to find himself in obscure conditions, in a monochrome where his colours might not prove fast. Given the present circumstances—the furnished room, the brute fact of Sydney, the desk at Harrods, and the examination already as good as failed—this should now have been overwhelmingly the case. But was not, by any means.

These women provided something new to Christian—a clear perception unmingled with suspiciousness. Their distinction was not only their beauty and their way with one another, their crying need of a rescue for which they made no appeal whatever; but a high humorous candour for which—he could frame it no other way—they would be willing to sacrifice.

Christian was happy. Grace had done that for him. She will make you very happy.

The degree of good faith being required of him amounted to a mild abandon, but he did not want to botch this afternoon. His chances in life seemed bound up with the colours of girls' dresses, the streaks of curtain at windows, a painted angel; and even with a tea-cosy of crocheted orange, felted with handling, that said everything about the landlord. Turned to him, there were the two long figures in light. He would have liked to think, Sargent; but feared something more disruptive, like Vermeer.

There were intervals when he knew that he was the one in need of rescue, that Grace might easily do better than take up with him, and that Caro would pass the examination ahead of all the rest. But health was hard to maintain: self-importance flickered up like fever.

There was something else now, with the three of them in that room, some event or at least a moment. Whatever this was, the excitement in it was displacing the calm, the charm. It was quickly past. Christian knew that Grace was as much as he could manage; she was already a departure, though of his own unexpected choosing. Caro was beyond his means. He was like a cabinet minister faced with a capital decision. On the brink of the sofa he renounced any possibility of Caro. There was deliverance in this, and a flow of propitiatory emotion towards Grace.

Now that Caro had proved too much for him, he almost disliked her.

Grace was telling about a customer who had sent back a dead canary in a box, for refund. Christian must soon make himself clear. A third meeting would be commitment of a kind, to a chain of new circumstances.

"And got it back stuffed, from Taxidermy, with a bill for five guineas!"

Christian was laughing out loud with relief. He could hear this laughter of his that showed what he could do when given a chance. In his laughter it was as if he already took Grace in his arms.

She came downstairs to see him out. Dora, now in sight along the street, performed her usual function of bringing matters to a head. He asked Grace to dine with him during the week, and she made an arrangement for Wednesday. They repeated time and place like vows, safe forever from the sharp heels of Dora on the path.

Christian quite strongly did not want to see Dora, but waited to greet her and hoped for credit from Grace. Dora's hair was netted in a veiling cap, like thatch under wire. She dropped her key, and bumped her head on Christian's as they both bent down for it. This in turn gave rise

to false little gasps of overdone apology. Christian knew
the type. She was one of those persons who will squeeze
into the same partition of a revolving door with you, on
the pretext of causing less trouble.

By the time he got home he had forgotten Caro. It was
years before he seriously considered her again, or before
she became the object of another cabinet-level review. Long
before Wednesday he began to wish for Grace, and when
the evening came was more charming to her than he had
ever been to anybody in his life.

4

"Have we missed it?"

Ted Tice was staring up the country road for the bus. Caroline Bell was looking round at roadside trees and tangling gardens that no Australian could take for granted. Signs of last month's storm were difficult to find: however hard you might look, the earth insisted there was nothing wrong. Tice stood ungainly, his character loose on him that day like clothes he must grow into. His question did not wake her.

They had little to say under the heavy trees. It was when the bus trundled and they got on board that they began to speak, starting up along with the ancient snorting engine and the metal shudder of flanks and the raised voices of other passengers. The bus enclosed them like social obligation. Or it was departure that loosened their tongues, a reminder, as they wound down the valley of the River Test. Caro, though leaning back, arm extended to brace herself against the seat in front, showed no desire to be mistress of the situation. Ted Tice looked down her profile of eyelid and lip, down her blue shoulder and breast and her bare arm to where her hand grasped the rusted metal of a seat-back. Her body had a more distinct outline when she was parted from her sister.

An hour had already passed, of this day they were to spend together. Ted Tice was glad of each additional mile, which would at least, at last, have to be retraced. Every red and noticeable farmhouse, every church or sharp right turn was a guarantee of his time with her. He said, "Are you thinking how tame it is, all this?" He meant the floral English summer, but could have been understood otherwise.

35

In fact he was not bold enough to touch her, but made his gesture to her head. "What are you thinking?"

Caro had been watching out the window, and turned the same look of general, landscaped curiosity on him. This man was no more to her then than a callow ginger presence in a cable-stitch cardigan. The country bus lurched over an unsprung road. The girl thought that in novels one would read that he and she were flung against each other; and how that was impossible. We can only be flung against each other if we want to be. Like rape, men say.

"I was thinking the summer is violent, rather than tame." It was her second summer of the northern kind, an abundance that overwhelmed—as did the certainty that it could be dismantled and remounted indefinitely: Nature in a mood impassive, prodigious, absolute. "Australian summer is a scorching, without a leaf to spare. Out there, the force is in the lack, in the scarcity and distance." Remembering distances of ageless desolation, she wondered if she was defining frailty. "For colours like these, you need water." But, even with water, in Australia the pigment might not be there. It was doubtful that pinks or blues lay dormant in Australian earth; let alone the full prestige of green.

She looked again out the window, full face like a child, and thought that here the very fields seemed intended for pleasure. As to the multiplication and subtraction of seasons, she had of course known perfectly, beforehand, how leaves fall in deciduous England. But still been unprepared for anything extreme as autumn—more, in its red destruction, like an act of man than of God.

They left an abbey afloat on a swell of trees, and passed through a town of overhead wires and small discouraged shops.

"Great Expectations," said Caro, who could read the billboard at the far-off picture-house. The bus halted, and retrundled. The regularity of suburban streets had been shorn back for a highway: the new road fanned out across a rise, houses splayed back like buttons released over a paunch. In a blighted field a capsized merry-go-round was turning to rust; a strung-up sign had lost its introductory F, and read, in consequence, UNFAIR. A barn squatted by the roadside like an abandoned van. The bus plunged forward. At its roaring, a small car withdrew into a hedge: an animal bayed.

Ted said, "It used to be, in England, that you were never far from countryside. Now you are always near a town." He had begun to look with antipodean eyes, because of Caro.

"I'll be living in a city ever after." Caroline Bell was soon to start work in the government office. "I have to wait until there is the post."

He thought, She already has the jargon then—but she went on, "Post, post. Like being tied to a stake in a field. Like a gibbet at a crossroads."

They smiled at this moonlit image of dangling Caro: Caro would swing for it. Whatever they said mattered to him. Instead of making phrases about towns and offices they might have been asking, "What will become of us?" or "Do you believe in God?" The girl felt a man's breath speaking on her neck. A river trailed willows at her side; a pale spire appeared, scarcely mineral. The bus plunged and bucked, determined to unseat them. We are flung against each other.

Where they got down, wrought-iron gates were folded back like written pages. Guarding this calligraphy there was a white-haired man, one arm missing and the ribbons of old battles on his chest.

"You're just in time." A notice gave hours of visiting, as if the great house beyond were a patient in hospital. The guard called after them, "Better look lively." And they laughed and did so.

Caro had taken up a song from Ted Tice and sang "Southerly, southerly" in a high voice, light and none too tuneful, as she lifted both hands to shade her eyes. For that instant at least, these two were no more than the world took them for—young, hopeful, and likely to become lovers.

"Of course we never saw any of this." It was the great house in which Ted Tice had once been a child evacuee from the blitz. "It doesn't even seem to be the same house." Resplendent indoor colours of silk and velvet and porcelain might themselves have been a prerogative of ruling classes.

Caro said, "Perhaps we took the wrong bus." They were laughing and looking out the windows. The house was all of stone. Outside, below the broad sill, there was a mass of mock orange; there were Buddleia bushes, purple and full of bees; roses as a matter of course, and sweet peas. The clippings of ornate hedges were being gathered up by gardeners—all England being trimmed and snipped, shorter and shorter.

"Does the Rape of the Sabines mean anything to you?"

The guide was reaching up with a white rod. Her voice was also on English tip-toe, though heard by the obedient crowd. They saw the picture, hugely Italian, swirl with outraged limbs; the red lips parted on the painted cry. Caro and Ted were laughing by the windows. The Rape of the Sabines meant nothing to them.

The tour shuffled. There was a restraining loop of twisted cord and a notice: VISITORS ARE KINDLY REQUESTED. Emotions were roused by a cascade of painted decoration falling from an immense height. There were goddesses, there were fantastic garlands, urns and balustrades, and any amount of gold. In such a room the house was felt to be harbouring some other, too lavish nation; and barely escaped treachery.

"These walls were boarded up in the war. And are by Rubens." The crowd became intent, not seeing the paintings now so much as the interesting and ingenious planking that had once obscured them. "The battle theme of the west wall merits special attention, if you consider the Second Front was planned in this room." Yes, it was true: commanders had sat here in battle dress and the map of France had hung, in its turn, over the boarded canvas of flung drapery and glistening flesh; and Mars in truth had covered Venus. A bald general had practised putts on the underfelt, while a prime minister, not to be outdone, had painted a picture of his own.

The crowd had not realized. They had been thinking the house long past its serious phase. And wanted to know, how was the table placed, and what about Montgomery.

"Yes, they were here." The dove-coloured guide had laid her rod on a table and was showing with her hands, like an artist. "All the architects of the invasion." As if war, too, were some stately edifice. She had removed her glasses and, with a small red impress each side of the nose, was a bird delicately marked. She was happy to please with her important information—the general's putts, the statesman's placed easel. And was glad, also, for the family in their great possession.

The tour shifted along to another loop of cord. A notice once more asked, or kindly requested, that they do or refrain from doing; and went on to say that the library was lined with books to within ten feet of the ceiling (which itself depicted the story—pastel, concave, and none too decent—of Deianira and Hercules). Far below, the carpet was figured in pale colours like reflections. On polished tables photographs stood at angles, in silver frames, and were signed. You could see, time and again, the great R after the name.

"Queen Alexandria, Princess Pat." The crowd picked them out, expert certainly in this. They prowled among chiffoniers and credenzas, and no one had the heart to deny. The dead and executed, the Russian and Prussian princes, struck no pity or terror: it was part of their privileged destiny, all one with the magnificence, the tiaras, the stars and garters, and long ropes of pearl.

A man in herringbone said, "That's the bleeder." Heads turned sharply, but were soon nodding for the affliction of the little doomed Tsarevich.

"Note the unusual group of the generations. And the Duke of Kent shortly before he was killed by Cecil Beaton." There was no lack of appreciation. A woman in paisley print was asked, most reasonably, not to touch.

"Indeed, it is the very same house," said Ted Tice. Where there was a sign, THIS WAY, they went downstairs together.

From outside, the house was seen to be sculptured. There was no imagining ribs, beams, architraves, or stages of laborious construction. Virginia creeper reached the flaking windows of the room where generals had charted death; and a great wistaria strangled columns in a silent portico. The house prepared for mouldering as for another phase of life.

Ted Tice sat with Caro on the lawn. The girl hugged her knees and said, "The creators of such a house should themselves be beautiful."

"Probably the house was as much as they could manage in the way of beauty." The ginger man lay back on turf, arms beneath his head, and recited in his regional voice:

"That they,
Bitter and violent men, might rear in stone
The sweetness that all longed for night and day."

Caro's dress moulded a blue kneecap. "Do you suppose anyone anywhere is longing, or rearing the evidence now?"

"If so, they'd best keep it dark, or they'll cop hell." By now, longing itself might be an admission of failure. Ted said, "Beauty is the forbidden word of our age, as Sex was to the Victorians. But without the same power to reassert itself." He might have been echoing Sefton Thrale: You'll be the ones to bear the brunt.

Ted Tice sat with Caro on the lawn. A silence can easily fall between those who do not consider themselves a topic. And in any case the air was filled with the blunt sounds and green smells of the pruning and cropping. England was being cut back to the roots for its own good; that is the way you build character. The gardeners in grey shirts moved to put a stop to growth, or to hold it in check. Green fell in every form, and was carried off in baskets.

"They are cutting down the very colour." Caroline Bell leaned forward and smiled to see her long belief justified. "The green we only knew about from books."

5

"Grey Winter hath gone, like a wearisome guest,
And, behold, for repayment,
September comes in with the wind of the West
And the Spring in her raiment."

You might recite it in Elocution Class, but could hardly have it in English poetry. It was as if the poet had deliberately taken the losing, and Australian, side. He had grasped the nettle. But a nettle grasped remains a nettle, and grasping it an unnatural act. What was natural was hedgerows, hawthorn, skylarks, the chaffinch on the orchard bough. You had never seen these but believed in them with perfect faith. As you believed, also, in the damp, deciduous, and rightful seasons of English literature and in lawns of emerald velours, or in flowers that could only be grown in Australia when the drought broke and with top-dressing. Literature had not simply made these things true. It had placed Australia in perpetual, flagrant violation of reality.

Little girls sang, sing-song:

"Come down to Kew in lilac-time (it isn't far from London!)."

Involving themselves in a journey of ten thousand miles. For a punishment you might, after school, write one hundred times:

Self-reverence, self-knowledge, self-control:
These three alone lead life to sovereign power.

41

The little girls licked nibs of tin and fingered pigtails, preparing for sovereign power.

History was the folding coloured view of the Coronation that had been tacked on the classroom wall—the scene in the Abbey, with the names printed beneath. The Duke of Connaught, the Earl of Athlone, the slender King in ermine. Dora bought a coronation mug at Woolworth's: Long May They Reign. That was History, all of a piece with the Black Prince and the Wars of the Roses. Grace and Caro had been allowed to stay up one summer night to hear the Abdication crackle over the short-wave. Something you'll remember always.

Australian History, given once a week only, was easily contained in a small book, dun-coloured as the scenes described. Presided over at its briefly pristine birth by Captain Cook (gold-laced, white-wigged, and back to back in the illustrations with Sir Joseph Banks), Australia's history soon terminated in unsuccess. Was engulfed in a dark stench of nameless prisoners whose only apparent activity was to have built, for their own incarceration, the stone gaols, now empty monuments that little girls might tour for Sunday outings: These are the cells for solitary confinement, here is where they. Australian History dwindled into the expeditions of doomed explorers, journeys without revelation or encounter endured by fleshless men whose portraits already gloomed, beforehand, with a wasted, unlucky look—the eyes fiercely shining from sockets that were already bone.

That was the shrivelled chronicle—meagre, shameful, uninspired; swiftly passed over by teachers impatient to return to the service at the Abbey. The burden of a slatternly continent was too heavy for any child to shift. History itself proceeded, gorgeous, spiritualized, without a downward glance at Australia. Greater than Nature, inevitable as the language of morning prayers: O God, who art the author of peace and lover of concord, in knowledge of whom standeth our eternal life, whose service is perfect freedom.

Sentiments of a magnitude to which only a very affected, bold or departing Australian might aspire.

In the true, and northern, hemisphere, beyond the Equator that equalized nothing, even bath-water wound out in the opposite direction. Perhaps even the records gyrating on the gramophone. Australians could only pretend to be part of all that and hope no one would spot the truth.

Once in a while, or all the time, there was the sense of something supreme and obvious waiting to be announced. Like the day the boys at the junction were tormenting the swaggie and a man from nowhere told them, "E's a yoo-ming being."

When fiery December sets foot in the forest . . .

They were living in a house with a tower and a view of the Heads. They had embroidered chairs, crystal dishes that chimed when flicked with a fingernail, and a frag-ment of oak from Nelson's flagship in a small velvet box. At school Caro was up to the Spanish Armada and the sad heart of Ruth, when the ferry called the *Benbow* turned over in Sydney harbour and hideously sank. Grace was on a blue chair in the kindergarten and still had Miss McLeod, who had come out after the Great War and would be superannuated at Christmas.

Miss McLeod played the organ for the school at morn-ing prayers. "Hush'd was the Evening Hymn," "For All the Saints," and, in season, "Once in Royal David's City." Everyone was C of E or something like it, except Myfanwy Burns and the Cohen girl. Religion was the baby in the manger, the boy with the slingshot, the coat of many colours.

Caro and Grace knew what had happened to them was drastic. They could tell by flattering new attentions that had nothing to do with incredulous, persistent loss. They were slow to give up hope of miraculous reversal, and each morning woke disbelieving to the weather of death. It would have been hard to have weather appropriate or con-soling, but this heat did not seem neutral.

Full fathom five thy father lies. Mrs. Horniman in the house with the English lawn said there was nothing she would not do. And on Christmas Day they sweltered beside the Hornimans' celluloid tree while a bushfire broke out over at Clontarf. Grace got a threepenny-bit in the plum pudding, but afternoon grew awful. The children were forbidden to swim because of the turkey, and Athol Horniman hit Caro with a cricket ball.

A few days later Dora told them, "It is 1939."

Dora struck them both as unfamiliar. They scarcely recognized her from before, when she had been part of a family of five. The present Dora seemed not to have shared in the life before the *Benbow*. There was only one thing—a memory, not yet defined as such, of Dora shrieking beyond a closed door and Father saying, "Look what a daughter."

It was hard to think where Dora might have been, for instance, on mornings of the great past when Grace and Caro were driven into town for new school clothes. Father dropped them off, the mother and two girls, in the important haze where metallic smells of town flowed along with the cars, sluggish between narrow ranks of buildings. A toast-rack tram, discoloured yellow, rocked them on wooden benches glossed with human passage. There were office girls with rolled hair and sailor hats of felt or straw; but there was no Dora, surely. The men sat in the open compartments at each end of the tram, their heavy waist-coats unbuttoned in the heat; flinging tobacco butts on slatted floors and leaning out to spit. In the rain, a canvas blind drew down for them on a rod. In the inside compartment Grace stood between her mother's knees and Caro swayed against an assortment of standing thighs. One and two halves, like the fare; and no Dora.

Dora's own mother had died when she was born, as happened in stories. Dora was twenty-one, but had given up Teachers' College.

Where they got down from the tram there were windows brilliant with coloured gloves and handbags and silk shoes, and shopping arcades lit like rainbows. The women passing along Pitt Street or Castlereagh had cooler faces and wore hats of violets or rosebuds, with little veils. Kegs of ale were nonetheless drawn on drays right past the best shops by pairs or teams of Clydesdales: chestnut necks straining in collars of sweated leather, great hooves under ruffs of streaked horsehair. And the driver collarless, frayed waist-coat open, no jacket, with his leather face and stained mop of horsehair moustache. Manure underfoot, and a bruised smell of dropped cabbage trodden by blinkered ponies harnessed to vegetable carts. Along the curb, barrows of Jaffas and Navels, or Tasmanian apples. All this, raffish and rural, at the fashionable conjunction of Market and Castlereagh streets.

At the same corner they would come upon the spectres dreaded by Caro and by Grace; and, from the looking and the looking away, by all who passed there. Apparitions of the terrible kind were dispersed throughout the city and might be expected at any shopping centre of the suburbs. For a dead and atrocious certainty they awaited you at this particular and affluent corner, which for that reason seemed not to be a street at all, but a pit or arena.

Some of them stood, including those with only the one leg. The legless would be on the ground, against shop-windows. The blinded would have a sign, to that effect, around the neck—perhaps adding SUVLA or GALLIPOLI. Similarly, on the placard GASSED that hung beside pinned medals, might appear the further information, YPRES or ARRAS. Or the sign might say MESOPOTAMIA, quite simply, as you might write HELL.

They took up separate places, perhaps having a dog with them or a child, or a gaunt woman silently holding out the cap. More usually, each alone. Who or what they had singly been, however, was sunk in the delved sameness of the eyes. Nothing more could be done to them, but their unsurpassable worst would be sustained forever and ever. Stillness was on the eyes even of the blind, closed on God knew what last sighting.

What music they made, and how they sang, that ghastly orchestra in lopped and shiny serge, with unstrung fiddles and wheezing concertinas and the rusted mouth-organ grasped in the remaining and inexpert hand; the voices out of tune with everything but pitched extremity. How cruelly they wracked, for Depression pennies, an unwilling audience with their excruciating songs—"The Rose of No Man's Land," and "The Roses of Picardy," and "The Rose of Tralee," and "Oh my, I don't want to die, I want to go home." The war of the roses, roses, and smile, smile, smile.

"Ighty-tiddly-ighty,
Carry me back to Blighty,
Blighty is the place for me!"

Even children—children who had not yet experienced virtue and might be ruthless in tormenting playfellows—were struck adult in pity: the Great War being deeply known to them, learned before memory, as infants know the macabre from dreams. Nothing would have truly surprised them, not if they had been explicitly told of the exploded horses, exploded men, the decomposing gestures of the dead, the trench-foot, trench-mouth, the starshells, the terror. The bully of a sergeant-major howling about clay piping to those as good as dead, the visiting statesman jocose behind the lines. They knew about Wipers and Plug Street and the Line. They had found it all out somehow from the speechless instruction at street corners and the songs of the roses and "Inky Pinky Parlay-Voo." Uncovered it in defiance of the brittle brown wreaths at cenotaphs, two minutes' silence, and the pools of remembrance where beer bottles lolled, and the monuments to war's sweetest symbols—the soldier, bronze rifle rested, supporting his decorously felled comrade, the marshal cleanly victorious on his flawless mare.

How long they were, how immensely long: the four years that would go on forever.

On Anzac or Armistice Day, Grace and Caroline Bell had been let through the crowd to watch thin-faced men walk in rows, in the decent suit if they had one, pin-stripe, with scraps of braid aligned in small rainbows on the breast, the poppy of red paper in the lapel, the sprig of rosemary. Being little children, Caroline and Grace Bell had been brought to the front of the crowd to see this, as having the greater need.

In the wringing of their hearts, knowledge had entered. Knowledge stood formidable and helpless in their small rib-cages as, glancing aside, they dropped tuppence in the extended cap, or ground the rosemary to death between their fingers for the smell.

The house to which they now moved with Dora was smaller, with camellia trees on the lawn but too many hydrangeas. At the back it was buffalo grass and spiked shrubs, and a rockery hewn from the sandstone slope. Indoors, the responsive crystal, the splinter of the true cross from H.M.S. *Victory* had become museum pieces, relics of another life. At each side of their own brief horizontal, the long streets dropped to the sea. They might almost, had they known it, have been at Rio or Valparaiso. Night followed night, nights of oceanic silence not even broken now by the screams of bandicoots in traps on the Hornimans' English lawn.

In the slit of two headlands the Pacific rolled, a blue toy between paws. The scalloped harbour was itself a country, familiar as the archipelago a child governs among the rocks: it hardly seemed the open sea could offer more. Yet, passing into that slit Pacific, ocean liners took the fortunate to England. You went to the Quay to see them off, the Broadhursts or Fifields. There was lunch on board, which Dora did not enjoy because of a small fishbone caught in her throat. Sirens were blown, and kisses; streamers and tempers snapped. And the *Strathaird*, or *Orion*, was hugely away. You could be home in time to see her go through the Heads, and Caro could read out the name on the stern or bow. Even Dora was subdued at witnessing so incontrovertible an escape.

Going to Europe, someone had written, was about as final as going to heaven. A mystical passage to another life, from which no one returned the same.

Those returning in such ships were invincible, for they had managed it and could reflect ever after on Anne Hathaway's Cottage or the Tower of London with a confidence that did not generate at Sydney. There was nothing mythic at Sydney: momentous objects, beings, and events all occurred abroad or in the elsewhere of books. Sydney could never take for granted, as did the very meanest town in Europe, that a poet might be born there or a great painter walk beneath its windows. The likelihood did not arise, they did not feel they had deserved it. That was the measure of resentful obscurity: they could not imagine a person who might expose or exalt it.

There was the harbour, and the open sea. It was an atmosphere in which a sunset might be comfortably admired, but not much else. Any more private joy—in light or dark,

in leaf or gatepost—savoured of revelation and was un-
countenanced; even in wistaria or wattle on mornings
newer, surely, than anywhere else could by now achieve.
There was a stillness on certain evenings, or a cast to
rocks, or a design of languid branch against the sky that
might be announcing glory. Though it could hardly be
right to relish where Dora was aggrieved, the girls put
their smooth faces to gardenias, inhaling December for a
lifetime.

Inland was the Bush, the very name a scorched and
sapless blur. Inland was a drought, a parched unvisited
mystery, a forlorn horizon strung on a strand of slack
barbed wire. Dora would not drive farther than Gosford,
and none of them had ever seen an Abo. At Easter, the
Whittles took them to Bulli Pass, where the radiator boiled
over and they all stood by the side of the road after rolling
up stones to the rear tires. Getting out to push, plump
Mr. Whittle reminded of a growing infant whose first impulse is to trundle the perambulator in which he has been
wheeled. Returning home, Dora sat in an unaccustomed
chair and said, "You will not get me to do that again."

Like a vast inland of their own littoral, Dora was becoming an afflicted region, a source of abrupt conflagration.
Compliant with her every mood, they wondered that her
life should be, as she told and told them, subjugated to
theirs. There was some misunderstanding here. Deep trouble
was having its way with Dora, as the girls were the first to
know. She might still take them into her arms—but vehe-
mently, as if few such embraces might be left to them, and
without providing sanctuary. Dora's state was coming on
them like nightfall, while they still affected to discern the
shapes and colours of normal day. Keeping up emotional
appearances, they were learning to appease and watch out
for her. Dora's flaring responses to error might now be
feared, or any kindling of her enchafed spirit. The bruises
of a fall must be concealed from Dora's shrill ado, and so
with other falls and bruises.

They were losing their mother a second time.

Caro was coming round to the fact of unhappiness: to
a realization that Dora created unhappiness and that she
was bound to Dora. No one would now appear offering
rescue, it was too late for that. In growing, Caro was begin-

ning rather than outstripping her long task. At least for the present, Caro was stronger than Grace, and was assuming Dora as moral obligation. Dora herself was strongest of all, in her power to accuse, to judge, to cause pain: in her sovereign power. Dora's skilled suspicion would reach unerringly into your soul, bring out your worst thoughts and flourish them for all to see; but never brought to light the simple good. It was as if Dora knew of your inner, rational, protesting truth, and tried to provoke you into displaying it, like treason. On the one hand, it was Dora seeking havoc, and, on the other, the sisters continually attempting to thwart or divert.

The girls heard it said that Dora was raising them. Yet it was more like sinking, and always trying to rise. In these children a vein of instinct sanity opened and flowed: a warning that every lie must be redeemed in the end. An aversion to emotion was engendered, and the belief—which in Caro was to last her lifetime—that those who do not see themselves as victims accept the greater stress.

In their esteem for dispassion they began to yearn, perverse and unknowing, towards some strength that would, in turn, disturb that equilibrium and sweep them to higher ground.

Like other children, they stopped on the way home from school to pull at socks or pick at scabs or stare up a garden path at some opalescent entry. Grace with a satchel and pale jiggling ringlets, Caro tilted to a loaded briefcase. At school both were clever, which was attributed to the maturing effects of their tragedy—just as, had they lagged, obtuseness would have been ascribed to the arresting trauma. They sought each other in the playground and were known to be aberrant, a pair.

The classrooms had rough sallow walls. The children were reading *The Merchant of Venice* under the specked reproduction of Lord Leighton's *Wedded*, and the water-colour of Ormiston Gorge. The classrooms were windows on the bay. Tendrils of morning glory crawled on wooden sills. It was always summer—and was afternoon more often than not, hot with smells of chalk and gym shoes and perhaps the banana uneaten in someone's satchel. Fatigued as businessmen, the girls carved names into desktops in expectation of the bell.

Caro and Grace walked home uphill in raging heat. Brick houses were symmetric with red, yellow, or purple respectability: low garden walls, wide verandas, recurrent clumps of frangipani and hibiscus, of banksia and bottle-brush; perhaps a summerhouse, perhaps a flagpole. Never a sign of washing or even of people: such evidence must be sought inside, or at the back. Caro was beginning to wonder about the inside and the back, and whether every house concealed a Dora. Whether in every life there was a *Benbow* that heeled over and sank.

You felt that the walls of such houses might topple inwards, that they would crush but not reveal.

Refinement was maintained on the razor's edge of an abyss. To appear without gloves, or in other ways suggest the flesh, to so much as show unguarded love, was to be pitchforked into brutish, bottomless Australia, all the way back to primitive man. Refinement was a frail construction continually dashed by waves of a raw, reminding humanity: the six-o'clock shambles outside the pubs, men struggling in vomit and broken glass; the group of wharfies on their Smoke-O, squatting round a flipped coin near the Quay and calling out in angry lust to women passing. There were raucous families who bought on the lay-by, if at all, and whose children were bruised from blows or misshapen by rickets—this subtler threat contained in terrace houses whose sombre grime was a contagion from the British Isles, a Midlands darkness. Britain had shared its squalor readily enough with far Australia, though withholding the Abbey and the Swan of Avon.

Concussed by these realities and worse, refinement shuddered and turned away.

The two girls walked home hand in hand, not so much like lovers as like an elderly couple, grave with information and responsibility. Coming home was to a Dora of outraged quiet, of which some cause must, sooner rather than later, be explosively made known. Or to Dora disfigured by tears from the affront of some neighbour, now marked down for life. Meaning was acoustical, ringing statistical: "They only invited me once in two years," "In all that time I was there to tea exactly twice." Any crisis of classroom or playground, inadvertently disclosed, might

set Dora to shrieking, "Peace! I want peace!" the house re-
sounding to cries of "Peace!" long after the girls were in
their beds.

Dora could always die, so she said. I CAN ALWAYS DIE,
as if this were a solution to which she might repeatedly
resort. She told them that death was not the worst, as if
she had had the opportunity of testing. She said she could
do away with herself. Or she could disappear. Who would
care, what would it matter. They flung themselves on her
in terror, Dora don't die, Dora don't disappear. No, she
was adamant: It was the only way.

How often, often, she drew upon this inexhaustible reserve of her own death, regenerated over and over by the
horror she inspired by showing others the very brink. It
was from their ashen fear that she rose, every time, a
phoenix. Each such borrowing from death gave her a new
lease on life.

Not that Dora was tolerant of the afflicted or of those
who had gone under. "We could all give in," she said, when
told that Miss Garside the librarian had completely
dropped her bundle. The maimed or blinded were a resented incursion on pity that was Dora's by right: Dora's
cry for help must drown out all others. She was quite taken
up with her own disappearance, which loomed the largest
presence in their lives.

The girls' early legends were all of the time that Dora.
The time that Dora stood up to the tax man, the time Dora
took no nonsense from the minister. "For once I spoke
out." Dora taking exception, umbrage, or the huff. Dora
lashing out, Dora pitching into, Dora breaking down. Dora
giving the dreaded news: "I had a good row." A good
cry, a good row, a good set-to. Dora was, furthermore,
convinced that if she pressed on kind intentions hard
enough they would disclose their limitations; and in this,
time after time, had proved herself right.

Dora had a vermilion dress with black buttons that
she wore for housework. The child Grace was asking,
"Why are you always angry in that dress?"

Dora scarcely knew how to flare. "In this dress—I'm
always busy. Not angry, busy."

Grace disbelieved.

"I don't care to be told I'm angry all the time. I certainly am not angry." Dora was very angry.

Grace trembled. "I'm sorry."

"Do you have any, do you have the slightest notion how hard I work for you. I am never done." It was true, housewives were slaves. "Then I get this flung at me, I am told I'm angry. Well let me tell you."

Grace went outside to cry.

Dora was twenty-two and had dark sloping eyes and, despite an addiction to boiled sweets, perfect little teeth. Caro wondered when Dora would be old enough for tranquillity. Old people were serene. You simply had to be serene, for instance, at seventy. Even Dora must be, if they could only wait.

Yet Dora was daily life. Dora shopped, and paid bills out of their small inheritance; and spoke with trustees about debentures. Dora took back *The Citadel* to the lending library and returned with *The Rains Came;* played bridge at Pymble, and had a wealthy cousin at Point Piper. Dora went to tea, and wrote thank-you notes on her blue deckle-edged. She wore a smart silk frock of the colour known as teal, and had her long dark hair waved and rolled. On prize-giving night Dora exulted over the girls' bound anthologies and the silver cup Grace won for Piano; and shed true tears for Caro's gold medal in French. It was this that set Caro to wondering about the backs of houses, and whether Dora was in some form inevitable to every household.

Supremely confusing was the Dora, all loving normality, who followed the release of the good row. At those intervals the girls became, for an evening or a day, young again. It was of course a confounding of all they knew for sure, through the certainty of suffering. But, like others in the clutch of absolute authority, they settled for the brief respite. It seemed easier to lie—to Dora, to oneself, to God —than willfully to precipitate the other Dora.

Into these hostilities came war. One year it was statesmen shrieking "Peace! Peace!" while marshalling, like Dora, for a holocaust. The next it was Poland, the Siegfried Line, the *Graf Spee.* A family from Vienna, Jews, took the house next door, and Dora reported, "He's an engineer, she's a children's doctor. Supposedly." Because a professional woman aroused mistrust. The two boys, Ernst without the second *e* and Rudolf with *f*, mooned on the lawn. Their father, slim and grey, pondered a row of freesias that in October had forced itself through from the far side of the earth.

The following June, the greengrocer's windows were smashed because of being Italian. Manganelli's at the Junction put out a sign: WE ARE GREEKS. Once again the men set sail for history, in darkness and without streamers. France fell. There was the blitz, the RAF, and Mr. Churchill. Caro's class put aside the War of the Spanish Succession to read a book about London, the buildings standing out like heroes—the Guildhall, the Mansion House—which every night the flames consumed on the seven-o'clock news. Dora seethed under rationing, but yearned to be where bombs were falling. She took the conflict personally, frenzied by Mr. Churchill. It was Dora's war.

The neap tide of history had, as usual, left them high and dry.

Caro was becoming flesh. Her hands were assuming attitudes. In shoes dull with playground dust her feet were long and shapely. The belt of her school uniform, which at the time of Dunkirk had banded a mere child, by the siege of Tobruk delineated a cotton waist. Her body showed a delicate apprehension of other change. Caro knew the sources of the Yangtze, and words like hypotenuse. Even Grace did homework now, sitting on the floor. Dora was knitting for the merchant marine, charging this calm activity with vociferous unrest.

Greece fell, Crete fell. There was a toppling, even of history.

One hot day Caro looked up Pearl Harbor in the atlas. Buses were soon painted in swamp colours. Air-raid shelters were constructed, and a boom, useless, across the harbour mouth. You kept a bucket of sand in the kitchen with a view to incendiary bombs. Mr. Whittle was an air-raid warden, and the Kirkby boys were called up. The noble rhetoric of Downing Street scarcely applied to dark streets, austerity, and standing in the queue. Colonial families arrived from the East destitute, and Singapore fell, fell. Orphans were numerous now; and the girls, in their civilian loss, no longer commanded special attention.

The school was moving to a country house, where the invading Japanese would hardly penetrate. Grace was too little to be saved by such methods, Caro would go alone. Caro would try out the fugitive state; if it came up to snuff, Grace might later be included.

Caro was installed one afternoon at the foot of the Blue Mountains. On the plain below, gum trees straggled back towards Sydney, bark was strewn like torn paper. The littlest children cried, but the parents would visit them in a fortnight if the petrol held up and the Japs did not arrive. There was also an ancient train as far as Penrith, but after that you were on your own. They knew about Penrith, a weatherboard town with telegraph poles and the sort of picture-house where you could hear the rain.

Grace waved out the car window: jealous, guilty, and safe.

It was Sunday. After sago pudding, they sang "Abide with Me," and Caro went out on the upstairs veranda. Fast falls the eventide. The darkness deepened in silence more desolate for the squawk of a bird they had been shown in illustrations. Incredulous response cracked in Caroline Bell's own throat. Smells of dry ground, of eucalyptus and a small herd of cows gave the sense of time suspended, or slowed to a pace in which her own acceleration must absurdly spin to no purpose. The only tremor in dim foothills was the vapour of a train on its way up to Katoomba. It was insignificant that Dora had taught them to abhor, and if ever there was to be insignificance it was here. The measure of seclusion was that Penrith had become a goal. Caro took herself in her own tender embrace, enclosing all that was left of the unknown. Caro was inland.

She had crouched into the angle formed by the balustrade and one of the high supports of the veranda. Bougainvillea was trained on the uprights; and a round plaque, cool as china, impressed her cheek. There were insects in the thorny vines, there was the scuttle of some animal in the garden below. Dora would have confirmed that death is not the worst.

In a room with six beds, all subsequently cried themselves to sleep. In the morning, Caro saw that the medallion on the balcony was blue and white, and Catholic. One of the girls told her, "Miss Holster says it's a Dellarobbier."

The house was at once seen to be peculiar. There was a lot to look at. It was owned by the Doctor, who was not a doctor at all but an architect; and Italian, even if on our side. He had withdrawn to a smaller building alongside—servants' quarters was a phrase that came readily enough to them from books, or from the old stone houses built by convicts. The Doctor wore a short white cotton jacket and a little white pointed beard and, although not lame, carried a stick. According to Miss Holster, he had seen through Mussolini from the word Go.

The house had 1928 in Roman numbers on the porch; or portico. For its construction, coloured marbles and blond travertine had spent months at sea, fireplaces and ceilings had been dismantled outside Parma, where the ham and violets came from. And whole pavements of flowered tiles uprooted and rebedded. The dining-room was said to be elliptical. All the doors, even for bathrooms, were double, with panels of painted flowers, and paired handles pleasant to waggle until they dropped off. There were velvet bellpulls, intended for maids, that fell into disrepair from incessant tugging. There was also the day Joan Brinstead broke an inkpot on the white marble mantel in the music room and ammonia only made it worse. Miss Holster had a canopy over her bed; but could not say why lemon trees should be potted rather than in the ground.

These rooms enclosed loveliness—something memorable, true as literature. Events might take place, occasions, though not during the blight of their own occupancy. At evening the rooms shone, knowing and tender.

In a forbidden paddock below the house, a wire fence surrounded tents, tin buildings, and thirty or forty short men grotesquely military in uniforms dyed the colour of wine. The Doctor's countrymen had come to the ends of the earth to find him, for the men who dug his fields and gathered his fruit were Italian prisoners of war. At dusk they led in the cows before being themselves led behind the wire. The Doctor could be seen in the mornings moving among them, white beard, white jacket, white panama:

once more the master. They learned that, like a baby, he slept in the afternoons. They had seen, or caught, one of the prisoners kissing his hand.

From the fields, or behind the wire, the prisoners waved to the schoolgirls, who never waved back. Never. It was a point of honour.

After two weeks of this, Dora came with Grace in the Marchmains' car, which had been converted to naphtha. Dora was at her best in the drama of reunion and had brought a magnificent hamper to supplement the dreadful meals. Caro showed off to Grace with the Marchmains' pale-pink Rosamund, her fellow exile. They had a picnic on the banks of the Nepean, Mr. Marchmain explaining about nettles and dock leaves. Sausages were cooked on sticks over a fire the Marchmains made. The fat dripped, reeking; sausage meat obtruded from split casing. Fending for yourself on a desert island would not be like this: there would be mangoes, breadfruit, milk from coconuts, and fish from the coral reef.

Dora sat on a corner of the spread rug, longing to be assigned some task so she could resent it. The girls swam in the river, repelled by the saltless water and the ooze. They played Moses in the Bulrushes, with Grace in the title role but Caro as the Princess. Across the river, the gorges began, melancholy, uninhabited. A friend of the Marchmains had once stayed up at Lapstone—for pleurisy, or so it was given out at the time. You could usually tell the real thing, though, by the hectic flush. Caro was thinking of Umbria, until yesterday a mere colour in the paintbox between Yellow Ochre and Burnt Sienna; and of flat Parma where the violets came from.

Caro would have liked to reveal the house, but feared Dora's reaction. Dora was not one to lie down under the news that a veranda was called a loggia, or a mural a fresco. Let alone villa for house. Any such divulging would somehow bring word of Caro's secession from Dora's rule. They walked about the corridors and looked in the oval dining-room without perceiving.

"This Montyfiori," said Mr. Marchmain, who was coarse, "appears to be a raving ratbag."

After tea the Marchmains walked down with Rosamund to the paddock, where you took turns for the pony, and

Dora went to put the Thermos in the car. Caro and Grace disappeared into the makeshift dormitory, where they sat side by side on a bed. They made little wracked gasps of an adult weeping that must presently be concealed. The huge heavy mechanism of their hearts dragged at their slight bodies.

Grace said, "I'll write."

They washed their faces in a bathroom varicose with streaked marble. The basin was shaped like one of those shells. Even the lav had a blue pattern inside, possibly Chinese.

Dora had found the matron and was reading the Riot Act about blankets. Marchmains were coming up the gravel. Now, authorized public tears, let grief be unconfined. Grace climbed in the car, abashed by escaping yet again. At that moment, Japs were the last thing in anyone's mind: the entire exercise appeared pointless except for the emotions to which it was giving luxurious rein.

Caro came home in winter, with the others. The villa dissolved into gum trees even as they twisted to see it for the last time, breath steaming the cold windows of a bus that took them to the Penrith train. No one, even so, would take a chance on waving to their fellow-prisoners.

Soon their flight to the mountains was part of the fabled past, a form of war service. Not before the Doctor had brought suit, however, for irreparable damage to his house. After all that palaver about Danty and the sunset, the old ratbag was asking a thousand quid, Mr. Marchmain reported, to fix up his caricature of a home.

Caro returned, as if from abroad, to a city populated by American soldiers. Dora confirmed that these were boastful, and self-indulgent in ways unspecified. Girls who went with them were common. Caro and Grace, in school uniform, were photographed by a lanky sergeant while crossing at the Junction; and put up their hands, like the famous, to ward off intrusion. It was a pity one could not have a better class of saviour: Americans could not provide history, of which they were almost as destitute as Australians.

The sisters had never seen black men before, apart from the Lascars at the Quay.

At school, Grace was studying the Stuart kings. From newspapers they learned about Stalingrad and Rostov-on-the-Don. Dora was part of a camouflage-netting group that met on Thursdays in Delecta Avenue and was rancorous in the extreme. In the relief of home, Caro was lenient. Once in a while she pictured to herself the Doctor's house, and the high rooms that created expectation. If you could have had the rooms, without the misery.

These pictures might be memories—unless it was too soon for memories. The moments would not say which of them might be remembered.

When you measured five feet tall you were eligible for extra clothing coupons. She would have undone her plaits into a pony-tail had it not been for Dora.

One morning a girl whose father had been in America for Munitions came to school with nibless pens that wrote both red and blue, pencils with lights attached, a machine that would emboss a name—one's own preference—and pencil sharpeners in clear celluloid. And much else of a similar cast. Set out on a classroom table, these silenced even Miss Holster. The girls leaned over, picking up this and that: Can I turn it on, how do you work it, I can't get it to go back again. No one could say these objects were ugly, even the crayon with the shiny red flower, for they were spread on the varnished table like flints from an age unborn, or evidence of life on Mars. A judgment on their attractiveness did not arise: their power was conclusive, and did not appeal for praise.

It was the first encounter with calculated uselessness. No one had ever wasted anything. Even the Lalique on Aunt Edie's sideboard, or Mum's Balibuntl, were utterly functional by contrast, serving an evident cause of adornment, performing the necessary, recognized role of extravagance. The natural accoutrements of their lives were now seen to have been essentials—serviceable, workaday—in contrast to these hard, high-coloured, unblinking objects that announced, though brittle enough, the indestructibility of infinite repetition.

Having felt no lack, the girls could experience no envy. They would have to be conditioned to a new acquisitiveness. Even Dora would have to adjust her methods to contend with such imperviousness.

Never did they dream, fingering those toys and even being, in a rather grown-up way, amused by them, that they were handling fateful signals of the future. The trinkets were assembled with collective meaning, like exhibits in a crime, or like explosives no expert could defuse. Invention was the mother of necessity. It was not long after this that the girls began to wave their uniformed hips and to chant about Chattanooga and the San Fernando Valley. Sang, from the antipodes, about being down in Havana and down Mexico way. Down was no longer down to Kew. The power of Kew was passing like an empire.

Now Caro and Grace Bell did not go home at once after lessons but walked along the beach below the school, getting sand in their shoes and stockings, picking up chipped shells and flinging them away. Seaweed sworled in dark, beady tangles, scalloped up by the tides, bleared by an occasional medusa. A boy or pair of boys would speak to them, boys in grey knickerbockers and striped ties. The uniforms were a guarantee: schools recognized each other like regiments.

Grace was a flower.

Caro's hair hung heavy on her shoulders, as no child's will do.

The sounds and smell of ocean made speech unworthy, or required a language greater than they knew. Because Dora's intrusions had made privacy sacrosanct, they exchanged no word on the dangerous preparations their bodies were making for an unimaginable life. And, in this respect, lingered in unusual ignorance.

Dora was too sore and disturbing a subject for their circumspect afternoons. Besides, they were supposed to love her; and, more to the point, did so. They would have given anything to see her happy. However, the threesome was beginning to irk them. People had to step aside as Dora marched the girls, on arms inertly linked, along streets or pushed them singly through turnstiles. They lived under supervision, a life without men. Dora knew no men. You could scarcely see how she might meet one, let alone come to know.

All women evidently longed to marry, and on leaving school held their breath, while accumulating linen and silver. There was a lot of waiting in it, and an endangering suggestion of emotion. Of those who were not taken, some quietly carried it off—like old Miss Fife, who came to tea with parasol and high collar, fondant silk to her calves, pointed shoes each clasped with single button: gentler than Queen Mary. There were others, unhinged, timid, or with whiskers—crushed by father, crushed by mother, or unthinkingly set aside.

In this, Dora was hard to place.

Caro was allowed into town on her own, on the ferry. There was the gangplank, creak of hawsers, casting off, smell of throttling engines, and the sea slapping at green encrustations on wooden piles. She heard the hooting approach of the city, tram-bells, the jarring of a great ignition. In the cabin, office girls held up little mirrors and patted powder off their curving fronts and concave laps with small reverberations at thorax or thighs. They dabbed behind the ears, then sharply closed their handbags to signal preparedness. This was not the groundwork for a march, three abreast, through the town; but a prelude to encounters.

Alone in the city, Caro was lifting a frayed book in a shop. "How much is this?"

"Fifteen and three."

Back on the teetering pile. The table was massed like an arsenal.

"Ah well. Let's say, ten bob."

Seeing it that evening, Dora said, "You have enough books now."

Dora knew, none better, the enemy when she saw it.

6

"We too," said Ted Tice. "We knew about things from books."

Caroline Bell sat on the grass with her bare arms about her knees. The turf was close as stitching: seamless England. The astounding trees were Weymouth pines, through which the sun came down in hallowed strokes like light into a cathedral. Matters must soon come to life for her that had only been known, like colouring, from books.

Ted said, "Like heat, for instance. Or love."

"The heat is intense," they had written home through the Forces Mail. Or, according to rank, "You would not half believe." The troopship, which was the old *Lancashire,* out of Liverpool, broke down in the Red Sea. Hearing her called "the old *Lancashire,*" they had expected something of the kind. Aden was a line of molten crags awaver with fumes of petroleum and colonial dejection. They passed into the Indian Ocean with no sense of release. Sunburn cream and soda water had long since run out. They sang war songs—stale, in 1946, with superseded poignancy— and marching songs that taunted immobility. In the evenings there was housie-housie or another sing-song; which met few requirements. Airless episodes of England continued to be performed, at Colombo, at Singapore.

In Hong Kong, Ted Tice, who was to take ship again at once for Japan, sat in a club for officers with a lieutenant of the Royal Navy. The club was on a side street within walking distance of the naval dockyard, and in the evening the officers came there in pure white and gold, as if in court dress. Under slow revolutions of a ceiling fan, the aftermath of war was coming to a halt. There was a smell

of starch, of lime juice and gin, mildew from canvas cushions, and, faintly from the street, the reek of China. Three
fair floral women on a sofa were clearly nurses off duty,
awkward as plainclothes police.

"You know what they say." Ted's lieutenant knew a
thing or two, lowering his voice. Hearing him laugh, one
of the women innocently turned and laughed too, from
good nature. She was about nineteen, a broad, guileless
face with long nose and irregular teeth. The sleeves and
bosom of her civilian dress were outgrown as a schoolgirl's tunic. Like Ted Tice's mother, who kept a news-
agent's shop, she had a Manchester voice.

(When Ted Tice first left home for the university, his
mother had said to him, "Tha dustn't have to say owt
about shop. If tha dustn' want." They had stared, like
children playing to see who will blink first. Unbearable, her
understanding; her lack of understanding.)

The naval lieutenant, who was not all bad, had been in
Japan. "It's an American show. You can do nothing without a permit from MacArthur." He gave an inevitable,
obscene example. "They treat us worse than Japs. They're
in the driver's seat now, and we're on the skids."

On the wall there was a framed photograph of an artless
king in naval dress. Even a king might be regretted now
he was on the skids. Chinese servants were carrying trays,
not yet apprised of change. The girl on the sofa said in her
Mancunian voice, "And I say he couldn't run a pie-stall."
She was speaking of the prime minister.

The lieutenant told Ted Tice, "Unless you have a girl."
Ted turned back to him. "I'm saying, don't get pushed into
a lot of cultured pearls."

Because of minesweeping, they were all day in the Inland Sea. The islands were irruptions, each fringed with the
single file of lean trees leaning. At home, even the wildest
coast had established itself with slow insistence, but these
islands were fragments of a cataclysm. Ted had never seen
so red a dawn, or villages of straws. Little boats like wrap-
ping paper flapped on alluvial waves, and a young Englishman looked down over a railing into faces stigmatized with
the cartoon image of enemy.

At the port, hulks lay about like rotting whales. There

were blitzed docks and, in the harbour basin, the upturned keel of a ship capsized at launching. On the pier, the erstwhile enemy, dressed in the colour called fatigue, pulled on ropes and uttered the cries by which a ship is docked. One of the ship's officers said, "You'll be going over the hill." The slopes above the port of Kure were terraced gold and green, there were red valleys of azalea. It was early in June. "Not that way, it's the other direction." And Ted Tice pronounced, like a lesson, the name of his destination: "Hiroshima."

It was like riding in state—the jeep being open, and khaki with authority. There were the bombed docks and ruined avenues of the port, and then the hillside grotto of a destroyed railway tunnel. The officer beside the driver was pointing out, "Here there was, apparently there used to be, you wouldn't credit it now." He said, "I'll fill you in as we go." Along the back of the front seat his heavy, extended arm was energized yet not quite human, like a turgid fire-hose. His name was Captain Girling.

They were descending to a vast ground without horizon, and at first there were small unfinished houses everywhere. Unweathered timbers were being ribbed into rooms, roofs were being woven slat on smarting slat. Men and women were bearing loads, were walking planks, were strung up against a hot tin sky. The jeep slowed beside a new-laid tramline. Where rails and road diverged, a youth leaned from the tram door to spit on them, and withdrew.

"If I could get at him," the officer said. "If only." This man was literally decorated, wearing the ribbons of many medals. He had a scar, just a line, as if a pillow had creased his sleeping cheek. This Captain Girling saw the flaw on Ted Tice's eyeball without looking into his eyes. In the back seat of the jeep they were showing, like children, what they had got—the cameras and watches and little radios with which the enemy had nearly won.

In the past, the demolition of a city exposed contours of the earth. Modern cities do not allow this. The land has been levelled earlier, to make the city; then the city goes, leaving a blank. In this case, a river amazed with irrelevant naturalness. A single monument, defabricated girders of an abolished dome, presided like a vacant cranium or a hollowing out of the great globe itself: Saint Peter's, in some eternal city of nightmare.

A catastrophe of which no one would ever say, the Will of God.

It was now that Ted Tice's life began to alter aspect and direction. He was used to thinking of his life—I have done this, how could I have done that—like everybody. Barely twenty, he would have imagined he had overcome a fair amount. There was Father, loudly angered; Mother, all untidy woe. Then there was his aptitude: a teacher coming round after school, "The boy has unusual aptitude." The boy, out of all the others. His name had been printed on a list, and the award covered everything, even the books—except, that is, for a coat; and the university was near the North Sea.

Due to the unearthly flatness where a city had been famously incinerated, the events he already called his life were growing inconsiderable before he had practised making them important. This derived from a sense not of proportion but of profound chaos, a welter in which his own lucky little order appeared miraculous but inconsequential; and from a revelation, nearly religious, that the colossal scale of evil could only be matched or countered by some solitary flicker of intense and private humanity.

Whether this amounted to a loss of faith, or to the acquisition of it, was uncertain.

It was at this period that Edmund Tice's fate became equivocal, and he ceased to make quite clear if he would win or fail.

Captain Girling informed them that, as a result of what they now saw, war had become unthinkable: "In that way, it has been salutary." He was pleased to justify an extreme. "You have to stop somewhere," he said, despite the evidence.

The rest were silent, doubting the world's stomach had sufficiently turned. On the other hand, there was the seductive, dangerous relief of contemplating Armageddon, which would absolve them from blame or effort.

Captain Girling said, "I'll fill you in." As if at a graveside. He believed it might be twenty years, and that was a conservative estimate, before effects would be fully known. Records were being maintained, there would be an institute, studies. "Well, that is your shop, over to you." They would now see survivors—who were confined to an institution, as artifacts of special durability are housed in a museum.

The jeep entered a corridor of finished new houses. Ted Tice heard, "You blokes are used to it." He wanted to say, "I have never. I am not a doctor." Imagination stalked ahead, aghast, among sights soon to be outdone. In front, Captain Girling was satisfied, seeing this young man's knees tremble. In the present setting, the merciful were at an even worse disadvantage than usual.

Ted Tice's manner of looking interrupted the smooth flow of acceptance, casting useless doubt on the inevitable. If he and his kind had their way, the world would be a bonny mess. So Captain Girling reflected, amid the atomic ruins.

All along the new street, there had been posted the tokens of normality: habitation, children, the silence broken. Aligned timbers were assembling the tableaux of daily existence. And small squat women had been gathering up the concave reflectors from searchlights, which had fallen everywhere like stones in an eruption. Filled with water, these dishes had been placed at doorways. And in each of them floated, rose-red and magnified beyond your wildest dreams, a frond or single flower of azalea.

Such families could not be considered survivors, being physically intact, and prepared to rebelieve.

When they got down from the jeep, Captain Girling took Ted aside: "Look here. Don't make a goat of yourself." Goat signifying anything unmanly, or humane. He was only giving sound advice.

And did not see why the bugger should laugh.

7

It was the fate of those mild hills around the Thrale house to be portentous in the view of Edmund Tice. There was the low road where he walked home with Caro, the surrounding crops and grasses, and the hills large with event.

"It was here the storm came up, the day I arrived." He was marking it all, making shrubs and hedges bear witness. Now it was dusk that was falling. He asked, "Are you cold? We'll soon be home." But thought instead that they would stop as they climbed the path and he would touch her and speak differently. In the fine evening air he walked less confidently than in the storm; alone, as yet, with what he had to offer.

Caro could not consider the approaching house her home, though she had no other. "Do you have your own place, at the university?" If one could have privacy, all must be well.

"I've a flat, two rooms, in a professor's house. Where they are kind, a happy family. He has been a great friend to me. Now he's moving to Edinburgh—I'm to go there for a few days, in September, before I set off for Paris." He paused, on the note of parting and departing. "In the family there are two boys—who like me. And a daughter, a bit older."

"Who likes you."

"Who can't decide to become a dancer or a painter."

Caro might have asked, How old? But was silent, and the wraith of daughter was soon gone from them. They stood on the country road while she turned away Ted's embrace. She herself appeared to wonder at the antipathy, and said aloud, "I don't know why." They walked again, a new gentleness on her part conveying finality: she could afford kindliness, refusing all the rest. She remarked, "I've been happy today." She would have gone on with him indefinitely, but would not love. There were necessities, of silence and comprehension, that she valued more than love, thinking this a choice she had made.

At the turn of the road he recorded, "It was here the rain came down"—his features smudged with twilight or from some new mood; recalling that noon when, decisively, a streak of light split earth from sky. They began to climb the country path, slowed by trailing brambles and by Ted's intention of halting.

Since his moods had come to refer to her, his watchfulness roused Caro's exasperation. As a child, Caroline Bell had abhorred Dora's ceaseless scrutiny and the sensation of being observed—while she read, played, or sewed —with possessive attention. She now said to Ted what had been left unsaid to Dora: "You must not be so interested in me."

He took her meaning at once—that was part of it too, his quickness with her thoughts. "I see it might irritate." Not promising change. In the night or in any pause she might now, if she chose, feel his consciousness of her. Through all the events and systems of her days it would persist, like the clock that is the only audible mechanism of a high-powered car.

She said that to him, about the clock, exorcising it with her laugh. And he replied, "It's not a clock you're describing, it's a time-bomb."

"So there's a limit, then. Time-bombs must have a stop."

"Not a limit. A climax."

He supposed she had some fear of physical love. He did not invent this to save his pride, having already noticed her quick withdrawals that extended even to the eyes, and the effort—almost charitable—with which she did sometimes touch; and from time to time a turning to her younger, lighter sister as to the one who had mastered this subject or was at least at ease with its inevitability.

As Ted Tice saw, it was not a matter of conquering her objections. She herself required a kind of conquering. And he had begun with devotion. Her demands would before long be tested by experience, as principle is tested by adversity, and it might be that she would temporize; but for the present imagined herself transcendant over what she had not encountered.

She wished to rise to some solitary height. From ignorance she had an unobstructed view of knowledge—which she saw, on its elevation, stately, pale, pure as the Acropolis. It could not be said that hers was a harmless vanity: like any human wish for distinction, it could easily be denounced or mocked; and, in its present elemental form, was clearly short on pity. Yet, as pretensions go, it was by no means the worst.

Ted Tice already understood his attachment to Caro as intensification of his strongest qualities, if not of his strengths: not a youthful adventure, fresh and tentative, but a gauge of all effort, joy, and suffering known or imagined. The possibility that he might never, in a lifetime, arouse her love in return was a discovery touching all existence. In his desire and his foreboding, he was like a man awake who watches a woman sleeping.

A bark, a bell, a farmer calling in an animal, a baby's wail. These were the only sounds, but they struck eternity. On the hillside below them, a door standing wide on the yellow light of a shabby hall was a declaration of peace. Compared with such forthrightness, the windows of Peverel, their now visible destination, were smudges of a veiled respectability where ardour was unknown. Much as you might blame Sefton Thrale, something drastic had occurred to his house in an earlier time. The nineteenth century has a way of darkening.

While they walked, Caroline Bell thought of Professor Thrale—his propoundings, tilted stance, and disavowals of his own humanity. Only the day before, he had, in his rapid and conclusive manner, exonerated completely the inventors of deadly weapons: "We merely interpret the choices of mankind." And when Caro objected—"Aren't scientists also men, then? At the very least, responsible as their fellows?"—he had closed the discussion with his scarcely patient smile, as if to assure a child that it would understand, or not care, when it was older.

Having no vocabulary for their work, Caro could not imagine the Professor's mornings with Ted Tice, which took place, ceremoniously, behind a closed daily door. She might picture two men at a desk and the Professor making notes in his tiny writing, but could think no further.

She said, "I can never ask you about your work."

They sat on a low piece of wall, which was still warm—in a southern country there might have been a lizard. There was an odour of privet or clover, in air so open you could smell the sky. From the geometric flake of yellow light, a man was calling, "Bessie, Bessie." Until at last a cry came back, displeased.

Ted said, "In fact no technical competence is needed to understand our disagreement, his and mine." Caro had not raised the disagreement, which was felt in the house, if not witnessed. He went straight on, "Which is simply this, that there is no site whatever in England for this kind of telescope. There isn't the visibility. They all know it. But for politics and gain, and out of littleness, will have it here."

It seemed to her an adult matter, graver than love. "Then where should it go?"

"There are good sites in the south of Europe. But it will never be allowed to go out of the country." He explained how the Professor was studying the calculated hours of daylight, pretending to believe. While he spoke, leaf shadows lengthened on the path, turning exotic; across Caro's extended foot, a thong of shadow like a sandal. Again there came the call, "Bessie," and the impatient squawk of response. Ted said, "I may publish a dissenting view."

"Obviously you must, if it's like that."

He had made it sound incontrovertible, but when he now began, "You see," and hesitated, she thought he might be indeterminate like everyone else. He resumed, "The only purpose of it would be to bring the press in and make a scandal. It wouldn't stop it, but would draw attention." He said, "So there's the matter of disloyalty, and the usual question of where loyalty lies."

From a change of pitch Caro might have expected an outburst, and was the more surprised when he asked, "Do you remember you read out the sign today—*Great Expectations?*" His saying "Do you remember" put the morning back in time, a distant innocence.

"At the picture-house."

"Yes. Do you remember how, on the first page of that

book, the boy helps the escaped convict?" More like interrogation than recall.

"He doesn't befriend him, though. He does it out of
fear." It was natural enough to be sitting on a wall in the
dark talking about a book.

"Fear can take other forms than helpfulness, and in that
instance it's remembered as compassion." Ted Tice's fingertips rested on the stone wall, to poise his body for some
new advance.

"In the war, I helped a prisoner get away. A German.
It was in Wales, where I spent a couple of years at a
school when I was sent on from that place you saw today.
A few miles inland from us there was a camp for prisoners
of war, and we heard that an officer—a general, of course,
the story went—had got out. There was a long stiff walk
to the coast that I took sometimes, when I was let, to be
alone and see the sea. The sea had a sort of prohibition
on it at the time, the beaches forbidden and the barbed
wire piled in hoops and the gun emplacements thick as
bath-houses. The ocean beyond looked like freedom. You
couldn't think it led to Ireland or America—it was infinity,
like the firmament. The open sea. I was sixteen, wanting
solitude more than anything and miserable enough when
I got it—except on those walks to the coast. And having
only the school in my present and the army in my future.
We were hardly ever allowed out on our own, yet in a
year or two would be in battle, possibly dead. In fact,
eighteen months later I was sent for the radar training, at
the very end of the war.

"Anyway, I used to walk from the school out to the
coast and stand up on the last hills and look at the sea
awhile, and turn and come back again the ten miles or so
to the school. Merely to have looked at something expan-
sive was a taste of liberty. I loved the country, too, which
was bare—just rough grass and bushes rocking in the everlasting wind. Worn-out colours that kept to a periphery—
as if there might be a core to existence, and here one drew
closer. Or, to put it the other way round, that place was so
obscure that it took all your conviction to believe it, or
you, existed. The weather was always foul, but I didn't
mind. Even that gave a sense of exposure, of space after
confinement.

"There was a particular curve of cliffs, it was like walking round a turn of the earth. And this one time there was a man sitting in a cleft of the rocks, looking. Not staring. So silent and unsurprised, he might have been waiting for me. I knew right off it was the German. As if I'd been waiting for him too. So the two of us, looking. He'd got a coat from somewhere but was half frozen. He'd been out on the hills nearly a week and was utterly beat, exhausted, and starving. The face had sort of drawn off from the eyes, you should have seen the hands."

Ted Tice said, "He was conclusive proof that war was real.

"Well, that's almost all of it. I gave him my sandwich, and pullover. And a flask of awful stuff we called beef tea. The police themselves would have done much the same. It's the not turning him in that makes the public outrage, but I didn't even think of turning him in."

It differed from every other secret Caroline Bell had known, in having no darkness. Dark had meant Dora, had meant words and events sordid with self. Struggling to the light from Dora's darkness, Caro had acquired conscience and equilibrium like a profound, laborious education. Exercise of principle would always require more from her than from persons nurtured in it, for she had learned it by application of will. Caro would never do the right thing without knowing it, as some could. Now there was this secret of Ted's, streaked with difficult humanity: something immediate yet scarcely touching the self, noble but not virtuous. Something it would be presumptuous either to judge or condone.

She was silent, then reverted to the logic of the story. "Did he get away?"

"Yes. He knew the way down to the sea, whatever he was expecting there, only he had got too weak to try it till I showed up. A few days later the word got round that he'd somehow been taken off by his own lot. We never knew how. But after the war the press got hold of it as a notable case of our stupidity—that was the headline. Because they'd found out he was a scientist with the missile installations, which was why his own crowd were so keen to get him back. That wasn't realized when he was captured, because he was in uniform and had military rank—

he'd got caught during a freakish journey in a destroyer, going back to Peenemünde on the Baltic. It was only discovered when he cut loose from the prison. Then, because of the rocket raids it ultimately came out that we'd let him slip through our fingers." Ted said, "One goes on saying we and our. It was I who let him slip through our fingers. So, after it came out who he was, I had the rocket raids to think about too."

"Where is he now?"

"In America. He makes their weapons now, and ours. The story of his escape is part of his public legend, almost admirable as presented in the magazines. I do not figure in it—perhaps the recollection would be incompatible with the life of power. Having been at someone else's mercy suggests that mercy may matter. I've sometimes thought it would be a difficult case to prosecute now—mine, I mean." Ted Tice's voice smiled briefly in the dark. "I see pictures of him from time to time. Quite unrecognizable, as if he's wearing a mask now, and the real face was the one I saw. The face we all might have in extremity."

Caro did put her hand out to him. He took it in his own, accepting mere kindness.

"I'm not trying to make a justification. It's the first time I've told this and I'm doing it badly. I'm no good at telling stories. I knew at the time he might be anything, one of the worst, and there was even the idea that in his own eyes he would be winning. Not that I thought it out then. At the time I had to act and that was the form action took— the permanent form, since whatever is wrong with it I wouldn't imagine doing differently. By now I mostly forget about it. If I remember, it can seem important, or irrelevant—depending on my state of mind. You cannot only give alms to the harmless. Anyway, the complications came in right away, with the concealment, which creates its own treasons. Even if you would not particularly want to divulge an experience, you should feel able to. I didn't know the sort of person I might have confided in, I had few friends of any kind. And couldn't be sure of understanding the thing myself, let alone telling it right. Also, naturally, I didn't look forward to the hullabaloo if it became a public matter. So it stayed hidden, till this. I would tell it now if I chose, but it serves no purpose."

Caro said, "Anyone would think such an action rightful in a book—like the child and the convict, as you said. Yet most would censure it in life."

"I was too old, don't you see, to be credited with a good impulse. Sixteen's too old for holy innocence."

The child Caro had not so much as waved to those behind the wire, let alone extended mercy.

Ted said, "A conscious act of independent humanity is what society can least afford. If they once let that in, there'd be no end to it. If he and I had been in a battle, I would have killed him, having accepted society's standards. As it was, I was left to apply my own. Well, I'm not putting myself up. I just had too many advantages to use them. Again, the complications come later. One's best instincts are no more reliable than the law and no more consistent. If you live essentially within society there are times when you'd prefer to depend on the social formula—and you discover you've somewhat spoiled that possibility. You've disqualified yourself from judging others by those rules."

"You mean you might have a good reason, one day, to turn someone else in, but have forfeited the right."

"Precisely." Eventually he went on, "All this comes back to old Thrale. I'm probably going to let the old bloke in for it over the telescope, but the righteousness of my position repels me. At least this time it can't be said I hold all the cards, or any of them."

"You have the truth."

Ted Tice laughed. "Freely assuming such a handicap ought to be convincing in itself." He turned in the dark and clasped the girl's hand again, his touch uncertain, deductive, entirely personal, like the contact of the blind. He asked, as he had asked that morning, "Caro, what are you thinking?"

"About the German. I wonder what he thought, and how it was between the two of you."

"Yes. Excess of elementals, like being unable to draw breath in a high wind. At another level, familiar small sensations—resentment, for instance, at this having happened to me rather than to a confirmed patriot who would handle it conventionally without a qualm. A degrading sense, too, of youth and limitations. Then there was the new possibility that nothing mattered, not even this, though it had taken the event to make that clear. On his side— who knows? No show of natural emotions, no sympathy or excitement, even fear in the usual sense. We had no words in common, but surely I'd have recognized any wish to share."

"Was this why you chose the sort of work you do?"

"Who knows?"

"You might meet him again someday. Things come round so strangely."

"I've thought that too. I've thought there may be more collisions of the kind in life than in books. Maybe the element of coincidence is played down in literature because it seems like cheating or can't be made believable. Whereas life itself doesn't have to be fair, or convincing."

There was something conclusive in this that soon made it necessary to rise and walk on. His story had created a closeness that was human rather than sexual, a crisis of common knowledge too solemn to desire. At the sight of the man and boy among the frozen rocks, love had removed itself to a respectful distance, where it lay in wait for tomorrow.

8

"Please excuse an oddly worded and badly written letter. I have torn a thumbnail, and this is the result."

Caro and Grace reached the postscript at the same moment. They were standing in the living-room of Peverel at noon, Grace holding the letter and Caro looking over her shoulder. Dora was going to be married.

Never having entertained the possibility, they were unprepared for the ease of rescue. Or for the realization that it could have happened earlier, and in time. Their shoulders touched in comfort of a kind, having so much to take in and being so greatly unburdened. Henceforth they might be spared something.

"Let's see the first page again." They shuffled the sheets to where it said, "Dear G and C."

Beth Lomax, the well-off widow from the Victoria League, had proved gratuitously rude soon after reaching Gibraltar. Having herself proposed the visit, had begun to treat Dora as an encumbrance. For once Dora had spoken out: Beth Lomax had heard a few home truths, and high time. Dora had then gone into town to book passage back to England. And in the shipping office, which was notoriously inefficient, had waited on a leather settee with a man who was lodging a complaint. Both, it turned out, had been pushed just that bit too far. They had gone out together to find a cup of tea, having neither booked nor complained. (As it happened, Major Ingot's trunks turned up next day at Algeciras, which struck them both as a good omen.) Since then they had been seeing something of one another, and discovering mutual interests.

Caro read with wonder: "We share the same tastes, and think alike."

"You are both grown now," Dora wrote, "and no longer need me." There was reproof in it as well as irony. The wedding would be in the Algarve, where the Major lived, or resided. Major Ingot—Bruce—was taking over the arrangements. "I have never had anyone to do things for me before, and am enjoying the luxury." The bridal pair would then travel to England, but only to pack belongings, as the Major was setting up in the Algarve where he had retired into import-export.

"Dora in Portugal," said Grace. It sounded historic.

"Oh Grace, thank God."

It was as close as they had ever come to assessing the damage.

Again they leaned to look. Dora would be often in England, as Major Ingot—Bruce—had his buyers to look up. After all, it wasn't as if she was going to disappear. She need not say, she said, that she loved them. It did not matter about her, they were all that mattered. "I have never asked anything from anybody, and don't mean to start now." The dress would be ivory crepe, day-length, with a short jacket; the hat, beige. There was a word they could not read, which might have been stephanotis. The Major was fixing up about photos and Dora would bring any that were half-way decent; but had never taken a good picture. It would be a relief to get away from this heat, worse than anything in Australia. Just be happy.

The letter was signed "D." Dora had difficulty with signatures, as with salutations.

A mechanical tone, already absent-minded, raised the possibility that Dora might have been unfeeling towards them always. Grace feared that Caro might point this out. There was also a swift, indecent consciousness of the fleshly change that Dora would, amazingly, be the first of them to undergo.

"We must cable." But they remained there together in a synthesis of confused remembrance. Grace would have liked to think something universal, but could only arrive at the outskirts of feeling. Caro might have been seeing Grace herself, in a pinafore, hauling by its spokes a little sky-blue chair.

They would have given each other a rare embrace.

"Not interrupting, I trust." Sefton Thrale saw the two women standing rapt in the sunlight and holding up their letter.

They separated, not ready to tell.

"I have Tertia with me."

He had Tertia with him, the daughter of a lord. So sleekly pretty, so fair and tall that she seemed an advertisement for something very costly. She had driven a car from the castle, and her hair was bound with a strip of pink silk that passed behind her ears. Her eyes were light blue—shining with what at a distance passed for sheer delight, and perhaps in childhood had truly been. Up close, however, the clarity was stinging, and neither gave nor received a good impression. Nothing about her appeared to have been humanly touched.

Circumstances had made Grace responsible here. She closed Dora's letter into its envelope and came forward, too polite to seem in charge. They murmured, you-do. Tertia offered fingertips in a gesture not so much exhausted as reserving strength for something more worth while.

"Has Paul come?" Three young women sat down while Sefton Thrale went on a favourite errand—to seek news of Paul Ivory, who must today arrive at last.

Having shaken hands, Tertia touched her bodice, her hair: an animal fastidiously expunging traces of contact. She was aware of intercepting, without rupturing, a current of high feeling—the sisters, in their private preoccupation, being not quite accessible to her aloofness. Like Christian Thrale before her, she found them insufficiently conscious of their disadvantage, and would have liked to bring it home to them. She perceived that, while Grace might eventually be set straight in this fashion, Caro would be a tougher proposition.

Tertia Drage plucked a leaf from her dress and flung it emphatically in the empty grate. It was something they were to notice again in Tertia—that she handled objects or pushed doors with punitive abruptness, seeing no reason to indulge an uncompliant world. The occasional human anger felt against inanimate things that tumble or resist was in her case perpetual.

No. Tertia would not have sherry. Thank you. She had

come in the car they could see through the open window. Caro got up to look. It was a low, open Bentley from before the war, a model sought by collectors. Dark green; slim and beautiful as Tertia. "What a marvellous car." Caro pushed the paned window farther, and stood looking at the car. Circular lamps, set over the mudguards, were glassily unlit like Tertia's eyes.

Tertia said, "Nineteen thirty-seven. And in showroom condition."

A half-grown cat came in over the window-sill. Caro sat again, taking the cat in her lap. Grace held Dora's blue letter. They could not recall whose turn it was to speak. The Professor came back, saying "I now have decisive information," but Tertia gave no sign of life. Outside the window, the car was kinder because suggestive of fluency and eventual animation.

Paul Ivory was motoring down from London, and should soon arrive. ("Motoring down" was the Professor's choice of phrase.) Ivory's car would swoop up alongside Tertia's, which would almost certainly put it in the shade or the wrong.

"I can't wait," said Tertia, meaning only that she would not. "I dislike reunions." She would assert "I don't like animals," or children, or the ocean, or the spring, confident that her distaste must have importance. Any contrary opinion must be, as she implied, falsely sentimental. Even so, she could not manage to put these two sisters in the wrong or shade. They were actually waiting for her to be gone so they might resume.

Caro recrossed her legs with care. In the sleeping catkin, weight slipped from end to end, as in a bean-bag. The true weight was in the blue envelope on Grace's lap. As to Tertia, Caroline Bell wondered what *Benhow* had capsized her into this showroom condition.

Grace thought that Tertia would soon say she hated cats.

"I can turn the car right there," Tertia said. "Can't I." Her observations were unsmiling, without doubt or delicacy. They were quoits that fell with a tingling, accurate thud around a post. She looked at the room, saying "Goodbye." To Caro she remarked, "Cats hate me."

When Tertia had gone out with Sefton Thrale, Caro

said, "Overjoyed at your happiness. What about something like that?" The only happiness Dora had in fact endorsed was their own.

"We can write it out. I'll cycle down and send it." Tertia's manner had infected them with flatness, and they would never embrace now over Dora's letter. Outside, the car rolled backwards to a herbaceous border, where it crouched to spring. Petrol was exhaled on candytuft. Then Tertia dashed away, scattering small stones.

When they had written out the cable, the second car came, short, closed, dark red. They could see the man with light hair at the wheel, and Ted Tice coming out from the side of the house to help him park. Grace said, "So many things are happening at once. It's a pity they could not be more spread out." Giving, childlike, the measure of their secluded, innocent, yet expectant lives. Ted disappeared from their view, but they could hear him call, "Left" and "Right" and "Mind out." The young man in the car moved his elbow from the open sill and took the wheel in both hands. He wore a dark, high-necked jersey. His hair fell over his forehead like a schoolboy's.

Wheels turned this way, that way, and off-screen Ted called "Hold it," like a film director. Grace asked Caro, "D'you want anything when I'm in the village?" but they were watching the red car coming to its halt. The engine stopped, and a young man got out: tall, graceful, and well dressed in a way that was unfamiliar to them.

Paul Ivory was the first Englishman they knew to dress, as everyone dressed later, in a dark-blue jersey like a fisherman's, and to wear light cotton trousers and canvas shoes.

Then came the moment in which Ted was most to blame, since it was he who stopped and looked, and lowered his hand. Whatever spontaneous antipathy announced itself between these two, Paul at least came on, introducing himself and making things possible. Even as his candid glance went over Ted Tice, sizing up and deciding. They did shake hands, but Ted stood impassive while Paul Ivory heaved a leather suitcase from the car and slammed a door. He might easily have moved away, for the Professor had come out of the house and was saying he could not be more delighted; but instead remained there, awkward and removed, as if dozing in the activity of arrival and determined that Paul Ivory should shine by contrast.

It was a show of instinct so pronounced that Grace half-turned from the window, waiting for Caro to interpret.

Caro was thinking that, in England, class distrust might destroy even the best, by distracting their energies. She was watching with some large feeling, less than love, in which approval and exasperation merged to a pang that Ted Tice should supply, in a little scene of varnished attitudes and systematic exchanges, the indispensable humanity. She was used by now to his providing strokes of comprehension that were strong experiences in themselves; but on this occasion he stood on gravel with his hands dangling, and had no apparent consciousness of Caro or anyone else. While she observed, and wondered what impulse worked on him.

Paul Ivory looked at the low window where the young women, standing, were almost at his level. He smiled out of a handsome, fair, and fortunate face, acknowledging pleasant surprise with such controlled openness that no surprise remained. And the sisters smiled back in the serious way they had for such moments. Only Charmian Thrale, at an open door, made a contrast between this auspicious arrival and the way in which Ted Tice had been washed up out of a storm; remembering how Caro had looked down that morning from the staircase, and gone away.

9

When Paul Ivory walked in espadrilles on the paths and passages of Peverel, the sound inaugurated, softly, the modern era. As did his cotton jerseys—some blue, some black—and trousers of pale poplin. The modern era, like the weather, was making these possible. Paul had brought the sun, and his luck, with him. Early on warm mornings, the girls pressed flowered dresses in a room by the kitchen where an ironing-table was covered by a worn blanket and there was an old stone sink. Ted Tice's fair-isle pullover and sea-green cardigan in cable stitch had been put away, perhaps forever.

Mrs. Charmian Thrale told Paul Ivory, "I recall you as a perfect child. The only child ever to captivate my father." It was her way of saying, What a charming and indeed blessed young person; and of sketching, most delicately, her own desolate childhood. Paul took praise well, unembarrassed, diffidently pleased. It was not usual at that period to see a young man frankly enjoying the fact of youth and taking justified pleasure in his own health and good looks. In his early and deserved distinction, he made the future seem less formless.

Paul's play would be produced in London in the autumn. In preparation he received telephone calls and registered envelopes. There were mornings when he must not be interrupted, because of adding or rewriting. The play was called *Friend of Caesar*, and had been announced in the press as presenting a contemporary family as an analogy of political power. Paul himself read this out with a smile. A celebrated actor had agreed to play the leading role.

Paul Ivory was a man of promise in a literal sense: cir-

cumstances had made a solemn undertaking to see Paul
prosper. His play would be widely and justly praised. Provincial towns and foreign cities would clamour for it, and
a famous director would make a successful film. The radiant pre-eminence of Paul's engagement with events was
far more bridal than his prospective betrothal to Tertia
Drage.

In its subtlety and confidence Paul's physical beauty,
like his character, suggested technique. As some fine portrait might be underpainted dark where it showed light, or
light where dark, so might Paul Ivory be subliminally
cold where warm, warm where cold—the tones overlap-
ping to create, ingeniously, a strong yet fluid delineation.
Similarly, his limbs might seem the instruments or weapons
of grace rather than its simple evidence. Paul's attenuated
fingers turned up at their tips with extreme sensitivity, as
if testing a surface for heat.

Sefton Thrale told Ted Tice, "Paul will make his mark."
Like praising a pretty girl to a plain one. And yet there
was the sense that Paul Ivory and Ted Tice were both
marked men, and symbolically opposed. It was not merely
that the world had set the two of them at odds. More
irrationally, it seemed that one of them must lose if the
other were to win.

Sefton Thrale had twice remarked that Tice would soon
be gone, and was mindful of the actual date.

Mrs. Thrale told Paul Ivory, at his request, about the
Vicar—who had an impediment of speech and had once
been a Communist, but had never, like the man at Thaxted,
hung the Red Flag in the church. The Professor put in, "He
is High, of course, very High," as if a clergyman were a
piece of hung game; recommending attention to the church
façade as a fine example of napped flints. And on the
Sunday Paul went to church in the village, involving the
household at Peverel in a religious gesture.

The two sisters, ironing blouses, watched the red car
drive away. Charmian Thrale might be noting the event
from an upstairs room. Paul cast his spell, as Ted his pall.
It was undeniably affecting, the thought of this tall, victorious male kneeling down, offering and receiving. Although
both Mrs. Thrale at the high window and Caro in the

kitchen were aware that women are not to be trusted with emotion of the kind.

Carrying the folded clothes into the hallway, Caro found Ted at the open door.

Ted Tice said, "Christopher Robin is saying his prayers."

She did not know whose part to take but, like Sefton Thrale, recalled that Ted would soon be gone. She put the fresh blouses in a basket on the stairs and went with Ted into the garden.

He said, "In two weeks I'll be gone."

"You'll be in Edinburgh. And, soon after, in Paris." Making clear he had nothing to complain of. She herself, in a month, would go to London to work in the government office. For Caro had come out of the examination ahead of all the rest; being a marked person in her own way, which was not theirs.

There was the brief, silent imagining of new life, even to the deal tables and scarred office chairs. Ted said, "I must imagine it without you." They walked out of the flower-garden and stood under trees, looking on the valley. An entire nation lay still with Sunday and summer. A yellow field, far off, was flat and bright as a streak of paint. From distant uplands, reaped stubble pricked the eye, reliable as old tweed. On the opposite rise, a chess-piece on the chequered board, Tertia's castle notched the sky with grey crenellations.

Ted said, "I've no charm at the best of times, and nothing is less charming than unwanted love. But as we're parting soon I must say it, that I hope you'll think of me and let me write to you. And eventually let me love you."

The girl heard his speech out with a stoicism that made her seem the sufferer: withstanding his appeal like necessary pain, treating it with careful respect. "Of course I think of you, and will write. I like you better than anyone I've known." She moved away—a blue dress passing like haze over a backdrop of dark trees and painted fields. "As to the rest, I can't see how it would ever happen."

"From my point of view, that is very hard." For the release of a few words, he was squandering the asset of silence. It was inconceivable that he could not touch or take hold of her light-blue body that had power over all his days. "You're as distant from me now as you'll be when we're separated. There's no happiness in this for me, our standing together here and now. But I'll think of it, later, as being close to you, and lucky."

She had clasped her arm about a tree and stood looking at him. It seemed the very landscape gloated, and that the tree allied itself with her—impersonal, established. Or that she leaned on the tree seductively, to taunt him. The hallucination vanished, but left knowledge of a kind. There was a heavy smell of vegetation steaming in the sun: England drying out.

"Ted," she said. "Ted." Mild exasperation. "When I start this work in London, I'll be on my own for the first time. It matters to me to be at liberty now, after years of Dora."

It was a reason, certainly; if not the truest reason.

Ted had heard of Dora. "Once people establish themselves as a cause for concern, they don't give up easily." Then he feared she might refer these words to himself. "On your side there's the anxiety, on hers the claim to it. That often passes for affection, even for great love. The very fact that you did well in that test"—he meant the examination where Caro had come out ahead—"confirms your ability to accept her burden; you have a certificate now to prove it."

"I don't tell her a thing of that sort. It seems to recoil." Caroline Bell having discovered in childhood that achievements can be transformed to hostile weapons. ("Everything falls in your lap, why should you care about a life like mine?") A childish struggle between the wish to show, or tell, and the need to hoard silent strength had long since been resolved. She said, "I'm not sure I can explain that."

He said, "I know exactly."

(When Ted Tice was eleven or so, his mother told him, "It was when I went to Lacey's, after leaving the mill, and worked on the invoices. It was your uncle Tony Mott got me the chance there, seeing I was a dab at the sums. Yes, it was your uncle Tony give me my chance. Well, come Christmas Mr. Dan Lacey handed other lasses at office two pound apiece in an envelope as a present. But I got three, along of being quick at the figgers. I'd never seen the like of two pound let alone three, me wages were twelve bob a week, took off me by my dad soon as I was in the door. An I knew well enough he'd take this off me too. We was in Ellor Street then, and when I got home that night I heard right off that my cousin Lorna—tha never saw our Lorne, that was Cec's only girl and died of the lungs, very month tha was born—well, that Lorna had got three pound, or three guineas it was, where she worked, though two was usual. An I was pulled both ways, I was put to it, you see, whether to show I was worth the three like Lorna or to say two and keep one to missel. An I did, I kept one back and didn't let on. It was the one time I was fly."

Ted's mother was sifting flour at the time, on a big kitchen slab that was their only table.)

Under the laden trees Ted Tice tilted back his head and saw the sky. This might have had to do with salt tears and the law of gravity. " 'Twas your uncle Tony give me my chance." Ah Christ: *My chance.*

(Ted's mother was saying as she sifted: "Lorna favvered her dad. She's in the family group, 'twas taken just round that time, but tha can't make her out that clear, she's at back and got her head down, poor Lorne.")

Ted Tice looked at the horizon. He remembered Uncle Tony, short and pink, who lived a little better than the rest of them, knew a chap on the council, and kept a tiger cat called Moggie.

He said, "Paul Ivory is marrying that castle."

"I suppose so." They both stared out at the solid, sunlit figment of history's imagination, on its dated elevation. As a spouse it inspired some apprehension.

Ted said, "Paul Ivory has to marry a lord or, at very least, the daughter of one. It is written. Written likewise that she be rich. He has no choice, it's mandatory. Turn right for the castle."

"Even so, I don't see why Tertia should oblige him." It was unnatural to say "Tertia" where no intimacy could exist.

"Maybe she feels beleaguered in the castle." They smiled to imagine Tertia on the battlements, peering glassily from behind machicolations. "Or there is an antagonism she enjoys. Or they know the worst about each other. That can be a bond."

"Paul might change. He is still young."

"His faults aren't those of youth. He has no growth, merely automatic transmission."

The girl had not heard Ted Tice on this note before—savage as his inferiors, with a malice that blurred his virtue. Disappointment was perhaps for his sake, that he should join in the general unmasking. She moved out from the shadow of trees and started back to the house. They had not disagreed. But some carefulness would now develop on both sides—a concern not to offend or expose. It was unclear why this had come into existence.

To Ted Tice, the defeat appeared to be of his own making, as if some great duty had fallen to him and he had bungled it. An image—of her strong will expressed in apparent passivity, while he urged an absolute need—baffled his intelligence with sheer waste. Otherwise he might have seen in it a virtual representation of the act of love.

In these warm days Tertia came and went, taking Paul Ivory here and there. Grace and Caro saw her sit at the wheel of her green car, her eyebrows raised, her pupils insensate as the bronze discs applied as eyes to ancient statues. Grace said, "I suppose she is a great prize." She had read this phrase, which was her way of declaring: They cannot be in love.

There came an interlude of calm brilliance when it was morning all day long. On one of these clear days Caro, returning from the village, met Paul Ivory, who was on foot. Seen this way, out of bounds, he was like a rider unhorsed; and she said this to him.

"My lost advantages." No one would have thought them lost, to see Paul laugh and make his graceful stride. Paul Ivory was a star: any firmament would do.

He had seen Caro from a distance and altered his course to intersect. Had observed, as he drew near, that her walk turned the progress of other women to a thump or shuffle. He would have said her delicate dark strength was virile—a sombre glow that might distinguish some young man. He remembered dark, vigorous young men who kept somewhat to themselves, yet retained this vibrancy of adventure. Then he thought how such youths often ended feebly, how quickly they grew sour or cautious, or became the foils of bitter women—their energies turned to blame or bluster, their pride morose. He had already seen that; and supposed that in the case of women such beings dwindled entirely, or at most passed some shred of their lost impetus to children.

Paul Ivory had also noted penalties of impulse. Had seen how men provide themselves, before their taste or character is formed, with wife and children—committed and condemned thereafter to the fixtures of an outgrown fancy. He was satisfied his own prospective marriage would preclude such dangers. An accusation of dispassion would not have troubled him. He was not convinced that passion was essential, or that the world had properly defined it.

The girl asked, "Shall we take the shortcut through the churchyard?"

"No graveyard can be a shortcut." Paul opened a wicket gate.

A torn kite was lying in the grass. Caro said, "There are often children playing here."

"Children like cemeteries. No traffic, no live grown-ups, and the headstones are child-height, companionable."

Caro, who usually came that way, showed the inscriptions. Here lieth all that could die of Oliver Wade. The earthly enchantments of Tryphena Cope are here subdued. On later stones, merely the name, and the years—of birth and death—connected by a little etched hyphen representing life. Eroded tablets tilted like torn kites. On the oldest the lettering was indecipherable: inaudible last words.

Caroline Bell said, "The dead in cemeteries give the impression of having all died normally and peacefully." Paul did not reply, but she persisted, "Do you think that's why they excluded suicides from consecrated ground, to maintain the fiction?" As they passed on in silence to the road it occurred to her that, since he was a believer, she had possibly offended. Paul's expression smoothly allowed her to think so. There was something cold in him that might wait to be given a chance.

Paul wished perhaps to punish her—for her being remarkable now, and for any impending ordinariness. All that was remarkable, if you boiled it down, was that she gave belief of a kind. You might not accept it but she gave it—being a believer in her own way, which was not his.

He said, "You emanate so much resolve, and all of it unfocused."

"I don't think you know me well enough to say that."

Paul laughed. "I can say it, then, when I know you better?"

Passers-by looked harder than was necessary, for these two made a couple whose fates could not be predicted with confidence. Having the world regard them as a pair made a fact of it.

"They're surprised to see you with someone at your side," Paul said. "You're so much alone." They had reached a turn where the castle confronted them across summer meadows. Everything else appeared to waver in the heat, but not the castle. "I see you alone in the garden at night. I look down and see you there alone."

In the transparent morning he created a moment of night silence: Caro unaware in the garden, and Paul watching. From his hidden elevation he created fragrant darkness round them both.

"To me it seems I'm not enough alone."

"Is that intended for now?—For me?"

"Of course not."

The castle was obdurate, the only detail not executed by Turner. In the valley a line of osiers flinched at the least breath of air.

"Women have capacity for solitude, but don't want it. Men want and need it, but the flesh soon makes fools of them." It was Paul Ivory's habit to suppose that girls knew more than they let on.

Taking the castle for her model, Caro would not be disconcerted. They were on the hillside path, near the place where she had sat in the dark with Ted Tice and talked of loyalty. Although no treachery was involved, she would not have wanted Ted to see her pausing there with Paul Ivory. Although she walked on in her straight way, inwardly she stooped and was vulnerable.

Paul halted by the low wall, as if he knew of her scruples and meant to flout them. "Do you send him about his business too?" He brushed the wall lightly with his hand, and sat there. "You know I mean Tice."

Caro sat beside him. Her soul seemed a cold, separate thing, while her body was weightless, humid, its contours exposed and scarcely natural. It was hard to say which was unworthy of the other. She observed Paul Ivory's appearance as if it were an event that might develop before one's eyes. He had the face of the future, skilled in perceiving what the world wants. When he said, "You know I mean," there was a clouding of his looks with something coarse that made her its accomplice. It was no more than she deeply expected of him, yet his tapping of that vein of expectation made complicity between them. When he said, "You know I mean Tice," she understood, also, that Ted's love was a stimulus to Paul and the cause of their sitting together on the wall.

The man was turned towards her, awaiting some kind of victory. He would have her believe that any or all suspicion was warranted and confirmed.

She was certain he was about to touch her—touch her breast or shoulder, put his face to hers—and already experienced the imagined contact with purifying intensity. At the same time she was fixed, subjected, fatalistic. And sat, fingers clasped, no sign of agitation, with the immemorial stillness of women at such moments.

Paul stood up and thrust his hands in his pockets. "Shall we go on, then?" Paul stood; while Caro looked up recomposing her flesh and blood. And Paul smiled, having had his victory.

Caro entered the house alone, and stood in the hall. There was a mirror on one wall, and she had lately taken to watching herself. Even when looking at a plain wall these days she might be picturing herself, if not with accuracy. Now her likeness was dark with the change from sunlight to shadow, or because her vision dimmed from momentary faintness. At a distance a door opened, and Professor Sefton Thrale called, "Charmian?" And Caroline Bell could not know why that simple fact should bring her close to tears.

It was a state of mind. Or it was because she had stood

long ago in a darkened room, a little girl of six years old, and looked in a long mirror cool as water. And, a door opening, had heard her father's voice call "Marian?"— which was her mother's name. That was all there was in it, that was the evocation: a small spasm of memory that could never elucidate itself.

10

Paul Ivory had been accepted by Tertia Drage. When this was known, the Thrales gave a dinner for the lord of the castle, inviting also a pair of neighbours known to have sufficient property in Kenya. The large locked drawing-room at Peverel was aired and reclaimed by help hired from the village. The opening of the room for such a purpose did not so much terminate its period of closing as make clear it was now a shrine.

Longer than broad, the room had Corinthian pilasters and a pale fireplace at each end. Windows went from floor to ceiling, draped with orange silk brought long ago from Swatow by a relation in Butterfield and Swire. The handsome curtains, though shredding now and dusty, might be drawn to conceal panes in need of reglazing. Two chandeliers had been carefully cleaned; but a third, in a basket in the attic, was a hailstorm of dismantled crystals.

By daylight, patches of damp made an atlas of the walls. Ted Tice, who was handy at such things, repaired an extra leaf belonging to an oval table. The panel, which had warped while out of use in the war, was laid on trestles, where Ted could work at it; and the village help, unconvinced of his standing in the house, despised Ted for his proficiency. There was an elderly hired couple who supervised—the husband tall but with distorted stance, as if he had once been seized and wrung; the wife buttressed by flesh and corset, an emplacement withstanding attack. This pair, the Mullions, were now retired from long service in some mighty house; but were glad, as they said, to give satisfaction from time to time. Service and satisfaction, their strong preoccupations, had neither unnerved them nor made them approachable.

Mrs. Mullion, in black, told Ted Tice: "The young do not understand the meaning of service." Because she had heard him sing "Southerly, southerly" in the drawing-room, yet did not believe he was a guest. Mrs. Mullion also disliked and feared Ted's accent, or rather the absence of any attempt on his part to flaunt or disguise it.

It was plain, however, that this hired couple went in awe of Paul Ivory, who neither sang nor repaired furniture and scarcely greeted them.

Ted was at the final stage of his repair of the table, which involved a touch of varnish and the fitting of a small brass hook. When Mrs. Mullion spoke of the meaning of service, he was working near an open window and might not have heard.

(Once—it was when Ted was ten and had his tonsils taken out, which was done at home—his mother had sat down on his bed and told him about the service and the satisfaction. "Thi father said he'd not do it again, go in service. Nor would he. We did it that one time, when we was first married and went as couple to the Truscotts at Ponderhurst. Being afeard of not finding work, and thi father still with the cough then from getting gassed in the war. Truscotts brought cook and maid with them when they come down, and driver, but were wanting a couple to look to the place when they were up in town whilst Parlyment was sitting. Well, pay wasn't much but there was keep as well, and the work not heavy.

"We'd been there six weeks it must have been when Mr. Truscott—Sir Eric as he is now—come to thi father and said as we were giving satisfaction and should look to stay on. But seeing we were a couple newly wed he should make clear that he and Mrs. T., wanting their quiet in the country, preferred we have no children. I wasn't there when he said it, but thi father called out to me and I came. And he says to Mr. Truscott, 'Say it again'—like that, right out, so you could see what was coming. 'Tell 'er,' he says. Well then your father gave it him good and proper. 'We're leaving here today,' he says—us that hadn't penny to our name nor mortal place to lay our head. And Truscott says, all red and fit to brast, 'You'll go without the reference then.' And thi father says, 'My reference from thee is, I wouldn't stand thi bloody lip. What's it o' yourn if we'd a ruck o' kids, or none?' And then he says what he shouldn't about Truscott and Mrs. T.—she wasn't a bad sort really, only gormless. Well, Truscott made to walk off, but thi father told him, 'I'm going to news-papers with this and they can print it, how a minister o' the crown talks to an Englishman these times.' And from being red Truscott goes white as this sheet and says, 'Tice, I'm sure we can settle this peaceable,' or peaceably. He'd the wind up right and proper. 'Let's sit down and talk sensible, I may not have explained missel. And have been lately under a strain.' Him that ne'er did hand's turn ex-cept to blether. Well, upshot was he give us fifty pound and we left next morning. We could live six month then, at a pinch, on fifty pound and keep oursel decent. There was the reference too, They have given every satisfaction. But thi dad said, Never again.

"A bit later on he told it all to Mr. Beardsley, yon par-son at Southport who stuck up for the working folk, and the idea was he might still go to papers with it for it riled him yet. But Mr. Beardsley told him No, because we'd took the fifty pound. So that was an end of it. And now Truscott's Sir Eric and has his picture with Prince of Wales.")

As to the hired couple at Peverel, the Mullions, Ted Tice learned afterwards that they had lost their grandson in an accident some weeks before. If you knew enough, antipathy would rarely be conclusive.

Caroline Bell took out a dark dress, bought abroad, which alone of her clothes created the effect that might in some future time, or very soon, be entirely hers. She hung the dress up in her room, where she could see it, like bunting for a festival. She had scarcely worn it, and liked to think how she had bought it with a pile of pastel-coloured banknotes on her last morning in France. Dora had subsequently gone to pieces over the price.

When the time came she took the dress down from its hook, and it slipped into her arms like a victim. She had drawn back her heavy hair and coiled it; and could see, in the mirror, how this became her.

Caro went downstairs in the early evening wearing her dark dress, holding the silk belt of it in her hand. She was ironing the belt in the room near the kitchen when Tertia came in carrying a mass of flowers.

"These must go in deep water." Tertia laid the flowers on a slab by the stone sink. She had a rustling, sweeping dress of silver. It was as if a salt gale had blown in; yet Tertia was only standing still and watching Caro iron, while the flowers lay on their cenotaph ready to die.

Caro set the iron on its rest and held up the belt—her head back, her arms raised, and the belt suspended. Being human, she could not help herself. She knew she had sometimes left her mark, but on this occasion had a taste to see the fact acknowledged.

"And what," Tertia asked at last, "are you going to put on tonight?"

Caro continued to hold up the belt—to one side, like an abstracted snake-charmer, so she could look Tertia in the face. It was a pity there was no one else to see Caro then in her beautiful dress, her throat and arm bare, her delicate raised hand, and her dark eyes fixed on their object. In this way for some moments she compelled Tertia Drage to admire.

And from the garden Paul Ivory called, "Caro." It was the first time he had spoken her name.

There was a pause, in which sounds could be heard from the adjacent kitchen. Releasing Tertia from the spell, Caro lowered the belt and fitted it with slow care about her own waist. She then carried a heavy vase to the sink and turned the tap. These modest actions commanded attention, and Tertia was not the first to see in Caro's most commonplace movements rehearsals for life and death. When the flowers were in the vase Caro looked again at Tertia and said, "In deep water." And laughed, and dried her hands and walked away.

That evening they were celebrating Tertia's betrothal to Paul Ivory.

Sefton Thrale showed the view over the valley in the dying light before bringing his guests indoors. The lately opened drawing-room was not quite willing to harbour life: a neglected room can no more be rallied for an emergency than an overgrown garden. It went without saying that there were bowls of roses, soft lamplight and, in each grate, a small fire burning. However, as the entering voices rang, the room retreated. It was an old room, unpractised in raw new sounds of struck matches and the ice in tumblers.

It appeared that Tertia's mother was a survivor of the *Titanic*—eclipsing Grace and Caro with their obscure, inglorious *Benbow* and its ineffectual displacement of Australian waters. Tertia's mother remembered being lowered to a lifeboat in her seventh year, and saved. Surviving to become a brawny chestnut mare, she had conceived and borne five daughters but no male heir.

There was the glacial flow of Tertia's moiré on the carpet as she sailed away from her mother, a pinnace from the flagship. How much time had been taken to prepare that evening's version of Tertia Drage—the sleek hair and molded silver dress, the smooth armpit, gleaming necklace and little pointed shoes; the enamel matching on her fingertips and concealed toes. Yet Tertia was indifferent, scornful, as if decked out in these trinkets and gauzes quite against her inclination. You might nearly believe in her neutrality, against all the evidence. Tertia had dissociated herself from human weakness: when she touched her dress with near-derision, mere life in others was made to seem commotion.

Yet she had begun the evening with a sharp defeat.

Tertia's mother said, "She spoils every dinner party she attends." Fond and proud. Crushing a billowing blue sofa, Lady Drage now became a creature too heavy for its element, a cormorant on the waves. An extra guest she had brought took his place on the hearth, where flakes of fire sprang up behind him. A tall, reddish man about forty, he cleared his throat with assurance but spoke little. He had a signet ring, old gold, smooth as a knuckle; and wore a Brigade of Guards tie.

Some talk of costs, and taxation, was a formality with which such evenings must now be opened.

Caro asked Ted Tice, "Do English people always speak of money?"

"Mainly the rich ones."

Mr. Collins from Kenya, seated in a leather chair, knew a joke about Australia, or Orstrylia; which he said was from the recent war, giving the setting as Tobruk, but which in fact went back to the Great War and the campaign in the Dardanelles. The story was as follows: A wounded soldier asks an Australian nurse at his bedside, "Was I brought here to die?" and "No," she answers, "yesterdie."

That was the joke. Caroline and Grace Bell were familiar with this story, which was often told to them when they were introduced. Ted Tice had not heard it before. It could be seen that tears came to his scratched eye as they did to the other, flawless one.

Mrs. Charmian Thrale gently touched a collar of pearls. Whiter than pearl, her throat might never have been exposed to light.

(In 1916, during the Battle of the Somme, Charmian Playfair, volunteering as a nurse's aide, was assigned to ambulance duty at Victoria Station where casualties were arriving on hospital trains. The loaded ambulance trundled back through dark streets carrying its racks of blanketed men—who, from their spotless newspaper anonymity of "the wounded," were suddenly incarnate as moaning, silent, or plucky inhabitants of rent, individual flesh. Enclosed with these spectres in swaying gloom, a nineteen-year-old girl put her hand to her soft throat. Yet moved as best she could, to supply water or answer questions, among the grey blankets and the red, rusty, or blackened bandages. There was a boy of her own age to whose whisper she had to bend, her face nearly touching his: "So cold. Cold. My feet are so cold." And, almost capably, the girl answered, "I'll fix that"; turning to adjust the blanket, and discovering he had no feet.)

Around Mrs. Charmian Thrale these impressions passed in ritual rather than confusion: the simultaneous preoccupation of girls with love and dresses, the men with their assertions great and small, the women all submission or dominion; an imbalance of hope and memory, a savage tangle of history. These welling together in a flow of time that only some godlike grammar—some unknown, aoristic tense—might describe and reconcile.

Mrs. Thrale shifted roses to make room for an ashtray. Her back did not touch the sofa.

Tertia's chestnut *mère* was saying, "Not Kenya, no never alas, but we of course were in Egypt when my husband was—oh picturesque I grant you, who can deny, Luxor, Karnak, but the beggars and what can one do. Nobody is more tender-hearted actually—to a fault my family always tell me—but it would not be a kindness, indeed dangerous to. Isn't that so, Guy?"

Her husband mechanically gave his endorsement. He sat between the women, a panel that had warped for lack of use. He had long since become the views he had never contested: perjured acquiescence registered in an inward shrivelling of lip and chin. Yet he suddenly said, starting from sleep, "In Egypt she suffered from the sun." And did look about, if not intently. "Pigmentation, that's the word. Parents had no sense, forced her outdoors as a girl, did a lot of harm." The remonstrance an echo of a time when he had imagined that his wife, of all people, needed his protection. Yet, between the fire and the ice, she had survived.

The dreaming dog, Grasper, twitched on the hearth, where the tall man in the Brigade tie stood impassive, lighting his cigarette. He had been introduced as Captain Cartledge.

The young people had drifted to the other end of the room, where they were grouped together, all standing. Their elders smiled to see this—someone at least was having a good time; which, it was hoped, would counter their own dullness. The galaxy of lovely young women, and, in Paul, one desirable young man.

Caroline Bell did not quite look young, bearing her new beauty like a difference of generation.

It was churlish of Ted Tice simply to stand there. It had somehow been agreed, on both sides, that he should not be one of them.

"In my usual way," said Tertia Drage, "I lost the car keys." My usual way, she would say, or my inimitable way, just like me—to connote distinction, even fame. If Tertia did it, it must matter.

Ted stood taciturn, the underdog; and yet prevailed. While Tertia, topdog, had suffered a defeat this evening and might again do so.

Ted had repaired the table in time, despite last-minute anxiety from Sefton Thrale about the hammering. Linen, silver, and flowers were deployed and candles placed, the table solemn as a dignitary lying in state. In its elaborate discretion, the table was their cue, a setting for behaviour.

Tertia told Ted, "I suppose you are a whizz at carpentry, that sort of thing."

"That's right."

"Lucky you. Runs in families, I expect."

"As in the Holy Family." This was Caro. And the man with the Brigade tie looked out from the elderly end of the room.

Paul smiled. "Saint Caro, Protectress of Carpenters." He was on her side, a side differentiated from Ted Tice's, or even from his own. Ted perhaps chose to have no side that evening, preferring no one should join him. He was not even guilty of showing that he judged. They were ranged so that Paul and Tertia, betrothed, faced the others, but in the talk Paul would sometimes cross over to Caro. It could not be said this was brave, yet it involved a certain risk.

Tertia now said, "All of you together in one house." As if this were absurd of them. "Like castaways on an island."

"Or a country house party," Grace remarked, "where a murder has been committed and all the genteel people are suspects."

It was agreed that Grace could never be a suspect. Ted Tice stood silent. Ruling Grace out made the rest of them appear more capable of violence. Grace was separate, not only in her mildness but in having fixed her affections. She had been claimed, and appeared as one of them for a last time and incompletely. For Grace, there had already been public avowals and secret disclosures, and the letters from Ottawa beginning Dearest. In someone's view, she had attained excellence.

These conditions might now have equally applied to Tertia—yet did not, although no marriage could seem more inevitable than hers. It was notable that Tertia never laid public claim to Paul by touching or by the other proprietary little exhibitions through which lovers show themselves complacent or insecure. On this night of their betrothal, Tertia forbore to link herself in any way with Paul and, standing at his side, conveyed a peculiarly hard detachment in what should have been the sweeter outline of her body. There was something in it of the disdain she showed for her carefully chosen clothes.

Paul now said to Caro, "Where did you get that dress?" —bluntly, and, it would seem, not praising.

It was then that Captain Cartledge joined them—making clear, by brusquely leaving the hearth and crossing the room, that he had been waiting the chance. Joined Caro, in fact, since he said at once, "Yes, the dress is beautiful" —exposing, by his compliment, Paul's withheld praise. A horseman, Captain Cartledge had ridden over to the castle from a friend's house nearby, not expecting to stay. Hence, he remarked, the wrong clothes, the tie. He had the complexion, lightly webbed, of outdoor living and indoor drinking, and was a high, handsome man who might have been cruel. There was boldness, or purity of a kind, in his walking up to Caro with the word "beautiful," which cut across their youthful feints and begrudgings with its single stroke of experience, making even Paul Ivory appear unformed.

Tertia in her silver cataphract could not be pleased. Nor could Ted Tice, though it would have taken more than the aversion to bind them. Tertia exchanged with Cartledge the same cold recognition she offered Paul. And Ted Tice saw that these two had, perhaps that very day, been lovers.

At the other end of the room the three old men discussed infirmities; exchanging symptoms in undertones as boys might speak of lust.

At table Captain Cartledge sat by Caro. Mahogany glowed like marble, the very flowers shone like glass or silver; everything was something other than its lustrous self, and the table a catafalque no longer. It was inconceivable that a dark countryside lay draped outside the copper curtains.

"You've searched each other's souls, then." This was Captain Cartledge on the intimacy of young people in a house together.

Caro said that soul-searching was at an end. Ted Tice would leave, tomorrow, for Edinburgh; from Thursday, Paul Ivory was to be some days in London, and, on that day also, Grace would choose, in Winchester, material for her wedding-dress. She pointed them out around the table like strangers; while Tertia, opposite, cleaned her plate with her same disdain.

"And you?" As if the rest were immaterial.

"I?" Making known that she chose to be immaterial, too, to him. "I'm going over to see Avebury Circle for a couple of days." She said that Ted Tice had written out for her, for Thursday, the changes of trains.

The Captain said, "The prehistoric monument," while the table listened without knowing why. "It is prehistoric," he repeated, as if this narrowed it down precisely. And, having done training on Salisbury Plain, went on at once about Stonehenge.

Suddenly, down the table, Paul Ivory spoke; lifting his eyes to Caro's and giving the slight, ironic smile with which people excuse themselves for remembering poetry or prose: "The heathen temple, do you mean?"

And Caro, unsmiling, both slow and instant in reply: "Yes. Older than the centuries; older than the D'Urbervilles."

Going back in the car Tertia said, "That elder Bell girl has a neck like a man's."

Tertia's mother was thinking that the middle classes kept their silver far too clean.

11

When Paul drove past the station and turned into the main road, Caro said nothing. Having gathered himself for an effort of persuasion, he took his time before addressing new circumstances. In these moments the girl's stillness was such as to create, paradoxically, a bodily alteration.

"You knew I wasn't going to London?"

She nodded.

"Wasn't going to drop you off at your train?" He would not have exchanged for anything the suspense generated by her short nods. "And you knew why. When did you realize these things?"

"The night of the dinner."

"You always know everything, then?"

She said, "I am inexperienced."

"Something we must rectify."

He was creating an exchange he might have had with Tertia. Caro wondered if he did this to women, made them talk in such a way, in such a voice, with the double meanings that diminished meaning, stretching the tension-wire between man and woman to a taut, purposeless antagonism. His banter gave an unearthly feeling that you were not hearing his true voice, and that it might not even exist.

She said, "Don't let's speak like this."

"It's how I talk."

"You might like a change." His present object, surely, being just that.

"You will never sound like Tertia, if that's what you mean."

She waited, fearing his disloyalty, or his loyalty. Paul

went on, "Or look like her, either. You must have noticed Tertia's eyes." He brought the car nearly to a halt on the empty road. "Look at me." The moment took them further, as if serious discussion had occurred or some harm been done. He had not yet touched her, and the certainty he would do so gave speech a finality: the last words of their dispassionate selves. "When women have eyes like hers, it's usually impossible to tell if they're crying." Paul might be accustomed to a likelihood of women's tears. "In Tertia's case, however, one may rest assured."

"You chose Tertia."

"I'm not here to account for myself." In this there was already the quick, overbearing petulance of the celebrated: Paul drawing on his future fame. However, he continued with no transition, "She was exactly the same at fifteen when I first set eyes on her, the most unphysical person I'd ever seen."

"Is that an attraction?"

"Let's leave Tertia out of it for the moment."

They turned at a signpost, leaving Tertia out of it. "We're heading for Avebury, if that's what you still intend."

"Yes. I want to see it." She wanted to see Avebury because Ted Tice had described it to her. She leaned her head to the air of the window, leaving Ted out of it.

They drove over a surprising countryside like a delta or reclaimed shore, low and scarcely sloping beneath a sky of high massed cloud. Caro said, "For this moment it is not like England. More like the centre of America."

"I'd like to live awhile in America, and use it the way their writers have used us. English writers can't manage American talk, they just write in their own prejudices. The English have a terrible ear for any speech except their own anyway, and as regards Americans we're all stone-deaf here—deaf, that is, to everything but the easiest awful tourist. That's why an articulate American gets told in England that he doesn't talk like an American: because he's spoiling the game."

He could not have found a better way of reaching her than by making sense. And, since there were infinite possibilities to Paul Ivory's utmost candour, could even have had this in mind. For Paul, sincerity was something to fall back on when other methods flagged.

He said, "A lot of people in England pass their time collecting negative evidence on almost any theme. Old Thrale is archetypal."

It was more unexpected than his betrayal of Tertia, for Paul was throwing over not only the Professor's adulation but his own winning ways. It was also remarkable how this repudiation turned Sefton Thrale's sycophancy to pathos.

"What does it mean, then? That you detest them all?" She meant Tertia, Thrale. But he took it to be the nation— or preferred it so, the public breach of faith being more presentable than a private one.

"I loathe the undernourishment of this country, the grievance, the censoriousness, the reluctance to try anything else. The going through to the bitter end with all the wrong things." Paul's face no more expressed loathing at that moment than Caro's expressed love; yet those were their prevailing passions. The car kept its even pace, a swift capsule giving form to their energies.

Paul said, "You know my father was a prisoner of war in a Japanese camp." Assuming Caro's awareness of this fact, Paul Ivory was quite forgetful of her own father's death by drowning. "When he came back in 1945 he had a jar of beef extract with him, a three-ounce jar of Marmite with a rusted top and the label off, that he had gone into prison with and kept intact for four years. Prisoners do preserve talismans, of course, but this might have saved a life for a few days, or kept a fugitive on the go for a week. Except that the idiot farce of preserving it—of withholding it, in fact—had counted for more. Well, that is England in all its bloodiness."

A child waved to them at a crossing. Paul waved back.

"The day after he got home he produced this jar of Marmite with the rusted top. Plonked it down on the lunch-table and told us in his graveyard voice it hadn't been touched in three years and so-and-so many months of starvation in the camp, and had been with him at every meal. Not bombastic, of course, the off-handedness being part of the larger vacancy. It was one of those occasions you can't rise to because you don't accept the rules. I couldn't stand it—the devotion to Marmite, the reverential baffled silence round the table. And I told him, 'Then its hour has struck, for God knows we're hungry enough here too.' And I unscrewed the bloody thing and dug my spoon into it there and then, to desanctify the Marmite cult before it took hold of me too and embalmed me."

They entered a lane where the heavy overhang of trees was a closing of curtains. Paul said, "Well, speak to me. Or is that a damned Marmite look on your face too?"

Caro said, "I think your story brutal and Oedipal, if that gives me a Marmite look." Summoning real courage for a heavy risk. "Why should you mock anybody's endurance or their means of survival? You, who've never faced death or even danger?"

Paul lifted his hands from the wheel in a show of hopelessness. But when they drove out from the screen of trees he said, "I might add, it tasted foul. I'm lucky to be alive." And they laughed, and gladly forgot all about Paul's father.

When Paul Ivory's father turned conscientious objector as a young officer in the trenches late in 1917, he had already published a volume of verse that, according to its pale paper cover, astonished by a lyrical precocity—astonished, presumably, because at nineteen he was considered old enough to leave the world but not to have ideas about it. Following a court-martial, and two years of detention that included an enforced stay in a mental asylum, he produced a second collection of poems, of the same lyric form and pastoral theme. And this was, in a public sense, his undoing. Lyricism had gone out with the war; peace had brought in belligerence. That a doomed subaltern had celebrated, under fire, the glories of his native Derbyshire had been affecting and commendable; that an adult survivor in civilian dress should stick, through extreme, violent, and controversial experiences, to the identical rambles and brambles was absurd. Rex Ivory was seen to have no sense of his era or his opportunities; to be, even more obtusely, unaware of new movements in contemporary criticism. And his second book, like his several subsequent collections, was received with curt contempt.

Shortly after this he married a well-to-do and bossy girl,

produced two sons, and disappeared into Derbyshire, apparently forever—his name once in a while providing a condescending footnote or obvious joke for writers on literary matters between the wars.

Joining, or rejoining, the army in 1939—a paradox noted only by himself—he was posted to Malaya, where in due course he was captured by the conquering Japanese. In Singapore, shared his prison hut with a statistician, a lanky officer of the 18th Division with whom he also divided a daily task of digging graves for comrades felled by malaria, dengue fever, dysentery, beriberi, gangrene, and the malnutrition of interminable rice. Clandestine radio kept the captives sporadically in touch with similar prisons throughout the East, and by this means the tall statistician, Ivory's companion, compiled slow lists of surviving, missing, and dead—keeping the records in cipher and burying them nightly in the earth; and training Rex Ivory as his accomplice.

In the third year, the statistician dug a last and longer grave, and bequeathed his archive and its maintenance to Rex Ivory. In the fourth year, when a liberating British fleet reached Singapore, the records were conclusively disinterred, and the scarecrow of Captain Ivory, the sole person equipped to decode them, was ordered to take fast ship for Colombo. From a devastated dock at Singapore he was piped aboard in his rags while the ship's company stood to attention on deck. The coded rolls crooked in his starved and scrawny arm were the only coherent record of the death of a British army.

Clothed and fed, Ivory was sent below to the paymaster.

"Disbursement to be made solely on submission of previous pay-slip."

"I was taken prisoner in Johore at 1500 hours on the afternoon of 8 February 1942 and have been in Changi Camp until this morning."

The paymaster got up from his metal desk and opened a combination lock on double doors. A bulkhead safe was seen to be entirely fitted with packets of banknotes in infinite coloured order, like bricks in a pastel façade.

"Help yourself."

From Colombo, Rex Ivory was flown to England where, after reporting himself at the War Office as ordered, he arranged to take the late, and at that time only, train for Derbyshire. His family were by now aware of his resurrection. As if he were some normal returning tripper, he preferred not to come empty-handed, and at the London station tried to buy a very small box of blanched chocolates displayed in isolation in a case.

The girl said, "The coupons. The coupons please." She pronounced it kewpongs, and was not a girl at all but a dour grey woman, for all the girls were gone to the war.

"What coupons?"

She looked in his face. Her alarmed fingers crimped on the tiny box as she then more slowly stared. "Where the devil have you been?"

Ivory said, "I was in a Japanese prison. Three years and seven months."

"Lose me job I will." She put the box into his hands.

These undivulged incidents, of paymaster and chocolates, were the peaks of Rex Ivory's return, although his story was soon one of the items of victory, for the newspapers took it up and he became "the poet Rex Ivory" in publications where an indefinite article had formerly done for him well, and rarely, enough. A *Selected Poems* went into print on coarse, flecked wartime paper, and there were no more witticisms about ivory towers. He read that he had been correct in spurning the First World War, and prescient in endorsing the Second; and he pondered the new idea that he had shown acumen. The BBC brought electrical equipment into the Dukeries in a van and a camera followed the well-known and prescient poet Rex Ivory as he walked away between flowering borders with a pair of Sealyhams borrowed from a neighbour. Despite his unrehearsed analogy between the British mental asylum and the Japanese camp, the interview was a success; because, when people have made up their minds to admire, wild horses will not get them to admit boredom.

Ivory's wife was amazed, and greatly pleased. And was pleased to amaze the great, and right, people with a distinction hitherto unsuspected by them or by her. To take social advantage of the surprise, she bought a house in London shortly after the war, when prices were lower than they were ever to be again. And Rex Ivory remained in Derbyshire, an all but invisible lode of authenticity.

There was one thing. In his jungle prison Rex Ivory had, as before, composed poetry—which he memorized there, since any scrap of paper was conserved for the coded casualty lists. An eminent publisher stood ready to sacrifice a portion of hoarded postwar paper to the awaited volume. None of this was unpredictable. What had not been expected was that the verses from the Malayan death camp, when transcribed, would be found to celebrate, exclusively and inexorably, the streams and hedgerows of Derbyshire.

There were other heroes by then, and other manuscripts. Public interest in Rex Ivory was waning, the paper shortage intensifying. At a top-level meeting held on a wet Saturday morning at the publishing house, it was felt that certain of the poems—in particular, one concerning a lapwing—invited critical derision. Availing themselves of an Act-of-God clause, the publishers withdrew from the contract. And *The Half-Reap'd Field* appeared, like earlier volumes, under an obscure imprint at the author's expense.

Ivory's two sons had grown into tall young men by attending the right schools, singing the right hymns, and making the right turns. "Quite right," Ivory said, when his wife recounted the directions taken during his years abroad. "Ah. Quite right." There was no reason to think there could be irony in it. Gavin, his elder son, was going into merchant banking. Right again. The younger, Paul, was still at the university. Born at the right times, they had escaped war by inches. In his family, Rex Ivory was a bereaved person, having lost familiarity. They had no idea of making good the loss, but would do the right thing and keep him company—at first all together and later by turns —until he grew accustomed to his solitary condition. That much at least was due to him: he had earned it by his interesting and advantageous behaviour in the camp.

Their best hope was that America would take him up. There had been an inquiry from Texas about his papers, and a questionnaire from Ann Arbor as to working methods. In addition, he had been interrogated by a visiting professor named Wadding, who was on his way to Scotland to establish the identity of Wordsworth's "Solitary Reaper" and the words of the song she sang. (An essay on these researches was later published in a scholarly journal

under the title, "Will No One Tell Me What She Sings?")
Ivory's wife felt that this American interest, which had
flagged, might be stimulated.

Rex Ivory objected to nothing. Yet you could not feel
he was passive.

"Unless it is passive resistance," Paul said to his mother.

"Your father has never been communicative."

By the time Ivory put on the requisite weight and a
civilian suit, the wife and sons had drifted upstream to
town. Ivory had visits from a few old friends who had
shared footnotes with him in the past along with the indefinite article. There was no petrol to be had, and one
friend, who had testified on Ivory's behalf at the 1917
court-martial, came a great distance by bicycle; another
rode up on horseback in the rain, wearing a velours beret.
There was no heating fuel either, and Ivory was always
cold. Of this he did make mention. It was said—not of
course alleging any fault—that his blood must have thinned
in the jungle. There were times when his wife came close
to saying, "Rex, dear, we are all cold."

When his father was dying, Paul came from Oxford with
three changes of trains. Lying mostly silent, suffering this
or that to be done for him, watching with his mute blend
of detachment and attention, Rex Ivory seemed much as
usual; as if dying had been long familiar to him. Paul sat
at the bedside—for they were taking turns with him again
—and knew he would never care enough to understand his
father's mystery. There was something there, but it did
not engage the interest. If the putative American biogra-
pher one day explained it, it would be a defeat for Paul,
even cheating—like looking up the solution to an exas-
perating puzzle.

> *"Never seen death yet, Dickie?*
> *Now is your time to learn."*

Paul had not heard his father say these words before,
but knew them for quotation and not, as his mother supposed, a deathbed confusion of names. A line from a ballad
by an imperial poet about an old adventurer who had seen
life and was breathing his last in the presence of a milksop
son. Paul could not accuse himself and was not even sure,

despite circumstantial evidence, that his father had seen life: events had imposed themselves on Rex Ivory, and could scarcely be called adventures. There had always been the absence of initiative—even the pacifism in the trenches might, if examined, turn to abnegation and withdrawal. Effort, quietly huge, had been expended in renunciation, as if human existence were some monumental jar of Marmite.

Thus the poet Rex Ivory, assessed by his younger son, shrivelled; and, at no great age, pined away and died.

12

A small flat road brought Paul and Caro, in the bloom of their youth, suddenly among the megaliths. Paul stopped the car. Caro unlatched her door and stared. Tremendous stones stood expressionless on curved avenues of grass. England had yawned open to disclose some other land, of fundamentals.

The little churchyard slabs——child-height, companionable—among which Caro and Paul had once sauntered became, by contrast with these huge and mighty forms, ephemeral leaflets promulgating a forgotten cause. Compared with this scene, all the rest of Creation appeared a flutter of petals and pebbles, a levity in which the most massive tree was insubstantial. The sweet village itself, through which the farthest monoliths were posted, suggested, with its few thatched and slated centuries, a frail masking of reality. Not that the dark boulders supplied, by their outlasting, any triumphant sense of durability in man's intentions. There could be no winning or even mattering here. You would have to pit some larger reason than mere living against these rocks: it was your mortality, your very capacity to receive the wound, against their indifference.

(At an earlier season Ted Tice had said, of another landscape, "It took all your conviction, there, to believe you existed.")

The ordered placing of sarsens was more inevitable than Nature: with Nature there is a chance, at least, of inadvertence. Gaps in the rows, where boulders had fallen and not been raised, seemed themselves balefully ordained, obscene as missing teeth in the smile of a tyrant.

110

Some stones were rounded, some columnar. That was their natural state, unhewn, untooled. Paul Ivory said, "Male and female created He them. Even these rocks."

The presence of Paul offered something like salvation, implying that the human propensity to love, which could never contradict Avebury Circle, might yet make it appear incomplete. Aware of this advantage, Paul awaited the moment when Caro's silence would be transferred back, intensified, from the place to himself. He was calm, with controlled desire and with the curiosity that is itself an aspect of desire. As yet he and she had merely guessed at each other's essence, and her show of self-sufficiency had given her some small degree of power over him—power that could only be reversed by an act of possession.

Preliminary uncertainty might be a stimulus, if the outcome was assured.

Caro had a wonderful danger to her, too, that derived not only from the circumstances but also from her refusal to manipulate them. The danger and the attraction were the same. There was, in addition, her young, resilient body, strong arms and throat, and her aversion to physical contact. Beyond the pleasure of defying his own circumstances, Paul pursued a further impulse to violate Caroline Bell's pride or her integrity.

She will not be so very different in the event, he supposed—with a mental shrug or swagger ineffectual even to himself. The thought was nothing more than a way of wounding.

He knew she would turn back to him glad of human greeting: Paul Ivory would be a solace by contrast with the unearthly field of monuments. And when at last she did turn, he repeated, "Look at me," and with infinite naturalness drew her against him and kissed her throat and cheek, and her mouth. There was a shock of sympathy not quite open to mockery. Her body strained both towards his own, and away; her breathing rippled in his arms, on his tongue. In these moments, if he chose, he might feel her change forever; might verify a crisis in which women confide their strength to men, like trust—so readily, if not unconditionally.

Beyond the girl's tilted head, Paul Ivory could see two or three people moving among the boulders, and a dog leaping for a thrown stick. But the coloured scene was detained, suspended, unable to keep pace with their own dual rush of life.

Caro's canvas satchel slid out from the open door of the car and lay in a small hollow of grass. She felt it go with absurd finality, a prized possession slipping away on an open sea. Within the awkward space of the car, arms, shoulders, and breasts agreed perfectly. Over and over, the distant dog leaped for the stick. In the shade of syringa, a man with a cap had set up a camp stool and easel and was selecting paints. These onlookers might think them any pair of lovers in a parked car.

It had not occurred to Paul that Caro's influence might increase with her submission. Or that she would remain intelligent. When she leaned her head back to look at him, he was aware of her judgment persevering like a pulse—even forming the most tender, if least magical, part of love. He put a hand to her face, his own fingers trembling with a small, convulsive evidence of unfeigned life.

He said, "Beautiful"—having learned this new, quixotic word. He traced the outline of her mouth with his finger, and her lips smiled under his touch. He said, "Shall we walk a bit?"

They got out of the car. Caro retrieved her canvas bag. Brief lack of contact was a sharp division from which they reunited. By the roadside, where grass was fine as moss, the earth interred chalk rubble, scraps of pottery, and human bones. Paul walked with his arm round Caro's waist and now called her repeatedly by name: two syllables like prohibited, pent-up endearments.

A notice hung on the back of the door: "The Management is not responsible for loss of valuables."

"So it's no use blaming them," Paul said.

Over the washstand there was another notice, splashed and faded: "It is regretted that hot water cannot be provided in the rooms." A streak of late light clipped one cardboard corner.

"How did you know such a place?" She was looking up at flowered wallpaper and a moulding of undusted acanthus. Beneath her head the pillow protruded from its cover, striped and soiled.

"Under quite different circumstances."

Caro remembered a deserted little bar downstairs, stale-smelling; a row of filmed bottles, bleared tumblers. On a counter, a veal-and-ham pie, bisected, pink, and larded—its centered egg blatant as a child's picture of sunset. She said, "The scene of the crime."

"What are you saying?"

"I was thinking about Avebury. Though crime is irrelevant to Avebury. Everything human is insignificant there"—lifting back her hair, resettling her head on his arm—"even human sacrifice."

"Things are the same now as then, only overlaid with hypocrisy." Certitude returned to Paul, and some scorn for a world in which he had, so easily, his way. The girl lay by his side, part of the general acquiescence. He stroked her heavy hair and said, "I have never suffered greatly."

For luck or exorcism she touched his hand to the maple veneer of the awful bedstead. "Then you still have something to fear."

"I mean, when there has been tragedy or risk, I have not felt enough. Whatever enough means." He was not warning her, just telling the truth. "If you can reach fifty without a catastrophe, you've won. You've got away with it. Perhaps even now I've had more good life than they can take from me."

By "you," Paul meant himself. "They" were undefined. Caro said nothing. By now she would have given up her life for him, but repudiated his wish to be indemnified, by arithmetical advantages, against experience. "Got away with it," he had said, as if life itself were a felony, a shiftiness exposed like stained ticking on a rented bed. As if, for all his authority, he were a fugitive. His father had perhaps renounced existence; but had not given it the slip.

She would have told him, "You can't have this without catastrophe," but was silent out of fear of loss—reminded how nothing creates such untruth as the wish to please or to be spared something.

Paul got up and dressed. From the bed Caro watched, languid as a patient emerging from ether, in pain and swirled by slow impressions that would scarcely focus; while the wakeful world, personified in Paul, went about its business. Suspension of will in this experience might almost have brought new innocence, had it not itself been so deeply willed. There was the offering and inflicting: a brief excuse for the limitless tenderness no man would otherwise indulge.

From ignorance she had gone, in one hour, to this superiority of common knowledge.

When Paul sat in a shabby chair to pull on his shoes, she at last rose and went to him, and knelt for his embrace.

Paul drew her body between his knees. Pressure of sleeves and trousers on her bare skin urged on Caroline Bell another sensation, from infancy, when her father would lean over her cot to take up the scarcely clad child in hard omnipotent arms of serge or flannel that smelt of the city and the great world. A particular memory, inapposite, of her father in evening dress on his way to some ceremony, wearing medals of war that swung from bright ribbons as he bent to kiss his elder daughter. And she was the child reaching up to a smell of tobacco and cologne and the dark male friction of the coat, while medals dangled like coins of small denominations.

The transformations of her twenty years were no more amazing or irreversible than the new change, within a single day, of solitary girl into a woman kneeling naked on a threadbare carpet at her lover's feet. The embrace, the room, a bar of light on the ceiling, a vacant luggage-rack in a corner could have been part of seedy insignificance the world over; or might hold the very source of meaning, like the kiss, or flagellation, in the silent background of a masterpiece.

"Caro," Paul said, "you'll catch cold." He was clothed and sat presiding, but could scarcely bear the renewed power it gave her, this kneeling at his feet. "You'll catch cold, my dear." The pale sun had gone to the ceiling, a thin draft came in at every gimcrack. Paul pushed back her tangled hair to discover the white skin at the margin where summer had not reached. "Maiden no more." Tears had formed at the corners of her eyes, but were not of the kind that fall or need be noticed.

A stained mug had held cocoa, there was a browning scrap of apple on a saucer, there were heavy, unaligned shoes on the floor, a shirt on a chair. The room's dark curtains and stern fixtures were not livened by mere litter and the smell of food. The books hardly helped, having nothing to do with the room: books of passage. It was a phase of Ted Tice's work that interested him less than what had gone before and was soon to come, and the books knew it. He was uncharacteristically cold here, and lay on the bed dressed and wearing socks. At night he had a heavy quilt. It was a joke to the family: "But it's a fine September for Edinburgh, not a day under forty degrees." Ted and Margaret had done this joke to death, as people do who hesitate to move on to the next phase.

The family were all out to Sunday tea, except Margaret, who stayed in to paint or to practise the piano.

Margaret must practise. Or might be avoiding some Donald or Willie—for Margaret, fair and stately, was the natural quarry of her father's students. Or had some reason, greater than her many accomplishments, for remaining at home. The piano was in a downstairs room at the back of the house, where she also painted. But in the Sunday suspension you heard all the notes, and even the hesitations of turned pages—of Schumann, César Franck. Willies and Duncans would have turned music for her by the hour, or, if young men were not turning music these days, would have walked her through cold daylight streets to eat a brittle chop in the smoky din of a students' hole. Any number of them hankered after the broad white brow and tender mouth of Margaret and were anxious to make some sort of showing for her sake. "She is a princess," said her mother, who was a Fabian socialist.

Ted Tice released the book he was supposed to read, and lay with one arm under his head, his other hand holding a letter. The book splayed awkwardly on the plaid blanket and, when he sighed, it sighed too and over-balanced to the floor. Below, the piano paused to inquire politely into the thud. The pause deepened. When the music was taken up again it was the music of songs as they might be played in a nightclub by a gifted pianist down on his, or her, luck. "Smoke Gets in Your Eyes," and all the rest.

*　　*　　*

I went to Avebury more or less as planned. It's more a symbol than a place—an expression of the inevitable. You once said that life didn't have to be credible, or fair. And that seemed clear enough at Avebury Circle.

Then last week I was in London overnight. The interview was with a man called Leadbetter, and the job begins next month. I get four pounds a week—it would have been three but for passing the test. This Leadbetter was spruce, diminutive, in his celluloid cubicle. A sort of miniature model of a man, a ship in a bottle. Our talk was like that too—a whittled-down representation of human discourse. When I questioned one of the conditions, Leadbetter told me I was a perfectionist, as if that meant sinner.

In the evening I went to *Richard the Second*. In front of us was a mountain of a man—the least movement and he blotted out half the English court.

"These Foolish Things" was followed by "My Romance." The songs were being played with too much style and attention. No longer a pleasant diversion, it was more like a lavishing, the utter waste of something inestimable.

I try to imagine you in your northern limbo waiting to leave for France. Ted, don't lose your precious time on me. There is no future I believe in as I do in yours, and no one else whose ambition ever seemed so clear a form of good.

"In front of us." Ted Tice was so sure, and so wished to be unconvinced, of the other presence in that phrase that he lost the capacity to judge—like a man who stares too long at a distant shape and cannot be sure if it moves or is still.

It isn't a matter of more time. Don't be disappointed in me. I wish you so well—only, am helpless to make your happiness. If by happiness is meant a sort of vigorous peace of mind, then I hope—against all morality—it can be conferred on you with no suffering on your part or even effort. (This may be the sense in which perfectionism, in my case, is linked to sin.)

Downstairs, Margaret was playing "I'm in the Mood for Love"; was playing her last card. And Edmund Tice, in the cold room with his arm beneath his head and a letter beside him, grieved for her as much as for anybody.

13

Caroline Bell's body was not white but nutritiously pale, like pastry or a loaf, even having the slight flaws—tiny tag of a mole on neck or breast, scar on the knee from a childhood fall—that might have formed in a process such as baking. When she raised herself on an elbow or lay with outspread arms, the space of her belly was a lap, the paired curve of shoulders was matched to an imminent embrace. This could not be guessed until she was naked: until then, sensation itself was clothed.

She was wearing nothing but a small round watch. "Soon they'll be home."

Even Grace was "they," that afternoon in September. Even Peverel was home.

In Paul Ivory's room, at the top of the Thrales' house, the bedstead was brass, the discarded, trailing counterpane a swag of white crochet. It was the room of the high incongruous window, whose panes of sun fell flat on a pure wall. On the white bed, Paul and Caro arranged head to shoulder, chin to temple, thigh to thigh, ingeniously.

"No one will come up here anyway. It being Sunday, I being hard at work, you being out."

"Where am I exactly?"

"On the road near Romsey, enjoying the walk." Paul kicked an entanglement of patient white crochet. "Oh Caro, how lucky this is." Sufficiency was like deliverance: he had been suffocating and now breathed freely. He was familiar enough with pleasure to know it might become jaded or reluctant; but joy was literally foreign to him, a word he would never easily pronounce, an exhilaration that had some other, reckless nationality. For this reason,

118

Caro's wholeness in love, her happiness in it, made her exotic.

Paul said, "I have locked the door."

In the brass rods and finials behind her head, Caro's fingers were vaguely grappled, like those of a woman dreaming. Her arm, which people thought strong, revealed an underside soft as an infant's and scarcely grooved in the elbow. Her other hand slipped through and through Paul Ivory's hair with all possible tenderness. In his mind he could see it happening, his fairness falling through her fingers in the white room. He told himself, This is real at any rate. And could feel her think the same.

He reached for the covering, drew it up to her chin. Then slowly down. They laughed: the unveiling of a monument. In the wall there was the window of blue sky, green leaves on a bough of elm. Once, an angular little plane passed slowly over, the silver-paper sort that might have taken children for joy-rides between the wars: a toy plane that had whirred in a grassy peacetime field while a man in overalls lunged at the propellor and shouted "CONTACT."

They were as much part of that aerial brightness as of the locked, earthly, domestic room.

"What if your sister hadn't gone to the concert?" Paul having learned the story of Grace and Christian at the Albert Hall.

"Our destiny, as well as theirs."

He had called it luck, but now she spoke of destiny. As if she said to him, You must choose. It was the way of women to require choices, sortings, and proofs; and then to attribute blame. The Judgment of Paul.

Caro said, "I never liked afternoons, till this."

In a corner there was a wardrobe so heavy you thought at once of men who had heaved it up the stairs fifty or sixty years ago, grunting and putting their backs into it. Over a chest of walnut drawers, there was a blurred photograph inscribed in ink with the date 1915. Even a mildewed snapshot of an English cottage, if it was labelled 1915, was smirched and spattered with a brown consciousness of the trenches. Even in a room of love. Beneath the picture, Paul's brush and comb were set out, along with a pigskin pouch and a bottle of French cologne: all blond on a lace mat. The band of his discarded watch rose in two brief arcs, ready for his wrist. Most objects of the kind were so solemn you nearly smiled, but Paul's possessions had their owner's electricity.

Paul said, "We should be somewhere in the sun."

"The sun is here."

He meant her to think of a simplified shore with palm trees or Italian pines. But she did not believe in this film set, which she stared at before closing her eyes. His urge to move on made an end, or denied a beginning. From her now prodigious knowledge, she could have assured him that what he sought was found.

"Well," she said, "it's here. The sun." She would have liked merely to have it recognized.

Paul preferred what he discovered for himself. "I had in mind real warmth. Heat, sand, the sea." He placed their hands together—young, smooth, and beautifully clean, with such superior fingers. "Lemon groves, vineyards, white walls." Taunting her with lack.

A test of wills, when everything might have had an easy virtuosity. "Why are you unkind?"

Women are born, he thought, with that question on their lips. And amused himself a moment searching for its male counterpart—I hope in time you'll forgive me. He said, "*A la guerre comme à la guerre.*"

"What war is there between us?" she wondered. Yet wondered too at how poor, in French, his accent was.

"No, it's all right. If you like it here." He laughed, and gave up the excursion for her sake. Like realization, his glance followed her outstretched arm and raised knee. He put his lips to her breast.

It was in that moment they heard the car. Not the rumble of a Hillman or Wolsey or the bronchial change of gear with which a van might mount the hill, but a swift, decided sound, a sound in showroom condition that made its way intently, playing on the house from far off, then on the wall and open window, like a raking beam of light.

It was then, in their primordial attitude, they heard the car.

Caro's head relapsed on the white pillow. Paul sprang.

"If she should come in," he said. "If she should come upstairs and find the door locked." Tertia was she, that day and after. Paul was already in his shirt, and held a tie; having snatched up, for this occasion, more formal clothes than usual. On the gravel, wheels were scattering stones. The castle itself had come to find them.

The machine stopped more conclusively than any engine ever.

"Paul."

A steel door slammed. "Paul."

There had never been such final sounds, such pauses, ultimatums, and high-pitched unquestioning calls. And Caroline Bell lay still.

Paul was at the window now. He was leaning out, laconic. "Good God." He was smiling and leaning and making room for his casual elbows. "Anything up?" There was the hard intimacy of tone, the naturalness with which he did not use her name. If he had even added so much as "Tertia."

Tertia Drage came right below the window: a pink dress, an upraised face. Perhaps she had not expected Paul to appear at once, but showed no surprise and, despite the standing down there, no sense of disadvantage. Any more than Paul did—standing easy in, merely, the shirt and tie; and, as far as Tertia was concerned, fully dressed.

Seeing them now, an onlooker might have judged them well suited.

"It's a glorious afternoon." Tertia said so without fervour. There was a strip of pink silk round her head, a leather driving glove on her right hand. "We should make use of it."

"What's the plan then?" They were at one in their competitive refusal to expose themselves by any show of spontaneity. Both were secretive, though not private persons, whose undercurrent of sarcasm allowed disavowal of any inadvertent sincerity. With Tertia, the archly antagonistic mood was already habitual.

She raised her derisory hand. "You know the possibilities as well as I." The sound of the motor had been a truer voice than hers, and more responsive.

Out of sight below the window Paul Ivory's bare feet had crossed themselves, negligent as his folded arms. Small fair hairs curled on his naked thighs. "Nothing too arduous," he said, or was saying, when from the fixing of Tertia's limbs he knew that Caro stood beside him.

He knew that Caro had come up behind him and was by his side at the window. Her bare shoulder, perfectly aloof, touched his own. He did not turn, but, as if he himself were Tertia Drage, saw Caro standing naked beside him at that high window and looking down: looking down on the two of them. It was he and Tertia, and Caroline Bell looking down on them. Caro's hand rested on the sill. She was wearing nothing but a small round watch.

Moments passed, or did not pass. Tertia stood impassive. Only that her arm stayed raised, her gloved fist clenched and extended like a falconer's. She was looking straight up at Paul; not staring but looking hard and fast at him only. She said, "It's up to you."

"I'll come down."

For perhaps the first time they met each other's eyes.

At the window Caro did not move. Paul withdrew and took up the rest of his clothes. His departure exposed completely the upper part of her body. Flesh-coloured light was striking her shoulder and making reddish streaks in heavy hair that fell over the collar-bone. Below, Tertia was walking around the car and opening the door. She got in, leaving the driver's seat free. In the room above, the bed creaked as Paul pulled on his canvas shoes. With no more than normal haste he took his own watch from the top of the bureau, glancing at it as he strapped it on. He might have been late for an appointment.

A door all but closed. Stairs thudded to Paul Ivory's quick feet. He appeared on the path below the bedroom window, and dropped his jacket into the car.

"You want me to drive."

"If you please."

Their voices were neither lowered nor lifted: you might have said, level. And Tertia was roughly pulling off her glove. There was the prompt roar of the car. As if someone swung on a propellor yelling "CONTACT."

Captain Nicholas Cartledge was waiting for a train. His tweeds were the colour and texture of fine sand. Beige and granular, he stood on an asphalted branch-line platform in a blaze of Sunday-afternoon tedium. The railway dollop of bitumen virtually annihilated an entire sweet countryside. Even the radiant day could raise colour only where rust had overflowed on cement, and in a stain of slack dahlias round a signpost. Nicholas Cartledge was impassive, neither patient nor impatient, occasionally leaving his small cloth bag on the asphalt, in order to stroll the length of the platform and return. Once a cuff flicked up, white, to compare time with the station clock; but he drew no apparent conclusion from a discrepancy. If someone had remarked on the boredom, he would have said, "It doesn't bother me."

He saw that the local taxi, an old green Humber that could be phoned for, had stopped at the station steps, and that Caroline Bell was getting out of it. With the slightest vibration of surprise he went down to help her and, before she had recognized him, was leaning in to pay the driver. She stood on the pavement holding out to him in the palm of her hand an assortment of half-crowns and sixpences. Cartledge said, "For pity's sake," and picked up her bag, no larger than his own, and a light raincoat. Relieving her of these things, he suggested expropriation.

He and she went up the wooden steps, and the pieces of luggage stood side by side. The dahlias limply circled the signpost, like sluggish water round a drain. Cartledge said, "Headed for London, I take it," and did not seem to wonder. He had an authority associated with imperviousness. Caro had scarcely spoken, and might not have remembered his name. She was decorously dressed, and showed— or betrayed, as the saying goes—no emotion whatever. Yet he might have said her appearance was wild, not only because that summarized an evident situation but because of an emanation of helpless shock.

She refused a cigarette, and did not want to sit down. They walked along the glittering platform, and back. Pale socks showed above his supple shoes. You could not say they walked together, or that he made any effort to close the distance she left between them. An elderly couple in black sat on a bench and watched with a perspicacity whetted by Sunday doldrums: "There's some story there." Inclined to side wtih Cartledge—who was the man, after all, and had those excellent clothes, one of the old school with his light hair and his expensive face, lean and polished. "A real old rake," the wife said, as Cartledge passed again where she herself sat motionless under a toque of rayon violets. "Or roué," she added, to reinforce. But soon resumed about her own Sunday: "Well, Fred it was a long time afore you talked me into visiting Maude, and it'll be longer next time."

Standing by their baggage, which provided a destination, Captain Cartledge shook ash. "It was clear you would come to grief in that place." He did not expect an answer, but after a while turned to look—at her head, her breasts. She watched him do this with dispassion that was, as he saw, a variant of whatever trouble she was in. Eventually he did say, "If I can help."

She might have been smiling at the irony. "To grief, as you say."

"There's nothing worse," he agreed, identifying the form of it. "You could not have come to a more sympathetic auditor." She had not in fact come to him, but his assurance would have required an onslaught to disrupt it. When the train drew in he threw down his cigarette and lifted their two bags. She walked ahead into an empty compartment, where she sat by the window, pallid and peculiar, for the old couple to remark on for the last time, as they passed, "More there than meets the eye."

"This will help." He spilled a few drops of it with the starting up of the train. She saw the initials NGWC in the silver. He dried the overflow from his fingers with a white handkerchief while she drank, then poured a very little for himself. The handkerchief had the same initials coiled in a corner. He said, "Take your time." He sat back opposite her, politely arranging his tailored legs not to touch, placing an elbow on the ledge of the little window. "There is plenty of time."

He did not mean there was time for existence to resume but that she would come to accept what must now occur. There was the silver and the linen, the granular tweed, and the dirty rim of the window. She had clasped her hands in her lap, a becalmed attitude she and her sister both adopted under stress; and held his gaze, unthinking, unblinking. Hills and dales wobbled past the window. A factory momentarily obliterated the view, and was swiftly withdrawn like the wrong slide on a projector. There was a damp, metallic smell in the compartment, an ancient reek of upholstery, a whiff from a nearby lavatory, and the more immediate taste of brandy.

He said, "I am at your disposal," but she would not be deceived, or scarcely heard. As to her silence, he would have said, "It does not bother me." He pondered whether it might have been the wall-eyed boy, before remembering that Ted Tice had already left—for Glasgow, Edinburgh, or possibly Paris. The fact of Paul Ivory was a shade more interesting, if only for caste reasons.

There were stations of rusted dahlias, from which the sun successively withdrew. In field after field, the hops were strung up. Somewhere near the front of the train the old couple dozed; and once the wife asked, between snoozes, "What do you think that word comes from— roué?" saying it rooey and getting no reply.

Caro's hair touched the window-frame. She did not close her eyes. Cartledge said, "It has not harmed your looks, you know."

She asked, "How much longer?" And his cuff went up. Then, "At what station do we arrive?" Not calling him Nick, as he had said to.

"You were intending to go—where?"

"There's a place in Gloucester Road where they take Australians."

"My dear, you make them sound like paroled convicts."

"We send friends there. Failing that, another of the kind in Cromwell Road."

"You'll be much better off in North Audley Street. Where I take Australians." He offered her the flask again, the sun glinting on it as on a gun-barrel. "I assume, by the way," he said, "that you left the inevitable note on the pincushion—some convincing and quite fictitious explanation?"

They swayed along among diminishing hops and burgeoning kitchen gardens. Two men in adjacent green back yards reached to each other companionably across a wall; or could have been grappling. The sky was falling redly on

the land now, and a hillside loomed like a haunch of beef.
Captain Cartledge shook cigarettes from an ordinary pack,
though somewhere there would be an initialled silver case
to match the flask. He said, "On Sunday nights they always
leave something out for me. Soup, chicken. My couple, I
mean."

So there was a couple, leaving a cold supper ready for
the Captain, giving a good rub to tarnished initials. Well
done, thou good and faithful servant. Captain, my Captain. Couple, my Couple. Captained, coupled. There would
be sheets, pillowcases, linen initials coiled to spring.

The Captain in his shadowed corner was cool above the
white blaze of collar and cuffs—apt streaks like markings
of a racehorse. He had not, as he might have put it, so
much as laid a finger on her. He said, "Better at any rate
than a dark night of the soul in the Gloucester Road." "At
any rate" put the thing in perspective.

There was beaded sweat at her hairline. If she blacked
out or went to pieces he would have bitten off more than
he could chew. But she remained distinct, integral, con-
temptuous, in her place opposite. He added, "Night brings,
among other things, counsel." From the syntax it was apparent he had said this before.

The sky was settling either into a rose-ripe composure
of summer evening or into an arc of monstrous contusions,
depending how you looked at it. They were crossing a
maze of tracks near the river, and there was a fine view of
St. Paul's. Caro was on her feet, reaching up to the rack
for her bag.

He said, "For pity's sake," as he had said at the station,
and lifted the bag down for her. They were standing, bal-
ancing, a few inches from each other and she had her
hands by her sides. Her lips were lightly drawn back so
that the lower teeth showed, and in that instant she might
have been considered cruel as he.

She looked in his face. "I have already made love today."

He staggered to keep his feet as the train belted for
home, then rocked on his toes, in control. He was taller
than she by about five inches. "I'm aware of the terms. All
the same, let's see if we can't offer you something short of

martyrdom." He glanced round the compartment. "All set?"

He was first on the platform. Following, she saw his quick sleeve raised: "Taxi." And got into his dark cab while he was still giving the address.

Part II

THE
CONTACTS

14

My dear Caro—

There are sixty thousand students in Paris, most of them in the corridor outside this room. Last week, however, the building was deserted for Easter and calm as a monastery. My window looks on a court-yard full of flowering trees—hawthorn, a Judas tree, and, very near, a big lilac coming out in purple pyr-amids. There is a fountain and—concealed—a thrush. During the holiday I drove with two French col-leagues to the mines near Lille, where we went down a pit. The coal-face straight from Dante, worked by boys of sixteen or so, mostly North Africans who spoke no French. Worse than this were the hovels they went back to afterwards, ten to a filthy hut. Hav-ing uselessly petitioned the Ministère du Travail on behalf of these people, my two friends are helping them form a union. We returned to Paris by way of the First World War cemeteries of Vimy and Notre-Dame-de-Lorette and a quarter of a million graves.

I work. I think of you. These are not alternating propositions—I think of you always. Since writing you last, I've been to a show of drawings by Leonardo, a one-man industrial revolution. Have seen a good play, *Le Diable et le Bon Dieu,* as well as Jean Vilar and Gérard Philipe in *Le Cid,* a judo championship, and Senator Kefauver on television. Kefauver dismaying enough, God knows, but I am regarded as his cham-pion here, there being so much facile and uninformed anti-Americanism among my colleagues. I dislike un-animity (or solidarity as it's perniciously called), and anyway the mindless Soviet and China worship bores me—particularly in this land of *en principe*.

The man I came here to work with continues to impress me, humanly and professionally. It is true he's made mistakes, in part because he has done so much. Those who undertake less can be more circumspect. (And those who attempt nothing—whether of the soul or the intellect—are safest, and of course most critical, of all. It's easy enough to denounce—all you need is ill will.) What an atrocious, sustained effort is required, I find, to learn or do anything thoroughly— especially if it's what you love. A vocation is a source of difficulty, not ease. To do is difficult enough. To be, more difficult still. Both to do and be demand an effort at superhumanity. Well, why not? Anything is preferable to the safe side of the line.

The students are early potatoes, forced too hard, the pace terrific. They come here at eighteen from the lycées, and after one year take the equivalent of B.A. All are "serious" and *engagés*. (I'm thoroughly sick of that word.) The place is plastered with Marxist literature, and one in four are Party members. Yet they spend their nights playing brutal practical jokes on the freshmen and yell like fourth-formers when meals are late. Fairly frightening on the premises, they are touchingly young and earnest when seen on the Boulevard Saint-Michel, where they pass what free time they can manage. They make me feel both sedate and gauche.

The new French government is identical with the one before, and will fall as quickly. Will we end up with Europe going facist again, "defended" by a German army with American commanders and American weapons, itching to cross the Elbe? (When you consider how real the Soviet menace is, it's remarkable that the countering dementia on our side can almost make you disbelieve in it.) One bright spot has been the death of de Lattre, raising some faint hope of a settlement in Indo-China. His funeral was a monstrous exhibition of militarism—schools closed, vast processions with Eisenhower, Montgomery, the cabinet, bands, choirs, clergy, troops, the lot. Lying in state at the Arc de Triomphe, Notre Dame, Les Invalides. A thoroughly Prussian performance.

If Leonardo had hit on the steam engine, Napoleon woud have dropped the atomic bomb, and to clamorous French applause.

Among the students, as with my colleagues here, there is often a background of poverty. There's no charade around this as in our countries—no dissembling by the poor, no fantasy of brotherhood on the part of the affluent. I remember the university people who used to come round Ancoats in my childhood, adopting our speech and clothes to show a kindred spirit—a sentimental condescension that does damn all for poverty. Membership in the proletariat doesn't come that cheap. What did it do for us, their guilt-edged security or the moral outrage they exchanged on their way home to their employed parents—and to their hot water and their books and music and savings-accounts, none of which they had immediate intention of sharing? What were their overalls to me, who'd have given anything to see my mother in a decent dress? In themselves, rags confer morality no more than they do disgrace.

The poor don't want solidarity with their lot, they want it changed.

(During the Depression, Ted Tice's father had taken him, a boy of nine, to hear a politician speak. Father and son stood in the crowd at the back of a grim hall, and to the child's questions the father returned his habitual response: "Don't talk wet." The speaker was a young Liberal with yellow hair, a lawyer from the district, standing for the first time. He considered himself one of the poor, but even the boy knew that this young man's parents had paid his education at the law—whereas the rest, lad and lass alike, were in the mill or at the works or on the docks at twelve or fourteen. If they'd luck enough to find the work. This youth was said to have a wage of three pound ten a week clear, and only one dependent, a paralysed aunt. All the rest was for himself. It was hard to imagine what he did with such a sum.

He was in earnest, he wished to change their lives.

A man standing at the side of the hall called out, "One wick of thi wages'd change a life here in this hall, if tha'd but give it." And the candidate's fair face flushed: "That's not the answer." And the heckler shouted back, "It'll do to go on wi', whilst tha't thinking up a better one.")

Ted Tice got up and went to his flowering window. He sat down again at his table and looked at what he had just written: "They want change." Even more than change, they want revenge. Men can make up soon enough with enemies who slaughtered them in battle; but never with the brethren who humiliated them in cold blood. They take reprisal on their own shame—that is what makes all hatreds, in war or class, or in love. And I too want revenge. On a new page he continued:

You will have seen the rumpus about the telescope. The *Observer* piece reached me only today. Old Thrale will never forgive himself for letting me in the house. But I remember vividly the moment when he did, and am grateful.

I seek relief from my pro-American role by attacking the United States ferociously to the pleasantest friend I have made here, a young American physicist whose main occupation is finding girls. We spend evenings together when he is not flat to the bawds. Through him I've met a dear little *étudiante,* a tall ballerina from the New York City Ballet, and a young curatress who is helping mount a vast exhibition of Mexican art and is very strong on pre-Columbian sexual motifs.

Ted was divided between the urge to show Caro, and the likelihood of her seeing through this. Reading over the last lines he crossed out "dear" and "young," and eliminated the ballerina. He rewrote the page, and went on:

Another of the Americans here was married yesterday, and I was in on the wedding, a prosaic little ceremony in a side-chapel of the American cathedral. The priest sounded as if he hadn't been paid. Afterwards, the champagne was enough to swim in, and I earned the extremely good dinner by listening to a woman telling me all about her citrus ranch and cottage at Monterey. The more annoying as there was, along the table, an interesting couple—a man called Vail, who subsidizes various cultural enterprises in America, and his wife. He looked like Orson Welles (though not as Citizen Kane). His wife, thinner than any model and very tall, was beautiful—a gaunt face with circular eyes. These two were enclosed in some unhappiness that, because of their intelligence and looks, engaged one's interest. It had never occurred to me before that unhappiness could be interesting in itself; God knows my own is not, to me. And I suppose this is the sort of thing novelists have to care about.

The man Vail also concerns himself with humanitarian and political causes, and surprised me, in the brief talk we did have, by having noticed the row about the telescope. (I should say that I thought well of him *before* this.) He had just come from Tunisia, which, like all the Arab world, seems to be going up in smoke. We had barely begun to talk when a dowager from Pasadena broke in to say that the world must surely improve now, as young people are all so *travelled.* Vail said, "That's not travel, it's dislocation."

Speaking of weddings, I saw that Paul Ivory's took place. I also saw that his play opened in London. I wonder which will run longest.

Ted put the pages together, then added: "I nearly resent these things I have described, because they are life without you. Caro, it is so long. If I could only see you." And signed his name.

Posting a letter to Caroline Bell was an instant of hope and contact, and anticlimax. Ted Tice went down scuffed and noisy stairs, and out into the street. Having dispatched the letter, he kept walking as quickly as the crowds would allow, so that good spirits would not drain from him along with the warmth of his room.

It was dusk, there were students in the cafés. Other young people, unable to pay for so much as a coffee, stood on the footpath in groups and talked fast without laughter.

Ted thought, It is grim and marvellous by turns, and I may never find out why; but at least it isn't raw or facile or paltry or sententious or dull. And the absence of self-delusion in itself is liberty.

The moment of exhilaration evaporated. It is degrading to fix passionate feeling on another being in the certain knowledge there can be no answering thought. As he walked, Ted Tice turned up the collar of his jacket. He had come out, as usual, without a coat. One of the men he had accompanied to the mines, a Breton going for the *agréga-tion*, drew away from a group on the pavement and walked with him. Ted thought how his American friend would have asked a question, "Had a good day?" something of the kindly kind. Americans might be the only people left who asked how one felt—still imagining one might know, or tell; or assuming an untroublesome, affirmative lie, some show of a willful unripeness like their own. After posting his letter to Caroline Bell, Ted was glad of the paired reticence with the Breton in the street: a companionship that broached his isolation but not his solitude.

When they reached the entrance of Tice's building, a group of students pushed past them, laughing and shouting. The Breton said, "It's melancholy, all this high spirits." The two men leaned against a wall that was dirty in the way that only institutions of learning can be dirty, with the pressure of too many soiled hands and hips and bottoms propped there in argument or love. Beyond them, the long street slowly flowed in human clusters, taut or flexible; active with opinion, suffering and lust. The Breton touched Ted lightly on the shoulder. "Just remember, my dear, that women grow old. See you."

Ted had another letter to write, which he had not meant to begin that evening—but did, being unable to work.

Very good to have your letter and your news. Yes, I do have a photograph—since arriving here I've spent most of my time and a fair proportion of my funds being photographed. I don't know what it is about me, everyone wants my picture, and in four or five copies too: the police, the university, the Comité d'Accueil. For you, herewith, one copy only, in which I look like the kind of person I disliked most at Cambridge. Since you are really coming over—good news—I'll try to get tickets for the May festival. They're giving Berg's *Wozzeck* and Stravinsky's *Oedipus Rex*. There will be plenty of ballet—the New York people, and the Marquis de Cuevas. Certainly you should see Golovine. As to tennis, everyone thinks the big match will be Sedgman-Drobny, will that be all right? I agree about what is happening at home—Attlee can count on my vote again next time.

I must finish a paper, so forgive a note only. We'll talk in May. It will be fine to see you. Let me know time of arrival. Yours.

15

At the time when Grace and Caroline Bell got their first employment—at Harrods and the bookshop—they had made over most of their small capital to Dora. By undertaking to raise them, Dora had incapacitated herself for earning a livelihood, and it seemed right that recompense be made. That was Caro's reasoning, at least, and all of Caro's capital went to Dora in the new arrangement, for Caro might soon expect to have some semblance of a career. Grace, whose employment at Harrods lacked even that degree of promise, had retained half her assets at Caro's suggestion. Explained to Dora, the plan ignited high passion. She wanted nothing, had never asked anything from anyone, had walked to save so much as a bus fare, and the one thing she would never give up to a living soul was her independence. "I will be dependent on no one, I ask nothing." Dora was outraged—irrationally but not unpredictably; and only after many days of tears and cries for peace was prevailed on to accompany the girls to a lawyer's office where documents were ultimately and emotionally signed. It was a further week before she spoke to them at all normally, or could bring herself to forgive.

Dora herself was confused by the indignation aroused in her by the sisters' gesture. By their action, they had deprived her, however temporarily, of her privileges of victimization. Until she re-established her prerogative of disadvantage, she was under a handicap. By her outrage she saw to it that tables were only briefly turned. The event was put behind them, unmentionable, and soon she was talking again about doing without, so that you girls might have everything when I'm gone.

At that time, Dora was not yet forty.

The signing over of assets had taken place shortly before Grace encountered Christian at the Sunday concert—Dora's umbrage on that memorable afternoon being attributable to it. A few months later, when Christian and Grace became engaged, Grace told him of the financial arrangement: "It seemed only fair."

Christian said quietly, "How like you, Grace."

"You would have done the same."

Putting the fair hairs back from her forehead, he was touched beyond her expectation. "I should like to think so."

Now Major Ingot appeared to have made their sacrifice irrelevant.

When the Major brought Dora to London in the late spring, Christian said he would give a small lunch, or luncheon, at a restaurant. Just himself, Grace, the bridal pair; and Caro—who would ask time off from work. Christian was by then married to Grace and the proper person to do such a thing, but had no affection for Dora, who he had seen in action now and then. There had been a convulsive scene, incomprehensible, on the occasion of Grace's betrothal; and letters from the Algarve had tended to take, from time to time, the unfathomable huff. Christian firmly (to employ his favourite adverb) believed that Dora could pull herself together—could be brought to her senses by a good talking-to, which, he contended, was long overdue and would do her the world of good. Even Grace still imagined there might be words, the words that could reach Dora and that had so far, unaccountably, not been hit upon. Only Caro recognized that Dora's condition was exactly that: a condition, an irrational state requiring professional, or divine, intervention.

Major Ingot was thickly built, though in no martial way, having a citified paunch and large pinkish jowl. Within the restaurant doorway he cut the oval sweep of a watermelon. His scalp was smooth except for a splaying of strands over the crown; his eyes, a hurt blue, were the eyes of a drunken child. At table he spread short hands on the menu, flattening out this plan of attack. A wedding-ring was already tight on his finger, like a knot tied there to remind,

or the circlet fixed on a homing pigeon. His neck made a
thick fold over his collar. Everything about him was contained, constrained, a fullness tied and bound. It was hard
to imagine him a soldier; although he had a desk-bound
corpulence that might have done for a general.

When asked by Christian about his military service, he
produced staccato information before ordering crab salad.

Salad was not reliable in Estoril, nor seafood either. On
the eve of departure, Dora had been poisoned by a plate
of king prawns. The bill of the Portuguese doctor had
come, with the medicines, to thirty pounds.

"And that," said Major Ingot, "made it an expensive
meal."

"Bruce was ropable," Dora told them. "And Bruce is
usually a patient body."

The Major redly glared endorsement.

They must return to Portugal within the month, there
was everything to be done to the flat. Curtains, upholstery,
Dora already had the swatches. In addition, Rastas, the
Major's Labrador, was in a kennel.

It was hard to imagine the Major's pleasures, difficult
even to picture him in the ingle of a pub in Algarve England saying, "Let me tell you the one about." Retribution
emerged as a main preoccupation: "They have made their
bed and must lie in it," "He will just have to take his
medicine"—making of life a military, or prison, hospital.
In the postwar scramble, the Major had been lucky; had,
as he explained, fallen on his feet. In the free-for-all, some
landed right side up, others came a cropper.

Around the table, the Major's punitive figures of speech
aroused antipathies that were scarcely coherent. The truth
was they were too reminiscent of Christian himself.

To revert one moment to the poisoned prawns. If I may.
For just such reasons there was a big future in the Algarve.
British residents liked what they were used to—Twinings
Earl Grey, Coopers Vintage Marmalade. Possibilities were
pretty well infinite—Tiptree, Huntley and Palmer, to give
a bare idea. Why not have a stab at it? Nor could the
liquors be disregarded, Gilbey's, Dewar's. "It is all there
for"—the Major made a deft, pink, snatching gesture
above the tablecloth—"the taking." No, the Major was not
thinking of getting into books. "It's a small turnover. Make

no error, I like nothing better than a rattling good yarn myself. But the turnover doesn't justify. Your average tourist is not a big reader. Guidebooks now—well, there you're on to a horse of a different colour."

There was no need to get mixed up with the Ports. The foreign residents out there were a well-to-do crowd, on the whole. Germans were coming back too, you'd be surprised. They preferred the Algarve to the Costa Brava, which had already been developed out of extinction. Furthermore, the government was stable. More so, he was sorry to say, than this lot we've got here at home. "These socialists wouldn't dare show themselves out there." If they did, they would soon laugh on the other side of their faces.

"I wouldn't live here if you paid me."

Thunder could be heard. Through the restaurant's glass doors, they saw a deluge.

As to the prime minister, the Major continued, "I wouldn't trust him with sixpence on the table"—slamming down the imaginary coin—"while I stepped out of the room."

Dora dealt out photographs, like trump cards, of herself in the sun. The Major said, "I'd have taken more, but I'd used up most of the roll on the dog."

Christian was surprised by Dora's good looks. He had always felt her nature did not come commensurately through in her appearance, and now that she was plumper and complacent—and kept the speckled veil, still suggestive of a bridal, turned up around her hat—it was hard to credit her awfulness. With her dark eyes and high colour, she might herself have been native to the Algarve or Alentejo; had it not been for the mouth.

Contrasted with Dora's rounded self-approval, Caro was hollow-eyed, the pale, impressive ghost at the feast despite a crimson dress. Only Grace truly looked her part, a sweet young matron with no darker side.

Dora was telling, "Bruce has an eye. And has picked up some exquisite pieces. Majolica, old rugs."

The Major agreed: "If I say so myself." (It occurred to Christian, like a warning, that this phrase usually preceded falsehood.) "I can go into any junk shop and pick out the one thing." Again, a show of thick, short fingers. "Of course, out there you have to bargain."

When it was agreed that bargaining went against the grain, there was a pause. Christian was thinking that in England a gentleman does not wear a wedding-ring.

Dora resumed: "Caro is looking so well. And happy." They all turned towards gaunt Caro, who held her wine-glass. "She must come out to see us." Dora was queening it. "And try her Portuguese." It was explained to the Major: "She has this gift."

Caro smirked a bit, to please.

Christian was thinking, A signet ring—well, that would be another matter. A horse of a different colour.

The Major said languages were unusual in an Orstrylian. He had a friend at Brisbane who was in dried fruit and nuts.

Christian lit a cigarette, and hoped his relation to the Major was not that of brother-in-law.

Dora remarked that her own language was good enough for her.

The Major was off on a story about an Australian nurse in a military hospital. He knew the soldier, actually, to whom the incident had occurred.

When the coffee came, Grace got awkwardly to her feet, cup in hand as if she might propose a toast. Above a blouse of lavender flowers, her face and forehead shone. She set the cup down as deliberately as if it, rather than she, were in need of care; and fainted.

Grace was to have a child.

The London theatre where Paul Ivory's first full-length play was given had a small foyer which, at the end of that afternoon's matinee, was emptying slowly because of the rain. Women shuffled out in single file, and a few elderly men waited under the awning, wondering what came next. Caroline Bell stood to one side, unfastening her umbrella while she looked through glass doors at a tawdry street.

Paul entered from a small interior door near the ticket booth: himself an actor on cue. Finding the crowd still there, he hesitated. And in that moment saw Caro, who had her back to him, her face obscured as if deliberately turned away.

Paul Ivory stood with his hand on the door he had just opened, a man who controls himself under an accusation.

The unfairness was not only that the woman had been placed in his path but also that, given her unawareness, the choice was left to him whether to speak. Even while registering injustice, Paul was almost physically swayed by the sight of Caro, and by the deliberate, detached authority with which fate had again produced her. Paul had measured his forgetfulness of Caroline Bell by the swift current of change and achievement in his recent months of life. He had not merely left her but left her behind. From the standing-room assigned her in the theatre of Paul Ivory's existence, Caro should pensively observe his performance, and applaud. Now, at the sight of her averted head, he had no choice, and must act under compulsion. He approached her with some consciousness of exaltation, obeying an impulse not necessarily to his advantage. Obeying his need as if it were virtue.

All this because a dark girl stood at a door with a furled umbrella in her hand.

"Caro."

So she turned, and again they stood side by side.

With his own sensations fresh in him, Paul saw her spasm of surprise and the sequence of quick, contradictory impulses. There was even recognition that she had run, or provoked, this risk in coming to see his play; and a flash that answered his own compulsion but was dourly mastered. Her lips closed to a deliberate curve he had not seen before because it derived from his desertion.

The lobby was by now almost empty. Lights had been turned out. They made a dark pair, standing by the doors.

She said, "Yes?" as if accosted by a stranger. But trembled in the raincoat with her whole body so that she felt the separate stuffs of her clothes, and her anatomy delicately beating within. In the same way her mind struggled, tremulous, inside the event.

"You were good to come, Caro."

"I am glad to have seen it."

"I'm hardly ever here. There's been a change in the cast, the part of Mandy, the tubercular son, and I wanted to see how it went." Automatic speech, anything to pass these moments.

She had never before seen Paul in a city suit. For his part he found her appearance extraordinary, large eyes and transparent skin: a formidable loveliness. He had expected to leave her behind him.

Impressions came and went in them, like quick tides.

Paul said, "Would you care to see backstage?"

They walked down a corridor of whitewashed grime. "Mind the steps." The stage had marks on it—a stroke of chalk, a stencilled arrow. The curtain, of stale, unclean crimson, was down, there was the glum furniture of the last act. At a time when Shakespeare was played in modern suburban dress or leather jackets, Paul Ivory's contemporary, working-class play was being acted out in royal robes. Father and Mother loomed as stage tyrants, crowned and majestic in purple and gold, while their subjected offspring cowered in cardigans and dungarees. This fairly obvious device had been called a stroke, or shaft, of genius in the press.

Caroline Bell accompanied Paul through a dingy labyrinth, never lowering her eyes. When they paused at a doorway she shook her hair back so that her face was entirely visible.

A man in overalls unlatched the door. Paul smiled his open, remembering smile: "Thanks, Collis." They went down a short flight, and Paul knocked on another door.

Caro was introduced to the great actor, who said, "If you do that again I'll have your hide." He was speaking to a dandified boy, who took grapes from a ribboned basket without replying. The embroidered royal robe hung on the wall. Paul said, "Feel it." Even a single fold was heavy to handle. The actor told her, "It gives the weight of bloody sovereignty all right." He had taken the colour off his face, and was wearing a lawn shirt and sponge-bag trousers.

A scalding radiator hissed in a corner. Caro loosed her coat.

Paul asked her, "What did you think of the Marmite scene?"

Before she could answer, the boy with the grapes said, "It's the strongest bit in the play."

Caro said, "I wasn't convinced a shopgirl would know the word 'Oedipal.'"

The actor laughed. "We've been through that. Don't forget it was a bookshop she worked in."

The boy said, "It's a bit heavy-handed, the king is dead long live et cetera. Otherwise it's okay."

The actor asked Paul, "Conder did all right, don't you think?"

"I've already told him so. He'll settle in. Mandy ought to look a damn sight sicker, that's all." It was to be noted that Paul smiled less with the actors—who, after all, were professionals.

The actor said, "Conder couldn't look sick enough to suit Valentine." Valentine was the boy with the grapes. This reference to his jealousy, while excluding the outsider —Caro—was, in the way of all exclusions, directed at her. The men exchanged a smile.

In the corridor the queen-mother sailed past them in long, sharp profile, eyelids and lashes heavily drawn in peacock colours, pencilled back to the hairline: the prow of a Greek trireme.

Paul said, "Performers never notice anyone but themselves."

He had done the right, or astute, thing in exposing Caro to his attainment, summoning up his auxiliaries. He said, "Are you working in that office now?"

"Yes. I had a half-day off, there was a lunch for my sister."

"Same old cast of characters." Confirming his advantage. They had reached the street door. "Me included." He put his hand on the doorknob and leaned against the wall, not really detaining her. "Me too, Caro." Behind him, aphorisms, all more or less obscene, were scratched or scribbled on whitewashed brick.

Her uplifted face, expressionless. She reached past him; but would not put her hand over his to take the doorknob, and hesitated, poised and thwarted. He saw she could not speak. She reached again for the door and kept her eyes on him, like a captive who edges watchfully towards escape. There was the everlasting, irritating, and alluring impression that she addressed herself to an objective beyond the small, egoistic drama of their own desires.

Paul said, "You always had some contempt for me."

"Yes."

"And love too."

"Yes." A flicker over her stare was the facial equivalent of a shrug. "Now you have a wife to give you both."

They stood fronting one another. Paul removed his hand from the door. "Caro. For pity's sake."

The figure of speech appeared to move her, and for an instant it seemed she might laugh. Again he pressed what he took for an advantage: "Have a bit of mercy."

She herself leaned back on the chalky wall, and closed her eyes. "How should you hope for mercy, rendering none?"

"These walls are full of dirty quotations, one way and another."

There was silence while she leaned there, austere with her umbrella, sheathed and closed. She roused herself and did step past him, then, to pull at the heavy door.

From behind her, Paul said, "You've got white all over your back." And in the most natural way in the world brushed his hand down her coat. Then passed his arms about her waist and put his mouth to the nape of her neck, and said, "Almighty God."

They walked in the wet street. Paul took hold of the loosened belt of Caro's raincoat and seemed to lead her through the rush-hour crowd—not pulling but establishing contact and mastery, so that she accompanied him like an acquiescent animal on a leash or rein. At the corner he signalled a taxi, and gave the driver an address. When they got in, he said, "We might take a look at my new premises. I'm fixing up a house I bought. You must tell me what you think." He held her hand as they sat in the cab—literally held it, since it lay in his with as much response as a coat belt. Caro sat without speaking, turning towards him her look that was neither sullen nor expectant but soberly attentive; and, once, a glance in which tenderness and apprehension were great and indivisible, giving unbearable, excessive immediacy to the living of these moments. Paul had seen that look before, when they first lay down together at the inn beyond Avebury Circle.

"This is it." Paul leaned forward to tell the driver. "You can let us off here. It's a cul-de-sac—once in, you can't get out."

The rain had stopped. The house was narrow and flat-fronted, a slot of brick severity between two pigeon-breasted buildings with porticoes. By the curb, a man working on the engine of a parked car nodded to them and went on singing:

> "Roses are flowering in Picardy,
> But there's never a rose like you."

Paul used a bright new key. There were smells of paint, plaster, and raw wood. Brown paper was spread on the floors, and each window had an X pasted on it like a warning of plague. Precipitous stairs were shinily white. The yard at the back was muddy and littered with workmen's discards, although a pile of flagstones showed it would be paved and planted in due course. A sink of pale porcelain stood in the kitchen, strapped and papered, ready to be puttied: a patient in bandages at a dressing-station.

In the dining-room the hospital motif recurred. Painters' cloths were whitely draped over trestles and a table. The smell of paint was antiseptic, anaesthetic.

Caro asked, "Is Tertia here?" The bull by the horns.

Paul pushed a painted door delicately with his finger. "Tertia is staying in the country till this is ready for her." Even a house required advance warning of Tertia. "You're my first guest."

The living-room took all the next floor, but was narrow nonetheless. Caro walked to the front, then to the back. They went up again. Paul switched on an unshaded light. "Up here is where I doss down."

It was the top room and the largest, not having stairs above. From the windows you could see the houses opposite, then a block of flats. There were espaliered trees that would be protective in the summer, or so Paul said. Several rugs on the bare floor were rolled and tied. The walls were dry, the windows had been cleaned. There were unattached lighting fixtures in a corner, door handles in a cardboard box; a pair of marble obelisks already decorated the mantel. A telephone had been connected and was placed on the floor. One window was half-way up, because of the fresh paint, and the room was cold.

With another bright key, Paul unlocked a built-in cupboard. "Let's have a drink." There was a package on an upper shelf of the closet, and a framed painting propped below. Paul showed Caro the picture.

She said, "Segonzac is a middle-class painter."

"Not every artist can be supreme."

"Obviously." She roused herself to meaning, as to a need for manners. "But there is a veracity—a keeping of faith, if you like—that enhances even some lesser talents. Something Mrs. Thrale said about your father—that he wasn't a great poet, but he was a true poet."

Paul put the picture away, since it had not served its turn. "Well," he said, "sit down. Drink to my new house." It displeased or somehow hurt him that Caroline Bell should recall his father. Caro sat on the pile of rugs. She watched Paul handle a silver flask with her same sardonic look, as if she were about to laugh. "There are no glasses— we'll have to use the cap, I'm afraid. What's more, we have to share it." He handed it to her. "A loving-cap."

She drank. She did not hand the cap back to him, but set it beside her on the freshly waxed boards. Paul said, "Hey, my new floors," and picked up the little container and drained it off. "Would you like another?"

"No. It tasted of tin."

"Tin my eye, that's sterling silver." He sat beside her on the rugs. "You must tell me what you think of my house."

"There is so little space."

"Now you're spoiling things."

"What is left to spoil?"

The telephone rang. The bell exploded in the unclad room, ricocheting off walls and ceiling like a burst of bullets.

Paul had to kneel to talk. "It is. But I'd like to know how you got this number. . . . Look, if this is going to press tonight you'd better read it to me. . . . Very well, you may quote me as follows. I have no response to Mr. Whatsit's remarks. I am not responsive to viciousness, and I find Mr. Whatsit's own writings the quintessence of vulgarity. . . . That's what I said. Certainly: Q-U-I-N-T, then essence. . . . That's right, exactly like vanilla. Actually, the word means 'substance of heaven.' Would you please read that back? . . . That's it, then. . . . Well, that would have to be after I return from Spain, where I go tomorrow, say the end of—yes, that's good for me. Call me then."

Paul put the phone down. He rose and stood with palms placed together, looking at Caroline Bell as if she needed solving: re-creating the frame of mind in which he had brought her there.

"Are you really going to Spain tomorrow?"

"Of course not." He looked round for the flask. "Let's have another of those tin things." He handed it to her. "How does it taste now?"

She took a little and handed back the cup. "Now it tastes as if it had your initials on it."

"You've turned such a bitch, Caro. You used to be—"

"What?"

"Angelic. But much less beautiful. That, alas, is the way it goes. Now tell me about my house, my play."

"You don't want opinions, you want approval."

"I do want your approval."

There was another detonation of the phone bell. Paul knelt again to talk. "Yes, this does seem to be Flaxman five— No, I'm afraid she isn't here but I can give her a— I've told you, she is not here but I—" At an interjection Paul raised, or hardened, his voice to proceed with his own speech—a slight restraint of eyelids showing he was too well bred to close them, even momentarily, in exasperation. "I distinctly told you Mrs. Ivory is not here." He said "Mrs. Ivory," instead of "my wife" or "Tertia," as a Party member might solemnly transform Russia into "the Soviet Union." He looked comical, crouching on the floor while standing on his dignity.

Caro said, "Tell them you're going to Spain tomorrow."

"I am certainly not going to stand here"—Paul crouched lower—"listening to—" He stared, then banged the receiver down, the force of the action taking him forward on all fours. He stood up, brushing his trousers. "Hung up on me, the bastard. He thought—pretended to think I was the servant."

"That's because you said Mrs. Ivory like that." Caro watched Paul wonder about the call, the caller, and Mrs. Ivory. Honourable Tertia. "What sort of voice?"

"Oh—educated."

God forbid Mrs. Ivory should take a lover from the lower classes.

Below in the street the man went on singing in a voice high and unsteady as an old recording:

> *"But there's one rose that dies not in Picardy,*
> *'Tis the rose that I keep in my heart."*

Paul closed the window. "If it's any satisfaction to you, this is pretty much the situation." He was speaking of the phone call.

"More troublesome than you expected, then."

This was scarcely a question, and Caro, looking up in lassitude from the bound rugs, might have been perfectly indifferent. Her venture at spoiling things by honesty had yielded nothing: honesty must be honestly intended, or its facts are worthless. But Paul considered a moment before saying, "It does create a new degree of isolation."

He was at his most sincere acknowledging displeasure, and his voice, when free of affectation, had a mature colour, resonant, almost beautiful. The clarity of his eyes, which threatened to become prismatic as Tertia's, was retinged by natural resentment. "That is of course because one is keeping up the public pretence at the same time. I daresay there's nothing new in it." Even the last remark had no sneer. Paul set his foot on the pile of rugs, close to Caro's hand, and went on:

> *"For aught I know, all husbands are like me;*
> *And every one I talk with of his wife*
> *Is but a well-dissembler of his woes,*
> *As I am. Would I knew it, for the rareness*
> *Afflicts me now."*

He sat with Caro on the rugs again. "Can you wonder that play is never performed these days?"

Beside the chill drama of Paul's marriage, played out in its interesting setting of worldly success, Caro's wound must blanch to a light stroke of experience that it would be tiresome to display. Caro would be instructed, not questioned; would be addressed, with knowing interpolations:

"That alas is the way it goes"; "Something we must rectify." Paul, not Caro, would interpret the degree of meaning in their respective lots. That had been decided, as he sat speaking intimately of his life to the person most excluded from it—in order to readmit her to the intimacy though not the life.

He lifted his hand to take hers. Then appeared to think better of it: a small indecision within a greater. "There is an interesting collusion in it, I suppose. Deceiving one another, she and I agree to deceive, on another level, a larger public."

"And does that appeal to you?"

"I've always had a taste for the play within the play." He smiled. "I have an idea. Let's go to Spain tomorrow."

"And send that man a postcard."

"Which one?"

"Both."

His laughter pealed up and down, like the phone bell. Twine stitches harshly imprinted themselves in Caro's elbow as she propped herself on the carpets.

"I have kept loving you." Through all the interesting things that have happened to me. "And you love me."

"Yes."

"Honesty's the best policy."

"That's a contemptible expression. Like 'Crime doesn't pay.' "

The same vexed tightening of Paul's eyelids. "Now we're to have a discourse on rhetoric, are we?"

Caro got to her feet, unhearing; her remoteness not intended to teach him any lesson. She took her umbrella from a corner, and walked out of the room.

The first flight of stairs, down which she quickly and lightly went, was too narrow for him to pass her. When he caught her up at the landing he did put his hand to hers. "Of course I shan't let you go." He said this with leniency, coaxing a child out of its caprice; but his hand was hot and uncertain, as he realized only in touching her. The steep little stairs rose above them, a white cliff-face that might or might not be rescaled.

"Let me leave here."

"Look, you wanted this, didn't you—coming to the theatre, then here?"

"That doesn't mean I don't have better in me."

"You've gone through enough doors for today."

"Let me go. This isn't how I want to be. Let me go on with my life. Or be at least as I was. Instead of what I've been all these months, since I knew you."

Vicious enough in themselves, the last words did not come out scathingly but as they might have been uttered by a person long cut off from speech and human society, who now ineptly articulated blunt realities. In Paul, however, they produced new tension; and the dim electric glow from above, like stage moonlight, showed his face bleached —scarcely male, scarcely young.

He said, "You look on me as a weakness in yourself."

"All my weakness is distilled in you."

Caro had the effect of interrupting the flow of Paul's will, so that his aspect slackened, in the way of all beings, even animals, who have lost conviction. A countering result was that Caro herself felt closest to Paul at such moments, and least surprised she should love him.

The climax of the sequence was that Paul, with an instinct for the fluctuations of resistance, once again embraced her, putting his arms inside her open coat as if entering her protection. Her umbrella fell to the bare boards with a tactless clatter. She did not raise her arms to him.

Paul said, "How cold. How cold you are."

They stood in this way, without change except for movements of Paul's hands on Caro's body—slight undulations on which the light played cloudily. Withdrawing, she said, "Why should you want this?" Her back to the downward stairs. The unfurnished ring to the voice, words bare as floorboards.

"I don't know." A contagion of honesty, the best policy. "It's the proof of everything I disbelieve."

She would have said, "Yet you believe in God," but could not implicate God in so much bungling.

Paul Ivory rested his palm against the wall beside her head, propping himself there to await her surrender. On the pure wall, the shadow of shapely fingers was huge: he had the upper hand. The light was turning his figure supple yet metallic, the colour of pewter. It is not often that Venus passes before, and occults, so bright a star.

He made a little distance between them so he might watch her yielding.

He had opened her dress, and the exposed streak of flesh within outdoor clothes was oddly shocking. There was the loosed raincoat and red unbuttoned bodice, then the secret slit of white. Unlike many images of Caroline Bell he later sought to preserve, this one did fix itself in Paul Ivory's memory: the stark wall, the stairs up and down, her red dress; and the flare of her breast which she left gravely revealed, like a confession.

16

You asked me about Paul Ivory's play. I saw it only last month. I was impressed, and perhaps surprised by his ease in handling the working-class milieu. I think you might be suspicious of it—some of the effects spurious, and a pat, clever ending that was nevertheless breathtaking. It looks as if it will run forever, so you may see it when you get back from France.

Caro stopped writing, and read the passage over. How sincere, judicious. How much easier it is to sound genuine when being derogatory.

Caro sat at her office desk remembering Paul Ivory's play and how, for an instant at the end of the final act, the audience had remained silent after its ordeal. Here and there in the theatre a click or tick, a slight crackle such as one hears at potteries among baked wares cooling from the furnace. And then the fracturing applause.

Good that you can go to the Rome conference before returning here—I saw something about it in the papers. In Rome I remember a palace designed on a nobleman's horoscope—that is to say, decorated with representations of planets and pagan gods. Mere astrology, but perhaps you'll manage to see it all the same.

It was thus assured that Ted Tice would pass his happiest hour in Rome in frescoed rooms on the bank of the Tiber.

There will scarcely be time to write again before you get back to England. Thank you for asking me to dinner, that will be lovely. Until one month, then, from today.

Caroline Bell posted this letter on her way home at noon. Saturday was a half-day at her office, and she stopped to buy food to provide lunch for Paul. She was living at that time in a top-floor furnished flat, rented from an office friend who had been posted abroad. It was near the Covent Garden market, in a building otherwise let to printers and publishers.

Noon came like glory into the narrow sooty brick of Maiden Lane, and expanded with architectural intention at the market. The city rose to the sun's occasion. And Caroline Bell was grateful for a bodily lightness never felt before, which she knew to be her youth. She walked with paper bags in her arms, smiling to think of her lost youth, discovered at the ripe and adult age of twenty-two.

Paul was in her doorway. He waited for her to come up to him, then leaned down from the step to embrace her. With the paper bags and a bunch of red flowers she made quite a bundle. "Why is this woman smiling?"

"I was thinking about adulthood, and adultery."

"Funny, I was thinking about adultery myself. Have you got the key?"

She gave it. They went up linoleum stairs, past doorways sealed with weekend finality. In an old building like this, dust settled quickly, and the unlocking of these small businesses each Monday were a mere deferral, each time surprising, of eventual, ordained oblivion.

Paul said, "Saturday afternoon in England is a rehearsal for the end of the world."

When they paused on a landing to breathe, he said, "These have been the best weeks of my life."

The flat was a large room with windows along one side and a blotched skylight at the far end. One wall was entirely covered by books on warped shelves, and the uneven floor was obscured by a big blue rug, nearly ragged, in which traces of reddish design could still be discerned, like industrial gases in a twilit sky or bloodstains inexpertly removed. A downward sag of ceiling, shelves, and floor was reproduced in a slump of studio couch that stood against the books and was covered by a new blue counterpane. There was a fine old table, scarred, and two chairs. The only picture was Caro's angel from Seville, on a wall near the kitchen door.

Everything was worn, or worn-out, even the smirched sky. The books supplied humanity, as they are supposed to do. Otherwise you might have said dingy, or dreary.

Paul sat on the fresh counterpane, his hands poised on his knees. Caro called from the kitchen, "Are you hungry?"

"I shall be."

She switched off the derelict stove and came back and stood beside him. He was turned towards the wall, looking at the books. "Very much a library, isn't it—Larousse, set of Grove, what's this, Bartlett."

"That's the reference shelf."

"While we provide the erotica." He drew her down on the sofa, so that she knelt while he lay. "This is our shelf, this sofa. This bed thy centre, these walls thy sphere."

"It's the name of a symphony, the Erotica."

"Here's something I want." The book was so heavy he had to sit up again and draw it out with both hands. He flopped it open on their laps, powdering the bedcover with reddish dust. "Unobtainable now. I can use it in what I'm working on." It was an edition of old plays.

"Well, you could borrow it, I suppose. I suppose you could." Caro lifted it off her knees and wandered about the room. She pulled curtains across, put the vase of anemones on the table. She took off her clothes.

He said, "To keep, I mean."

"It isn't mine, you see." Caroline Bell laced her hands together on the crown of her head. Her extended torso became both commanding and vulnerable.

Paul thumped the book to the floor at the bedside and lay down, watching. And in the veiled light, with an antique density of books behind him, might have done for a Victorian illustration: young body relapsed on blue and red, white-shirted arm dangling towards a fallen book. *Childe Harold, The Death of Chatterton.* Caro said as much.

"Thanks. Now come here."

She came to the bed and lay by him. Paul said, "To

think this waits for me, day and night." He took locks of her coarse hair and spread them in dark rays round her head. "Hair like a horse."

She said, "My love. My lover."

"Do you remember, the first time, near Avebury, I told you I'd never felt deeply. Or enough. I want to tell you now, this is the most I ever felt for anything or anyone, what I feel for you."

She touched his face. That day at Avebury she had touched his hand to the veneer bedstead; and he had said, "Whatever enough means."

Paul sometimes still thought she looked foreign—by which he meant she never quite belonged to him. He said, "Possession is nine points of the law." But this was much later, when he lay looking at the dusty room and thinking that youth was a help, because these particular moments, of languor, and underclothes on chairs, would otherwise seem a portent of deeper weakness. The flowers, now, were flat, red, garish.

He said, "I was sleeping."

"And I was watching you." She might have meant, watching over; but that did not occur to Paul, who showed his slight facial tension of displeasure or alarm.

He said, "Unnerving to be watched in sleep. That's the way men lose everything—their hair, or their heads, or worse." He would not tell how he himself had watched Caro's sleep, on the night she had first come to his new house. Watched her breath and her slight movements of dream, and skin so transparent that he might imagine the innards shaping her and the small, complex reproductive organs with their ability to change the world. As the sun came up he had watched over this phenomenon—sufficient in its beauty, so that you might hardly believe reason and articulation and human wakefulness need be added; let alone the capacity for mating.

He would not tell this and further increase her strength.

He reached his hand down to the floor beside the bed. "I can take it, then?"

She knew it was the book.

17

In the government office where Caroline Bell worked there was a young woman called Valda. That she was called Valda was to the point, for she objected to this. None of the other women there objected to being Milly, Pam, or Miranda with their appointed Mr. Smedleys and Mr. Renshaw-Browns. None of the other women objected, for that matter, to being girls.

By that epoch the men themselves were no longer Bates or Barkham to one another, but instant Sam or Jim. Those who had irreducibly formal names, such as Giles or Julian, even seemed to be lagging dangerously and doomed to obscurity. There was one older man in Planning who would say Mister to his subordinates—"Mister Haynes," "Mister Dandridge"—like the skipper of an old ship with his first mate or boatswain. But he too, among the women, permitted himself an occasional Marge or Marigold; although at home calling his charwoman Mrs. Dodds.

When Caro asked, "If they make a true friend, what will they call him?" Valda told her: "They're hoping to put true friendship out of business."

New, compulsory congeniality among males was at least, however, in Valda's view, a loss equally shared. Unlike the outright seizure of June or Judy.

Soon after her arrival Valda had drawn attention to herself. Her little Mr. Leadbetter, the administrative officer, had come out of his hutch, ears up, holding a button, and asked if she would sew it on. This, he estimated, would not take a minute. Valda politely consented. And, laying aside her paper, brought from a desk drawer a housewifely pouch of needles and coloured threads. With Mr. Leadbet-

158

ter's jacket aswoon in her lap, she narrowed her own eye to the needle's and was soon stitching. Leadbetter stood to watch her. His shirt was striped and blue, his trousers came to his armpits, depending from canvas braces, also striped, that had long ago been made to last. It was pleasant to doff his armour and watch the handsome Valda at her humble and womanly task. When she had done, when she had wound the thread and broken it off, he was grateful.

"Thank you, Valda. I am not handy with such things. And would jab myself to pieces." It was important to show appreciation.

To this, Valda replied, echoing his own benevolent thoughts: "These are small things to do for one another."

The following week Valda came into his office, where he was reading over a penultimate draft, and asked him to change her typewriter ribbon.

Mr. Leadbetter stared.

She said, "I am not handy with machines."

He was baffled and displeased. "Have you never needed a new ribbon before? Were you not trained to do these things?"

"It will not take a minute."

"You had better get one of the girls to show you." It was incomprehensible.

"They will dirty their hands." She said, "It is a small thing to do."

Now he understood. He went out and got one of the other girls—the real girls—in a rage. "Miss Fenchurch needs help with her machine." It was the first time he had not called her Valda, but respect was accorded only from pique. The second girl looked with ingratiating timidity at him, and with terror at Valda, and at once bent to the machine as if over a cradle.

When the time came, Mr. Leadbetter wrote in Valda's file that she tended to be aggressive over trifles. "Tended" was official code for going the whole hog.

There was a small inner room like a cupboard where, morning and afternoon, these girls took turns to make the tea. A list was tacked to the wall, of all the men and their requirements: Mr. Bostock weak with sugar, Mr. Miles strong and plain. Valda's Leadbetter had an infusion of camomile flowers, which he bought at Jackson's in Piccadilly; these were prepared in a separate pot and required straining. Another notice cautioned against tea-leaves in the sink. The room was close and shabby. There were stains on the lino and a smell of stale biscuits. On one spattered wall the paint was peeling, from exhalations of an electric kettle.

Sometimes when Valda made tea Caro would set out cups for her on a scratched brown tray.

It was something to see the queenly and long-limbed Valda measure, with disdainful scruple, the flowers for Mr. Leadbetter's special pot (which carried, tied to its handle, a little tag: "Let stand five minutes"). To hear her reel off the directions: "Mr. Hoskins, saccharin. Mr. Farquhar, squeeze of lemon." She filled the indeterminate little room with scorn and decision, and caused a thrill of wonderful fear among the other women for the conviction that, had one of these men entered, she would not have faltered a moment in her performance.

When Valda spoke of men more generally, it was in an assumption of shared and calamitous experience. None of the other women entered on such discussions—which were not only indelicate but would have mocked their deferential dealings with Mr. This or That. Furthermore, they feared that Valda, if encouraged, might say something physical.

Watching the office women file towards the exit at evening, Valda observed to Caro: "The lowing herd wind slowly o'er the lea."

There was another male faction in the office, of ageing young men who spoke bitterly of class divisions and of the right, or absence, of opportunity. For these, equally, Valda had no patience. "They don't quite believe they exist, and are waiting for someone to complete the job for them, gratis." She would set down the biscuit tin, switch off the electric kettle. "Oh Caro, it is true that the common man is everlastingly embattled, but he has a lot of people on his side. It's the uncommon man who gets everyone's goat."

Valda would tell Caro, "You feel downright disloyal to your experience, when you do come across a man you could like. By then you scarcely see how you can decently make terms, it's like going over to the enemy. And then there's the waiting. Women have got to fight their way out of that dumb waiting at the end of the never-ringing telephone. The *receiver,* as our portion of it is called." Or, slowly revolving the steeping teapot in her right hand, like an athlete warming up to cast a disc: "There is the dressing up, the hair, the fingernails. The toes. And, after all that, you are a meal they eat while reading the newspaper. I tell you that every one of those fingers we paint is another nail in their eventual coffins."

All this was indisputable, even brave. But was a map, from which rooms, hours, and human faces did not rise; on which there was no bloom of generosity or discovery. The omissions might constitute life itself; unless the map was intended as a substitute for the journey.

These at least were the objections raised by Caroline Bell.

For her part, Valda considered Caro as a possibility lost. Caro might have done anything, but had preferred the common limbo of sexual love. Whoever said, "When you go to women, take your whip," was on to something deep, and deeply discouraging.

Valda would watch Caro, and think along these lines. She would think, Oh yes, let them show her their whip, or some comparable attraction.

18

When Paul Ivory made a two months' trip to North America, he wrote from Los Angeles to Caroline Bell:

My dear, I shall be glad to move on from here—not because of film people and exhaust fumes and limitless cemeteries that make Stoke Poges look like headlines, but simply because I've discovered I can expect only one letter from you at each place I visit, and when I've had it I might as well move on. Having wanted all my life to come to this country, I now streak through it madly looking for your next letter. A diabolical plot on your part, for which I can never hope to get even.

The letters, when I catch up with them, move me to the heart—an organ which in my case you invented anyway. I find it strange to be affected by your wisdom when it stops so short in respect to me. From these letters I try to follow your moods, with the moon as an independent check; but always there is that fine solemnity—towards what? the world? me?—that acts as a degaussing belt (it's a thing they put on ships to demagnetize them against enemy mines and radar). I find I do not want you to retain any independence or protection from me, especially in the form of good character.

Having said this, I acknowledge that my unprecedented equanimity this past year derives from your own; as you must be aware. Contagion of a kind, one of the risks of venery.

This is being written at midnight in a big bed in

a little room overlooking a garden—part of a suite provided by my masters here. It is precisely a room I have imagined, so much so that I attempt to put the final and most important factor into the picture—but it doesn't work. There is also a white sitting-room, a terrace with marvellous plants, a bathroom, and even a small kitchen. But the main thing is the bed, which puts the world in perspective.

I'm just back from the sort of dinner called stag. (How we rush to claim our horns.) The monarch of this glen scarcely addressed me, which is supposed to be a good sign. Everyone extremely tough in keeping with the tradition, and I did a lot of smiling of the kind you dislike. Things can be accomplished here, so long as you don't expect to retain your immortal soul—I was instantly parted from mine on arrival; presumably it, or something like it, will be restored to me by the hat-check girl at my departure. On the other hand there is not much listening or questioning, but a great deal of expounding. (Conrad, was it, who said the air of the New World is favourable to the art of declamation?) That is to say, there is a formula, and I must be fitted into it.

So far, California offers the greatest contrast imaginable between the works of God and the desecrations of Man. California is a beautiful woman with a foul tongue.

In the hotel in Washington last week I ran across Christian Thrale, who was there, as you no doubt know, for some conference. I liked him better than usual, but am not sure whether this was for intrinsic reasons or because I could say your name.

I am shocked and impressed by my love for you.

19

In August of the following year, Caro was sitting in a lofty tearoom waiting for Ted Tice. This restaurant of a London department store overlooked Piccadilly on one side, where light was discreetly veiled; some sound of traffic from the Circus was modified to prewar rumble by walls of antebellum solidity.

Admitting only seemly sounds, the room sheltered none but the decorous. All tables were occupied by women. Waitresses like wardresses kept a reproving eye on performance, repressively mopping a stain or replacing a dropped fork. Something not unpleasant, a nursery security, came along with this. Yet in such a setting you might sicken of women—sicken of their high-priced, imperious, undulant gender, their bosoms and bottoms and dressed hair, their pleats, flounces, and crammed handbags: all the appurtenances, natural and assumed, of their sex. In such density they could scarcely be regarded as persons, as men might be; and were even intent on being silly, all topics sanctified by the vehemence brought to them.

Caro felt her abnormality: to be the only one watching, the one not talking, the one who did not particularly want a car or carpet, or a service for twelve. The one who lacked place and protection, yet was not free. At the table next to hers there were two sisters—slim, calm, distinguished, both with honey hair and long clear eyes; the older engaged to a little sapphire ring, the younger perhaps seventeen. Their manners with each other were perfect—delicate, courteous, loyal. Offering menus and sugar as

164

politely as if there were no blood tie. If you could be like this, the renunciation of temperament might be worth it.

When Ted came in, the room of women pulled itself together. As he passed among them they were inclined to deny shallowness and to cease rummaging in bags. It was a power he was acquiring: part of a third possibility unforeseen by those who wondered if Edmund Tice would succeed or fail.

Since returning from France, Ted had been working at Cambridge, where once again he lived in furnished rooms. A measure of early recognition was unharmed by his attitude to the proposed telescope, for others had unexpectedly rallied to his position. A woman met through his work had been his mistress some months, but had recently returned to Jodrell Bank. Throughout an autumn and winter they had made love on Saturdays, keeping aloof the rest of the week—an arrangement not unlike a dull marriage. When this young woman left for Manchester she had nearly cried, at the same time giving Ted a little smile and turn of the head, as if to say: Hopeless. He realized she had found him an uninspired and selfish lover, and had no mind to tell her why.

"What a funny place to meet." Ted seemed larger than before, and more adroit. His hair, already receding from his forehead, still stood up in thick ginger curls. The vertical groove was deeper on his brow. He dropped his newspaper on a spare chair and sat down. When he looked about him it was as if to foresee an end to such a room and its women; as if he knew of drawing-board plans to storm this citadel. It became plain that the lofty room would soon be divided into two floors, the tearoom becoming a cafeteria with self-service. This had not been clear until Ted arrived and took in the situation at a glance.

Sometimes, in such a place, Edmund Tice would think of gentlefolk in rainy towns and damp parsonages. Would imagine families restrained and civil, their gardens, their domestic pets with literary names; the glazed bookcases with volumes of Sir Lewis Morris or Sir Alfred Comyn Lyall; *The Light of Asia*, an embossed school prize in mock leather. He would know that to die out is different from mere dying; killed off different from killed. Something—memory, belief—was to die that had not died before, or at any rate half so quickly; exterminated by those who had the approved, knowing attitudes, though perhaps no greater virtue. He was to play his part in this destruction and, like others, would mourn when all was safely dead.

Ted came to London regularly to see Caro. "I enjoyed walking through these grey streets knowing it was to see you." A simplicity requiring no reply. "Tell me what you've done all day."

"Listened to people's grievances." Caro made room for a platter of coloured cakes and meringues like spiralled shells. "Not that the grievance isn't real."

"That's the trouble with grievance. It's usually justified." When Ted had ordered tea, he asked, "Is there anything there you could care about?"

"Not really." And not in the way you intend.

"Does no one ever leave the place?"

"The men, never. The women, only to get married."

"Unless you marry me, I'd frankly prefer you stay in the deathly hole." He thought she would be exasperated, or smile; but she would not receive the remark, and it remained between them. He went straight on, with a consciousness of fatal timing: "My own work is not like that. It's necessary to me, and lucky. Yet you are as necessary to my life as knowledge is to my work, and I've not been lucky in this, and God knows I will never be truly whole or fortunate without you."

"People can't be possessed like information."

She was not combative, or even agitated. She was calm from some great resource of joy, achieved and anticipated, that could only be love.

The discovery was like violence in the pink, trivial, and fairly harmless room that had known no greater upheaval, until now, than a crash of flowered crockery.

He saw that it could not be new. But she had grown careless, and did not trouble to dissemble. Today, she had the assurance of an acrobat, rising to her adventure in grace and wasted courage. So it was all explained. Her hands and hair explained themselves, her forearm sloping back into a sleeve became the soft wrist of a woman in love: all of this desired and handled and awaited by someone, offered to someone. Ted dwelt on it with sickening defencelessness, a revulsion.

He was certain—and yet afraid of an obsessive mistake —as to her lover's identity.

She said, "You make me unkind." Sorry for him and unsmiling, she nevertheless sat there with that other life flowing through her, making her cheek rosy and his pale. He watched the glow of her flesh where it disappeared into her clothes and thought that her body, which was unknown to him, was already changing.

When she looked at her watch he said uncontrollably, "Don't go."

"I'm a bit late already."

Like a detective he noted callousness, the lover's indifference to the unbeloved. And there is nothing I can do to alter or stop any of it. She can destroy me and there is nothing I can do. I can't prevent her from sleeping with her lover this night, or from loving it and him.

The incapacity was unfairly shameful to him, like sexual impotence, and was bound up with some immense, contingent humiliation—perhaps the helplessness of all humanity to foretell or shield themselves from chaos.

When they parted he got a cab to Liverpool Street, where he waited an hour for his train, unable to read or to telephone a friend he had promised to call. The roof of the station made a sky of leaded grime, its girders and fittings insoluble. On the platforms, people milled like refugees. Ted Tice revolved and revolved the same impressions, while the same slogans intersected them from billboards. The refusal of time to pass was stupefying, and he recorded, with no detachment, the multiplication of moments in that hour. Squalor intensified, the waiting passengers appeared to age, nothing and nobody was kind or young, or ever had been. From his dirty bench he watched them as they scurried or loitered, characters from Realism without self-doubt or remorse, and with no sensations worthy of his tears.

Climbing at last on board his train, Ted Tice wished all loving at an end if this was a sample.

"Hullo." From a habit that characterizes nurtured love, or resentment, Paul seldom now used Caro's name. "The car's round the corner."

Coming through grey streets, Caro had forgotten Ted

Tice; and in her mind already told Paul, I am so happy to see you.

Back that day from a fortnight in Italy, Paul was sunburned. Men and women passing glanced at him for his expensive, imported health, and at them both for the pair they made. This had been the case when they first walked together, on a country road. Paul's presence, unlike Ted's, caused people to forget rather than recall themselves. In addition, Paul, who had a new play called *Equinox*, was sometimes recognized by strangers.

When they were in the car, Paul took her wrist a moment.

Caro asked, "How was Rome?"

"Baroque." A grim drizzle misted the windshield. "This morning I was sitting in sunshine on the Pincio."

"A shame to leave." She would have said, I am so happy to see you.

He smiled. "What a stately mood you're in." Paul drove carefully, stopping to let a trio of schoolboys cross. The children tipped their caps to Caro, as they had been taught. Paul said, "They think you're Queen Mary."

"Surely I wouldn't be in front with the chauffeur."

"Now listen, you must be sweet to me because today, within an hour of my return, I had an unexpected approach." He said a name and, when Caro showed ignorance, went on in irritation, "The only important director to come forward in the last ten years."

"Come forward" intimidated with its sense of owning up: "Would anyone answering to the description please come forward?" "Unless someone comes forward, the entire school must remain after class." As if this important man—whom Caro now identified from press reports—were somehow willing to take the blame.

By the time Paul had told his story, they had reached Covent Garden and left the car. In an hour or two, in his own house, he would tell it all again to Tertia; who, having married a man of pledged renown, would receive it as part of her due.

They went up Caro's stairs. Paul now had a key of his own. Turning it in the lock, he said, "It's now you must be sweet to me." But was clearly invincible this evening, and distracted by tributes paid. It was useless to attempt reversal, to propose one's own mood to Paul—who so hated to feel himself under direction that he sometimes could not tolerate the mere recommendation of a book; or was angered if Caro, by looking her best, should seem to compel his interest. The lightest claim on his affinities might be repudiated with savage energy, like a threat, when he was in that beleaguered frame of mind.

Striking out in this way, he might also, on occasion, accidentally wound himself.

Caro lay dressed on the bed, and Paul sat beside her, preoccupied. His hand rotated on her breast, but from force of kindly habit, absently fondling a domestic pet. On the coverlet her own hand lay open, upturned, extended to a fortune-teller.

She watched him with love that was like a loss of consciousness.

Paul was thinking of the play he might write for the man who had unexpectedly come forward. "It's hard to surprise anybody now, I don't mean it in a cheap sense. The lack of surprise that develops with age, in individuals, has now occurred in an entire population. I suppose it began with the First World War. Why should you or I, for instance, be surprised at anything by now?"

"You could still be surprised at the person who does it. Someone you know well might still surprise you with an action that was monstrous, or noble."

"Even then, love or hate can take the edge off it." This evening Paul was impartial, even clinical, regarding hate and love. The world, in being sweet to him, had met his desires for that day, and his present energies were channelled in such a way that sexual gratification itself was sublimation. "The ability to surprise is a form of independence. And proprietary feeling can be so strong that it will not concede such a revelation."

Caro said, with no strategy of surprise, "Ted and I were talking about possessiveness. I had tea with Ted Tice."

Paul made no answer. But an hour later remarked, "It is hard to be interested in Tice." Perhaps Ted Tice had never left his mind. He got up and said, "I hate this part. Socks and shirts. Leaving."

"Going home."

"You can save some man from this," he said, "by not

marrying him." Being quick with the socks and shirts, he hummed with intention—a machine switched on if not yet in operation. He sat again on the bed beside her. "Do you know that Russians always sit down for a moment before departure?"

"That's the only time you sit down."

"My God. Complaining like the classic mistress." He knew she would never hold out against the suggestion that she might begin to get on his nerves. He had no wish that she should be secure in his love; and might have held it was recurring loss that bound them.

"But I am the classic mistress."

He held both her hands. This gave an impression of restraining her from doing harm. "Don't be censorious. You look like a schoolteacher."

"The Classics mistress." They both laughed, but then she said, "What will happen to us?"

"Who can tell?"

This produced resentful fear—as if a trusted surgeon suddenly came out with "Now it's up to Nature," or "We're in the hands of the Lord." As Paul had pledged eminence to Tertia, so he had promised mastery to Caro; and, now that he finally exerted it, must not recant.

His marriage vow that evening was the stronger.

Caro's timing was fatally insistent as Ted's: "There must be an end somewhere to deception. Ultimately there must be the truth."

"And do you think the human need to deceive is not also part of truth?"

"Of reality, not truth."

Paul said, "We need a theologian and a semanticist to settle that." He smiled, still holding her hands. "I'm glad they're not here." And went on, most reasonably, "These days you want all the cards on the table. You had that enigmatic charm before, capable of anything."

"It was this I was capable of." Love had become her greatest, or sole, distinction. "Not all capacity is adverse, like 'capable of murder.' "

He released her hands, with a show of resignation: restraints were useless, she might commit violence in any case. "I mean, you used to amaze me."

"How shall I amaze you now?" Since she was obliged to keep his existence at a certain pitch.

He laughed. "Tell me something interesting about Tice."

A silence that was also a faltering made the moment interesting.

To the woman, the hiatus was a sensation remembered. One summer, helping in the garden at Peverel, she had picked up a dead rat, or rabbit, on a spade: a weight differently inanimate from that which had never had life.

"Well?" He did not so much want disclosure as to intrude on whatever virtue she privately retained. Which might be nothing more than the sacred custody of someone else's sin.

"Well then, Scheherazade?" Paul flung down his jacket and lay again at Caro's side. And she told him how Edmund Tice had spared the German scientist who was his enemy.

Paul Ivory wrote to his mother:

My dear Monica,

How wise you are to stay on in Barbados. We have had four (patriots might claim five) fine days since you left. The summer being now over, England has little to look forward to, ever. Actually, I like this season, whiteish stubble in fields and the woods beginning to go rusty. From which you'll gather I've been in the country, staying a few days with Gavin and Elise. My sister-in-law continues to take over— while Gavin is speaking she explains, *ad alta voce,* what he really means. It is like a film with subtitles.

This in fact gave me the germ of a play—the eclipse of a man who takes up with a woman of character, even of genius (patently not Elise, but you get the idea). I might call it "The One Flesh." In consequence I've been pondering such phantasmata as Messieurs Récamier, de Staël, de Sévigné, and Mr. Humphry Ward. What do you think? Of course I don't know what it would demonstrate—probably nothing more than that, on any terms, mariage is hell.

Your informant, or informer, was accurate in thinking she saw me at the opening of the Pinero revival.

A bad play: I had been told it could not be overlooked, but think it should have been. Afterwards
there was a party, at which the prime minister briefly
appeared, looking very ill: the Sea-Green Corruptible.
Your friend was also correct in reporting that I have
been seen with the same woman on a number of recent, and less recent, occasions. I should have thought
this constancy would reassure rather than disturb you.
As Lord Byron wrote—though not, I think, to his
mother—"I have not had a whore this half-year, con-
fining myself to the strictest adultery."

Your loving son

Caro stood by the windows of Paul's bedroom while
Paul, at the fireplace, fiddled, not nervously, with an
obelisk of rose-veined marble.

Tertia Ivory was pregnant.

Tertia was at the castle: gravid Tertia in her fastness.
Hold fast, the race is to the swift. Somewhere beyond
Paul Ivory's city room a landscape shimmered, the castle
swelling on its impregnable ancestral rise.

Paul said, "You knew the probabilities at the outset."
To exclude love was to fortify himself. He owed this much
to his legitimate descendants.

To discover how passion could debilitate, you need only
look at Caro.

She said, "I didn't realize you would take so much. Or
that I would give it." Both these statements were false.
Her mouth turned clumsy with incomprehension, with
comprehension. Her body, motionless, expressed an un-
lovely struggle.

"Isn't that your temperament, though?" Disengaging, if
not quite blaming: a doctor who ascribes to emotional
causes the malady he has failed to treat. "I know it is
hard." Paul was lenient, indulging the offence of love.

"Hard?" She might never have heard this sour word.

Paul had told himself he would have to go through a
bad time with her, and had certainly taken into account
her point of view. He dreaded the bad time as one dreads
process, not outcome. His mother had once said to him,
"The truly terrible things are those one cannot alter, to
which one is indefinitely committed." (She might have

said "endlessly," though that was not her style.) Paul's present suffering was not of that doomed kind. He could foresee an end to Caro.

Paul's bedroom had long been completely furnished—rugs spread, chairs stationed, pictures hung, and curtains parted on a pot of white, clothy flowers at one window. Everything was maintained in perfect order—although, by an oversight, the flowers sometimes shed gold particles of dust. On the dressing-table, silver fittings were aligned—brushes and hand-mirrors of outdated, even antiquated, kind, each embellished with a crest. In the closet there would be Tertia's clothes, which now, for a while, she would not wear. These objects were precise, and glittered; or became blurred; or altogether ceased to exist, while the man and woman stood there.

Paul remained by the fireplace in expectation of Caro's outburst. He did not like to be kept waiting. The coming storm would set him at liberty: what she was to say of him, to him, would put her in the everlasting wrong. His escape was assured by the degrading violence of her pending emotion.

"Now I'm off," she said.

He helped her on with her jacket. His conventional, unblessed touch was the true dismissal. Composure in others always thwarted him, and hers at that moment denied him the offence of a scene. That he had loved Caro more, and far more, than he had cared for anyone else gave her stature: she was either unique or an inaugurator. Paul resented this historic position she had established for herself in the momentum of his life, and because of it would have liked to see her broken.

She glanced at the room, not to be seen looking for the last time. Nothing testified to her presence. Her eyes rested on Paul with a darker questioning than he had ever endured; and he turned away, not to be tempted to some acknowledgment he himself might fear.

They went downstairs in single file, both of them recalling the earlier scene on the landing; Paul imagining his own huge hand, the whip hand, a shadow on the wall. Seeing also, in his mind, her dun raincoat and the folds of scarlet parted at her breast. It was from this time onward that the image would recur to him—vivid enough at that moment to make him almost doubt that Caro's present face looked out from a dim mirror in the hall, a face the colour of nakedness: the new Caro he had created, to whom he was now putting the finishing touches.

Her mouth was a wound that might never heal. Merely by standing at her side he could yet hope to provoke the storm of tears that would formally release him, like a dissolution of vows. He had never seen her cry, except for joy.

And in perfect obedience to his wishes, as to a law of Nature, Caroline Bell made a primitive gesture of bereavement, and spoke his name. And wept aloud without so much as covering her face.

20

"I am more sorry than I can say," Mrs. Pomfret's letter began, "to be the bearer of bad news, or tidings. But feel you would want to know."

The Major had left, or abandoned, Dora. And, since he now declared himself insolvent, was providing no support. Dora was remaining in the Algarve flat to establish possession, but was otherwise without funds. It seemed that Dora's capital had unfortunately been transferred to the Major's name at an early stage of the marriage, and was quite irretrievable in the view of Mr. Prata, far and away the best lawyer of the province.

"Her main concern is that you should continue happy and not be bothered by this. You know, even better than I, her fierce pride. But her state is pitiful and I told her flatly I would write to you as above. Without wishing to worry you unduly, I obviously have a duty to let you know that she has spoken, and more than once, of taking her life."

Caro telephoned Christian at his office, because Grace was expecting her second child. When she had read him the letter, Christian was silent awhile before saying, "This could have been foreseen."

Caro the culprit. "Is there anything to be done through the embassy?"

"I have made it a firm policy not to mix the official and the personal. Not to abuse, that is, my position." It was Caro's turn for silence. Christian soon resumed, "I'm sure you see that." In his admonishing formality he might easily have added, "Caroline."

An obscene absence of decency caused childhood panic,

as if a lavatory door-handle would not turn. "You have nothing to suggest?"

"I scarcely see how I can intervene at this stage. Without knowing more."

In the space now constructed for the utterance, Caro said, "Then I will go."

That exacted, Christian became cordial with relief. "It does seem best, if you can swing it. What a shambles. I'll talk to Grace tonight and call you back first thing."

That evening he told Grace, "Your sister is more trouble than a barrel-load of monkeys." And added, "I mean Dora."

Grace was shivering. "What will she do, without money?"

"Get a job, like millions of other women. Take her mind off herself for a change. It could be the making of her."

But the making of Dora had occurred long since.

"She would not be good in an office."

Christian now came out with it. "If it hadn't been for the damfool nonsense of handing over your own money to her, this wouldn't arise." Grace sat shuddering, and Christian got up and loped about the room. Tall men with thin shoulders begin to stoop comparatively early. "Handing it over. On a platter. Just like that." He picked up and flung down a coloured magazine, by way of illustration. "I always thought it insane."

"Caro gave up everything."

"That was daft enough, but her business. It's involving you in it that I resent."

Grace had drawn her legs beneath her on the sofa and looked thoroughly misshapen. "That's unjust. I'm as much" —she nearly said "to blame"—"in it as she. It was Caro made me keep half."

"Very magnanimous, since the entire thing was her idea."

"No."

"Allow me to refresh your memory. You particularly told me." Christian dropped into a chair. His voice was hoarse with what had been rehearsed for years. "Besides, it's just like her. She has this notion of herself."

"What notion?" As if she did not know.

"Of being different. Or better. Sees herself making large gestures." Derisory whirl of hand and arm. Christian might have respected the characteristic in a person of acknowledged standing; but who was Caro—an Australian who had worked in a shop——to be high-minded? "Rank egotism." Unsure what this use of the word "rank" conveyed, he added, "Delusions of grandeur."

"There must be worse delusions than that." Grace did not have the vocabulary for argument and was only aware, confusedly, that there was general dislike of any person with a sense of destiny—even when destiny was little more than a show of preferences. The Thrales stared at their cream-coloured rug, their brocade chairs, and the Staffordshire figure of Dick Turpin, from all of which enchantment had unaccountably seeped away. "How can Caro get leave from the office?"

"She must have some holiday saved up."

"Only a few days. And she was going to France."

"I'm sorry, but Caro will just have to learn she can't do everything."

"What about money? How will she pay the fare? Her salary is almost nothing. And then there's Dora."

Christian came and sat beside her in a chair. "Listen, Grace. You are making me out a Scrooge. A Whatnot Legree. I tell you we will do what we can when the situation is clear. Or clarified. I simply refuse to commit myself in advance, blindfold, to another of Caro's"—the word he was groping for was "harebrained"—"wild schemes. On the phone she obviously took the fare in her stride—after all, it isn't much. And it's amazing what someone like Caro often manages to salt away over the years—we'd probably be surprised. The thing is, you and I have responsibilities. We have children, which neither Caro nor Dora does."

"We are choosing to have children, for our own satisfaction. Caro has been landed with Dora, and no satisfaction." It was an answer Caro herself might have made. "Besides, Caro will have children herself one day."

The assumption was disturbing. Christian had supposed Caro might one day marry (he recalled the unappetizing Tice, who had behaved shabbily over the telescope), but had not got as far as children. In his alarm Christian could not know it was Grace's last stand, and was ready to waver from surprise and fright. But in that moment Grace gave

in, gave up, on an outburst of weak, womanly, and oblig-
ing tears. "Oh Chris, Dora will be so awful. Poor Caro."

At once he had his arms about her, and there was no
need to do more. "Poor little Grace." Eventually he said,
"You know I'm fond of Caro." Grace wiped her eyes,
while meaning flowed slowly back, like a stain, into the
cream rug; twill cushions miraculously reinflated; and a
pair of Spode plates, mounted on a wall, renewed their
encircling spell.

Grace said, "I suppose Dora will come back to England."

Christian would not announce it yet, but was determined that when Dora returned to London she should be
sheltered by Caro. It was only logical, two working girls,
a saving in rent, and so forth. He was as unshakably and
righteously resolved on this as if it had been a moral cause
or high ideal. It would have surprised him to think he was
avenging himself for the spectre of Caro's fecund marriage.

After dinner, Christian sat reading in his habitual chair,
his feet propped on a cushioned stool. This was his cus-
tom in the evening—not quite recreation but an interval
between working days. And in fact, in that position, shafts
tipped in air, he somewhat resembled an unharnessed cart
or dray. Grace, who was leaning against sofa cushions—
holding a book that seemed, fetchingly, too heavy for her
—suddenly began again to cry. Christian came and sat by
her.

"Please don't say things like that to me, please don't."

"Like what, for heaven's sake?"

She clutched the book and sobbed without control. "Like
allow me to refresh your memory."

In the morning the administrative officer, Mr. Leadbetter, told Caro, "I fear I must deny your request for
compassionate leave." It was among Mr. Leadbetter's functions to guard the department's slender store of compassion. Caro was silent. "I see, Miss Bell, that you have made
your submission"—he took up a yellow paper—"as a
matter of urgency." He read over a paragraph or two of
the application. "I am of course sorry that your sister, or
half-sister rather, has domestic difficulties. But if we made

one exception we would naturally be in no position to hold the line on similar cases."

Leadbetter's unwindowed cubicle was like an enlarged elevator—one of those that in a hospital accommodates stretcher cases, or, in a museum, transports statuary. In this case, the space was occupied mainly by a metal desk, and Leadbetter appeared as the desk's attendant or custodian: Going Down? He held the document, a yellow targe at his breast. His hair was prematurely grey with anticipation of his pension.

"I am sure you see that?"

Caro's silences were giving annoyance in these days.

"The arrangement is intended for emergencies—ill health, say, of parents or a spouse. Or, of course, decease."

Although she had Mrs. Pomfret's letter in her handbag, it would have been cheating to bring up Dora's everlasting death.

"Besides, Miss Bell, you do have annual leave accruing." Leadbetter consulted another paper. "Allow me to refresh your memory. One week has in fact accrued. I suggest you ask your supervisor whether you can be released for one week's leave at short notice." Now he had disposed of her, and without broaching the small, costly and heavily rationed fund of official compassion, he grew, like Christian, quite solicitous. "I trust you will be able to settle matters to your satisfaction."

When Christian telephoned, Caro said, "I have some annual leave. Accruing."

At lunchtime Caro took out a loan at the bank, using her pension as security. She drew a salary advance, and bought escudos. When she got back to the office Valda told her, "A man called."

Expectation of Christian made Caro aloof even to Valda. But when she took up the written message she found that Ted Tice was in town for the day.

In the evening Ted drove her to the airport. He had a small secondhand car that became silent on the smallest rise. In the car he asked, "Do you have money for this?"

"I dug some up." Planes were loud and low in the sky. Along the side of the road there were electric advertisements for soft drinks and boot polish. In the changing lights, Ted's profile shone green, then red and blue.

"Because if you need anything, ever, you need only tell me."

"Edmund Le Gentil."

"My fear is, you will never need anything that I can provide." He neither wished to impute high motives to his anxiety for her nor to underrate a selflessness inseparable from love. He had seen how people grew cruel with telling themselves of their own compassion: nothing made you harder than that. He said, "Caro, when will you let me deliver you from these awful people?"

She could scarcely bear it, that Grace might be included.

Ted Tice was observing suffering that had nothing to do with Dora. Caro's flesh was no longer luminous. Her body had grown so slender it was impossible to imagine the strength that must still be there. These changes gave him no hope, for in her misery she belonged as much, or more, to another man.

He never ceased to marvel at the waste. On each side, so much high feeling, and none of it transferable.

He said, "Today is my thirtieth birthday. If I'm not young soon, I never shall be." He was saying he would accept any terms. "Also today the final decision was made to put that telescope in Sussex."

At the departure gate he kissed her. It was the first time he had ever embraced her and seemed hardly to matter, her substance being neutralized by grief. In his arms her body was light and dispassionate as a dress.

A bus that left Lisbon at daylight brought Caro through foreign fields to a provincial city. Countryside gave way to new residential blocks and to streets busy with morning. Pavements were being hosed, shutters flung up or apart. The sun was not yet warm, the mild air still free of fumes. Along every curb, parked cars, like pack animals, waited to start. The most prosaic shop-window was exotic; a display of kitchenware, installed in coloured tiers, was a pagan altar.

The block of flats in Rua das Flores was called The Chisholm and might have been at Hammersmith. Dora lay on a twin bed, a sodden bundle. One averted one's eyes from the empty bed alongside, as from an open coffin.

"I gave him everything, that's why he hates me. Everyone has always hated me. You hate me too. Why have I gone on. Why. But this is the end now, at last." You could certainly hear her through the wall.

Caro came and went to the kitchen, the bathroom, bringing aspirins and tea, and a brioche she had bought across the road. Dora's face was a skull, the eye sockets crimson: a boiled wooden doll from an exhibit, the first doll ever made in colonial Australia. Sometimes she thrashed, at times was inert. Once she gave a scream like a flash of lightning. "I will be better dead."

"As if I could eat," she said, when Caro brought the tray. "Did you get this from the place across the road?"

When she had the tea she sat up against a soaked pillow and at every question thumped her head from side to side. Her dark hair hung down in mad long tangles. "Everything gone. I have nothing. Can't you grasp that?" She would tolerate no denial. "I'm telling you, there's nothing, it has all gone. You can ask Ernesto Prata. Who is," she added on another shriek of tears, "the best man in the province." Her head banged sideways on the pillow, as against a wall.

Caro changed the pillowslip. She made scrambled eggs. In the kitchen, leaned her forehead against a cabinet of pink Formica.

"Don't worry," Dora called from the bedroom. "I won't bother you for long."

Later that morning Caro telephoned Mrs. Pomfret, who said she would be round at tea-time. Dora put on a silk dress and lay on the living-room sofa, a brown bag of sweets at her side. "You'll be all right once I'm gone."

Caro stood out on a narrow balcony. In the foreground, television aerials were Chinese calligraphy, were a fretwork of masts and rigging in an ancient port. Beyond the brick apartments and the bungalows, a glade was green in the wasted morning. To the right of the golf course, an old garden glowed like civilization. In the orchards, almond trees remote as happy memories. She thought how she had betrayed Ted Tice's secret to Paul Ivory, and that Paul had later said to her, "What a good turn you did me, telling me that." There was nothing here to hinder her from thinking the worst of herself.

"Can you imagine for one single moment what it means to look for work at my age?"

Caro came inside. "I work."

"You're young." Dora's head was vehement again. "Can't you realize I have no one."

"I too am alone."

"You have friends."

"You have Mrs. Pomfret, here."

Dora said, "It's funny how I always manage to attract the one or two. Who take to me. I don't know why." She allowed Caro to draw the comb through her hair. "What I would have done without Glad Pomfret I don't know. The only one." Glad Pomfret had come round within an hour of the Major's departure, although it was her Bridge day. "I've never had anyone to do that for me. It doesn't seem much to you, but." Glad Pomfret had known from the first what he was, but hesitated to interfere.

Glad's own husband had been a handful himself, but was dead. "Cancer of the heart."

"I've never heard of that."

"The right ventricle. He was a big man," said Dora, "but at the end shrivelled to nothing."

Caro could clearly see Sid Pomfret on a hospital bed, a swag of deflated rubber. Dora had an ability to bring deliquescence before your eyes.

"They opened him up but he was riddled. In no time he was gone." Dora sighed. "Those are the lucky ones."

Caro said, "Mrs. Pomfret is bringing a Miss Morphew."

"I don't trust Gwen Morphew." Dora bent her head so that Caro could make the coil at the nape. "That's Glad's paid companion." Ernesto Prata, Glad Pomfret, Gwen Morphew, they were like the cast of a play. On the other hand, the Major had become, simply, he. "He took the antiques, the pieces. He even took the wireless. If you could have seen his face. The cruelty of him. The cruelty."

"Dora, don't cry any more. Your poor eyes."

But Dora was hooting for the cruelty. "I'd put nothing past him. Nothing. I'm lucky to be alive."

Caro sat with her arms about Dora, and for two pins would have resumed long past pleadings: Please Dora, oh Dora don't. In any embrace, Dora would apply her stranglehold. Caro, whatever her frailty, was now irrevocably cast as the strong one who overcame without effort; Dora would be the victim, and pitifully weak. There was no reversal of roles in this, only a change of tactics. They had made the exchange in mid-air, as two mountaineers pass between them, at the critical instant, the rope that hoists them to the ledge.

"This awful place. So alone. If only we could get back to Sydney," Dora was howling, "where we were all so happy." Tranquillity recollected in emotion. After a while she said, "At least Grace had the sense to keep half." It was Dora's only reference to the sisters' loss in the debacle: Grace was respected for her foresight, Caro had been the fool. "Grace is so happy, so fortunate. Christian is reliable, someone to turn to. I've never had anyone to turn to. Not one."

In making a fool of Caro over the transfer of the money, Fate had aligned itself on the side of avarice and calculation. Fate had teamed up with the Major, Christian, and Clive Leadbetter, and the righteous had been forsaken. Caro had to wonder at it, the unfairness.

Mrs. Pomfret came at four, in a large dress of turquoise wool with matching turban. There was a cameo among folds. Miss Morphew was lean, slate-coloured, and had a slight tremor.

"Ernesto Prata is my own man," Glad Pomfret said; meaning lawyer. "And the best in the region." Mrs. Pomfret preferred a straight chair because of fused vertebrae. Caro brought more tea and the remains of the brioche, along with some macaroons found in a tin. A quartet of white doves, released from a garden, wheeled outside the windows. Dora observed that pigeons were said to carry viral hepatitis.

Caro asked, "Is there work here for Dora while this is being settled?"

Mrs. Pomfret pursed, pessimistic. "It is a pity she never picked up the language. Even though circumstances are different, I have picked it up." She uttered the expressions for good morning, good evening. "It is not all that hard to pick up." Portuguese might have been viral hepatitis, or some object by the wayside for anyone's casual lifting. Mrs. P. settled turquoise folds. "Even Miss Morphew has picked it up."

Looking aggrieved in a new way, Dora said from the sofa, "I read somewhere you couldn't learn a new language after thirty. Not properly."

Mrs. Pomfret told Caro, "Naturally, Dora does not hope for a career like yours."

Caro struck out hopelessly: "I am an ill-paid clerk, in a dull office."

Mrs. Pomfret's smile was sadness itself. "That seems, you see, a lot to her."

Dora moaned in realization. Miss Morphew was leaning for another macaroon.

"Dora was unwise," Mrs. Pomfret adjudged, "in signing over to him." They had all taken up the he and him, out of deference to Dora. To so much as name Bruce Ingot would have been a declaration of treason. "A woman should never make over capital. Not even to her nearest and dearest."

Miss Morphew said, "Dora was too trusting."

Dora whimpered. "He won me over."

It was hard to imagine the Major in wooing mood. One suspected he had never courted anything, except disaster.

Dora wailed, "Forget me. I am determined to trouble no one."

Miss Morphew helped Caro take away the dishes. In the kitchen, she ran the tap and said, without looking in Caro's direction, "Prata is in with the Major. Try Salgado in Rua do Bomjardim."

When Dora got her settlement she stayed on in the Algarve throughout the winter. "I long to leave this awful place, as you can imagine," she wrote to Caro, "and these unspeakable people. Thank heaven England still stands for something. But might as well get the winter out of it here, as I will never see it again. Also, it is advisable to stick it out till spring, since I do not trust Manoel Salgado." Later she wrote that she had reached breaking-point with regard to Glad Pomfret. The main thing was that Caro should continue perfectly happy.

Christian said, "I was sure something would be worked out."

Mr. Leadbetter, meeting Caro in the corridor, reminded her that his door was always open.

One Sunday afternoon Nicholas Cartledge telephoned Caroline Bell. "Am I never to see you again?"

"No."

"I've tried you a number of times."

"I was in Portugal last month."

"Lucky you."

21

On winter evenings and weekends, Caroline Bell walked through the city alone, in labyrinthine suburbs to the north or south. From these expeditions—which never lacked an expectation, scarcely sane, of coming face to face with Paul Ivory—she would return home, perhaps wet, always cold. And, removing her shoes, stand in the kitchen trying to warm herself by the stove.

Repayment of the bank loan had done away with heat for the winter. She understood how people had burned fine furniture during winters of the war. She understood why men spoke to her in the streets. She understood many acts of destruction and survival formerly incomprehensible.

She stood in the kitchen and thought, What a cold country.

Caro lay in her frozen bed and stared at the skylight, which was a sheet of clotted ice. She lay in darkness or in moonlight, remembering how, one evening of the previous year, she had come in from work to find Paul sitting at her table writing; and that he had got up and embraced her and asked, "How does it strike you, to find a light on and someone waiting for you?" He had put his mouth to her hair and said, "I have wished that Tertia did not exist." Now it was Caro whom, for his convenience, he wished away.

Love had not been innocent. It was strange that suffering should seem so.

Her mind shifted uselessly on silence, ravening as much to give as to receive. A sense of waste made incredulous tension in eyes and breasts and stomach. Her mind shifted on silence, like a ship on the disc of ocean that represents the globe.

Caro, on her knees, said, "Christ." Possibilities of mercy were remote. God was powerless, only Paul could extend mercy. God had nothing to propose but a relinquishing that amounted to her own disintegration.

Or there was death, which made no commotion but from time to time broke the silence with a bronze reverberation.

On the child Caro, Dora Bell had inculcated a moral obligation to find the world abominable and to speak readily of doing away with oneself in protest. This corruption was now reconsidered by Caro the woman as, possibly, a cheap rendering of sacred truth. For Dora, death had been a recurrent, ostentatious reminder of existence. For Caro, a single death, unadvertised, would suffice.

Like Paul, to whom there were other resemblances, death had its own key and awaited Caro's return at evening. Its unpresentable spectre must be socially got round when there were visitors—whose dull, rational, living exchanges seemed the manifestations of a normality grotesquely uninformed, piteous as the flowered wallpaper in a gutted building or the piano intact in a blitzed and roofless room.

There was the afternoon, the Sunday afternoon when Cartledge telephoned: "Lucky you."

Callousness was of course immeasurable. Caro herself had walked with Paul in a graveyard and joked about suicides. She lay on her unconsecrated bed and wondered, "Did I come here to die?"

Caroline Bell watched the room dwindle in the early dark. The skylight made a gash of paler grey.

I had a dream that I was lying on a long slope, and a great stone, greater than the stones at Avebury, rolled down at me. I saw it coming and could not rise, but was not afraid. When it got close, I turned my face to it as if to a pillow, as if to rest at last.

A pathos as bad as if it were someone else's death. Confuses the issue. No issue, died without issue. Once, for two weeks, thought I was to bear Paul's child, and feared to tell him. The deed of death has no hypothetical existence—or, having its hypothesis in everyone, must be enacted to achieve meaning. Then meaning is total, as for nothing else.

A phenomenon known as the Black Drop.

It is no less than logical. There are dying conditions as well as living conditions. Venus can blot out the sun.

Don't remember coming out here in the hall. So terribly hot. Was it impossible then? No longer like someone else's death, now it is like my own. No more thoughts, thing itself, itself. Darkness what darkness, and I have not even.

Returning from work one evening, Caroline Bell found a letter from Major Ingot. Taking it upstairs she put it on the table while she lit the gas for her dinner, then sat down to read it. She kept her coat on because of cold.

The Major asked that a compromise be arranged. Otherwise, prospects were dim for keeping body and soul together. "I don't have your advantages," the Major wrote. And "Day after day, it was a tongue-lashing or the waterworks. Or both, like as not. Cry, you've never seen anything to equal it. You'd not believe, you can't imagine. She was all for dying one day, disappearing the next, till I'd half a mind to take her up on it, and no error." In extremity, the Major's social pretensions had dissolved, or perhaps he believed the unaffected idiom might touch Caro. The Major could not know his timing was badly off.

Caro gave the letter to Christian, who told her he would soon settle the Major's hash. He said, "I am going to drop a word through the embassy. After all, there are some benefits in having access to official channels."

When the spring came, Dora took a cruise to Capetown with a new friend, Meg Shentall, whom she had met in the Algarve in a tearoom called The Lusitania.

In a park without flower-beds or streams, on undulations of November leaves, Caro was walking alone. Branches fissured a white sky, the bark on ancient trees was corded like sinews of a strong old man. On a free afternoon given in recompense for late office hours, Caro had come there without purpose, scarcely noticing the intervening streets crossed in her mute private delirium. Inside the park, lack of intention struck her wretchedly and she grew physically uneasy, ears aching from cold, feet slipping on dun leaves. The smell of earth was decayed, eternal. Flat colours offended, a dreariness full blown: Nature caught in an act of erasure.

She stood on the path, shoulders narrowed and hands up to protect her frigid ears; still and watching. And might have been taken for a woman aghast at some cruel spectacle. But the single person approaching was reading a letter and had not yet seen her.

That Paul and Caro should meet in such a way, by accident, might appear the calculated act of a fate that preyed on helpless lives. What would in retrospect be made reasonable—since they had occasionally met by chance when they were lovers, and the park was familiar territory —at that instant amazed with predestination. In this they were both egotistical and humble—the two of them facing each other on the ceremonious avenue, the leaves shifting and drifting on the ground or inertly falling; the senile bark, the pinched white light.

Paul came on, of a colour with the pale scene—hair, light coat, trouser legs. Caro lowered her hands from her bare head, but he had already seen her in that attitude and took it to refer to himself, her gesture of apparent terror. Paul was coming from a protracted lunch at a hotel overlooking the park. The document he held was a contract, in which magic formulas—"hereinafter referred to as," or "payable in United States dollars"—assured his safety. Through these defences Caro broke like whiteness or darkness, elemental. He saw two things distinct on her face: that, having perpetually conjured the sight of him in fancy, she could not be sure this was he and almost thought herself deranged; and that she feared to exasperate him with this meeting that was none of her doing—that he might say to her, Am I never to be free of you? Her very silence was the speechless dread of displeasing. As a man might imagine a clothed woman naked, so in that moment Paul saw Caro nearly unfleshed, her disclosed pulses tremulous as the cranium of a newborn child. Her fear, or rapture, pierced him with unusual shame, as if the encounter exposed him in a colossal lie; as if this meeting itself were truth.

Observing them, one would have thought it planned— the way they stood facing, the man with the paper rolled in his hand, the woman waiting. You would certainly have imagined a meeting, rather than the farewell of which they were trying to be worthy.

They could have sat on a bench, or on the damp leaves pitched up here and there in burial mounds. Had they sat, however, would have touched; and some reticence, you could scarcely call it honour, deterred Paul from this. He held the contract, clenched and now forgotten—though unclenched, later, it might again become imperative—and made a slight gesture. And perhaps spoke, saying "Caro." While she looked from the daunting stature of her agony. They were converging from extremes, two opposing commanders who meet while their forces slaughter, not to make peace but to exchange a high, knowing, egoistic sadness before resuming battle: two minutes' silence, their brief armistice.

At a distance, a woman in a raincoat stooped to let a dog off a red leash—a lean white dog blotched with black, who soon bounded up to them and stood gasping and with legs wide, awaiting orders. Even this dog, to whom the deathly park was paradise, stared, noting what was not usual. Though the dog pranced from side to side, they were not drawn. The dog then barked a bit, reproving all who are not kind to animals. And the owner called, "Split! Split!" Paul and Caro were moving slowly along the path, while the dog scampered round their circumspection, circling it like a quarry before losing interest and loping off to be released.

They were two persons who conduct themselves well in some outrage; who rise above.

Trees moved past them in procession. Standing by elaborate though open gates, Caroline Bell had her hands in the pockets of her coat and, as far as she willed anything, wished to stay in the park, which had become a core of endurance now and her enclosure. Standing, she was again conscious of sore ears, although her body had otherwise dissolved to a rise and fall of breath and blood. It was simplest to stand, and be free of explanations.

The dog had found a dead rat, or mole, and was snuffling.

Leaving the park, Paul walked the length of the Mall, then took a cab home. In his hallway he put the contract down, with its creased guarantees, on a table and hung his coat on a stand. The living-room was pallid as the cold sky—walls, carpet, and chairs all of the bleached condition called neutral. Two small Sisleys, hooded by strip-lights explicit as price-tags, were drained of colour as if left out in the rain. In this ashen room, Paul's wife sat on a window-seat, looking out through what might, or might not, have been a glaze of tears.

"Tertia," he said—quite gently for anyone, let alone Paul.

22

In her room Caroline Bell would fall into long reverie, remembering though not pondering sights, episodes, and sensations, or lines she had read; like an old woman ruminating on the long, long past. She was coming to look on men and women as fellow-survivors: well-dissemblers of their woes, who, with few signals of grief, had contained, assimilated, or put to use their own destruction. Of those who had endured the worst, not all behaved nobly or consistently. But all, involuntarily, became part of some deeper assertion of life.

Though the dissolution of love created no heroes, the process itself required some heroism. There was the risk that endurance might appear enough of an achievement. This risk had come up before.

(At age of nineteen, Caro—travelling in Spain as a nursemaid—had spent a week at Granada with the young and antiquated English family who employed her. A wide balcony ran the length of their hotel near the Alhambra, looking out to the Sierra Nevada. Directly below this terrace there was a steep drop to the town on the valley floor. On crystal mornings and ripe afternoons the hotel guests would sit out on long chairs in the white presence of the mountains, and ask for rugs to be brought to them, or cups of tea on trays. They would turn pages of books from the hotel's library—where titles and authors, long forgotten in their own countries, clung on in exile. The sanatorium atmosphere was not dispelled by the proximity of Moorish monuments and gardens of perfect roses. It was as if you had died and gone to heaven.

At dinner in the Edwardian dining-room—where Caro's

192

employer sometimes noted, on his starched, projecting cuff, the years of wines or names of dishes, or might scribble his suite number on the broached bottle of sherry—there was a trio that played, in an alcove, so discreetly that even gipsy selections turned demure. Each evening, between the entrée and the *pastel,* this trio of piano, violin, and cello would go sadly, softly through *Adelaide, Caprice Viennois,* and Schumann's *Arabeske;* resuming, with the coffee, with a selection from *The Land of Smiles.* And a handful of guests would, quite as mournfully, applaud.

Caro's chair was placed so that she faced the cellist— a woman of thirty or so with white skin that, contrasting at throat and wrists with black crepe, suggested the pallor of torso beneath a dress voluminous as a nun's. This woman was passing visibly from Madonna youth to dedicated spinsterhood in calm renunciation. Once in a while her dark eyes would meet Caro's with melancholy, recognizing tenderness, as if to affirm a bond. As if to state: You and I will make no part of that enervating and degrading struggle.

Each evening the cellist's gentle confidence in Caroline Bell's willingness to waive her claim on destiny cast its pall. Later, in her hotel room, the girl would stare in the mirror to discover why she had been picked out as a kindred soul. In some moods, a dispiriting response raised the prospect of solitary, chaste, ineffectual decades. At other times a vital, coloured image in the mirror obliterated the cellist's pale acquiescence and the threat of the waxen body in its dark shroud.)

Very early one spring morning the phone rang at Christian Thrale's bedside, and he learned that his father had suffered a minor stroke. With perfect composure his mother gave details, while Grace raised herself on her elbow and a wakeful child called from the adjoining room. Christian said, "I'll catch the eight-twenty."

Sefton Thrale lay in a hospital bed at Winchester, his firm expression withered, his carved jaw an unshaven jowl, his breath a laboured sigh. At the foot of the bed his wife stood listening to a doctor: "There is some slight impairment." As if he were a damaged object in a shop, his value now reduced. There was a rail at the edge of his bed like a small wicket gate. He saw the white ceiling, white counterpane; on a table, a red tincture of anemone.

Charmian came and put her hand on his: "You are going to be well." His eyes made some effort, a frightened child trying to be brave. The bluster of existence had ebbed, and he could have been signalling that it had all been an imposture anyway. She said, "Christian will soon be here." He knew who this was, but the name struck him as an odd choice. He remembered them all indistinctly— a blur of Christian, Grace, Tertia, and many others, of whom his wife was the accredited representative. All of them so fortunate, compared with this.

The rich man in his castle, the poor man at his gate.

When he next woke, Christian was there. Sefton Thrale remembered this had been promised, and was reassured by his own ability to make the recollection. He said, "I knew you . . ." and finished, on a long exhalation, ". . . were coming." Christian, however, understood his father to say, "I knew you would come," and was moved.

His wife stood at the foot of the bed, and gently touched the outline of his feet, then covered them with a blanket.

In the succeeding days and weeks, the old man, as he had now conclusively become, revived considerably, made progress with the therapy, and began to distinguish among the nurses—which ones he liked, which had it in for him. When the doctors came he had small witticisms, and some complaints. Like a ball lobbed to a great height, he made his few last diminishing bounces.

In compensation for, or extension of, his own feebleness, he noted signs of ageing in Christian—hunch of shoulders, first crescent of paunch; and a gesture Christian had developed of passing his hand up over his face and brow, as if casting off a web. Sefton Thrale did not know why these details should give him satisfaction, but observed them with listless self-indulgence and made no effort to overlook or find them touching. The doctors had said that whatever he enjoyed was good for him.

By Whitsun he was able to write an occasional note to friends. His handwriting, which had always been minuscule, enlarged with this ultimate flourish of reality. He did not ponder his errors, or think tolerantly of his enemies: to admit qualities in his opponents would be, by now, to recognize the wrong he had done them.

He was allowed to go home in the summer, and at Peverel a nurse was engaged for the nights. It was she who found him dead one morning in September, when he had seemed over the worst. Obituaries were not as extensive as they might have been, but there was a distinguished funeral, and people travelled by rail from London to attend. The service, like a good connection, waited for the train. There was music, there were flowers. The congregation stood, knelt, and sang. And a diminutive young minister commanded a fair measure of attention with a text from Galatians, as well as the inevitable Corinthians. During other parts of the service the chancel arch was seen to be late Norman, an early example in England, and it was noted that a dry-cleaning ticket still attached itself to the coat of an usher.

Tertia's mother, some years a widow, sat in the middle of a forward pew: the grey turret of her tulle hat itself like the lantern of some solemn abbey or cathedral.

"Even so we, when we were children, were in bondage under the elements of the world." With this text, the life of a scientist was ingeniously eulogized, while Grace Thrale dreamily recalled the childhood bondage of bushfires, drought, the Murrumbidgee in flood, and the Southerly blowing cool over Sydney after a blazing day. She held her mother-in-law's gloved hand, knowing that Charmian Thrale allowed her to do this out of civility, so as not to seem ungrateful, but that it could seem condescending, or even a way of showing that the balance had tipped at last. Grace thought leniently of Sefton Thrale, who had been as kind to her as it was in his power to be.

Lately she had seen her little boy—her second son, Hugh —take up the old man's stick as he sat feebly in his chair; and whirl it, swing it, toss it, in innocent mockery. A pang was perhaps more for herself, or for mankind, than for Sefton Thrale, who was abruptly gone.

Now with his love, now in his cold grave.

At the end of the pew, pressed against a clustered pier, Caro had set herself to remembering Robert Browning:

> *There's a great text in Galatians,*
> *Once you trip on it, entails*
> *Twenty-nine distinct damnations,*
> *One sure, if another fails.*

These damnations were distinctly given as adultery, fornication, lasciviousness, and the like, all of which she had practised. It was a curious, almost idle thought that she was so great a sinner. Perdition weighed as nothing beside the laceration of departed love. Beside that, an old man's death was a mere distraction. She leaned her cheek on frigid sandstone, as she had once, in childhood, leaned in egotistic desolation on a majolica plaque, not knowing change was at hand.

"There are also celestial bodies, and bodies terrestrial: but the glory of the celestial is one, and the glory of the terrestrial is another. There is one glory of the sun, and another glory of the moon, and another glory of the stars: for one star differeth from another star in glory."

The congregation stood for the last time, and Sefton Thrale was over the worst for good: his mortality mitigating all, at least for a while. Poor old man. Ted Tice's strictures now seemed too exigent. Death could so easily put the living, however rightful, in the wrong.

Christian's back was the back of a man who takes his responsibilities seriously. In commendable control, he was also seen to be so by commendable effort: already, in bearing and breathing, no longer a son.

Professor Thrale left a larger estate than anyone had foreseen. Although his widow had the use of Peverel for her lifetime and an adequate income, virtually everything went to Christian, who in this way became quite well-to-do. Explaining the will to Grace, he said, "I feel we should keep it to ourselves." He meant the legal content, but could have been understood more explicitly.

Part III

THE
NEW WORLD

23

Girls were getting up all over London. In striped pyjamas, in flowered Viyella nightgowns, in cotton shifts they had made themselves and unevenly hemmed, or in sheer nylon to which an old cardigan had been added for warmth, girls were pushing back bedclothes and groping for slippers. They were tying the cords of dressing-gowns and pulling pins from their hair, they were putting the shilling in the meter and the kettle on the gas ring. Those who shared were nudging each other out of the way and saying, "And it's only Tuesday." Those who lived alone were moaning and switching on radio or television. Some said prayers; one sang.

It is hard to say what they had least of—past, present, or future. It is hard to say how or why they stood it, the cold room, the wet walk to the bus, the office in which they had no prospects and no fun. The weekends washing hair and underwear, and going in despondent pairs to the pictures. For some, who could not have done otherwise, it was their fate, decreed by Mum, Dad, and a lack of funds or gumption. Others had come from the ends of the earth to do it—had arrived from Auckland or Karachi or Jo'burg, having saved for years to do just this, having wrung or cajoled the wherewithal out of tear-stained parents. Not all were very young, but all, or nearly all, wished for a new dress, a boyfriend, and eventual domesticity. No two, however, were identical: which was the victory of nature over conditioning, advertising, and the behavioural sciences—no triumph, but an achievement against the odds.

Among the awakening women, that New Year, was Caroline Bell.

Caro had passed another examination and moved to another flat, where there were high ceilings, and draughts at long windows. Learning the address, Christian had remarked, "I didn't know there was anything cheap round there."

"It's over a shop," Caro told him, by way of reassurance.

For the first time she had a table and two chairs of her own, and a gold-coloured rug from India.

In the morning she was closing one of the windows, had drawn it down and was leaning both hands on the hasps. On the inside sill there was a sprinkling of soot and flaked white paint. A branch of quince blossom, brought by Ted Tice the week before, was propped in a glass vase. Caro was standing at her second-floor window in a green dressing-gown and thinking of the women, of whom she was one—the women, waking yet dormant, who were getting up all over London.

Across the street a man on the curb looked up at her; looked up in the same swift, focusing way that she looked down. He appeared to have arrived at a destination, and might have been a figure in a spy story keeping watch on a fateful house: a wide, tall, motionless man in a dark-blue coat, who held a black stick and stood with feet apart and his bare dark head raised, confident that the house, or the world, would yield to siege.

She leaned, he looked. From her arched figure to his inexorable one was no great distance, and their eyes now met as they might have done in a room. There was momentary, complex stillness until, with a show of normality, Caro lifted her hands and dissolved the spell.

He slightly bowed, as if he came from a graceful nation, France or Italy. They resumed their motions of interruption, crossing roads or rooms. Caro's bare feet on the yellow carpet, Caro's thin fingers yanking a dress from a hanger; the man's wide hand raised for a cab.

All the girls of London shuddered, waiting for the bus. Some had knitted themselves unbecoming brown Balaclavas, with worse mittens to match. Some held a boiled egg, still hot, in their glove—which warmed the hand, and could be eaten cold at lunchtime in the ladies' room. At that hour all London was ashudder, waiting for the bus.

At Caro's office that day there was a deputation from South America. Four exiles had come to plead for their imprisoned comrades: Let a governmental message be sent, merely a message, proposing mercy. Pleading of this kind was not unusual when executions were to take place in other lands. What would be unusual would be if the message were dispatched.

On this occasion there were the four applicants, or supplicants, and a man from the United States who had taken up their cause. Only these five, and Caro, were punctual in the meeting-room. Northern winter overlaid the summer faces of the four exiles like sallow illness; featureless with it, they were the more submitted to present extremity. Later on they might become distinct with eloquence, but for the present remained an amalgam, a team. Their clothes were too light, and too light-coloured, and too American, to do them any good here. Only the man from New York was well dressed, having a dark-blue coat open over a good flannel suit.

It was the man from the curb in Mount Street.

He crossed the room to drop his coat and stick on a spare chair. He said to Caro, "Let's hope this is a good omen." Again he had an easy grace, though not from a graceful nation.

Eight men were to be hanged. Or shot, that was not clear. Two officials had now entered the room with their air of punctilious humanity that portended refusal. To be perfectly frank we do not feel that intervention by Her Majesty's Government would be useful. And must also take account of the long and singularly close cooperation between our two nations.

The American said that was precisely why. He was the spokesman, a public man who had founded something—perhaps a foundation, or it was an orchestra, or a museum, or all of these. He had lived for a time in the Latin country in question and had recently been advised, officially, not to return there.

Attention was paid him here because he was wealthy and did not come from a gimcrack country like the other petitioners—or the auditors themselves. For these reasons consideration was shown him, although it was made plain he had not the authority. When he described certain tortures, the two officials became disconcerted, withdrawn, fascinated, as if he were discussing in public the act of love. His four companions were growing discernible, their faces retinged by feeling: old sepia photographs whose unnatural flush had been externally applied. One was chopped and stocky. Another, exhausted and elderly—leaning forward to rock his body as if in pain. The third had highcoloured Andean features, and shabby teeth outclassed by a gold bicuspid. The fourth, who was tall and personable, had ginger, kinky hair and the dense freckles of a freakish pigmentation. His compatriots would turn to this fourth man, making him a leader.

This freckled man had large properties—orchards, pastures. In his case, a possibility of self-interest comforted his official hearers by introducing an element of the rational. Ted Tice had once pointed out that an independent act of humanity is what society can least afford.

The distinction of these men was that they entreated on behalf of others. It was this that gave them an authority the authorities would never have. The one who bent forward had a huge tie-clip, shiny, dragging on a flowered tie; and fingered this lucky charm. He had a pencil, like an unlit cigarette, between his lips; and a cataractal rheum on both eyes, like an old dog.

Caro knew there was no question of it. She had heard that yesterday: It is quite out of the question, let ourselves in for, no end to it if we once, interference in the internal affairs of, do more harm than good. There had also been a call to Washington, eliciting the reply, "Counterproductive."

"Any loss of life is always to be regretted. If only we were in a position to assist. I do not mind telling you I feel for your situation very very. Speaking on a strictly personal. I am bound to point out, however, that under existing conditions charges of physical abuse cannot of course be verified."

"Even if we produce a man with no balls?"

"Mr. Vail, you will not convince me by losing your temper."

The American sat at his ease. "You are right to reprove me. And I am right to be angry."

He made present something more than speaker and listener; something more than mere men.

What if the families of the condemned were to make a personal appeal?

Unfortunately we do not feel that would make the slightest.

It was rumoured that the pope?

That is, obviously, an option of which His Holiness may choose to avail himself. We have received no indication to that effect. We did hear that the United Nations secretary-general was considering intercession.

"Surely you are being humorous."

A silence, truthful and juridical, conveyed that sentence was pronounced. You will be taken from this court to a place of execution. The leaning Latin man sat back in his chair, as if reviving from a faint or fit; the impression of a convulsion reinforced by a dry white fleck at each corner of the mouth, and by the pencil lodged between his teeth. The stocky petitioner had his face in the light, pockmarks and capillaries visible. All four were expressionless in the irresistible silence. And the morning had gone by.

The four exiles were leaving for some other last, hopeless rendezvous. Their reality intensified with defeat, dividing them conclusively from the two figmental officials who had received them. Pocked perforations and gilt tie-clips were invested with some grandeur, or stood at least for a preferable exposure.

Escorting them out, an official would confide in a lowered voice, "I myself wish to God," and so on. And then in the men's room wash his hands and dry them on a paper towel.

The man from New York was detained by a senior official. "But I'm certain there was an arrangement about lunch."

"A misunderstanding then."

Consternation was real this time. The lunch had been with a member of the cabinet.

"If you would just wait while I ring up. Please." The

suplicants had not pleaded for the lives of their martyrs with such abandon. No, unfortunately he was late for another engagement, and left.

Papers must be locked in a red portfolio, and Caro stayed for this. It was also assumed she would, from a housewifely instinct in fact minimal in her, set the room to rights. She stood leaning on the conference table with damp hands, and, but for ineradicable mistrust of Dora's antics, might have sobbed aloud. Incrimination and disgrace were growing on her, in that place, like old-maidishness; it was like sexual frustration to be always yearning for some spasm of decency that in this context could never occur. That one's thoughts should as much as follow four unprepossessing men into a cold street was a breach of contract here, as if a soldier in battle conjured to himself the harmless private affections of those in the opposing lines. There were rules of combat in which the victory went to those who could emerge with no pang of realization.

"Forgot this." His stick.

He let the heavy door click at his back, and there they were in the attitudes of the early morning. He had walked a distance before missing the stick, and brought cold fresh air with him. Though touching her fingers to her face, Caro was scarcely abashed, the morning's episode being more shameful than tears.

The wide man sat on the edge of the table, and the cold came out from his good clothes. His broad hands waited on his thighs. "Can we go out somewhere?"

They were crossing the flapping and shrieking of a street. The restaurant was upstairs, there was a pub downstairs. It was a place that was always full because tourists came to see the government eating. You're in luck, sir, there's been a cancellation. He might have been accustomed to luck of the kind. They sat by a window in a thin film of sunlight and Caro thought, Now he will let me down. Now he will say, Oh I see their side of it too.

He said, "Shits, aren't they." And handed the menu, which was a typed slip. All the room was men, except for Caro.

"When will they die?" She meant the prisoners.

"In a month or two."

She said, "Almost the worst was the panic about the lunch."

"Or the best." He smiled. His hound-face had lines, at eyelids and mouth, that were now at rest but might be put to use. His dark hair, greying, fell loose over his forehead. His body, too heavy and indolent for the precise little chair, was that of an active man who had taught himself to wait: an incongruous patience that could trouble those who wondered what might be restrained. He said, "Men go through life telling themselves a moment must come when they will show what they're made of. And the moment comes, and they do show. And they spend the rest of their days explaining that it was neither the moment nor the true self."

"They might at least think how soon, historically, these things recoil. My colleagues today, for instance."

"The British temperament in particular has never been one of speculation. In extremity, Archimedes went on with his theorem, but Drake went on playing bowls."

She said, "Some men—or many—are both Archimedes and the soldier who slays him."

He took the menu from her. He was something over forty. A vein corded the back of his hand. There was his watch, a cuff of striped shirting, the grey flannel sleeve. He watched her following these details, which she considered as carefully as if they had dressed an arm projecting from fallen masonry: clues to the undisclosed.

His name was Adam Vail. "What is your name?" he asked. "I know your address." Saying "*ad*dress" in the American way.

The two officials of the morning had inevitably entered, and were eating whitebait.

Vail said, "They will make you the culprit, about the lunch." You could see them doing it already, above the heaps of tiny fish. Not wishing to believe in any moral mastery, they were relieved to attribute something salacious. From the whitebait perspective, Vail's arms around the table rim appeared to offer an embrace, into which Caro leaned.

These two men would be saying she slept with him, and might write that in a file to relieve their feelings. From knowledge of the imagined intimacy laid on them, he and she faintly smiled, and grew intimate.

At a hotel whose chimney-pots could be seen from Caro's window, Adam Vail had two large sombre rooms with heavy curtains. In the sitting-room there were cut hyacinths in a thick round glass pot on a low table, beside a sofa like a brocade Zeppelin. Letters had been stacked on a desk, along with catalogues of paintings in glossy colours and a pile of unopened packages.

Between the windows there was a picture in an elaborate frame. "A dealer hopes it will grow on me. You're the first to notice it, everyone else has taken it for hotel furnishings. I'm not sure if you get a good mark or not." He stood by a table where there were bottles and glasses set out on a tray, and watched Caro move through the expensive shadows of the room. Saw her sleeve, of some dark-reddish colour, burn in lamplight, and the strand of chain on her neck. At her window and in her office he had twice seen her solitary, habitual, but not resigned. His thought re-enacted an instant when he had looked up at a window, his glance drawn by a branch of blossom in a vase.

She had no unoccupied zone of objective feeling. He supposed men might find irritating or formidable her air of awaiting some solemn event that could not possibly be their own approach.

He said, "It has no suspense." Watching her, he was thinking how, in some great pictures, every particle of the light is usual, daily, and at the same time a miracle: which is no more than the precise truth. He said, "Some paintings transmit the suspense of life itself." He thought most men would hardly dare to touch her, or only with anger, because she would not pretend anything was casual. It was unflattering, what she was apparently willing to dispense with in consequence of this belief.

He poured liquor into glasses and talked about the picture. Parted on speech, his lips were dissimilar: the lower, jutting and conclusive; the upper, thin, delicate, and considerate to the point of weakness. Which was certainly better than the other way round.

Caro Bell sat on ballooning damask and held a glass of vodka, and the man Vail sat at her side. Their feet were outstretched towards the flowers and the low table in shoes of identical fine brown leather. To think they could both have excellent shoes.

"What are you laughing at?"

"At the democracy of shoes." The lamp was burning velvet creases in her sleeve and lap. Through a doorway a low light showed slippers aligned on a white mat. There would be a sheet folded neatly back, a good dressing-gown ready on the counterpane, new books beside a bed: all this a form of freedom, since he made it so. Even when he rolled his body round to bring out a handkerchief or produce cigarettes, it was an un-English roll suggesting fresh energies, opinions, sights, affinities, a landscape. There was a time-change to him, a resetting of a mental watch. Everything else was this time yesterday.

Soon he and she would go downstairs to dinner, like guests in a country house. He said that on Sunday they might take a drive, if she was free. "A spin, I suppose you'd say. Can I handle the wrong side of these roads?"

"You can. And no one's said spin for years." Except, possibly, Sefton Thrale. She agreed she would love to see the Fens. It was long since Caro had loved a prospect.

The glass bottom of the bowl of flowers had been set over a telegram that lay on the table. Through bevelled water the print rose up, unevenly magnified: "EXECUTION INEVITABLE," like a lesson in elocution. Adam Vail said, "Small letters grow larger when seen through a vessel filled with water. Seneca points that out. It was an early concept in optics." He said, "Seneca is full of good things." He grasped the rim of the vase and shifted it, and the letters relapsed into insignificance: ineffectual insects that had terrified beneath a microscope.

On Vail's bureau at the hotel there was a photograph of an adolescent girl: "My daughter." Father and daughter resembled, but did not get along. "Josie blames me for her mother's death. Blame generally shifts around a bit with age, at least I have to hope so." In a wallet there was a photograph of a thin woman in a jersey and trousers. "My wife killed herself." He said, "My wife took her life," like a rhyme.

"Do you blame yourself?"

"She had often said it, that she would. She'd had every kind of treatment. Eventually it becomes hard to know how to handle it."

Like Dora: I can always die, always die.

Caro said, "There is the damage on both sides."

He asked, "Have you been close to someone like that?"

Once he said it was possibly reported that they saw each other. "But I will make sure no harm comes to you."

"Who would watch us?"

"My countrymen and yours. Because a man with no axe to grind is a revolutionary nowadays."

"You only hold them to their proclaimed principles."

"That is what modern revolution means."

"The first morning, in the street, you like a figure in a spy story."

"They will turn it all into a spy story, if they can."

She asked, "Why do you need that stick?"

"I got the habit of carrying it in rough places." He handed it to her and the weight was surprising, like an opinion out of character. He took it back and pressed the catch to show the blade.

So this man of peace went armed with a sword.

There was a photograph of a whitewashed house in the sun: lemon groves, vineyards. In the distance, a white town blotched by poverty and weather. "The Lipari Islands."

"Then that's how it's pronounced."

"When Josie was little she called them the Slippery Islands." He put the picture down. "You shall see them, the islands."

He asked, "Is there someone else in love with you?"

"You're in luck, sir, there's been a cancellation."

Nothing could have been more seductive, or improvident, than his receptivity and generosity of mind: I will take care that no harm comes to you, perhaps you have been close to someone like that, you shall see the islands.

There was a night of extraordinary silence. "What time is it?"

Caro had a clock by her bed. "Nearly four."

"Then they're gone."

Tomorrow there would be a brief paragraph on an inside page: EXECUTIONS CARRIED OUT.

She laid her head on his shoulder, and drew breath so that her breast might fill his palm. She said, "What were you thinking, that first morning in the street?"

"Foreseeing everything but you."

24

Christian Thrale credited himself with special sensibilities towards pictures. In galleries where art had been sagely institutionalized, he walked and paused like all the rest, yet believed his own stare more penetrating than most; and, when others strolled ahead, would linger, patently engrossed beyond the ordinary.

Christian furthermore believed that there was an English way of regarding works of art (and in that he was perfectly correct). He would not have said this, but felt it. Phrases such as "The Rokeby Venus," "The Portland Vase," "The Elgin Marbles" held, for him, more than passing proprietary meaning. They summarized a proper custody and appeared to state a desirable case.

He did not much care for private collections unless magnitude had rendered them impersonal. Although happiest, or safest, in the great museums, he would once in a while take in, as he put it, a loan exhibition; but this happened rarely. When—declining the catalogue—he entered the carpeted rooms of a private gallery on a Saturday of bitter cold, he was departing from habit in the way that had, at the Albert Hall eight years earlier, brought Grace into his orbit and altered a number of lives. Once again it was a case of weekend work, the sight of a poster, and himself alone. Today, the very poster had been headed "Retrospective." A shade of all this was passing through his mind when he saw Caro, whose sudden materialization was consequently both startling and inevitable.

Caro had kept her red coat on indoors, and was standing with her cold hands locked inside the sleeves. Her hair hung on her shoulders in indecorous black streaks and coils, her lips were painted scarlet. She was leaning her weight back on one foot like a dancer in position, and behind her was a big man who might, in his stability, have been her partner. (For some time after the event, Christian's recollection would work on the image of Caro standing that way, with the man Vail at her back ready to raise her aloft.) In the painting before them the heads of two women appeared, aflame, facing one another but not aligned.

"There it is, then," Adam Vail was saying at that moment. He had lent the picture, which belonged to him.

From the other end of the room, Christian observed them. He himself remained transfixed, poised by their immobility. When they both moved, Christian was released and moved too, in their direction.

Adam Vail leaned forward to stare at the picture. "I think they've chipped the frame." He reached in a top pocket for his glasses. There was gesso where there should have been gold. Vail put his forefinger to it, and an attendant at once came over.

"Not to touch the exhibits, if you don't mind, sir." When Vail stood back, he went on, "Sorry, but that's the way accidents 'appens."

When Christian saw them alone again and smiling, he went up. As he did so he felt himself at a disadvantage. He usually saw Caro in his own house where he was—not to put too fine a point on it—in the driver's seat. This day, before he so much as spoke, he had a sense of intrusion or irrelevance. He wondered if this were simply due to the act of accosting; and did not think to attribute it to Caro's power on that morning of her beauty.

In an effort to establish dominion, he kissed Caro—which was not quite necessary and which he felt she saw through.

That the man with her was American did not provide the customary advantage either. Vail would not talk loudly or instructively or about himself, or make ungainly gestures, even when provoked. This composure of speech and hands warned Christian against any customary staking out of his conversational position: Vail's honesty would have transparency in return, at whatever cost to the respondent. Altogether a need arose to extend oneself that crossed Christian's awakened retrospect with a memory of Caro years ago, when she had compelled him to rise to one of her occasions: a summer afternoon, actually, when he had brought yellow flowers to Grace.

By now the three of them were turned towards the painting, and Christian was soon absorbed, as was his way, beyond the ordinary. Caro was about to speak when he said—and it was somehow against his better judgment—"You will never, of course, get me to like that series." They had not, of course, tried to. After a moment he continued, "This example does have considerable authority."

He knew he said "authority" because the American brought the word to mind. There were other Americans in the gallery, raising dogmatic voices, wheeling and slicing with unconfident hands, features contorted with reckless vehemence. But not this one, who did not even accept Christian as an antagonist. Christian now recalled having heard the name of Adam Vail; and felt a quick, unworthy distress, as if Caro had outwitted him. He remembered a magazine article in which Vail, asked if he considered himself a mystery man, replied, "No more so than anyone else."

The introduction to the exhibition catalogue had been written by a leading—or major, or brilliant—critic. Caro read out a sentence and asked, "What does it mean?"

Vail looked over her shoulder. "They come to think they've had something to do with painting the pictures."

The three of them wandered round the rooms, more or less together. Christian gave no more opinions, but tried out a series of bombastic thoughts: So that's how the land lies, the way the wind blows. He had seen how Vail looked over Caro's shoulder, his body not quite touching hers: grey wool divided from red by a vibration. After a while Christian said he must be off, and left them; giving Caro another blunt, incommensurate kiss.

He walked home perplexed by a sensation, sharp yet heavy, close to disappointment. Possibly he had imagined Caro cut out for some dénouement that would vindicate, or redeem, the cautious order of his own existence—a culmination, even tragic, that only she seemed fitted to enact. Or perhaps he had wished, for the greater common good, to see her sink into vapid domesticity like other women, sink into it as housewives sink exhaustedly into arm-chairs at evening. He detested the idea that she and Vail were lovers, but less for the imagined carnality than because Vail was personable, resolute, and rich. The satisfaction to Christian in withholding compassion from Caro had sprung directly from her need, her poverty. There was no power whatever now in letting Caro jolly well fend for herself. And he allowed himself, like a luxury, the honest thought: I might have helped her.

At home, Christian sat in his usual chair. And his little boy clambered over him as though he were a playground fixture.

One day in May Caroline Bell asked, and received, an extra hour for lunch. When she returned to the office she learned in the corridor from Mr. Bostock that Valda had refused to prepare tea or procure sandwiches at lunchtime or ever again.

Entering Mr. Leadbetter's office, Caro was asked to close the door. Leadbetter put down his ball-point, signifying the personal. Had in truth taken up the plastic pen in order to make the gesture of setting it aside. He folded his hands. "Perhaps you can enlighten me, Miss Bell." His enlaced fingers parted, then closed, as if to play cat's-cradle. "Miss Fenchurch has some grievance?"

"She does not like to serve food. It's an imposition."

"And is that not somewhat absurd? The purveying of—ah—victuals being an accepted part of her functions?"

"By whom is it accepted?"

"By every woman here except Miss Fenchurch and, I now take it, yourself. Had there been a wider sense of unfitness, the girls would have expressed it generally."

"Most people have to have unfitness pointed out to them. At first there is usually only one person who does that."

Mr. Leadbetter had, as he was to put it to his wife that evening, seldom been so vexed. "And do you not find this a paltry and selfish attitude? The men in this office are, after all, forgoing the lunch hour altogether, remaining at their desks for extra duty. The girls are merely asked—required—to help them discharge onerous extra tasks."

"The men do nothing that lowers their self-esteem. On the contrary, staying at their desks exalts it."

"I see that you are highly defensive." Not raised to such figures of speech, Clive Leadbetter had hit on them in recent years. Sometimes he said "highly defensive," sometimes, "highly aggressive"—it amounted to the same thing. Similarly, would accuse: "Aren't you a little too positive?" or "Rather too negative?"—propositions, interchangeable and unanswerable, that had never failed to confound. He could not imagine what people meant when they said the language was in decline.

Caro said, "I withhold my analysis of your own attitude."

Leadbetter's unlaced fingers came down on the blotter with a synchronized slap. "Miss Bell, do you really not find this incident utterly grotesque?"

"I know that any adherence to a principle can be called grotesque, and even made to appear so. At least for a time."

"You call it a principle. A tempest in a teacup."

"Mr. Bostock said, in a teapot."

He was now at white heat: molten Leadbetter. (To his wife that evening he would say, "I don't even mind insults, but will not tolerate verbal abuse.") "Miss Bell, since you yourself find our ways so unsatisfactory, perhaps you should seriously consider returning to—ah—New Zealand."

In a long pause he was made to feel her superior strength, and the fact that she had been withholding it for years out of charity.

"In fact I have come to give you my resignation."

His mouth opened and closed: like a horse with carney. "And may I inquire the motive?"

"I am going to be married."

Then he hated her, for her liberty and her looks and

her happiness, and that remark about the teapot. The Gatling jammed: words would not so much as sputter. However, since even she could only be delivered by male intervention, he eventually smiled and made his last attack. "I had already assumed something of the kind."

25

Grace Thrale was on her way out of Harrods through the rug department, which had the space and solemnity of a cathedral. Aisles had been devised among the spaced stanchions of the building, and thick rolled strips of carpet stood or lay like the fallen drums of columns in a temple. Wilton was piled on Axminster, forming floral platforms. And Grace was smiling, though not at these.

"Grace." Ted Tice caught up with her in a Moroccan transept. "Been lodging a complaint?"

She stopped, and stopped smiling. "Ted."

"How are your boys?"

She smiled again. "Rowdy." They walked, and halted. "Are you in town for a bit?"

"Only the day. I needed some things for my new place. I manage for myself." His collar was wrinkled, his shirt front showed the ogival mark of an inexpert iron. He held up his package. "And I just bought a pair of binoculars."

"So you sometimes look at the earth."

"Only in concert halls." Ted was cheerful: She will tell Caro we met. "I phoned Caro, but no reply."

Grace had never seen him so confident, or unsuspecting. He might be thinking time was on his side. She had pondered it all in a moment, while they talked of her children, and knew she would speak. "Ted, do you have a minute? Let's sit down." His expression at once stilled in apprehension, with the sense for bad news one develops from infancy. Grace sat on an upturned drum of ruby wool. Nearby, a rose-red parody of Persia was flung down by a salesman, though not for prayer.

"Ted." She had never used his name so much. "She is writing you today."

In that instant Grace somewhat resembled Caro, as always when matters grew serious. Ted could see it, the turn of head and the clasped hands. If he put his fingers to the nape, he would find the cord there, prominent as Caro's. He said, "She is getting married."

"Do sit down." A hostess receiving.

"I prefer to stand." A Victorian hero on the carpet, or carpets.

A salesman paused, and tweaked a nine-by-twelve.

"Thank you we're just looking." Staring at one another, Grace and Ted created a tension not easily absorbed into rugs.

He did not so much as ask, Who?

"His name is Adam Vail, an American." Grace obtained a respite describing Vail, as if in the process she hoped to put Ted Tice at his ease. She rambled, "He is kind, and interesting. He is very strong, I mean his character." This pierced Ted; but in fact Grace was making an instinctive contrast with her own husband.

Ted said, "I have met him." He thought, I am behaving well, but in fact it has not yet touched me.

Grace babbled, "Fortyish, very nice, they will be in England quite often."

Ted Tice's face was youthful for the last time, as is said to happen in death. "When will it be?"

"Well, very soon, two or three weeks. You have to have, they have to have papers. Not being British, you see. You —they—go to Caxton Hall. Where foreigners are married. Dora has to get back, she's in Malta with her friend Dot Cleaver. Then there's a daughter, there is Adam's daughter, coming from New York, she is fourteen. Fifteen." Grace was getting to an end of details and would soon be starkly left with a man's anguish.

A salesman brushed by, with a customer. "We have it in celadon or kumquat. Or can order in mandarin." This pair was engrossed, a happy couple.

Caro would have known what to say: not the right thing, but the truth. Caro would have spoken truly or kept a true silence. In accepting to be the sweet one of the sisters, tame and tractable, Grace had by no means intended to cast herself away. She had enjoyed being sweet, and being thought sweet, but had believed she held in reserve an untapped bounty of more difficult humanity; which was not now forthcoming. Ted's suffering was not obscure to her—indeed, her imagination occasionally played out such matters in some Austro-Hungarian empire of the heart. But she could rouse no true instinct with which to feel his pain or comfort him. And was suddenly afraid that sweet people might have little imagination.

On any day of the year Grace Thrale might be smiled at in the street by an elderly couple or by some young mother herding her noisy brood: saluted, that is, as a kindred spirit. Caroline Bell never attracted this delectable complicity. There were times when Grace wished the world were not so sure of her, so confident that boredom had claimed her. Yet in her daily existence feared the smallest deviation from a habit as an interruption that might bring chaos. Grace no more wanted adventure than Dora wanted peace. She did not convince herself, as some women do, that she retained capacity for a wholly different existence ruled by exalted and injurious passions: Grace knew perfectly how the practised conformity of her days gratified her own desires. Yet one might cling to security and still be bored by it. In its first appeal, security offered an excitement almost like romance; but that rescue might wear down, like any other.

In the evenings, putting away dishes or silver, this still golden Grace could sigh herself, mentally, into a squat housewife with a dowager's hump.

She offered, "If you like, we could go up and have tea." There was a place upstairs where women sat among their packages and were asked, Milk or lemon?

"Grace, my dear, you were running when we met. Let me go on down with you." Ted Tice saw—but it was incidental to his state of mind—that Grace Thrale, who had been his timid ally, had changed allegiance and thrown him over for the prize of Vail. He would get out from this broadloom solemnity, these sarcastic rugs and mechanical inquiries from the staff. Grace stood up, and they moved on into Lamps, heading for the stairs. Behind them, the salesman yawned: "Or there's always goat."

Ted was aware of a blue velvet suit—no, only the collar

was velvet, the rest speckled wool, a suit all to do with Grace's life and customs, like the gothic indictment of the iron on his own shirt. He acknowledged her body, twice convulsed by childbirth and reassembled, shapely as a suit, heroically normal. He likewise would maintain motion and equilibrium, though ripped asunder; and had kindly said, "My dear."

On the ground floor they passed stacked bolts of the materials women never wore now—georgette, heavy crepe, pongee. There was a serious, dry smell of stuff that must be measured, cut, and sewn. A man in black expertly placed lengths thumb to thumb: "Three and a half yards, madam?" A high voice asked, "And where are Remnants?"

Grace went ahead through a series of heavy glass doors. Shoppers coming and going handed the doors back and forth in the formal motions of their dance: "Kyou," "Kyou." Outside, a cold afternoon showed the season merely by reluctance to darken. A stout doorman wearing war ribbons cryptically signalled taxis; a trio of street musicians in ancient serge bawled about Tipperary while a fourth held out a khaki cap weighted by a single, central half-crown.

Grace said, "I can't bear these singers. Let's walk a bit." They moved together along the shop-windows, where mannequins in print frocks raised orange arms against tropical settings, in ecstatic, vital contrast to the waxen matrons lifelessly passing.

"I'm certain I'm delaying you, Grace."

Grace could not bear his good manners or the thought that this man in his crisis indulged her as a dying officer might joke to a rattled subordinate on a battlefield. She leaned against a glassed tableau of beachwear and looked in his face, trying to make up for years of willful insipidity in an instant.

"As this has come about, won't it be better for you? Now there's no false hope. It will be awful at first, but—" Grace's handbag slid to her elbow on its strap and she grasped her own jacket by both lapels as urgently as she might have clutched at Ted's. A consciousness of Dora flickered. Let me not sound like Dora, I'm sure you'll be very happy. She said, "Now you are free."

The cicatrice of stitching on her gloves was an imprint

on his brain. Earrings of pearl stared, white-eyed as fish. There was a streak of flowered scarf, inane, and the collar blue. Grief had a painter's eye, assigning arbitrary meaning at random—like God.

Ted thought, I was really better off inside the shop. I was pretty numb in there. After all, the claustrophobic building had provided shelter of a kind, with its avenues resembling city planning, its racks and trays overflowing with daily life, its suburbs named Millinery and Haberdashery in memory of childhood. In the open street Ted Tice was grappled, and experienced bodily lightness of a sort that accompanies physical peril. He would get through these moments as a duty in preparation for the next phase, the realization that was to take him over and maul him.

Whatever might have been thought an hour before as he was buying binoculars, or some few minutes past, no one glancing at him now would have called him a young man.

He took one of Grace's gloved hands and placed it against his own jacket, where it did finally and diffidently clasp his lapel. Earrings hammered, silk daisies panicked on the scarf. At her back a silver plastic palm tree was jagged as forked lightning.

"What I have done has been for hope of her. What I do now will be for lack of her." He let Grace's hand drop, and the bag fell again to her wrist. "Do you call it freedom?"

"That may not always be true." Grace was thinking that a woman would not have prejudiced the future with such a proclamation.

They walked back to the corner, where the shoppers bandied the doors back and forth. The singers were on to "Danny Boy" now, the half-crown solitary in the cap, the pennies expertly shaken under the lining. It was Christian who had told Grace about this trick.

They crossed to the entrance of the Underground. There was vibration in the road, a subterranean breath from the pit-head. A red-fleshed woman was peddling little wads of heather to people dashing up and down the steps, but did not aproach these two who stood silent. Grace thought, I suppose you'd get to know when it was hopeless.

In the rush of tunnelled air they turned to stare at one another. A look two persons might exchange who, having carried an immense weight to some forlorn halt, now set it down and meet each other's eyes. Grace had come as far as she could; Ted would go down alone.

The photograph showed a substantial jaw, hound-dog eyes; the face expressionless, as if the intrusion merely tested or strengthened endurance. An accompanying paragraph referred to a previous marriage and a daughter. A big man with an overcoat bundled on, standing in a bleak portico.

At his side Caro was a novice at public life. Not dressed in wedding clothes, she had nonetheless unmistakably just been married. Where the picture was cut off, the backs of their hands met—her right hand, his left, not clasped but transmitting the private message for all the world to see.

"There's one here too." Tertia knew what Paul was staring at, and raised her own page slightly to show an indistinct image. There was a heading, and below the photograph a caption said, "The couple is shown leaving the edifice." In Paul's newspaper Caro was an Australian typist; in Tertia's, a senior official. It was also stated that the couple had met while working on a humanitarian enterprise initiated by the British government.

"So that awful sister got those girls fixed up. Dora or Flora, I saw her once at the Thrales. You have to hand it to her. She brought them to London and launched them."

Paul said, "They're not the Gunning sisters, you know." Though seeing them for a moment just that way—eighteenth-century beauties in pastel silk with upswept hair and translucent glances, taking London by storm, being the Rage. In Tertia's newspaper Caro's eyes were lowered, she was a grey blur that did not even carry flowers. The man was large, an un-English physiognomy, big head, heavy, impassive. Caro was now endorsed, valuable: an obscure work newly attributed to a master.

Tertia exchanged newspapers with Paul. "Flora-Dora pulled it off." To see how much Paul minded.

"I rather like to think of Caroline Bell with billions."

"No one ever said the Vail man had billions."

"Where does the money come from anyway?"

"Catfood."

"It says here, bauxite. Whatever that is." Paul elaborated: "Penthouses papered with Picassos, yachts, private planes, limousines."

"Bodyguards," said Tertia. And "Lovers."

Paul folded the paper to read it—neatly, like a clerk in a train. "At any rate the astrologer didn't get her."

"What does 'at any rate' mean?" Tertia turned pages with her brutal gesture. Upstairs, a child wept, laughed, spoke, then mumbled, acting out the ages of man.

Tertia suddenly said, "Nick Cartledge. Who used to stay with us." She could have been protesting at last.

"What about him?"

"He's dead."

"What of?"

"Liver complaint."

"Well—he certainly worked for it."

Tertia put the paper down. Nicholas Gerald Wakelin Cartledge. For her, it was an untimely death. She said, "The old roué," trying to shrug off mortality itself; but sat there changing into a woman who knew the dead.

After a time Paul said, "That word means, broken on the wheel."

Dora told Dot Cleaver, "He is no Phoebus Apollo. As you can see." Dora would say Phoebus Apollo, or Pallas Athene, or Venus de Milo, distinguishing these immortals, by full title, from the terrestrial Glad or Trish. "It is an awful picture of them both, oh simply awful. And the snaps are no better." She showed. "I'd had a nasty knock from the car door, you can see the pain in my eyes." Dora had moved that day into Caro's vacated flat, which was filled with flowers. "They will be in Italy by now."

Dot Cleaver said, "When I first went to Rome, I did everything. Everything. I took the guide-book, I did everything. Well, that's over with, now I just please myself. You absorb more of a place that way."

Dora gave a sigh that influenced the entire room. She observed, after a time, that even the weariest river winds somewhere safe to sea.

"A cup of your nice tea?" Dot Cleaver arched her brows, body, and wrist, grasping a china handle that was itself a mark of interrogation. "Then they go to New York."

"Oh yes, they have everything they want there, all their interests, books, plays, music."

Dot Cleaver had recently attended an enthralling recital, but could not recall the programme. "In any case, they'll be over to see you in no time."

"Why should they bother. I don't blame them." Dora's ambition now was to be cast off. That was to be the culmination of her long alienation, the vindication of her overmastering belief in enmity, ingratitude, and whole congeries of wrongs. She had already told Caro, "Don't feel you have to see me." Her process of testing, now finely honed, was never at rest. Provocation had become the basis of her relations with the world.

Caro had said to Grace, "She is curious to see how many cheeks we still have left to turn."

He tore out the page, folded it, tore again along the fold. Then trimmed the picture and paragraph with scissors. These methodical actions seemed to have been leading somewhere, and when he had completed them Ted could scarcely believe he was left with a photograph of Caroline Bell's wedding. The accompanying legend, though conventionally phrased, was not quite comprehensible—as if written in uncials, or Cyrillic.

He stared into the dim little picture for some familiar thing that might give him a claim on her. But her clothes were new, uncharacteristic with occasion. In her left hand, a small object, certainly not a prayerbook and most probably a purse. The photograph banished him completely, declining association: an extra cruelty, when her possessions had always enchanted him—a green silk belt, a notebook covered in blue cloth, a white dish in which she kept oranges. In the photograph she turned away, forsaking all others.

The clipping lay on his desk, larger now that the superfluous, constricting tissue had been trimmed away. The whole room could not confine it or contain the injury. Ted Tice put his right hand on it, and hung his head—aware, like an onlooker, that this bowed posture required, for its own caption, a dated phrase: "He went under." A grown man with lowered head is a foolish sight, and scarcely a man.

There was no one to whom he need excuse himself. Obligation was the first detail erased by grief.

He thought he would go out and tire himself with walking. Or would get drunk, like a disappointed man in a story. But looked, without moving, at his sweater and cap and a striped scarf—outward things whose reasonableness he would not believe in again.

26

So Caroline Bell lived in a house in New York City and took the name of Vail. From the top of the house, which was in a row of short buildings faced with purplish stone, there was a view of the sky. To the south, a range of skyscrapers obstructed the late sun as surely as the mountains of the Taygetus bring early dark down to Sparta. The rooms were not numerous but relatively large, because dividing walls had here and there been removed. In this house Adam Vail had been born.

There were many objects over which Caroline Vail could never wish for, or assert, jurisdiction. Chairs, books, pictures, a screen from China, a leather folder fraying on a desk, a jade saucer, a convenient, ugly little light beside a bed—everything was habitual except Caro herself. She had contributed four boxes of books, a chipped plate from Palermo, and an angel painted on Andalusian board. From time to time she would look at these memorials, or at her clothes in cupboards and drawers, in order to believe.

A photograph at the time would have shown her more hesitant than formerly. The process of acquiring equanimity had brought its own disruptions, and some sacrifice.

Caro received letters on her marriage from several men: "He's a lucky man, dear Caro, who gets you"; "I hope he realizes his good fortune." There was an element of relief at not having had to assume the privilege themselves. Her own release at leaving an entire nation to its devices was, if not commendable, also natural.

In straight streets Mrs. Vail attempted to make the city over in the image of other towns, to discover its sources of continuity and solace, its places of refuge and glory. When this proved impossible, observed freakishness, fads, and obscure forms of endurance; as well as flagrant forms of self-assertion and conformity. Where morality was concerned, fashion was indiscriminate, giving the same weight to whim as to conviction. A ceaseless milling of persons was unnatural, ludicrous, determined as the acceleration of an old movie. There was anonymity and extreme loneliness, but little reverie and no peace. Apartments were cabins in the great liners docked along the streets.

The city posed its conditions like a test: those apt in its energies became initiates; the rest must fail, depart, or squander irrelevant strength.

In modern buildings opposite the Vail house, all ground floors were doctors' offices. In the early mornings ageing men and women would arrive without breakfast to ring these doorbells. Otherwise there was little passage of humanity on the short block, and few children. Signs of life were often associated with death or extremity: in the night, fire engines and ambulances could be heard on nearby avenues, and the revolving lantern of a police car circled private rooms with mistrustful light; convoys of trucks trundled, purposeful as if provisioning an advancing army. In winter, the tires of cars spun shrieking in filthy snowdrifts, and derelicts fitted themselves to icy crannies of the immense and all but continuous buildings.

The panorama was splendid, the detail grim. Glossiness created, or eased, a lack of contact. When summer came, plane trees obscured the view from Caro's windows, and seclusion was complete.

In the first weeks Caro would lie on her bed or stretch on a sofa, reading or merely still. The house was hushed with her stillness, which was not languor but renewal. Meanwhile, Adam Vail went swiftly through the rooms and hallways of long association, and nimbly up and down the stairs of all his life. Habits of home gave agility to his body that was heavy in repose or love.

The house had a light smell of plants and polish, and oils used to preserve books or furniture. In the beginning Caroline Vail noticed this smell, which she could not afterwards rediscover. In her stepdaughter's room there was a scent of calamine lotion, there were creams for adolescent complexions, there were tablets for pain; there were comic books, two guitars, and recordings of Italian opera. There were books to do with animals in far countries—Ethiopia, Kenya. These belonged to dark Josie who, at the time of Caro's arrival in the city, had gone to Africa on safari with the family of a schoolfriend, Myra.

Adam said, "Myra is bad news."

Fitted into the frame of Josie's mirror there were photographs of mother and child.

Adam's sister, Una, came to lunch. Una was handsome, with an air of fashionable disbelief. She smoked her cigarettes half-through and, as she put them out, rattled a golden chain on her wrist. Her laugh, which began on a loud peal, was also abruptly extinguished, incomplete. She looked at Caro with open interest that might have been kind.

Una was having an affair with a bureaucrat. She told Caro, "My friend is a diplomat"—diplomat being a term, like architect, whose disgrace had not yet caught up with it. That evening when her lover asked her, "How's the bride?" she dropped into a chair and crossed her legs: "Well." After a time she said, "This is no case of the second Mrs. de Winter." Eventually she lit a cigarette. "Bride's okay. Dark hair, dark eyes, dark horse. Late twenties, maybe thirty. By no means a dope. Talks, laughs, shows British teeth." As Hansi went on with a crossword puzzle Una put out her fresh cigarette and added, "Intolerant."

"Intolerant of what?"

"People like me." Reaching in her handbag, Una said, "Loves Adam." She brought out a tiny enamel box. On the table at her side there were similar boxes, arranged in rows.

Hansi mixed drinks and gave one to Una. She made a slight motion in his direction with the glass, and in her other hand held up the box. "Brought me a present." She handed it to him. "Adam must have told her." She drank from her glass, then took the box back from Hansi. She set it on the table with the others and said, "Cute."

"Ask me something," said Adam Vail. In the night they would waken and make love. "You never have questions."

"Now I have to learn what doesn't come through questions."

One afternoon, when she lay on a sofa reading, he came and took her in his arms. "Don't go into a decline."

"It's an ascent."

He got up then and moved about the room, rattling objects, slamming drawers, crackling a newspaper. His wife went on reading, regretting that so considerate a man should be driven to this and mildly surprised at how little restraint he was showing. He need only wait and she would give him perfect happiness. It was for this her energies were gathering, and for other proper purposes.

Una was going abroad for the summer. Una, who had been divorced, said she could have a great summer at last: "For eight years I was nailed to the cross of East Hampton." Una jangled a new bracelet. Her handsome face had a costly sheen, she wore what the ancient Romans called summer jewellery. Soon, from the Mediterranean, she and Hansi sent a postcard of pink bungalows on a beach.

Adam said, "It's a place for millionaires at the end of their tether."

"Why should millionaires always be at the end of their tether?"

"They're the ones who can afford to be." He touched her face. "You look fine, yourself."

"The beginning of my tether."

Caro took Adam's arm in the street and stood to look. A show of professionalism in machines and buildings was reproduced, with less success, in persons: existence had been turned over to the experts. "We"—she meant, people from elsewhere—"will always be amateurs compared with this."

Adam said, "Our great and secret fear is that America may turn out to be a phenomenon, rather than a civilization. Hence, in part, the scale, the insistence, the need to prove the great mysteries obsolete or serviceable. We want our lust to be loved and called beautiful. To receive the homage due to love."

Adam Vail linked his wife's fingers with his own. "Hence also a compulsion to account for ourselves. As I at this moment."

"But if Americans themselves say these things."

"Just don't you go agreeing with any of it, that's all." Vail laughed. "Oh Caro, we are much worse, and perhaps better, than you so far secretly think."

Adam was taking Caro to see a friend who lived at 149th Street. When they came home, Caro said, "Why should anyone stand it?"

Una, who was back from Sardinia, told her: "The American Negro is overadjusted to his problem."

Adam said, "But not for much longer."

One September evening Caroline Vail sat by a window with a book of poetry.

Adam asked, "Won't you say aloud what you're reading?"

She began, and spoke some lines in a voice high, thin, and unfamiliar:

> *"Primaeval rocks form the road's steep border,*
> *And much have they faced there, first and last,*
> *Of the transitory in Earth's long order;*
> *But what they record in colour and cast*
> *Is—that we two passed."*

She laid the book down without keeping the place, and turned her face away. "Sad," she said. "That's why I'm crying."

Adam stroked her head, her shoulders. When he put his arms round her, her body could scarcely be seen. "Who knows why she is crying. Who knows why Caroline is really crying."

In the autumn Grace wrote that Paul Ivory had a tremendous success with a play called *The One Flesh*. She also reported, more diffidently, that Ted Tice had married the daughter of a scientist. Soon there was a letter from Ted with the same information, and a new address. He hoped Caro and Margaret might one day meet. He wrote, "Here, among the young, we have a clinging to one's times that is like a substitute for patriotism: a pledge of immaturity. For anything in the way of enlightenment, you need people who do not have contemporaries."

When Ted wrote "the young," Caro lost her own claim on youth.

Speaking of enlightenment, Ted went on, the great telescope had been inaugurated at its site in the south of England, with a ceremony attended by the Queen. Owing to a complete absence of visibility, Royalty had managed to command nothing but a show of vapours.

Dora wrote that Gwen Morphew had mysteriously come into money, and had left Glad Pomfret high and dry. It was best to expect ingratitude, then nothing surprised you. Dora, whom Caro could now provide with a house near Dot Cleaver's, wrote of domestic difficulties. She did not wish to be be a worry to Caro in her happiness, and it would all work out somehow. One thing she had learned, and the hard way, was to trouble no one.

"It is almost true," Caro said, "that she is not a worry to me in my happiness."

Caro took her stepdaughter to a recital by a great guitarist. Walking home, the girl said, "It was okay. What I could hear of it."

"Next week we'll have better seats."

She took Josie to the ballet, and Josie said, "Myra's at the double-header." She meant that Caro could count herself favoured.

If Caro did, it was not for that reason.

Adam Vail made a trip to Chile and Peru. "Next time you will be with me."

Una told Caro, "Adam is obsessed. You must have realized that. He is obsessed by people's sufferings. It is something you will have to face."

"I have faced those who do not care at all." She did not see why Una should instruct, who had not succeeded.

One day, however, Una said, "I think it's great," and crumpled a Kleenex.

Caro lay in a hospital bed after a miscarriage, and Adam Vail flew home from Lima. When Caro closed her eyes, darkness restored her to private existence. Someone said, "Now I have to hurt you." The pain was an extension of experience, so new and astonishing as to have intellectual interest. In the dark it might be Paul leaning over her: "Now I have to hurt you." Like other suffering, the apartness of infirmity was either unreality or full reality at last.

Once she had stood apart in a hot corridor and contemplated her own death.

In the dark her thoughts were redistributed, through displacement of hope.

Adam said, "There are two of us to bear it."

"It wasn't this I meant to share."

When Caro was better, Josie told her, "I was ambivalent anyway. I felt very threatened." Confidence in her own simplicity could inspire cruelty scarcely credible. She was often angry, and when crossed would lower her head and weep: "I am being put in a position." Her great weapon was her weakness, the massive deterrent to which all deferred. There was the dread that Josie too would take up death as her lethal instrument. "I am so afraid," she would say; putting the fear of God into all of them.

Caro said, "If she wouldn't try so much to classify her emotions."

"Are you asking that she renounce her American birthright?" Adam said, "She will grow up, grow older."

Caro recalled childhood hopes centered on Dora's seventieth birthday. "We have to bring her round before that."

Only Una would occasionally repulse Josie's attacks, and was unafraid of the girl's tears. Una remarked, "Bite something often enough, kiddo, and it bites right back."

Una told Caro, "You get the message."

"Even those messages she is unaware of sending."

Josie had the eyes noticeable in troubled young women, eyes that are sidelong even when direct. She had the inanition that announces self-engrossment. She was already setting up an apparatus of blame, in apprehension of failure.

To Caro, Josie would state the obvious: "You're not my mother." To be sure of the hurt, she would have liked to see the blood.

"For one thing, I'm not old enough."

Caro told Una, "Josie's belief in her innocence is her warrant for doing harm."

Una said, "Like America."

Alone together, Myra and Josie mocked Caroline Vail—her voice, manner, and opinions, her habit of touching her hair. Josie told Myra, "She can't have children."

"That's why she's trying to take you over. Well, tell her she can cut that right out."

Caro could feel the wish she be cut right out. From far off she could sense Josie Vail thinking of her with resentment; as she might, even now, feel Ted Tice think of her with love.

Myra told Josie, "Can't you see the way they're using you?" If Myra had anything to do with it, Josie would never believe she herself might be an object of affection.

All this was plain as if Josie had reported it: the rehearsed unkindness, the direct and sidelong glance, the doubleness of phrase made all apparent. When Myra was present, Josie must prove herself: "How can you talk such shit, Caro?" In Myra's absence, the girl was loyally abusive, in order to have something to report.

Nothing creates such untruth in you as the wish to please.

Myra's eyes were downward, lank hair concealed her cheeks. Myra was for the present strong, because consuming another's life. Caro would wonder what particular *Benbow* had taken Myra to the bottom.

Adam said, "She mistakes suspicion for insight."

Caroline Vail found herself unsuitably immune to the judgment of Josie. She only wished to restrain the girl in her worst assaults, knowing that, if you wrong someone enough, you cannot bear to be with them.

In secret Caro dwelt on the release from emotional obligation, and could see how indifference might become seductive. What Josie took for exposure on Caro's part had been an offering of trust—a test the girl had failed, over and over. Trust would be offered repeatedly, but not indefinitely.

Adam touched his wife's arm. "Perhaps you mind more than you show."

"When you realize someone is trying to hurt you, it hurts less."

"Unless you love them." Adam hoped Caro might one day almost love Josie, as she would the city—through contiguity and shared experience. He thought it would be a pity if only the lovable were loved.

He wanted to say, "It was her mother"—having seen the child's interest in the universe turned to envy and mistrust.

But felt the indelicacy, and inaccuracy, of accusing his dead wife, who would even yet come to his mind as first known, in irresistible youth and beauty.

When young, Adam Vail had admired as intellect his first wife's plausible instinct for human flaws, and had not seen in this the portent of disaster. He, who wished above all things to be rational, had allied himself with unreason on her behalf. Out of allegiance to her, had put others unreasonably in the wrong. One cause of this was his pride, which could not admit his own defencelessness; another was the persuasive force of his wife's antipathies: single-minded in delusion, she was spared the equivocations of sanity. Gradually it had come about that she needed still another enemy, and only he remained to fill the role. It seemed she had intended this: all the while he imagined he was comforting or reclaiming her, she had been preparing their doom. Then began her threat of death, to command the straying attention of the world. To the utterer, the threat is an addiction that requires increasing dosage. Bystanders, on the other hand, are slowly immunized.

Adam told Caro, "There is no greater tyranny than a continual state of desperation."

He, who considered himself a man, had become, with his first wife, vulnerable as an intimidated child. She acted on him like a wasting disease: all healthy links to life were infidelities to be rescinded. His maturity shed daily, he relapsed into a sullen stupor from which the only sporadic arousal was physical desire. In fear, he felt his will contract, grow small and smaller, until it was a hard, shrivelled nut inside her breast. He had intended magnitude; and was a small hard thing in a shell.

Within the incubus of her infirmity, she was so strong and he so weak.

Adam Vail began to dream that he was strangling his mad and therefore guiltless wife. He dreamed, also, his own suffocation. Insufficiency of space and breath became a waking preoccupation: in the streets he pushed a way through crowds, unable to extend his pace or self to full dimensions.

One day she came to the top of the stairs, and called his name. Her hand was dark.

He said, "Charlotte. Charlotte."

"I've hurt myself." There was blood from a gash.

His horror was as much for the release, the exoneration, as for the event.

His wife had saved him by going so far that, with all his compromises, he could not follow her. It was then he had learned the patience now apparent, and laboriously renewed his ties with life. Not guilty by reason of insanity, his wife was yet incapable of innocence.

Madness might sometimes give access to a kind of knowledge. But was not a guarantee.

Caro said, "We must bring Josie round." Caro had mellowed with new youth, and was content. If this could happen to her, why not to Josie? She had once told Paul Ivory that capacity need not be adverse.

Optimism was vindicated, like prayer, when Myra's father was transferred, with all his family, to California.

Una's lover Hansi had a suite at the Carlyle and an entertainment allowance. From time to time would fly to Delhi or Tokyo for a congress he cheerfully designated useless. He often held a book in his hand, any book, on which to prop the word puzzles he also carried. These puzzles were his only known mental exertion. Hansi would say of himself, "Old Hansi was on his uppers when God in his infinite mercy created the international conference. May this providential, improvident, and peculiarly iniquitous racket, designed to support the moral and mental degenerates of our modern world, flourish forever."

Josie could hardly, and did not, contain herself. While Hansi sat deciphering anagrams, Josie would belabour him for his shoes, luggage, vicuña coat, and grey Mercedes, his suite at the Carlyle, and an illegal arangement to do with free liquor. Hansi laughed, yawned, and pondered a palindrome.

On a single occasion, Hansi broke silence. "At twenty, a man inactively ranting against social injustice is a promise; at thirty, a windbag. At age twenty-five, I, Hansi, spotted the era of the windbag approaching, and I clammed up. While, it is true, proceeding to profit from the organized international windbag industry: that idea whose hour has struck. I have my own form of ineffectuality, but I don't dress it up as morality. I decline to join those who babble about reforms for which they will never lift a finger. We are in the age of the open mouth and un-lifted finger; of those who must talk faster than the world can find them out. Is not that the basis of all modern state-craft, not to speak of battalions of the socially conscious who likewise will never see action? When they excavate the new Pompeii, the intelligentsia will be discovered squatting petrified on the floor, mouths agape to denounce materialism, with their built-in cost-of-living adjustments turned to stone in their pockets. I who am in due course to die do not salute them."

Josie said, "And what in hell is all that supposed to mean?"

Adam told her, "Hansi fears that aimlessness and bom-bast go together."

"I must correct you," said Hansi. "I do not fear but know it. No process of reform is currently acceptable that involves the sacrifice of one hour's sleep, one day's pay, or one chance to deliver yet more of one's own bluster. I assert this not as a moral statement but a factual one. Re-form, my dears, is neither banners nor bombs. Reform is unpaid labour, is poverty, is solitude, is the composition of innumerable letters by the midnight oil and the engage-ment in ignominious struggles with a duplicating machine. Reform means years spent in the mastery of uncongenial and arid themes. Reform is giving up dinners, holidays, and sex in order to pore over deadly documents in a base-ment. Is to be isolated, ignored, insulted, and possibly run over by a government truck. Reform is concentration and endurance. Reform, my dears, or any merest particle of it, is no more wanted at that price by our modern altruists than it is by good old Hansi. My intention, like theirs, is to wrest as much money from my employers as possible, turn up my hi-fi, indulge my appetites and tastes, and sleep long and sound each night. Unlike theirs, however, my own intention is openly declared." Hansi unfolded his double crostic. "I speak generally and shall be glad to allow any proven exception."

Josie remarked that she had never heard such shit.

Adam told her, "It's logical. Those who continually

criticize the achievement of others must achieve something of their own or become ridiculous."

Caro said, "Still, what they achieve might be simply character."

Always, Josie noted, thinking of herself. It was intolerable to her that anyone should distinguish themselves, even by their thoughts.

"Certainly," said Hansi. "But persons of character tend to keep their counsel. I can confirm, and conclusively, that they are not to be found expounding on the windbag circuit. As example of said character," he told Josie, "take your own father. Who has never reproached me. I consider it most handsome."

27

Returning from ten days in Sicily, Ted and Margaret Tice took a house handy to everything. The handiness made it possible for Ted to walk back and forth to work, and for his wife to go out to paint in a studio room she rented with another young woman, who was a musician. These days the will to paint was not strong in Margaret, as she believed she had all she wanted and must be happy. However, though departure for the studio was an effort every time, she was perfectly at peace once there and would overstay the hour, breaking off work only when she heard the cellist climbing the stairs. She did not know what she found in that bleak, unheated room, and, while connecting its serenity to her marriage, could not discover where the connection lay. It was years before she realized that the stairs, the room, the easel, the canvas, and the tubes of zinc white stood for safety.

In her paintings at this time, sombre forms represented the phenomena of earth, or of dreams.

So they set up house, each within walking distance of safety. Ted's parents came to visit, also Margaret's. Hooks were screwed in place, bulbs were sunk into lampshades and window-boxes, and a friend spilled wine on the unrolled Piranesi that had been a wedding present. Margaret shopped, and Ted picked up the library books on his way home. "Our Ted takes marriage seriously," his mother said to Margaret, but it was rather that he had taken it up and was doing it thoroughly. He had little taste now for varnishing bookshelves or hammering things home, but was to be seen diligently at work with brush or toolbox. He too became handy, along with everything else. Self-sufficiency appeared complete, a training for survival on a desert island.

Margaret's mother said, "Ted has thrown himself into domestic life. He's flung himself into it." It might have been an abyss.

Habits were established and seemed, in a month or two, lifelong. Once in a while Ted Tice would take up or put down a newspaper with a gesture beyond his years.

Passing through decreed phases, Margaret Tice was first a bride, next a young housewife, and then an expectant mother. Later, would be constrained to talk of schools, join a tennis club and a committee. Would hear herself say, as if it were some other woman, "I never use cornstarch" or "I can clean up as I go along." She felt this happening to her like symptoms of mild illness, and did not resist. But, with unintelligible nostalgia for a life she had never lived, knew that all would have been subtly and profoundly different had her husband greatly loved her.

On a night in the first summer of their marriage they had gone to dinner at the house of one of Ted's colleagues. For such occasions, scientists' wives were trained in self-effacement—except for those who, scientists themselves, could put their own foot on the conversational hearth. Others, like Margaret, might provide themselves with a sweet excuse ("She paints"; "She's musical"), but must expect to be ignored.

Ted at these gatherings was often morose, detached. Respected by his colleagues, he was only sometimes liked. In his dealings with assistants he dispensed a cool indubitable justice—where they would perhaps have preferred a more culpable, and human, partiality. The same objective strength was even less welcome, brooding in a living-room.

In his work Ted had for some time been studying a faint blue object, possibly a star. He had just returned from Palomar, where the controversy of red shift had now begun. It was known that he had things to say, but did not choose to tell them here. It was uncongenial, this notion of taking his own good time.

The dinner was being given for a physicist who had received a celebrated prize: an elderly monolith, with bluff body and desiccated face, who presided glumly at conferences and gave the government influential advice. His taciturn importance was implacable. Women attempting conversation with him heard their voices rising to a squeak: it was like scratching one's name on a historic monument. Even when seated he continued to recall some massive object. Slumped in an indigo chair, wearing a shabby grey jacket with brown leather pads at the elbows, he now resembled a ship of war gone rusty. When Margaret Tice appeared beside him, he half rose from the waves, exposing a Plimsoll line of sagging belt. Ted watched his wife: she was a slope of green in a straight chair, her eyes large with civility, her hand smooth on her knee. The old man-of-war gradually began to address her: speaking was his idea of giving attention. Accepting his monologue, Margaret was receiving what she seldom had: a man's undivided interest.

It was a warm night, windows open to a garden. Ted was remembering light of evening, how many summers past: the table and the talk of youth; two girls, both beautiful, one a gazelle. He came back from talk of quarks and quasars, as if from sleep, to hear his wife say—it was of some book the old man had mentioned—"Yes, I first read it at a time when I was unhappy, and have gone back to it often. I still find it . . ."

"When I was unhappy." What did she conjure up, or exorcise, by these words, seated there in green calm? He was jealous of her unhappiness and had to wish himself the cause of it—for who else should lay claim to her distress? In due course Margaret got up and went to speak to a friend. The physicist stood also, flying his skull and crossbones.

"I don't mind telling you, Tice, that I find your wife a most discerning woman."

Ted stood helplessly watching his wife cross the room: a most discerning woman. If she discerned what was often in my heart, if she knew what I sometimes dream. He wished to persuade himself that Margaret too might have secrets, giving her resources that would spare them both.

Someone came to the open window and threw a cigarette butt accurately into a dark pond in the garden. There was the flicker, the sizzle, and a small protest from insects or a frog.

The old physicist stood by the window, hitching his belt.

Recalling a night of war when he had done fire-watching on the roof of the Savoy. The black river reflected, red and white, the flames and searchlights, the earth rocked and shuddered with the impact and recoil of armoury. And a burning plane twirled down from the sky, shedding its pilot, who plunged in his separate fire. The plane exploded in fragments before reaching earth, but the blazing man plummeted to the river, which—as if he had been a cigarette butt—sizzled him out forever.

The old man remembered how, at the end of that night, he had not returned home but had gone to the flat of his mistress, a learned woman with a pile of yellowed hair. Now long since dead. She had saved him some of her ration, but he could not eat. He had sat on the bed with his face in his hands and said, "The sound of it. I can still hear it." In fact he had experienced worse—and, as a young officer crawling with lice and through mud, had attacked the Hindenburg Line. But at daybreak sat on a bed and wept. "I can see it." The fiery squib. "I can hear it." The doused flesh.

Ted Tice wrote to Caroline Vail that he would pass through New York on his way to Pasadena, where he was to spend some weeks. Caro replied, By all means come to lunch. And on the morning of his arrival went out to buy flowers.

It was a day in December, cold and very clear. Ted got out of the taxi at a corner and walked the last few blocks. On Caro's street, the houses were at first all the same, expensively uniform—black or gilt numbers over the entrance, panels of etched glass either side of the door. Doors were mostly black, too, with a prosperous gloss; one or two had been painted red. The last terrace was less regular, and when Ted came to Caro's house it was to him lively and graceful—a vivacious child between stodgy parents. This was a sorcery he could never get the truth of—whether the house was really distinctive, or if it was only for him it held incomparable charm.

He stood on the top step, more unnerved than he had been years before when he waited in the rain at Peverel. He thought, Now it will never get easier, only more piercing. Through a glass strip, saw a polished floor, mirror, white wall; a small picture of playing cards and a wine carafe. This time the newspaper on the table was explicit as the still life. An umbrella-stand of blue-and-white china was a monument. To come and go at will, forever, across this threshold was not simply a happiness denied him but held so large a meaning that it seemed scarcely permissible to anyone.

The enchantment would have been childlike, had it not been part of a man's forlorn obsession.

He rang, expectant as if something were to be decided—when all decisions had long since been made.

A rush of footsteps on stairs, and Caro, who had never in life before run to meet him, pulled open the door and was smiling. She was tall, high-coloured, strong, and beautiful. Her wide face was wider and sweeter. A current of warm air came out from the hallway. Ted stepped forward, and they embraced. Caro put her arms about him, her body rested on his in pure friendship. "Oh Ted, you look splendid."

It was true. The groove on his forehead, the streak in his eye were attaining distinction; the groove bisected, now, by a horizontal crease.

He came in and took off his muffler. "I had a lot to look forward to today."

The house was filled with light to its remotest interior. At the solstice the sun entered not only frontally but also, through a rear window, obliquely.

A girl with lank hair came out from a room and stood to look, as a domestic animal might saunter out to size up a visitor. Not as Caroline Bell had once stood on a stairway, presiding over his life.

Ted saw Caro's happiness, she had achieved it and glowed with it. That was why she had run to meet him—she could be generous to him, as to all the world. He said, "Excuse me," and blew his nose. The warm indoor air was making his eyes glitter.

Afterwards, Adam Vail said, "I like him. He looks like a slashed self-portrait by van Gogh."

At the end of that winter, Adam and Caro flew to London. There were whole days of sleet, the balance of payments was urgently off, and two new books had been pub-

lished on Guy Burgess and Donald Maclean. Tall buildings were rising, flimsy but all-powerful.

Dora made scene after scene. She had saved these up,
like treats. The remaining good in Dora wanted the two
sisters to go on and live. The other, prevailing Dora detested their escape and had been balked of the hope that
they would say of life, the three of them together, "How
terrible."

Dora told them, "I never ask God for anything. But I
do say thank you. There was a quadriplegic on the telly the
other night and I thought, Well I must be grateful for
something."

"Dora, we're here to see you."

"There are fifty-two weeks in the year. You come for
two of them."

There was something practised about these pat speeches,
their readiness, their conciseness, the fixed, accompanying
look that had been polished before a mirror, that touched
Caro's soul with despair. She longed to provide Dora with
the famous and elusive peace.

Adam told Caro, "Peace is no good. She is terribly
bored."

"But her days are filled with drama. She is always having
it out with Dot or Daph." It was like a message in Morse.

"She is one," said Vail, "for whom the Death of Sard-
anapalus would be insufficiently eventful."

Caro took Dora down to Kew. Dora said, "You loved
camellias. Then."

Caro wanted to deny camellias, as if they had been a
trap. Ashamed of this, she would have liked to explain:
she wished to share her peace of mind, not to offer it up
as a sacrifice.

Kew did not meet the case. Dora now wished to go to
New Zealand, where she had a friend at Palmerston North.
"Trish Bootle wants me." It was another of Dora's sun-
derings. "I'm wanted there."

Adam said he would get her passage on the best ship.

"Anything to be rid of me."

"We'll take a return ticket."

Dora told Dot Cleaver, "It's his easy solution, of writing
a cheque."

Informed of the situation by Grace, Christian said, "Vail

was a fool ever to get mixed up in it." But Christian was in fact content that Adam should take on Dora. It seemed something—like Lend-Lease, or the Marshall Plan—that an American should do. He told Grace, "I carried the burden long enough."

Christian was thinking about age these days, and fearing to be saddled with the decrepitude of others. Dora was heading for fifty. Her legs were slightly bowed, she was losing her figure and her looks. Every few weeks, her hair was streaked with grey. His mother was becoming what he termed a worry, alone in her old house with only a daily woman and a red cat named Hotspurr. She would be better off in a home. Christian said this to Caro, who replied, "She has a home. You mean an institution."

Commemorating some long past show of preference, Christian told himself that, in Grace, he had made the right choice. He had seen how people came a cropper by giving way to impulse. It was to his judiciousness, at every turn, that he owed the fact that nothing terrible had ever happened to him.

28

It was not until a summer of the nineteen-sixties that something terrible, or at any rate highly regrettable, happened to Christian Thrale. This came about while Grace was at Peverel with the children—which will suggest the nature of the occurrence. Grace had hardly been gone long enough to be properly, let alone acutely, missed; and certainly not long enough for Christian to have telephoned, for he was frugal in these matters.

It was early evening on a Tuesday, and Christian was standing at his office window observing the bloom of silky light extending in reconcilement over London: looking at forests of leaves spread like open hands, and white colonnades and porticoes, and roads that shone like rivers. In the park could be seen a streak of turf, a dab of water, the blue tilting steeples of delphinium. The evening bore the cachet of a huge success magnificently consummated after many botched attempts.

Christian was enjoying not only the manageable rapture of sundown but the novelty of his own high pleasure in it. He had merely glanced out, not expecting anything but weather. Though traffic rumbled, the mnemonic light had a quality of silence—yet seemed no simple fact of nature, for one scarcely felt such a radiance could exist without such a city to encompass. There was human engagement in it, as at some momentous passage of human greeting, or leave-taking, with the world.

Christian, moreover, was aware of himself looking: a sandy man of more than average height and intelligence—yet always keeping at hand the bolt hole of the average;

the yardstick, rather, by which departures and excesses might be measured.

A door opened at his back. He did not turn, being pleased to be discovered in the act of survey and reflection: a sandy man with narrow shoulders who had retained perspective. In childhood Christian had, like many children, defined himself as sensitive. Like many adults, he had made no reassessment in the light of later promptings. In office affairs he frequently cautioned, "If we lose our humanity we are done for." Although at other times he had said, "We have to draw the line somewhere," and "It's not for me to say."

A crisis had blown up, and what luck, Thrale, you are still here. A meeting was being called, since cables must be sent that evening. What luck, as Talbot-Sims had just gone down in the lift.

Christian could not feel What luck, thinking of Talbot-Sims spurting for home, for dear life, flying free across London in what he visualized as an open car, although Talbot-Sims was known to travel exclusively by Tube. Drooped over the willow pattern of his blotter, Christian assembled papers, and assumed with reluctance the willing expression he normally wore with ease.

Christian Thrale was now rising in his profession. Those peering into the oven of his career would report, "Christian is rising," as if he were a cake or loaf of bread. They did not say, "He will go far," which would have suggested temperament, but from time to time remarked his gradual ascent: "Christian has risen."

The conference room looked towards the park. Only the room did so, the men present being focused on a table, on papers, on one another; on themselves. They stared into the glossy grain of that table as if into a tank. Revived by a fresh draught of importance, they rustled, they murmured, they struck matches and matched watches; because there was a delay. The first rank of the stenographers having got clear, having somehow packed themselves along with Talbot-Sims into that escape hatch of the downward lift—and the doyenne, Miss Ratchitt, being home today bilious—they were waiting for a girl to take the minutes.

This was an aggravation when every moment was precious.

It was like the delphiniums, when she came. For this emergency she had been called back from the ladies' room, where she was preparing to go home—perhaps, who knows, to go out. In those preparations she had literally let down her hair, which was yellow like ripe corn; and had been given no time to redress it. Merely combed back, it fell over her slim blue shoulders and streaked down her spine. And even the worst man there, of whom there were several, yearned for it. Christian could not recall having seen her before in the zones of encounter, lift or corridor. But perhaps with the hair down it was different.

When she came, it was like the delphiniums.

She sat in a heavy chair—that no one, to put it mildly, pulled out for her. Never having pulled it out for Ratchitt, the contrast would in any case have exposed them. Behind the arras of his expression, Christian Thrale watched, entranced. The movements, shy, deliberate, with which she laid her lined notebook on the table and folded it, and restrained an extra pencil from rolling. The elbow poised on the table, the head inclined long-lashed to the page, evoking the schoolgirl she had lately been.

Around the tank the flickering intensified before falling ceremoniously away. It was a ritual moment, as if the soloist flung back coattails over the piano bench or fixed the protective pad between Stradivarius and jowl. Gentlemen, shall we begin. I need not stress that these proceedings take place in the utmost confidence, I trust that was made clear also to Miss—I'm afraid I don't know your—

Cordelia Ware.

Miss Ware. Very good. The cabinet will conclude its deliberations within the hour and we are informed that.

It fell forward, the flag of hair. An arm came up to pass it uselessly back over the shoulder. A page hastily turned. A gazelle in the room. China in the bull shop. Everything frail and fair, cheek, ear, wrist, and the earnest curve blue from waist to shoulder.

In view of the events of the past week the significance of such a decision can hardly be overestimated, the far-reaching consequences. Would you make a heading of this,

Miss— I'm afraid I don't recall your— Gentlemen, time is not on our side.

She was taking the minutes. The minutes flew, it was she who took them. Every moment was precious and time not on our side.

Christian remembered lines:

> *How can I, that girl standing there,*
> *My attention fix*
> *On Roman or on Russian*
> *Or on Spanish politics?*

The verse ended, "O that I were young again, and held her in my arms." He remembered that, too. If you learned the stuff young, you never lost it. You're as old as you feel. I feel old. Another page flickered, the wrist arching anxiously. The same gesture casting back the hair. Time was on her side. She wore a round watch, inexpensive, with a band of black ribbon—grosgrain, they called it in the ads. She was sinking him, he was listing like a ship. O Christ, it is the Inchcape Rock. This is ridiculous, and how very unjust. Years of happy marriage decidedly not foundering in any such rut or reef as is here implied. Spain this year and the Swan's tour in '63. It is true the office. But not to the extent this girl's effect appears to insinuate.

So Christian tacked, zigzagging on a course of yellow hair and blue flowers. His shipmates might have been bound to the mast, their ears stopped with wax. They seethed, they droned. They plied the ropes. They knew the ropes. As to the humanitarian aspect, deep concern will be voiced. However, this will be done confidentially in order not to exacerbate an already delicate. They were at the stage of leaning back, ties askew. A sensible precaution, Bickerstaff. A good point, Barger. Pertinacity commended as at school—with Christian, on this occasion, not among the bright boys.

There was no following her when at last she was sent away to type in some room where lights were now switched on and cleaners would have to be excluded. The contents of the wastepaper basket would be burned. On dune and headland sinks the fire. The captains melted away, the kingpins departed.

Roaming a grey corridor, Christian was accosted by a bleached colleague, Armand Elphinstone by name. Christian had sometimes told Grace, "I don't hit it off with Elphinstone." Adding, "I daresay it's my fault."

Elphinstone churned loose change in the pockets of unpressed trousers. He shrugged shoulders tweedy with dandruff, pin-striped by fallen hairs.

"And why, may I ask, are we always disorganized. We had no preparation. That meeting could have been called at least an hour earlier. I must say. I don't know how we can look the standing committee in the face." In Elphinstone's pockets invisible sixpences percussed, with a bunch of keys forming the brass. He looked away. "And sending that girl in half-dressed."

So he too. Even the blanched Armand.

There was no use hanging about. Elphinstone had rather spoiled things.

The following day there was something else. Christian's own secretary was leaving for her summer holiday.

"And what have they got in mind for me?" As he asked her this, he knew.

"They're giving you a girl from the pool. I'll show her the main things. A Miss Waring. Or Ware. Of course there'll be chaos by the time I get back."

The first day, she had on a dress of worn brown velvet, her hair smoothly coiled. Christian was a man of few words all morning, thumping down this or that for three copies: this has priority, do that in draft. He could only keep it up till lunchtime. By afternoon he was wanting to sound her and needing her good opinion. She sat taking his dictation, and he could hardly believe he had her there at his tender mercy: he felt tender rather than merciful. When she closed her book he said, "I hope you weren't kept too late the other evening."

She lifted her eyes, blank.

He felt he had given himself away. "The evening of the cabinet announcement."

"I missed the train. We live at Dulwich." Hesitant, as if she trespassed on his interest by so much as a reply. "One of the girls let me stay at her place."

"You did not have to cancel anything, I hope."

"It was my father's birthday."

What lives we give them, Christian reflected—not without gratification. He could recognize a pleasure in displacing her father, with whom he must necessarily stand—one was aware of such things—in rival status. Her eyes were so clear, upward, almost circular, washed like grey glass. He saw she wished to please him: I hope to give satisfaction sir. Her voice, like her dress, was doeskin, an excellent thing in woman. The father had called this child Cordelia.

When he heard her typing he made a pretext to stand awhile by her desk. There was something nearly sexual in this, like the relation of tenor to accompanist, she seated and subsidiary, he standing and commanding. She faintly sweetly smelt of talcum or shampoo. Her fingers, grubby from carbon, unnerved by his proximity, turned six copies to scrub at an error. A *Style Manual*—what style could there conceivably be in all this?—was open to instructions of inane and infinite tedium. I have the honour to be, sir, Your Excellency's humble and obedient. On the surface of the desk there was a dusting of molted rubber over the clawings and droppings of a score of previous, vanished secretary-birds.

Excellence and honour. With less satisfaction, he wondered, Why do they put up with this?

He all but placed his hand on her brown velvet shoulder. Could very nearly feel the smooth life curve into his palm —and at that instant would have let her off, wished her safe from all his harm, while she was so anxiously, innocently bent to her rubbishy task.

"That one is of prime importance," he said. "The rest can wait."

From his room he heard her storming the keys, the rip of the roller, arpeggios of sentences, the andante of an indented passage. A distraught exclamation for a false note. It was curious that a machine could reproduce the anxiety of the person operating it. The imagined globe of her velours shoulder stayed, palpable, in his hand still cupped to its contour.

Evening rose like dawn. The city inhaled it like a breath of immense relief. A wave of excitement lifted Christian from desk to window—where the metropolis once more lay helpless and expectant under a dusk phenomenal as an eclipse. A cautious man would have looked through special glasses, or through a hole cut in cardboard. With the naked eye, Christian gazed. He was one who could still see the sky. Who knew his Yeats. His Freud.

Not for nothing were these names prefaced by the possessive pronoun.

He was tempted to ask her outright to go to dinner with him. But no, not outright, and not the first evening. Let a decent interval elapse, and hope the weather would hold. There was prodigality in this—they had so little time. In thought he said "they"—and could not think unjustified this newly possessive pronoun.

The following day was hot. The city opened all its windows as Christian rode to work in his car. Down to tower'd Camelot. As if by assignation, she wore the dress of the cornflowers—was it?—and her hair down. He had heard that girls were ironing their hair that year, in order to wear it long and flat, but did not think that would apply to her. It would not be possible to do this oneself—perhaps their mothers did it for them. He tried to picture the little kitchen at Dulwich, neat as a new pin, the mother shapeless in flowered apron, and she with her head laid on the ironing board. It was like an execution.

It was a simple matter to detain her after work. There was no difficulty in manufacturing a crisis—most crises in that place being manufactured ones—by retarding some memorandum into the afternoon. When she came back at two from her hasty sandwich (he assumed the sandwich, noted the haste), he struck. At six they were alone, he attentively reading over, she pounding. He got up, went to the gents' to spruce. He ran water, ran a comb, ran a critical eye. Smiled into a square of quicksilver that was cracked from side to side. Walking back along the inert grey arteries, he could hear the machine still racing, like a heart.

He had plumped for the magisterial assertion: "I am going to drive you home." Had of course hoped she wouldn't look quite so bowled over. "Let's face it"—with this interpolation Christian habitually reproved a widespread tendency to shirk—"we're going to be another half-hour here, at least. Might as well"—foregone conclusion—"have a bite of dinner somewhere, then I'll drive you."

He thought he detected slight equivocation—he would not call it suspicion—mingling with her astonishment. She must be pleased, however, even thrilled. A girl who passed her days turning carbons would welcome any diversion. Your Excellency's humble and obedient.

Not that he regarded himself as any diversion.

"You are kind," she said, without causing him a qualm.

She was in the car at his side. They were crossing a river, the river, after Chablis and Dover sole. It was by no means dark. Ahead, the smooth common was an innocence of late cricket balls and unleashed terriers and elderly couples safely benched. (The hanky-panky would come later, with nightfall.) The trees, though; he had never felt it before—such trees, like clouds, like screens, like great bouquets. She was doing this: first cornflowers, now trees. Light-wingéd Dryad, beechen green, Rima the bird-girl that was her type, the constant nymph what was her name Tess of the—no, not that: Tessa. All this at Clapham.

He would have liked to stop the car, there and then, just to look at the trees, and would have taken her in his arms almost incidentally. But the decent interval must elapse. She had said so little, everything correct and nothing foolish. She was quite still, and looked at the evening and the trees, her head tipped towards the seat-back though not reclining. They drove on, along suburban avenues for which he felt the kindliness one summons for a boyhood friend who has not prospered.

"You turn left at the college."

He turned.

"It's along here on the right. This one."

He had been confident of a row of demoralized asters, three front steps, a porch of frosted glass glumly bulging from brick. And could not have been more irritated if she had deliberately deceived him. Not that the house was grand: a pretty house, white but eighteenth-century, banked with fuchsia along a brief crescent of raked gravel. But it was a house, precisely, of the sort he and Grace had looked at and decided they could not afford.

Every window was lit. It was like a party house described in a novel: "ablaze." (Christian himself preferred to switch lights off when not in use.) Or it was a ship, festive and stately with all her canvas up and pennants fluttering. On the ground floor a silk curtain belled through French windows, like a spinnaker.

He pulled up at the door. The car turned shabby in the glow from the house. He remembered plastic toys on the back seat.

"You'll come in." She was almost social on her own territory.

"I'll be getting back. It's late." He was being rude, but the house was a menace. He could feel the father's eye on him, see himself blinking in the lights, shown up as if at a police station. I must warn you that anything you say will be.

Even so, heard himself announce, "Another time." And boldly leaned across her lap to manage the door, laying his hand over her own ineffectual grip as if sealing a contract.

"Up and push," he said. Then, "Give it a good bang."

A Scots terrier scrambled down the steps to her, all muzzle and paws and sprout of tail. He heard her say, "Here, Hoots. Here, Hootsie," in a kind of ecstasy.

He withdrew to town in confusion. He had been prepared for his role, genial but restrained, master of the situation in the modest house of the begonias and new-pin kitchen; helping them over their natural diffidence. Had even been ready for a possible Socialist brother whose surly challenges could be gracefully debunked. But distinctly not prepared for the equalizing properties of Lowestoft, Regency, bound editions, a faded but valuable Samarkand; and, perhaps, attributed-to-Hoppner over the original fireplace.

He disliked, moreover, the sensation of the narrow squeak.

He could not help associating his present impetuosity with his first encounter with Grace. Was there not, in fact, a recognized condition called the Cophetua Complex? Or had he made that up?

Reaching home, he put in a call to Grace. This, which should have been a help, was not. A neighbour had dropped in, it was too late to bring the boys to the phone, just one second I have to turn something off. Jeremy had been sceptical about the authentic Round Table, which they had paid to see that morning, and Hugh had sulked.

"Anything going on at the office?"

"This dust-up in Africa's got us jumping. Then there's always the secretary of state. And we're short-handed as usual. They've given me a temporary."

"Miss Mellish got away, then?"

"There'll be chaos by the time she gets back."

He put the phone down and took off his shoes. Blinds were down, to protect the fading chintz. On the closed piano, Grace's music lay folded. He could see the House of Ware, its white sails crowding. The girl bending, the doorway lit like a stage. Her face and hands active with love as she reached to the dog scrabbling at her ankles, her knees. He could hear her speaking, in her voice of an articulate doe; he could feel the very burr in the animal's coarse coat. He could scarcely wait for tomorrow.

Next morning Christian stowed the toys away in the trunk of the car. The weather was holding, the decent interval elapsing. A Friday sense of near-abandon enlivened the department, as if something other than an English weekend lay ahead. There was a lull, even in Africa, where crocodiles idled on sluggish waters between walls of motionless bamboos.

The sight of Cordelia Ware in pink printed flowers dispelled the defeat of Dulwich, exorcising the spectre of Detective-Inspector Father.

Only Elphinstone had a cold. Elphinstone was flying to an important conference in Brussels that evening, and was concerned about effects of cabin pressure on the ears.

Christian stood by Elphinstone's desk. "All set?"

Elphinstone coughed. At first phlegmlessly, like faulty ignition, the engine turning over and over till it caught. He pulled a handkerchief from his pocket in a flurry of lint.

Christian turned away and looked at two framed photographs hung beside the map on the wall: Elphinstone's grandfather in diplomatic dress; and a weeding party of British residents once organized by Elphinstone at the English cemetery on Capri.

The map was so old that India was pink.

At last Elphinstone replied. "I have no problem." He said the word "problem" with sardonic emphasis to make clear he knew it for an Americanism.

"You know I'm on call tomorrow." Christian was duty officer for the weekend. "If anything blows up."

Elphinstone was all sympathy. "You're not having much of a summer, I must say. Losing your weekend." He raised the clotted handkerchief to his face and looked at Christian over it, like a bandit. "And working late."

Christian took his eyes off the trowels, grins, and brandished dandelions of the English cemetery, and stared Elphinstone down. "Not to worry."

When Christian went out, Elphinstone hawked once more into his handkerchief, and spread it to dry on the window-sill.

In innocence of this, in all innocence, Cordelia Ware glanced up from her scruffy papers as Christian came through—her look a refreshing contrast to Elphinstone's. Christian sat at his desk signing papers and vengefully slinging them into boxes. He felt rage, and some triumph. Elphinstone's eyes above the bandanna had been something to see. An incompetent, an intolerable fool imposed on us, let's face it, because his grandfather negotiated a disastrous treaty in 1908. God, if the public only knew.

The afternoon wore on, wore out. Steadily relieved of the ballast of early departures, the entire floor became airy, buoyant. Miss Ware—Cordelia—brought him the incoming. The lull persisted, extending over continents, taking the wind out of Africa's sails. The official boom swung ineffectually to and fro in the global Doldrums. There were copies for information, and the text of a ministerial speech which would not now be delivered owing to altered circumstances. There were papers marked PUS, for the Permanent Under-Secretary of State, on which action was neither contemplated nor required. There was a postcard of the rocks at Etretat from Miss Mellish: Hope all goes well.

"Mellish is in Monet country."

"She sent me one too." She handed it to him. The same rocks: I forgot to mention, just leave the filing for my return.

They stood, each holding a card, ticket-of-leave, with time running out.

He could not be mistaken in this stillness. The phone rang.

It was an opposite number in a parallel department. "Look here, Thrale. We're not getting the picture on the Brussels meeting."

"What more do you want? We're sending one of our best people."

"No reflection on your nest, old boy. Merely a matter of communication." The word "communication" was given the arch inflection Elphinstone had conferred on "problem."

Grimacing to the girl, Christian waved the receiver in a show of exasperation. He had never committed improprieties with Miss Mellish. He was in a fever for the day to end, or begin. The voice twanged on, irresistably drawn to jargon but unwilling to take the blame.

With impatient ball-point Christian scored, on the blotter, the outline of the colored postcard, his *carnet de bal*.

All at once she was saying, "If there's nothing more," and holding her handbag. She had a scarlet cardigan over her arm and was mouthing Good-bye, Mr. Thrale. It had never occurred to him that she would of her own accord leave promptly. Before he could get the phone down she was gone; and in the corridor nowhere to be seen.

He lost his head completely and strode out to stop the lift.

Only Elphinstone was poised between the lift doors, ready to plunge. Elphinstone grinned at Christian over his shoulder, and raised his fingers in a Victory sign. He might have been making a parachute jump. As he disappeared his hand went to his heart, fumbling for the rip cord.

Back in his office, Christian stood at the window where it had all begun. He was unsure of what he had intended, but definitely not this prospect of brooding through a failed evening. On a last clangour of filing cabinets and desk drawers, the office fell silent. All across London, girls were gliding in and out of cars, and younger men were leaning over saying, "Up and push." Couples were lifting trays and calling, "You bring the ice," and the garden furniture from Harrods was outdoors at last.

Only Christian stood disconsolate by his office casement.

Had it not been for the crimson sweater, he might not have spotted her. She was crossing the street below, walking slow and heading for the park. Or, it could be, for the

Underground—but one does not walk that way toward a train, lifting one's head to the sky and hitching one's woolly casually over a shoulder. She had slim legs and little flat shoes; and, like all her movements, her walk was charming.

He left the web, he left the loom. In three paces was at his desk slamming drawers and snatching pen and spectacles. He retained enough presence of mind to grab up an envelope of weekend documents as a prop.

When, in the street, he had her in view, he held back in imaginary relish of the sweetness of it. Stalking her, he knew an assurance of happiness such as he had seldom felt as an adult and which was incompatible with childhood. Christian had been in love as a lad, then as a young man ready to take a wife. But not as now when, quite out of any context, representing no forces other than those beyond his control, he watched Cordelia Ware in a frenzy of tenderness, confused between worship and condescension.

He overtook her as she was turning into the park. And was the soul of amiable surprise: No Dulwich? She explained, the evening was so beautiful, and the park. They passed through the gateway together. They were drifting past banks of iridescent flowers and among cornelian trees. They crossed a bridge and sat on a bench alone. The office envelope, whose wadded warm sensation had grown repugnantly alive in Christian's hand, was stationed on his other side like an overzealous accomplice.

Here there was a vast repose, the earth all grass and the sky all heaven; although waterfowl were squabbling over the flung crusts and a newspaper was carried past with an atrocious headline. Somewhere overhead, Elphinstone was safely airborne, swallowing hard to protect his ears and taking an extra mint from the proffered dish to be on the safe side.

She sat straight, not in a gym-class way, with her fingers intertwined on her crossed knee. And, with the evening on her hair and her pale skin, was all light. She was looking at him, grave and listening. Like the Muse: patient, but accessible only to those acting in good faith.

"Will you dine with me?" It was his most humble speech to her yet.

Pink flowers rose on her printed breast. "If that is all right," she said.

He did not know how to treat that appeal to his authority, and let it pass. Anything now seemed possible. The whole world, like the weekend, lay before them. He had not forgotten how she had once spent the night in town with a friend. Even at the time he had filed that info for possible future use.

"Won't they expect you at home?"

"I'll telephone."

He did not wish to learn what she would say. To hell with Inspectre Father. They would sit between grass and sky while the light lasted, and later he would take her to dinner at a little place off Duke of York Street where one went on red-letter days.

He had cashed a cheque that morning.

The limitless expansion of likelihood shed new tolerance on every mortal thing: the subdued honkings of human enterprise that reached them from the road, the screech of an intemperate fowl almost at their feet, the couple on the nearby grass whose undulations beneath a spread mackintosh were like some lewd wink in their own direction; the iron dukes and stone admirals fixed atop pedestals and columns. All were appropriate to this earth, even the Guardsmen in their vermilion Mao jackets and Afro busbies, and the distant reticulation of a rising skyscraper against whose erection Christian had lately signed a petition.

Christian was removed from pettiness, as one is only by immeasurable happiness or grief. His preoccupation with importance had unfitted him for greatness: he was a man of vicarious consequence only; but in those moments understood the large hearts of heroes.

In this mood the evening passed. Christian took Cordelia's arm at the first green light and did not release it until they reached the restaurant. Over dinner he talked of Spain, where she had never been—"Let's face it, Madrid *is* the Prado"—and the Hebrides, where she had. He discovered that the house at Dulwich had belonged to her grandfather, and that she had three brothers, and an uncle deafened by too much quinine during a decade in Bengal. In addition to the Scottie there was a fringed cat called Ruffles.

All this—the Grecos, the Cuillins, the uncle, and the

ruffled cat—paraded glittering through space in one narrow room.

They walked back toward the car through the broad
streets and capacious squares laid out in narrower times.
Scarcely a vehicle passed them. Not a soul ascended the
steps of the right clubs or issued from the little petuniaed
porticoes of the great corporations. You could hear a foot-
fall, or peal of laughter, all the length of that noble and
unearthly promenade.

Christian unlocked the car door for her, and stood holding it but blocking her entry.

"I must see you."

"I know," she said.

He let go of the door, which lurched slowly open like a
shutter on a derelict house. Into the back seat, from which
that morning he had put away childish things, he hurled his
envelope of bogus papers. He drew Cordelia Ware into his
arms.

They—they—had almost three weeks before Miss Mellish
returned. As luck would have it, luck held. The weather
also. Africa continued quiescent, Cordelia's parents left for
the Dordogne, and Grace felt the extra fortnight would do
the boys a world of good.

Even Elphinstone, though back from Brussels, was having extensive work done on his teeth.

Christian Thrale took Cordelia Ware by her perfect little
elbow in vacant evening streets, and drew her to him on
park benches. He leaned his cheek on her smooth coiled
head, and took her golden tresses—there was no other
word for them—loose in incredulous hands. She in turn
slipped her arms about his neck, or lifted his palm to her
face and kissed it. In his Hillman Minx they crossed and recrossed the Rubicon at Battersea Bridge. *Iacta alea est.* They
sat, as he had dreamed of doing, beneath the elegiac trees.

As far as Christian was concerned, these delicious proceedings left, quite literally, something to be desired. While
the virginal aspect of this girl had first attracted him, Time,
gentlemen, was not on our side—what with Grace consult-
ing timetables and Miss Mellish pushing the boat out from
the Normandy beachhead.

She said, "I am happy just being with you." Her hand

along his arm in one of her precise and fragile gestures. "You cannot decently complain of that."

He laughed. "Then indecently I complain." It would be unusual if she turned out to be—girls these days were not. At least, not by the time one met up with them.

It is hard to say which of her attitudes most delighted him, the intently curved, or slimly upright. Or which of her movements, chaste and extravagant as those of a ballerina. She had this way of looking—you would not have said "trustful" exactly, but "believing." She applied to one's judgment. She put simple questions with genuine inquiry, as if wishing to discover how the world turned. The look, the appeals, the inquiries had the effect of assigning responsibility. Christian enjoyed being the framer of constitutions, the dispenser of unalterable law.

"Your Socratic Method," he told her, taking her upturned face between his hands and smiling down from the stature she conferred. She did not ask what this was, but maintained undeflected her unfathomable openness. It was hard to see how a look could be both level and uplifted.

Never in any circumstances did she use his name, his Christian name. His remarking on this led to a small misunderstanding. "I thought," she said, "you would not like that in the office."

He had assumed as a matter of course she would not use it there. Some things went without saying.

One day she asked him, "Do you mind the deception?" He said, "Somewhat to my surprise, no." He could not leave himself there, and went on, "I just don't want people's feelings to get hurt."

He did not mean hers.

It was not until the end of the final week that he had, as the old saying goes, his way with her. The Thrales lived in a crescent of Victorian dwellings that had once been ivory, robust, slightly irregular, like a mouthful of sturdy teeth; but were now pared, drilled, recapped, and made uniform. It was here that, locking doors and drawing curtains, Christian finally lay down in his matrimonial bed with Cordelia Ware.

The question of beds, indeed, could not be gracefully resolved. It was either the children's, or his own. She made, in this regard, one of her inquiries: "Do you mind it?"

"Not in the least." He added, "This is my side anyway."

It was curious how abandon begot precaution. It was that very evening he began to make himself clear. "I shall never forget this. Any of it." Surely she could not, to employ her own phrase, decently complain of that. He told her, "I shall be wildly jealous of the man you marry. I hate him already."

She lay looking at the ceiling, eyes wide as if she could not close them. After a while she asked, "How shall we go on now?"

"My dear, I don't know." After all, he was not an oracle. She was looking up, scanning the heavens. "We'll have to play it by ear."

The following day he telephoned to Peverel. Grace had been to Winchester and seen Jane Austen's grave. "I wish you had been here, Chris."

"The only one I like is *Pride and Prejudice*."

"I mean here this summer. It will never be so beautiful again."

Their days apart, and nights, their divided pleasures pained him. Grace was speaking of the Close, the roses, the labyrinth of streams, and the meadows beyond the school. She said that, from Peverel, the view over the valley this morning was, in a word, splendour. He broke in: "I can't hang on forever. This is costing the earth."

For three weeks Christian had felt himself an explorer in his native city. Not because he had taken Cordelia Ware much about, unless you count once to Chiswick, once to Greenwich, and the Wallace Collection, where they did not get upstairs. But because the visibility had cleared for him as for a smogbound pilot, disclosing roofs and spires and gardens and the congested flow of roads at thrilling and dangerous proximity; revealing birds in flight and cats walking on walls. The curves of earth and water had become landmarks not to be taken for granted. Above all, he had perceived in the human form the sweet glory of the elms and oaks of Battersea: he saw men as trees walking.

Now, on a Monday filled with normality, a morning of wives ringing the butcher or going through trouser pockets before sending to the cleaner, Christian travelled once again by Underground. And Miss Mellish was in early, sorting the backlog and murmuring, "I don't know I'm sure."

"We managed." Loyally. "And not badly, considering."

Miss Mellish, who had been unlucky with the *fruits de mer* and whose back had gone out at Château Gaillard, was forbearing. "She's willing. Which is saying a lot these days."

Christian agreed. "Of course it's not like having you."

"That's experience, Mr. Thrale. I was just as green as that girl myself, in the beginning. The very same. We all have to begin somewhere."

Christian could have cried out for the pain of it.

Later they brought him a form to fill out, on the performance of Cordelia Ware. He wrote that she was willing; that she could take responsibility; and that her work looked neat on the page.

Grace came home, carrying a heavy suitcase and a crock of lavender honey. The two boys were empty-handed. Jeremy switched on jazz; Hugh rampaged through the house: "Where's Bimbo? I can't find Bimbo."

"Bimbo's in the trunk of the car."

All things were being brought to light, set to rights. Except Cordelia Ware. Limitless vertiginous space was contracting to a decent acreage. A place for everything and everything in its place.

Cordelia Ware was back in the pool.

Christian's situation had abruptly become a predicament. To feel for his isolation in it, one must realize that Cordelia Ware had been the only unpremeditated episode of Christian's existence since Grace Bell. Any other precipitate action having been sanctioned and demanded by the social order and—even when carried out single-handed—performed in mighty concert. In the Cordelia Ware undertaking he had ventured out on his own. It was a mutation as of fish to land. And Christian, gasping on the bleak shingle, knew himself a creature of the ocean and the shoal.

It was the point at which, in an old book, the protagonist might awake to find it all a dream.

In his solitude he said, "I blame myself." An accusation that seldom rings entirely true. If Christian placed blame elsewhere, then it was, curiously enough, on literature. He blamed—but that was not the word—the promptings and colourings of language, that put sights in his eyes and sentiments in his heart. He felt himself importuned by echoes that preceded utterance, betrayed by metaphors and exaltations that, acquired young, could never be eradicated.

Literature was a good servant but a bad master.

In the pool, Cordelia Ware sat straight at her long-carriage Underwood. Budgetary figures were being prepared: the machines hurtled violently from point to tabulated point like shuttles in a textile factory. She no longer bent intently to the page and, relieved of that anxiety, had grown proficient. The supervisor told her, "There you are. The experience has done you good."

The supervisor, who had had a nasty moment with brakes at an intersection, wore a neck-brace of foam rubber. She explained: "Whiplash."

There was no window. Cordelia looked at the wall where a window might have been.

Most of this Christian somehow and reluctantly knew. His time was not his own. Africa was tuning up: unpromising sounds rose from roofs of corrugated iron, and even from the Plexiglas civic centres, where it had been hoped that air-conditioning would lead to compromise.

Christian contrived to meet Cordelia Ware at lunchtime during the second week, in a pub rather far from the office. Although he was prompt, she was already there when he came; and if she had had the sense she was born with would not have looked so hang-dog. The weather had changed. The very mornings were now crepuscular. Everywhere there were signals of autumn, even of winter—dark afternoons, spirals of petals and blown leaves, and the miners threatening strike.

Christian put the newspaper in his raincoat pocket and sat beside Cordelia Ware. "The whole world," he cautioned her, "is going up in smoke." If only this would give her a sense of proportion. If only the tinderbox condition of the globe would obscure, minimize, or even make irrelevant his own dilemma.

"It will be a bitter winter," he announced; and she looked, looked. "If the miners go out." He could not say whether that stare was steadfast or implacable—neither being entirely desirable. "No one can deny, of course, that a miner's life is intolerable." If we lose our humanity.

She said, "People are on their side. There is that." Tepid shandies were handed over the counter, and he paid. "I mean, they are heroes. What with the risk and the pit. We all know it is frightful. In an office there is not even that."

He did not like this. "Aren't you dramatizing?"

She leaned back against the Edwardian effect of quilted plastic leather, her head frankly reclining. A young man at the bar looked at her white throat. Christian put his hand on her knee, beneath the table. Forgive me, Cordelia; and you have some cause. Her eyes at once met his: No cause. He did not understand his own irresolution—wanting now this, now that. Still less could he see why vacillation should at present seem his only virtue.

In books and films The Girl brought matters to a head. We must not meet again, this is Good-bye, Mr. Christian. Like most banality, the formula was now seen to originate in fundamentals. Cordelia Ware was evidently not about to avail herself of her unbearable and commendable prerogative.

She took up a parched sandwich whose lifting corners bared a scaled sardine. She left the tough crusts with the half-gherkin on her plate. When they went out the man at the bar looked at her openly, tenderly, ignoring Christian's claim or seeing through it.

In the street Christian said, "You had an admirer in there." He did not mean himself.

"Yes."

Having drawn the man to her attention, he was displeased to find she had seen him. In no time obviously she will take up with someone else. You iron your hair, you nickname God's creatures, go thy ways.

In the taxi she sat straight in a corner with her fingers laced on her knee. So many fingers—there must have been the right number, but it seemed a veritable lattice of fingers, fingers. Beside her, the window was pitted with sudden rain. The cab darkened. She was almost facing him from her corner, her hair the only bright thing and her eyes the colour of rain.

The window clouded like a spoiled mirror. Christian

said, "My word, it's close." He was wondering how to make his necessary separate exit from the cab in the sudden downfall; or downpour. He was wondering if after all he did not love this incomparable girl.

When she got back to the pool, the supervisor was saying, "There are not enough long carriages to go round." They might have been preparing for a state procession. Scrolls of lined paper were distributed like proclamations. "If you roll it in reverse it goes flat."

Cordelia Ware sat at her long-carriage Underwood with head bowed, as if saying Grace.

Christian, coming out of a discreetly later lift, looked about with upward head, a hound that had lost the scent. From the region of the pool, there came the sound of typewriters ticking in measured desperation: last messages from the bridge. He remembered her bitter speech: the risk and the pit.

"Back to the salt mines." It was Elphinstone, himself late from a root-canal job. They loitered. The news was ominous. Could not have come at a worse time either, what with Barger still on Mykonos and Talbot-Sims on Acromycin. Elphinstone had the latest about the secretary of state.

"Dropped a brick and lost his marbles. The Emperor Augustus, what?" Reaching the end of a corridor, they wheeled and walked slowly back, like a palace guard. "I happened to have the opportunity, as you know, of observing him at close quarters." Elphinstone had once briefly sat in the front seat of a car in which cabinet members were rear passengers. "There is, quite frankly, no discretion. None whatever."

They were at Christian's door. Yet Elphinstone detained, Elphinstone deplored. "Take it from me, Thrale. I cannot claim to have achieved much in my life. I must say. But whatever I have achieved has been by observing the rules. We cannot be too"—he began to say "careful," but substituted "scrupulous."

Whether these words were intended for Christian was debatable. And the debate engaged him throughout that afternoon. Culpability unfelt for Grace or Cordelia was, in regard to the office, deeply stirred. And what of the rising cake of Christian Thrale? Perhaps Armand meant well—

and, as an old friend, had spoken in time. Or was worse to follow?—Christian called into a room quiet with authority, a door closing, a chief saying, "Your private life, Thrale, is of course your own business," and meaning of course it was not.

> *And they cross'd themselves for fear,*
> *All the knights at Camelot.*

But he was letting imagination run away with him. Run, in fact, riot.

His offence had been so brief, to bring down this fearful retribution. It was absurd, really, if one could not have a little true love without lifelong consequences.

Reasonable speculations commuted madly, repudiated at the frontiers of belief. The most innocuous appointment became a summons to social and professional doom. He completed the day's tasks with attention wrackingly divided. Hanging like a dead weight from a strap in the Underground, he thought, This cannot go on. I am behaving like—well, like Raskolnikov.

The risk and the pit. That evening he was distraught, though he did not show it, throughout a benefit performance for which Grace had bought expensive tickets months beforehand.

Next morning there was an appalling development. Cordelia Ware appeared in his office. She stood in the entry—he later fancied she had leaned against the door-frame, but this grotesque embellishment merely reflected the dread the incident inspired.

Through a stroke of immense good fortune, Miss Mellish was not in sight. Christian got up from his desk—and it seemed that year he was ever sinking down or rising up at that desk, as at some anchorage or place of prayer. "Cordelia," he said, coming over to prevent her approach. "I cannot possibly. This is not the place for. The last thing either of us wants is."

It was hideous. From her expression she might have done anything: wailed, wept, made havoc of his draft report. He took her elbow—the sensation charged with almost clinical impersonality, as if she had been a patient in a hospital—and steered her for departure. Her very submissiveness alarmed. He was talking, talking. "We mustn't lose our. Let things get out of. This serves no useful. Cordelia do be." She had not said a word.

She went. The terrible receded, with laboured breaths, into the highly regrettable. A time and place for everything. She does not know her place. The position had already been filled.

The woman was clearly neurotic. From the outset there had been that unresolved fixation on the father. All things considered he could congratulate himself on a narrow squeak. There was no telling what she might or might not. It would be dreadful if—but that was out of the question. Only in plays. Ophelia. The awful apparition in his doorway was in retrospect suggestive of a mad scene.

Everything in disarray. The trees shredding, the shrubbery tousled with rain. The sails of Dulwich furled and the wind whistling in the shrouds. It was time to call a halt, there and then. With some difficulty, Christian arranged to meet Cordelia Ware after work. He telephoned Grace, blaming Africa. Rising at six from the launching pad of his desk, he could only remind himself, like a child, that at this time tomorrow it would all be over.

To make a long story short—which was the way Christian put it to himself in later years, in the synopsis of remembrance—he made himself clear, once and for all. There was nothing for it but the clean break. It was, as he told her, the hardest thing he had ever had to do. I blame myself. If I have hurt you, Cordelia. IF, she said; and in such a voice. If, as I say, I have hurt you. He had never seen anyone cry in a restaurant before—not even at another table. It was bizarre to think he had originally been attracted by her reserve.

He said, "I believe I have learned my lesson."

She leaned her elbow on the table and her brow on her hand. Strands of hair stuck along her cheek and trailed over her ear. In his heart, as the unconscious used to be called, he knew he had asked for trouble. But loathed every second of it.

One could only take so much of this. Attempting rational discourse, he told her of the previous evening's concert, where he had been much affronted by interruptions of untimely applause, and by the shushings that countered these. The motion of censure revived him: the world had once more proved unworthy of Christian Thrale.

He did not mention the music.

She appeared not to take these observations in. They might have been a bait to which she would not rise.

There was an instant when he saw it flash on her, that he was paltry and pathetic. He could see her take the measure of his bluster. Could see her recognize, also, that the realization had come too late, when she was already in the trap.

He thanked God he did not have the car, and took her to the train. Inevitably they had just missed one. People glanced in their direction, and away. She said, "Please go. Please." But he stuck it out to the bitter end. After all, he had been young once himself.

The following summer, Grace Thrale bore her last child and third son, who was given the name of Rupert.

Part IV

THE CULMINATION

29

In America, a white man had been shot dead in a car, and a black man on a veranda. In Russia, a novelist had emerged from hell to announce that beauty would save the world. Russian tanks rolled through Prague while America made war in Asia. In Greece the plays of Aristophanes were forbidden, in China the writings of Confucius.

On the moon, the crepe soul of modern man impressed the Mare Tranquillitatis.

On the Old World, History lay like a paralysis. In France, the generals died. In Italy a population abandoned the fields forever, to make cars or cardigans in factories; and economists called this a miracle.

Protesters with aerosol cans had sprayed Stonehenge dark red.

In London there was foul weather, and the balance of payments on the blink or brink. There were two new books, and a musical, on Burgess and Maclean: England was a dotard, repeating the single anecdote.

Paul Ivory had a new play, *Act of God*, about an Anglo-Catholic priest.

Josie Vail had thrown an assistant professor's files from a campus window. She had followed her guru to India, and lived two years at a commune in Arizona. Now preparing her doctoral dissertation on marketing techniques, she lived in Massachusetts with a sociology drop-out, younger than she, who referred to her as the Empress Josephine. His name was Burt. Together they would discuss Josie's castrating tendencies, and Burt's need for these.

"I suppose," said Una, "it was her mother's death that turned her so conventional."

271

Burt and Josie referred to their contemporaries as the kids. As exemption from action, they pleaded their youth, as if this were a disability. Josie explained that Burt was keeping his options open; not realizing that options have a season of their own.

Una said, "They're worn out with proclaiming their moral supremacy."

Una continued to shine. With the pendulum of the era, she had swung by night and by day; had shimmered in beads and sequins, when not in ragged jeans. Her name was on the letterhead of many charities, she had a house on the Vineyard and another at Puerto Vallarta. Cosmetic attention to face and figure, and to her strong, good hands, had become a ritual it might be risky to disband. There was some loneliness now to Una, and an ignored or buried vitality: in her wealthy sparkle and disused allure, she was like an abandoned mine.

Adam Vail's features had grown leaner. He had had an illness, never diagnosed. Most men become indeterminate with age, but Vail was strengthening. His patience and his energies were inexhaustible. In a crowded place, he drew sober attention, as Ted Tice might do. Yet stared at nobody, they stared at him.

Josie was kinder to her father, whom she patronized but could not recall disliking. When she came to New York she had her old room, where she sat cross-legged in front of a colour television.

"Pa doesn't look at it. I don't blame him, at his age there isn't the time. I'm young, I'm interested in everything, right?" Complacent as a matron of fifty.

Caroline Vail observed that knowledge was for some a range of topics; for others, depth of perception. She yawned at her own lie, and at the orange television. Josie was no longer young, and feared to turn thirty; she feared to work on her dissertation, lest she complete it. She feared to call things by their simple human names lest they somehow respond in kind. She did not know what to adopt in exchange for adolescence.

Now, when it no longer mattered, Caro almost loved her.

Caro said she and Adam would be away some months, in a country of South America.

Josie switched the television to another channel. "Do you have to do that?"

"There's no real risk, as yet."

"I guess not." Josie would have acknowledged, if she could, that courage can be required even where no risk is involved.

If she could, she would have touched her stepmother. But it had developed, over years, that they seldom embraced.

A man stood on a white porch and looked at the Andes. He was over fifty, white-haired, thin, with a stooping walk that suggested an orthopaedic defect, but in fact derived from beatings received in a prison. His appearance was slightly unnatural in other ways—pink, youthful lips and light, light-lashed eyes: an impression, nearly albinic, that his white suit intensified.

So many of the women eventually attracted to the poet Ramón Tregeár had experienced initial revulsion to his looks that distaste might by now seem a necessary prelude. Imprisoned in reprisal for certain writings, and released by a change of government, Tregeár had lived in the countryside two years. His city-bred person offered the polite excuses of exile. He maintained his perfect dress, that marked him out. In addition, he had done that which set him apart from the generality of men, and this had played its part in his attraction. There were women who loved him for the degradations he had undergone as much as for his having withstood these.

To have risked one's life for a principle, and survived, gave as much strength as a great renunciation.

If the present government fell, as in all likelihood it would, Tregeár would in all likelihood die—by decree, or in some necessary accident.

A woman sat on the veranda, at a table by herself. Two men talked nearby. She, not minding the exclusion, looked at the mountains, the valley. A book in her lap. She was not young, but supple, slender, with a weight of heavy hair bound at the back of her head. Youth, perhaps, had never been her strong point. Tregeár was drawn to her as he might have been, in an old photograph of famous persons, to the unidentified "friend" who stares away from the camera or bends to pat the dog. Also, women visitors were few.

He asked if he might sit beside her. She lifted a newspaper from a chair so he could put his straw hat there. Raised to him, her brow and eyes were secure and beautiful. He could not see the title of her book.

The valley, which formed a single vast paisley when seen from the air, at eye level revealed green rises and declivities. Fields, vineyards, and orchards were of every tinge and texture, tree trunks flickered like exposed stitches, watercourses slithered. The wave of growth broke at the foot of the Andes in a crest of green.

It was October, and therefore spring.

Caroline Vail sat on the veranda and said again, No, it was not like Australia. She was thinking, All these places glimpsed in transit. She could not remember who had once said to her, "Not travel, but dislocation." It might have been Adam, or Ted Tice.

Bauhinia, jacaranda were banked nearby. On a low terraced garden of flowers and shrubs, a gardener had been at work all morning. The master of the house, in a linen suit, sat at some distance on the veranda, talking to Adam Vail. Vail's stick was propped, a black stroke, on a white chair. Sheets of paper lay on a cane table between the two men, and from time to time one or the other of them would pick up a page and read carefully, before resuming the discussion. They were speaking in Spanish, and the man in linen was the freckled petitioner Caro had seen with Adam years before on a winter morning in Whitehall.

Three women lived in the house—the owner's wife and her sister, and an adolescent daughter. They did not sit on the porch with the men, though not questioning Caro's right: she was interested in justice, and therefore like a man. The three women were black-haired, high-coloured, statuesque; three rose-cheeked Latin women with pale throats and shoulders they protected from the sun, bodies for shuttered afternoons and cool evenings, bodies soft as the soft beds where they lay. They were physically distinct from the servants, who were Andean Indians.

In her own setting, Mrs. Vail would be considered dark. Such were the illusions of context. There might be places

—Ethiopia, Bali—where Latin women similarly blanched.

As visitors were few, Tregeár sat beside her and said, "I never supposed my life would turn on these matters"—meaning the discussion at the other table. "Nor, I suppose, did you."

"Well," she said, "I am not surprised." She dropped the newspaper on the ground. "Yet I can't think that all the rest—what went before and still goes on—has been unimportant."

"On the contrary. The rest is the reality that has a right to happen. Any proper struggle against injustice is an access, merely, for a more normal confusion. For myself, there's nothing I'd like better than to go back to squabbling about usual things."

It seemed hard, all the same, that such a man might have to die so that Dora, or Clive Leadbetter, could waste the world's time.

Caro asked if he could not leave the country before the government fell. He gave no answer, but after a time said, "Vicente has compromised himself for me."

The woman looked over at the freckled landowner at the cane table, to observe his virtue. "He's on the right side."

"Better than that, he has no side. Even a right side imposes wrongful silences, required untruths. As the timid say, there is strength, or safety, in numbers; but solidarity is an extension of power, that is, the beginning of the lie. The only proper solidarity is with the truth, if one can discover it." Tregeár still smiled. It was the smile of a primitive, having little to do with what was said. "In any group there are masters and followers. Even the right side rather dislikes a man who stands alone."

Long ago, Valda had said, "It's the uncommon man who gets everyone's goat."

"Vicente is also brave because I'm not a famous man. For most people it's easier to support an eminent person in deserved disgrace than an obscure one who has been wronged."

Caro sat beside this obscure man who had risked himself and lived to tell, offhandedly, the tale. She said, "There are those, too, who befriend the weak because they feel themselves unworthy of the strong. Because they cannot bring themselves to honour abilities greater than their own." But who are the weak, she was wondering; who are the strong? This man had actually displayed the heroism most people confine to their fantasies. He had left nothing, in his nature, to be resisted or exposed. Because of him, one could look on the green vega as a place where one man at least had earned a right to be.

She said, "There are many, too, who don't mind being wronged."

"One of our poets said, 'Disorder also holds its charm.'" His enunciation gave immortality, as slow motion makes any human action beautiful by an appearance of control. "'El desorden,'" he said, "'también tiene su encanto.'" He took his straw hat from the chair, and smiled. "Will you see the garden?"

The sun was already high. Man and woman walked into the garden. Caro turned to look back at Adam, who lifted his hand and watched her light-blue descent into the flowers with the repulsive, stooping hero. Through the cotton dress you could see the shape of her legs moving, like limbs of a swimmer.

An old, chained dog lay in a patch of shade, lolling tongue, swaying tail: a lapped old boat, weathered and tethered in a calm port.

There was a wall where different jasmines had been trained up, one or two of them already in bloom. Tregeár reached for a frond of flowers, while the gardener paused to watch. Petals shook from blue sky. "Gardeners and librarians hate to see their charges put to use." Ramón Tregeár showed the Spanish jasmine, Cape jasmine, jasmine from the Azores. There was a huge plant in a terra-cotta tub. "That's Florentine. Il gelsomino del Granduca. One of the Medici, the Grand Duke Cosimo, imported it into Italy from Goa, where he sent expeditions for tropical plants. They all came from India, or Persia, if you go back far enough."

On such a morning you might love the white-flowering earth as if you, or it, were soon to die. Left to herself, Caroline Vail might have run through fields or gardens.

A boy came through cypresses holding a tennis racquet

to his face. Squinted at them through the mesh. A smaller child toddled behind, calling out "Andrés." Below the trees, the garden ended at a small *barranca*. Man and woman turned their backs on the landscape and followed the children up the path, up the steps. The boy held up his mask, like a fencer. The dog lay on its side, a grey rock now, yellowed with age or lichen. On the woman's hair and shoulder, white petals clung like flakes from a defective ceiling.

At night in her soft strange bed, Mrs. Vail dreamed of flying over mountains and coming at last, not to this fertile valley but to a long flat land, an arid interior, boundless. Far below, occasional oblongs and squares of difficult cultivation tilted like paintings askew on a blank wall. Small depressions were neuritic with cracked mud. From this she woke in relief that she had done nothing wrong, at least in the dream.

In the morning she wrote to Ted Tice:

Your letter came as we were leaving. How sad to miss you this time. After some adventures, of the flesh rather than the spirit, we are among friends in a beautiful place where the earth is still supreme. There's a poet here who has been imprisoned and tortured for writing truth. Two years ago he was released. When this new government falls, it will be all over with him. He is old at fifty, his skin colourless, his bones awry. He walks like an athlete who has had an accident—perhaps a tightrope walker who had a fall performing without the net. His voice is beautiful. His poems are very good. I am going to try to translate some of his work.

She might have closed the letter, but kept the pen in her hand and eventually wrote

Dear Ted, I am content. Yet even in this silent place there's the foreboding roar. As if a jet plane passed over paradise.

Adam Vail came to where his wife sat writing and put his hand to her neck, beneath her hair. When she leaned on him, he moved his hand forward over her throat, into her dress. He said, "You might tire of this life, and leave me."

"I can't believe my ears."

30

"I like this eclecticness. Most eclecticness is too dark."

"I'm glad." Ted was lying with his eyes closed and, when she asked, "What's that picture?" he answered without opening them. "It's a mandatory group of sunflowers. No hotel can be licensed without hanging one in every room. Like listing the charges on the back of the door."

"You're putting me on. I like this hotel though, it's the best. On the lake too."

He would not spoil her prestige by saying the room was space rather than a room, it was geometry on a floor-plan. On one side, two windows exposed the lake, itself frozen grey like a dirty window. Melted splotches of lake were lathered by drifting ice. A wind ripped into the building day and night, walloping these encrusted windows as if beating rugs.

"Most of us work indoors at the center, the girls I mean. I mean, without windows. Getting assigned to the conference was like coming up for air or something."

It would be only polite to ask about herself, her life, her parents. Social obligation weighted Ted Tice as he lay with one arm about her naked shoulders, for he did not want her to come alive with longings and belongings of her own, or to add to his consciousness the details of one more life. Until she spoke of these things, she would remain typical, a random sample; once she mentioned them, she would, however typical, become singular. But he fatally began, "How does it happen that you . . ." opening his eyes and seeing, of a darkened room, only the ceiling on which an unlit fixture hovered, and the wall with the jagged picture,

279

and the top of the pea-green chair on which she'd draped her clothes.

His misery in that place had all been typical, a random sample. The city was cursed with sleazy inevitability—the most sombre thoughts acquired a picked-over character, and pleasure came ready-mixed for quick satiety. He had brought a girl to the hotel because the city expected it of him: loneliness had been industrialized. Yet fornication itself was very solitude. When he thought, here, of his wife and children and his own rooms, they seemed like health, and he could not feel that was banal. And when he invoked the presence of Caro it was to pit her strength against a city, or the world.

". . . and after that happened I realized, uh, I was mixed up with negative things like needs. I mean"—her arm wheeled in darkness, palm outward—"I was too involved, right?" Her spread hair, raised knee, and the outline of brow and breast were lovely: they almost made the room come alive out of its floor-plan. How lucky she is, he thought, to have got away with it. With features like hers she might have been sensitive. A generation earlier and this episode would have had to mean something to her. She would even have had to pretend it meant something to me. That deception is the one thing we are being spared.

"We've all got our personal hang-ups. You married, right?"

"Yes." This question, which she was more than entitled to ask, called for more than a frigid affirmative, yet would not bear enlargement. "Englishmen don't wear wedding-rings."

"That's what I heard." She took his hand and felt the fingers, then unexpectedly put it to her lips. "You're nice. Know that?"

"I don't think you've had much evidence of it."

"No, you're nice." And mechanically, "Great." She laid his hand on her young and beautiful breast and after a while said, "Happily married, right?"

"Yes," he said, feeling the absurdity of the answer in the circumstances but once more wishing to be let off. "This is very nice, but I don't do a lot of it." Everything he said was stale, sententious. He spoke to her from the lofty height of his all but continuous virtue.

"Ever loved anyone besides your wife?"

"Long ago. Before I was married." Caro had become the long ago, the legend.

"Oh— That doesn't count."

"Yes. It does count."

"It counts?"

"It counts." Inanely. How one shows one's weakness, I am like those people—not like, I *am* one of them—who must talk about what obsesses them, their lover, child, cat, dog, enemy, employer, servant, office—even while aware they are boring others and exposing themselves. The craving is compulsive in that respect, virtually erotic. "Perhaps it is the only thing that counts."

"Wow."

Possibly she felt her role too plainly signalled, for she soon got up and carried off some of her clothes. Water gushed in an uproar of plumbing, a tin cupboard clanged, there were twin puffs of a deodorant. When she came out of the bathroom, hands to her golden hair, Ted was half-dressed and thinking there was nothing more melancholy than doing up a zipper at one A.M.

He knew she was going to say more about Caro. It was the only interesting thing that had passed between them.

"Listen," she said. "We relate. We communicate. Wouldn't you say we communicate?"

We also, then, are part of the floor-plan: two rooms with a connecting door, of lust or loneliness. Ted sat on the edge of the bed. "Come here."

She stood with her palms on his shoulders, meeting his eyes in the half-dark. A good-natured dog that comes and puts its paws on you and looks wtih God knows what, if anything, in mind. But she said, "Do you ever see her?" with a rational, crucial lowering of tone, as if the jargon— which she had employed even in the act—was, for her too, an affectation to be set aside for the authentic.

"About twice a year."

"Still sleep with her?"

"I have never slept with her." Proclaiming this with grotesque pride, for it gave the scale of his devotion. And the girl said, "Fantastic," and seemed properly awed— though perhaps thinking also, Some kind of a nut.

"She'd be about your age, right?"

"A few years younger."

The girl signified that, by that stage, three or four years could scarcely matter. She said, "You should—"

"Should what?"

"Well— You only live once, for Christ's sake."

This girl was assuming that Caro loved him. Ted put her away from him and stood up, saying "We'd better get you a taxi," before the truth could strike her.

31

Adam and Caro returned to New York from South America during a heat wave. There was a demonstration against war. At the end of their street a row of grey trestles was guarded by two policemen on reddish horses, and by other police on foot. There was the smell of blistering tar and the sweat of horse and man. The street was cracked, the gutters unkempt. Trees had been hacked at, or were diseased. The Vails' door, which now had a complex lock, could be relocked from the inside, then chained and bolted. All of this took time. When they put their bags down in the hallway, Vail turned on the radio, which said, "Non-ferrous metals declined and cotton futures closed higher." They could hear the mounted police speaking by machine and, beyond the barrier, the neutral wail of an ambulance. In the locked house man and woman embraced, because a measure of safety can be attained under almost any circumstances.

Letters were stacked on a table. A folded newspaper half-disclosed a presidential scandal: "It's an outrage," said a Harvard professor who asked not to be identified. Dora wrote from Palmerston North that she would never forgive Trish Bootle as long as she lived; and was seriously considering Ireland.

"At her age," said Caro. "To go where nothing is familiar."

Adam told her, "Seneca said of Hannibal—who in old age offered his services to any king at war with Rome—

that he could live without a country but not without an enemy."

Caro could see the epitaph tilting in Irish grass.

In the mornings Caro sat at a table to translate the work of Ramón Tregeár. These poems had been invented in a prison. When the poet wrote her, "But then I held it only in the head," she thought of Rex Ivory digging graves in Malaya thirty years before. As Rex Ivory in the death camp had celebrated Derbyshire, so Tregeár in his prison hell had recalled the love of women.

Tregeár said he would soon send the remaining pages if things went well. And she wondered if she would ever see them. The volume would be called "Luz a Medianoche."

After some months a publisher returned her sample pages, explaining about the market. He noted the Miltonian title; and made a literary joke on the translator's name: "C. Bell." Another publisher, who had issued an academic study of dissident literature, returned the manuscript with a comment on the Koestlerian title; adding, "We rather feel we've done our pro bono publico stint for this year."

Adam Vail spoke in Spanish on the telephone. He went across town to be interviewed on television, and was introduced to the network's news chief, who said, "We think we're pretty gutsy, Adam, to be running this interview."

Caro, who went with Adam to the studio, was shown to a darkened room where, it was said, the picture would be clear on a large screen. She sat waiting in a velvet seat, and three men came in and sat in front of her. She had seen them in the corridor, carefully dressed men with dyed hair and tinted contact lenses. Not knowing she was there, they remarked that altruists rarely gave good value.

"You need only look at Stevenson."

"Stevenson. He went into orbit the last years. Committed one day, uncommitted the next. Maybe he really believed there was this peace proposal, so he clung on."

"I think he fell for it, that there was this peace proposal. I believe he died convinced. That if you could get Bundy and Rusk to a dacha outside Rangoon, Hanoi would deliver the goods."

"He couldn't get through to the White House though. Rusk stopped him."

"What was to stop him picking up the phone, Chrissake, dialling the White House? How long did he think this?"

"Autumn of sixty-four."

"No, I say June of sixty-five. And he was dead in July. One month then."

"Sixty-four. Who knew from nothing in sixty-four? Least of all our news service."

"I'll never forget, we did a programme on Stevenson. When he died. Embarrassing thing to replay now—not that it's gonna get replayed, like hell replayed. Jesus it was like nothing—some shots, the first convention, the second campaign. Speeches, puns, Stevenson conceding. Conceding, Jesus, conceding all right. A nothing programme. Not a word about Kennedy, about Vietnam."

"What about the Bay of Pigs?"

"I'm telling you, nothing. All right, I ran it, all right so I'm wearing a hair shirt. But we showed nothing. When the programme was over someone came in with the word, Washington on the line, the White House is very pleased. You bet they were pleased—God when I think of it now, the sigh of relief that must've gone up. Not a word about Kennedy, the war, nothing."

"Kennedy, that's what we're talking about—Vietnam, the sixteen thousand. The Bay of Pigs. Face it. The Bay of Pigs. Any idea if this crackpot, this Vail's gonna bring up the Bay of Pigs?"

"Remember the crackpots that used to borrow money from Ed. Remember they used to come round his office, Ed I got this story, Ed lend me ten bucks. Well there was this one little guy, Ed said maybe there's something in it, Sam you go down to Florida with him. Sam came back, God Ed what a nut. This nut thinks Kennedy's gonna *invade* Cuba. This time you bought it Ed, Jesus what a nut."

"He didn't believe it?"

"Well he thought, God if this is true, so he couldn't believe it. Afterwards—"

"But we couldnt've run that story anyway, it would've been treason."

"Still I always wondered, why didn't the press, they had that story, the whole Bay of Pigs bit."

"Theyd've been crucified, they couldnt've run it."

"But you know what Kennedy told them later, If you'd run it."

"Sure, if you'd run it you might have stopped me."

"*Saved* me. You might've saved me. That's what he said, If you'd run it you might've saved me."

"Kennedy, that's what we're talking about. Vietnam, the sixteen thousand."

"More than that. The appointments. Dean Rusk, Mac Bundy, McNamara."

"Lyndon *John*son."

"Johnson thought it was Korea."

"Johnson thought it was the Alamo."

"Munich is what he kept saying. Christ Munich. Where they been."

"We gonna teach them this lesson. Little brown men, this lesson. That's what they were saying, and that's why you'd never have got them to the dacha outside Rangoon. Mac Bundy at that dacha, don't make me laugh."

"So who we gonna accuse? Who are they? The Pentagon? Would it be Westmoreland, Abrams, Walt?"

"Christ Walt. He's the one who told me, you could find yourself shot in the back. That was Cam Ne, that wasn't even My Lai, it was Cam Ne and I said where *are* these people, a whole town disappeared, where are the people. They been relocated, he said looking in his milk, they're in refugee camps, been dispersed. It turned out the U.S. army didn't go in at all, it got handed over to the South Vietnamese, they had it on their list along with other hamlets that hadn't paid their dues, oh jesus oh god. Waste them, that was the terminology, waste them. So who you gonna accuse, finally would it be Rusk and Johnson, wouldn't it be them, wouldn't that be logical? Put them in the dock? Imagine."

"At the end Rusk kept going on aspirins and alcohol."

"I didn't know about the aspirins."

"Cambodia Laos, they make Vietnam academic. Better face it. South Vietnam's got an eastern seacoast, that's the only reason they need it now. Once they surround it, once they're in Cambodia Laos, what do they care. You can't get a story on Laos. Well hell you get a lot of stories but it's a realm of myth situation. Who's gonna risk their neck, you can't ask correspondents to risk their neck, what American's gonna die there except a lot of pilots we're not allowed to mention. Aside from one or two of them those are second-string correspondents in Laos Cambodia anyway, there's an information gap, everyone knows it, you can't find out what goes on."

"This is bouncing it off another cushion. Are we talking about what we can't get a lead on or about what we don't have the guts to report?"

"Look I can put on thirty-three stories about a mail strike in Italy or Princess Margaret Jones easier than run one on Cambodia Laos. Then there's risk, what about risk, it's your word against theirs, Washington comes in strong, it didn't happen. Says it didn't happen, what you gonna do?"

"Yeah look at San Jose. Nixon said worst violence he'd ever seen, holes in the car, rocks, people were throwing rocks, Agnew said it, they all said it. Worse than war. By Monday they were saying like it was mostly verbal violence. Then after the vote, maybe there wasn't any violence. No indictments, nothing. Supposing I ran a story that night, supposing I said election gimmick. Supposing I said the president is lying, is LYING, you want to imagine what they do to me. Nobody's gonna take that kind of risk."

"Maybe that's what's wrong. Maybe that's why television."

"Not just the government, not the government even. Can you imagine the calls, can you imagine. And not the viewers even. The calls from the ownership, from the brass."

"I'm saying maybe that's what's—"

"But if everyone ran it. Let me finish. If you got all the newscasters, if you got the lot. Hopefully."

"Anyway what good would—a week later, so who'd care—he lied, so he lied. Teddy lied, Henry lied, Laird lied, Helms lied, Nixon lied his ass off, George Washington swore he didn't chop down the goddamn cherry tree, so who in hell cares one week later."

"Care like hell in election year."

"Not about war. War isn't an election issue. We gave

them the longest chance, Nixon'll say. Winding it down, pulling it out, not our fault. Peace is at hand, okay? Look at the kids—the frenzy died with the draft card, with the risk to their own skins. The economy, the dollar, the buck. That's what election year's about, the buck."

"Honor. If I can finish. Honor of the United States. You don't get me, I'm serious. Honor's as good a gimmick as any other. That's what Nixon could do. Put it in the lap of the public, I'm standing on principle, I'm stopping the war. Leaving. Now. Put it up to the world, *you* defend the gooks, okay? You rassle up that goddamn dacha outside Rangoon."

"No one can propose that. No one has the influence."

"The president. No one else has the influence."

"What about the influence in this room. The collective influence."

"We now pause for the underarm commercial."

"I mean it. The collective influence."

"Anyhow, here it comes, here's the picture. Altruists always have some axe to grind. Remember we needn't run this in full."

The next morning an editorial appeared in a leading newspaper:

Mr. Adam Vail did a clever job in his television interview last night of depicting "serious aggression" practiced by giant American corporations in Latin America with, as he claimed, the connivance and covert support of the United States Government. He will draw enthusiastic if automatic applause from irresponsible elements in our divided society. At times, Washington may have acted clumsily in Latin America, but Mr. Vail wielded his verbal brush far too broadly when he suggested that clandestine efforts from the United States Government would insure, as he put it, that at least one elected Latin leader would "not get through the crucial next six months." His worst distortion was his assertion that intimidation of voters had in some areas been carried out with funds from official United States sources. There was an element of dangerous misrepresentation in Mr. Vail's remarks, of which his television audience should be aware.

Adam put the paper down and said, "I never like to see government spelt with a large G."

Before his arrest, Ramón Tregeár gave the remaining section of his manuscript to a friend who was leaving the country. When the pages were delivered to Caroline Vail, she found a note among them, addressed to herself: "If my death is spectacular, you will be able to publish these. People are inclined to rush to the scene of the crime, or accident." A young man who brought the envelope told them Tregeár had been imprisoned on an island off the coast of South America, in conditions not conducive to survival. At the end of the year it was learned he had been brought back to the mainland in failing health, and had died at a prison in the capital. It was the freckled Vicente who wrote this news to them from Mexico, adding, "He led captivity captive."

"And ascended," Adam said. "Having first descended into the lower parts of the earth."

The story of Tregeár's death, when disclosed, was atrocious. And, as he had predicted, resulted in a favourable reception for his work outside his native land, and its clandestine distribution in the city of his birth where, in former years, he had had few readers.

32

"Are you glad to be home?"

Margaret had never asked that question before. She stood at an open suitcase, sorting what should be hung from what must be washed, disposing of shirts and shoe-trees. She flung a dressing-gown on a bed. While Ted Tice, too, spread socks and ties about like regalia, saying, "It's not a return, it's a resurrection."

"I'm not even sure, this time, what countries you've been to."

"Nor I, at this moment." But for the decorum of unpacking, which made things proceed by stages, he would have made love to her there and then. Had she been his mistress, he would have drawn her down on the bed. In its way, marriage imposes formalities.

Ted Tice had driven through London early that morning on the top of an airport bus, skimming trees and chimneys and making top-heavy arcs round corner pubs. He had peered, like God, into backyards of hawthorn and clothes-lines; and through an attic window had glimpsed a tousled bed. At an open doorway, he had seen fresh sunlight on parquet and the tall, engrossed figure of an elderly woman reading her letters. A black cat crawled out between lace curtains to settle, loaf-shape, on a sill. A man with a cap on the back of his head and a gold watch on his wrist hosed a footpath in the Fulham Road. All this could be normality—unless what he had left, the feature-less world of airports and installations, was normality now, while these rational human scenes dwindled to anachronism.

The last segment of his journey was the best: he had

never enjoyed a train trip so much, taking conscious pleasure in familiar irritations of grime and delay. His very fatigue gave sensations of well-being, for he would doze, and wake over and over to the luxury of reassurance. His present greeting to his homeland was excessive, for his having undervalued it before. A note of apology ran, too, through that morning's praise of his entire domestic district.

"Listen, before I forget—"

"These are for the children, can you put them somewhere?"

"Oh yes, how sweet. Your letters are on the desk, I've done the bills."

"Anything interesting?"

"You'll have to see. I opened a telegram, but it was nothing. There are a few newspaper clippings about the ring-road. Did you see yesterday's paper, that man you knew in America died?"

"Vendler, was it? I heard he was near the end."

"Yes, I think that's the name. We can have tea in the garden."

"Shall I carry that stuff down?"

"Thanks, I can manage."

Ted went to turn the bath on, then walked through the bathroom into his study. A congenial gloom of curtains closed, of table, chair and pencils in abeyance; the desk an altar on which paper offerings had been laid for his safe return. It was an archaeological instant, he could tell how the room was without him: the moment of living entry into a tomb.

He had got into his head a phrase of piped-in music from the plane and began to hum as he stood over his letters, his loosened tie dangling forward. The mail was divided into professional and private, there was also a pile with circulars, clippings, appeals, and a folded magazine marked in red. Long expected, the death of Vendler was still a blow. There was no telling who would win in a wretched little struggle that must now take place for that position, or how the work would meantime be carried on.

Ted remembered he had liked Vendler the man, and was conscious that this came as an afterthought. He would write the widow with particular kindness, to clear himself of any taint, or suspicion, of heartlessness.

It was not Vendler who had died.

Dies in America. Suddenly at his home after an active career marked by and culminating in, considered aloof, nevertheless loyal friends such as, recently awarded, travelled, resided, founded, collected. Married twice: first, and then to the former . . . One daughter from his first union.

Had suffered a stroke. Dead and gone, at one stroke. Peacefully. Adam Vail lay at peace on a bed, his sword-stick at rest, or impotent, in a closet.

The scientist Vendler was alive, reprieved: still useful and likable. It was to Caroline Vail that Edmund Tice would write with particular kindness.

And the former Caroline Bell, where was she now? Where did one write, to express shock and sympathy? The shock real enough, he could scarcely focus on words or objects. A glass paperweight rose and fell, pounding with the dim room and the darkened self in the mirror on the open bathroom door. Ted Tice had never fainted in his life, but now supported himself with his palms on the desk.

The bath was full and had started overflowing into a chromium outlet below the taps. He went and turned it off and, in relieving that minor emergency, felt some easing in himself. When the churning and gushing stopped there was a subsiding, also, of the flow and overflow of realization. The mirror showed, merely, a glaze of feelings, not all of them shameful or shameless: he had never found a mirror, or words in the mind, to reflect the power or pain of his obsession.

He returned to his study and replaced the clipping as it had been. He would be seen to have changed: his mood of the morning could not be re-created, they had seen the last of that. He should not be known to have touched the table in the meantime. The morning had been a mood of premature rejoicing—hours in which he had forgotten Caro, and been free.

His hands were trembling terribly. He had often thought his love might be madness.

When he had bathed and dressed he went downstairs and into the garden. The tea-tray was on a table in the shade. His wife came out of the house with a ginger cat in her arms and stood in the sun, awaiting her cue. The grass was slightly overgrown, the flowers so delicately blurred in tangled colours you might have thought they'd been let go wild. It was the sort of garden Margaret loved; she planned it all. Ted had often praised it, except for one wall, where she had planted small bushes, each of them different. Once he had said, "That's too calculated. It looks dispassionate." She thought it a strange criticism for such a man to make.

She had an excellent carriage, which made her tall. She was always the same, calm, distinguished; innocent, except insofar as the hurt had made her otherwise. Her hair was very light, and shone in fine little curls in the sun. Eyes large and blue, not unquestioning. As she came forward she put her face to the cat's fur, offering the caress her husband might decline.

She shifted the cat in her arms, since it seemed to expect something more. Ted stood in the shade, by the table. They were quiet, facing each other: not united, not opposed.

He said, "If you knew your beauty."

Even the cat listened. Margaret said, "If I did, what then?"

"You'd set the world swinging."

They knew he meant, You would find a man who truly loved you.

33

When Rupert Thrale was thirteen and had trouble with his back, his mother took him to a new hospital across the river. After the X-rays had been studied, it was again Grace Thrale who sat beside him in a waiting room while he turned pages of a book on marsupials and tested a loose green rubber tile with the toe of his school boot. When, at the name of Thrale, they got up together to be shown to a doctor's empty office, they walked with arms touching. And, as they sat alone beside a desk, Grace leaned forward out of her anxiety and kissed the boy; and the door opened.

The man who came in saw the mother bending forward, her arm extended on a chair back, her throat curved in helpless solicitude, her lips on her son's hair which palely mingled with her own. In the next instant she turned and looked. And Rupert, getting to his feet, disowned her caress.

What Grace Thrale saw was a solid man of about thirty in Nordic colours—high-complexioned, blue-eyed, bright-haired, and dressed in white—standing at an open door.

The tableau was brief; but even the boy remembered it.

The three of them sat at the desk, and the young doctor said, "Don't worry." He put a row of photographs up on a metal rack and lit them: the notched segments, the costal arcs, the grey knuckled frame of a bare existence with its deathly omen. "These are what we call the dorsal verte-brae." He pointed with a pencil. And Grace Thrale looked at her son's mortality—all the respiring tissue blazed away, all that was mobile or slept, could resent or relish. It was as if she stared at an ossified remnant in a child's grave.

There was to be a corrective operation—which was delicate, infrequently performed, and involved a rod of stainless steel. It did not affect growth. "You'll be better than new, I promise." The Doctor addressed himself in this way to the boy, without heartiness, in a low clear voice and slight Scots accent, including the mother by a filament of experience that was almost tender. His face, in its revealing colour and kindness, might in another era have been beautiful. His hair glowed, gold enough to be red.

When they were leaving, he told Grace she should make an appointment to come with her husband. "We should talk it over with the surgeon."

Christian Thrale was about his country's business, conferring at Dar es Salaam. Grace would come alone on Thursday.

At the door there was a projecting sign: Angus Dance, M.D.

On Thursday he lit the photographs and showed with the pencil. He said it was tricky but would be all right. They had the best man in London to do the job. Grace Thrale sat side by side with Angus Dance to look at the plates, and, handling one of them, left a tremulous print of humid fingers. When the surgeon arrived, Dance got up and stood in the sun by the window, where he was white and gold, a seraph, a streak of flame.

Grace told him her husband was coming home, to be present for the operation.

"You'll be seeing my colleague. I'll be on leave that week." He saw she was disturbed. "Just for a few days." When the surgeon left them, Dance sat to fill out his portion of a form. He told her he was going to his parents' house, near Inverness.

"What's Inverness like these days?"

"Oh—like everywhere—full of Japanese." Reading over the form, he said, "We're neighbours. I see you're in the Crescent. I live around the corner, in the place that's painted blue."

They agreed they did not like the shade. Grace said she often walked past the building, taking the shortcut through the brick passage—which, originally reserved for pedestrians, was now abused. She knew he said conventional things to calm her; and was calmed by his humane intention.

The Doctor said, "Rupert will run me down there one day on his bike and I'll be a cot case." He gave her back the form and touched her sleeve. "You'll be anxious. But there is no need."

The operation went so well that Christian Thrale was back at Dar es Salaam in a matter of days. The boy would be in hospital a month or so. Grace came every morning and afternoon, bringing comic books, a jigsaw, clean pyjamas. There was a cafeteria where she had lunch.

"How was Inverness?"

Doctor Dance was carrying a tray. "The gateway to the Orient. I'm glad Rupert's doing so well." His upright body gave a broad impression, both forcible and grave. He had short muscular arms, on which the hair would be red.

They sat down together and Grace conveyed Christian's gratitude all the way from Tanzania, even bringing out a letter. Relief gushed from her in forms of praise: the nurses were so kind, the surgeon, the therapist from Karachi. Sister Hubbard was a saint, and Rupert would be spoiled beyond repair. She then said, "Well—why should you hear this in your time off."

Her light hair was sculptured down from a central parting and fell in wings over her ears. Once in a while she would touch it, a ring glinting on her raised hand. Her nails were of a housewifely length, unvarnished. "What about your journey?"

He said he always took the train. His parents lived an isolated life, but now had the telly. The house, which was in the Black Isle, was always cold, not only from heatlessness but from austerity. "They like it bare. Predictably enough, my sister and I tend to clutter." There was only one picture in the house: "A framed photograph of the *Tirpitz,* which was sunk the day I was born. Or at least the news came that forenoon that they had sunk it." His sister was also a doctor, and lived in Edinburgh.

Grace pictured the old crofters in the stark house uttering monosyllables like aye and wee and yon; the maiden sister, a ruddy, tweedy pediatrician called, in all likelihood, Jean. "They must miss the two of you."

"My father still does consultant work. He's an engineer. Then, I run up fairly regularly. And Colette is going to them for Easter. It's really harder for her, since she's married, with a family."

That evening Grace asked at a dinner party, "Does anyone remember what year we sank the *Tirpitz?*"

It happened that Grace Thrale and Doctor Dance spoke every day. There were the X-rays to light up and look at—each of these tinged with the bloom of deliverance; there was Rupert's bedside, there were the corridors and the cafeteria. Once they stayed ten minutes talking on a stair. They soon dispatched the neighbourhood topics—the abused brick passage, the hideous new hotel nearby that took groups—and Grace found out that Angus Dance was divorced from a student marriage, voted Liberal, had spent a year in Colombia on an exchange programme, and kept a small sailing boat at Burnham-on-Crouch. He had done prison visiting at Wormwood Scrubs, but now lacked the time. One day he had a book on his desk, about the Brontës.

Mentioning his marriage, he said, "Young people aren't doing that so much now." Younger than she, he already considered himself an elder.

Grace told him how her parents had died in the wreck of an Australian ferry when she was a child. Next—so it seemed, as she came to relate it—there had been Christian. Recounting these things, she felt her story was undeveloped, without event. Years were missing, as from amnesia, and the only influential action of her life had been the common one of giving birth. The accidental foundering of her parents had remained larger than any conscious exploit of her own, and was still her only way to cause a stir.

This vacancy might have affected growth. Compared with his variousness, she was fixed, terrestrial; land-locked, in contrast to his open sea.

These exchanges with Doctor Dance were Grace Thrale's first conversations. With Caro, there had been inarticulate union: the childhood silence on a Sydney beach. With Christian there was the office, there were the three boys, there were the patterns and crises of domestic days. She had not often said, "I believe," "I feel"; nor had felt the lack. Now beliefs and feelings grew delightful to her, and multiplied. Between visits to the hospital she rehearsed them. She held imaginary discourse with Angus Dance, phantasmal exchanges in which Grace was not ashamed to shine. There was a compulsion to divulge, to explain herself, to tell the simple truth. The times when she actually sat by him and looked at X-ray plates generated a mutual kindliness that was the very proof of human perfectibility. After these occasions there was consciousness of exertion —a good strain such as the body might feel from healthful, unaccustomed action.

One day, passing a paper from hand to hand, their fingers touched; and that was all.

"I suppose," said Grace Thrale, "that Angus was always a Scots name."

"It's a version of Aeneas."

She could not recall what Aeneas had done, and thought it better not to ask.

He was changing her. She wished more than anything to match his different level of goodness—his sensibility that was precise as an instrument, yet with a natural accuracy; his good humour that was a form of generosity; his slight and proper melancholy. It was virtue she most desired from him, as if it were an honour he could confer. He could make an honest woman of her.

The bare facts of Grace Thrale's love, if enumerated, would have appeared familiar, pitiful, and—to some—even comical. Of this, she herself was conscious. It was the sweetness that was unaccountable.

Because the condition struck her as inborn, she raked her experience for precedent. She dwelt on a man she had known long ago in London, before her marriage—a moody schoolteacher who often broke appointments or came late, and over whom she had suffered throughout a cold summer. Only the year before, she had heard he was now a headmaster in Dorset, and had looked up his name in the telephone directory. He provided no prologue to Angus Dance. In contrast to the schoolteacher, on the other hand, Christian had appeared a model of consideration, a responsible lover whose punctuality had from the start prefigured matrimony. Angus Dance had no precursor.

Grace put the end of a pen between her lips. Hugh, her middle son, said, "Why do you look that way?"

"I'm thinking what to tell Daddy."

At night she was alone with Angus Dance when she lay down solitary in the dark with her arm half-clasped about her body. She thought that Christian would soon return from Dar es Salaam. The knowledge that he would at once make love to her brought mere acceptance.

The week after Rupert came home from hospital, Mrs. Thrale ran into Doctor Dance in the street. They met at a site of road repairs, and could hardly hear each other for the electric drill. Grace stared at his clear, hectic skin and tawny head, his noonday colours, while concrete particles exploded and the pavement thrilled. Consciousness shivered also, on some inward Richter scale.

"Let's get out of this." Dance went through a motion of taking her elbow but did not in fact do so. They were both going to the cake shop, and agreed that the woman there was grumpy but the croissants good. When they crossed at the corner Grace said, "We all miss you." She heard this speech turn coy with trepidation, and a little tic started up in her cheek. He smiled. "Now, that's going too far." But added, "I miss you all too." Saying "all" both made it possible and detracted: a pact, scrupulously observed.

In the shop Grace had to wait for the seedcake. Angus Dance shook hands. "Doctors are always overdue somewhere. I hope we meet again."

When he had gone out, the grim woman behind the counter said, "So he's a doctor is he. He has a lovely face."

When Christian praised the seedcake, Grace said, "I got it from that nice woman at the corner."

Every spring the Thrales gave a party—drinks and little things to eat. They called this decorous event "our smash." Grace went over her question in silence: I would like to invite that young doctor. We might ask Rupert's doctor, who lives practically next door. What about asking that Doctor Dance, who was super with Rupert?

To the question as ultimately phrased, Christian responded, "Good idea." He had it in mind to ask someone very senior from his department, and supposed a doctor would mix.

Grace telephoned the hospital. Dance knew her voice: "Hello." He did not say Mrs. Thrale, and had never done so. He wrote the date of the party, and six to eight. "Is it a special occasion?"

"It's my birthday. Not that we tell people."

She had a new dress that displayed her breasts. Christian said, "Isn't it a bit bare?" He traced the outline of black silk with his fingers on her flesh. "Happy birthday, Grace darling."

Although they had a couple from Jamaica to do the drinks, it was Grace who opened the door to Angus Dance. Before entering, he bent and kissed her cheek, murmuring "Birthday." He gave her a little packet, which was later found to contain lavender water. Grace trembled under the astonishing kiss, from which she turned away with the male impress of jacket indelible on her silk and female arms. When Christian came over from the foot of the stairs, discarding his party face for the serious theme of Rupert, she moved back into the curve of the piano, where Dance soon joined her.

"Who plays?"

"I do." For once she did not add, "My sole accomplishment." He leaned to look at stacked music. She had put the Chopin on top to impress. She saw him turn the sheets with deliberate, large hands; she watched his almost spiritual face. Authority had passed from him in this amateur setting, and his youth was a blow, a disappointment. Authority had in fact passed to her. She presided, a matron, over her household, her associates, her charming children: mistress of the situation.

She did not know how to address him now that he was disestablished. At the hospital the nurses had called him Doctor, as women with a family will call their own husbands Father—or Daddy.

They spoke about the community centre, and Grace told him the art show would open on Sunday. Dance said, "I might look in."

Rupert appeared with Dance's whisky, and other guests were introduced. In an oval mirror they had bought at Bath she saw the room, tame with floral charm and carpeted, like England, wall to wall in green. And herself, in this field of flowers—practically indistinguishable from cushions and curtains, and from ornaments that, lacking temperament, caused no unrest. In the mirror she could see, rather than hear, her husband saying "Let's face it," and watch her eldest son, Jeremy, blond and beloved, behaving beautifully. She saw the rings on her fingers, and a bracelet that was insured. Look as she might, she could not see Angus Dance in that mirror (he had been taken to the dining-room for a slice of the ham), and knew she never would.

The head of Christian's department had a Common Market face. He put his drink down on the Chopin and said, "I don't really know you well enough to tell you this story." Grace watched the room rippling in mirrored waters: such slow movement, such pastels; and, again, herself—upholstered, decorated, insured, and, for the first time, utterly alone. A big woman in violet leaned against the mantel, purpling the view. Christian's chief said, "Now comes the bawdy part." Grace listened abstractedly to the end of the joke. When she did not smile, Sir Manfred was displeased; and looked at her white flesh as if to say, You started it. He took up his drink and moved off toward the bookcase: "I'm a voracious reader." He had left a circular stain on a nocturne.

She saw, or knew, that Angus Dance had come back into the room. Making sure about some cheese puffs, she found him close to her, talking to a black-haired, blue-eyed girl who had come with the Dalrymples.

And why on earth not? A man like that could not possibly be leading a celibate life, abstinent in tribute to her own romantic fancies.

"Grace, I've got the info for you on the *Tirpitz*."

It was their oldest friend, whom she at once wished dead.

"Don't say I ever let you down. A promise is a promise. Twelfth of November forty-four."

Grace folded her hands before her. Sunk.

"Capsized at her moorings. We'd disabled her with midget subs the year before, but the RAF gave her the coo de grass in forty-four. Somewhere in the Arctic Circle, up in the Norwegian fjords, don't ask me to pronounce the place, it's one of those names with dots over the top of it."

Angus Dance was back to back with them, well within earshot.

"Damfool Germans brought her well within our range,

you see. Always be relied on for the stupid thing. Utterly gormless. Well, does that take care of everything?"

"I'm grateful, Ernie."

Ernie spoke no German but could do a good accent at parties. "Effer at your serffice." He clicked his heels.

Angus Dance was fetching an ashtray for the Dalrymple girl. He had said, "They sank." For Grace and Ernie, it was "We sank"—even the schoolgirl Grace had attacked the great battleship *Tirpitz* with all her ringletted might. Angus Dance was out of it, free from guilt or glory. For him, Ernie and Grace might as well have rioted on Mafeking night.

Grace revolved a cold glass between her palms. Ernie ran a proprietary finger along the black waist of the piano, in the same way Christian had done with the rim of her dress. "She took a thousand men to the bottom with her."

Sir Manfred was disengaging himself from a questioner. "I don't recall the figures off hand. Why don't you call up my secretary?"

A pencil was brought out, and paper.

"Miss Ware. No, not Waring, Ware. Cordelia Ware. She's a bit of a battleaxe, but she knows the statistics backwards." Sir Manfred added a telephone number, and lumbered towards Grace. "So sorry, I've got to run."

People were kissing her, one after the other: "Dored it, dored it. Simply dored it." Angus Dance left on a wave of departures, shaking hands.

When it was over, they brought the Spode out from a safe place. Someone had broken a goblet of cut crystal.

Jeremy remarked, "You did say smash."

Two calico cats were let out meowing from the upstairs bathroom, but would not touch leftovers. Jeremy and Hugh put the chest back between the windows. Rupert, who was not allowed to lift, helped Christian count empty bottles. "I liked Doctor Dance the best."

I too.

Christian half-turned his head to where Grace stood, and lightly winked. "So we have a crush on Doctor Dance, do we?" He had assembled the bottles in a box. "I liked him myself."

Later still, winding his bedside clock, Christian asked,

"Why on earth was Ernie babbling on like that about the *Tirpitz?* Or was it the *Scharnhorst?*"

Grace was drawing the black dress over her head. "I think it was the *Scharnhorst.*"

He could have called next day to thank for the party but did not, although the phone rang all morning and Christian's chief sent flowers.

"It was a success, then," announced Jeremy, who was becoming worldly.

Grace was turning over the mail.

Christian said, "I don't know when I've seen a finer bunch of marguerites."

Grace Thrale was now embarked on the well-known stages of love: the primary stage being simple, if infinite, longing. She might, in a single morning, see a dozen Dances in the streets. Then, high-strung to an impossible phone bell, whose electric drill reverberated in her soul, she constructed myths and legends from a doorway kiss. That was the secondary phase. Tertiary was the belief that all significance was of her own deranged contriving, and any reciprocity on the part of Angus Dance a fantasy. She had no revelation to make to him. He had even seen her best dress.

If he knew, he would make some joke about her time of life. Even the kindest man could enjoy a savage laugh on that theme.

The trouble was, the very abundance of her feelings sufficed for mutuality. So much loving-kindness also made it appear moral.

The phrases mixed and alternated. If he came on Sunday, to the art show, she would know.

Grace lay awake, then slept uneasily.

Christian said, "You're up so early these days."

"It's that dog next door, barking at daybreak."

Rupert cackled. "Like a rooster."

"If that persists," said Christian, "I shall speak firmly to the owner."

Rupert said, "It was that fatal and perfidious bark." He spilled his breakfast laughing.

By now, Mrs. Thrale had committed adultery in her heart many times.

On the Sunday, Christian took the boys to a horse show. Christian knew quite a bit about horses——their dimensions and markings and matings, their agilities. The boys, too, could adroitly use words like roan, skewbald, and gelding.

"We should be back by six."

Grace said, "I might look in at the art show."

When they had gone out she made up her face with care. She put on a heavy blue coat that was old but became her. It was a raw day, almost lightless; heavy clouds suggested snow. In a shop-window she saw herself clasping her scarf together—hurrying, aglow.

A woman at the door charged her 10p. The floor of dirty wooden boards was uneven, and scrunched as she walked in. She was almost alone in the hall but could not bring herself to look about for Angus Dance. A fat man in a mackintosh stepped back to get perspective and collided: "Sorry." There were two or three elderly couples who had nothing else to do, and a dejected girl who was perhaps one of the exhibitors. The paint was in many cases green and red, in whorls; or had been applied thinly in angular greys. She knew he would not come.

When she left the place it was getting dark and there was sleet. She did not want to go home; it was as if her humiliation must be disclosed there. She shrank from home as from extra punishment—as a child, mauled by playmates, might fear parental scolding for torn clothes. But stumbled along with no other possibility. Pain rose up from her thorax, and descended like sleet behind her eyes. It was scarcely credible there should be no one to comfort her.

She thought, My mortification. And for the first time realized that the word meant death.

Alone at home, she went into the bathroom and leaned both hands on the sink, pondering. This anguish must be centred on some object other than Angus Dance. Such passion could scarcely have to do with him—the red-haired Doctor Dance of flesh and blood and three months' acquaintance—but must be fixed on a vision. This mirror, in its turn, showed her intent, exposed, breathing heavily. She had never seen herself so real, so rare.

She had just taken off her coat when they came in from

the horse show, speaking in a practised manner of chestnuts and bays. Christian had been jostled in the Underground: "Perhaps I'm not suited to the mass society."

Grace said, "Perhaps we are the mass society."

Monday was Mrs. Thrale's day for the hairdresser. She said, "Mario, I have some grey hairs," and put her hand to her brow. "Here."

He took her head between his hands, under a light, as if it were a skull held *norma frontalis*. Alas, poor Grace. After a while he said, "It is not a case for dyeing."

He released her. "You are not ready to dye."

"No."

"Being fair, you can wait a bit."

Grace sat in a plastic chair and he said, "It is worse for the dark ladies."

When she was settled under the dryer with *Vogue* and *The Gulag Archipelago*, the immemorial pathos of the place struck at her. There was hardly a young woman present, except the shampoo girl whose hipless jeans and prominent pectoral arch made Grace Thrale's soft flesh appear historic. Grace looked down at her own round little arms, stared at them as into a portrait by an Old Master. She thought of her body, which had never been truly slim, and showed a white mesh from bearing children, and now must passively await decay and mutilation. Her hands, clasped over a magazine picture of a bronze man on a beach, instinctively assumed an attitude of resignation. She read, "The Aga Khan in a rare moment of relaxation." But perceived herself in that instant entering into a huge suspense, lonely and universal.

That night Grace dreamed her own death.

The following morning she made an excuse to telephone the hospital.

"Doctor Dance has been out with a heavy cold."

She said it was not important, and hung up. The bad cold arousing scorn, she said aloud, "I would have got there," meaning to the art show; which was perfectly true. She went upstairs and made the beds, and thought in derision: Scotsmen are scarcely Latin lovers.

Equilibrium did not last. On her way downstairs there was the same thoracic pain, a colossal suffering, grandiose,

of a scale and distinction to which she, Grace Thrale of
London W8 7EF, hardly seemed entitled. She sat in the
kitchen and thought, I am overwrought; and perhaps am
mad. Oh God, I must break myself of this.

Break, break, break. You said smash. A crush.

It occurred to her, in her isolation, that books might
have helped. It was the first time she had reckoned with
the fact she did not read, that neither she nor Christian read
—and here was the true discovery, for she had relied on
him to maintain a literary household. They had dozens of
books, on shelves that took up half a wall; not to speak
of the Penguins. And would send to the library regularly
for the latest. She had the Iris Murdoch in the house, as
well as the Solzhenitsyn. Voracious readers. But a state of
receptiveness in which another's torment might reach into
her own soul, through which her infatuation might be
defined and celebrated—there was none of that. Christian
confidently presented himself as a man of letters: "I'm
rereading Conrad this winter." But *Within the Tides* had
lain on his night table since December.

Christian came home and kissed her. "I have spoken to
those people about that yipping dog."

"You haven't."

"Certainly. You can't go sleepless forever. They have
agreed to keep the animal indoors."

She wished he had not said the animal.

He thumped his briefcase onto the hall table. "And I
actually used the word yip."

In her dream, Christian had been weeping.

Grace got up in the night and went downstairs. She
took *Wuthering Heights* from a shelf and stood by the
windows in the moonlight, keeping the ceaseless watch
of her passion. She had no right to utter the name of Angus
Dance, or to give him an endearment even in thought—
never having done these things in life. She might as well
have called on Heathcliff, or Aeneas. The book, an old
edition, weighed in her hand. She knew she would not read
it; but wondered if you might open at any page and find
truth, like the Bible. She passed her other hand down her
body, and thought her small feet irresistibly beautiful as
they showed beneath her nightgown.

In the morning Christian said, "Perhaps we need a new mattress."

When the marguerites began to fester, Grace put them in the garbage. The card, still attached, said, "With homage," and had an ink line through the surname. She swirled water in the vase and remembered: "I didn't laugh at his off-colour joke."

Christian was worried, but said, "You certainly don't have to take insults to further my career." To forestall her thoughts. After a moment he asked, "What was the joke anyway?"

"I couldn't for the life of me work it out." They both burst out laughing. No reply could have pleased him more. Perfect, sheltered Grace. Once, during a holiday on Corsica, he had turned her face away from the spectacle, as he called it, of a fistfight.

Late that day she met Angus Dance in the street. She had bought narcissus to replace the daisies, and stood holding them downwards in her hand. She could think of nothing to say that would equal the magical silent discourse of her reverie.

He said, "Are you all right?"

"I haven't been sleeping properly." She might as well have said, I love you. "Except with pills."

"What are you taking?" For a moment authority passed back to him.

They then spoke of his heavy cold. And she would bring Rupert in for a checkup at the end of the month. Despite sleeplessness, her skin glowed like his own.

He said, "Do you have time for a coffee?"

So Grace Thrale sat at a Formica table and Angus Dance hung his flannel jacket on a peg. He wore a pale woollen waistcoat knitted by his mother. His hair in itself was enough to attract attention: his Northern Light, his blaze of midnight sun. They scarcely spoke, though leaning forward from a delicate readiness, until the girl came to take their order. Both his accent and an oddly aspirated R were more pronounced. Grace thought her own speech indistinct, and made an effort to talk out.

"I have been wondering how you were." All things considered, the boldest remark she had ever made. She was surprised by her definite voice, her firm hand efficiently taking sugar, when the whole of Creation, the very texture of the firmament, was wrought, receptive, cream-coloured, like his sweater.

He said he ought to go to Burnham-on-Crouch to see about his boat, which was up on the slips for scraping and red lead. Some recaulking was also needed. "I don't feel up to it, somehow." The commonplaces, the withholdings, were a realization in themselves. Her scented flowers stood between them in a tumbler of water, pent within a green string.

Grace asked, "What is your boat called?"

"She's called *Elissa*." He made room for the milk. "I'm not much of a sailor—the genuine ones are fanatical. I took it up after a bad experience. I suppose it was a means of motion when everything was standing still."

"Was it when your marriage broke up?"

"No. This was a later repudiation." He smiled. "I don't know that any of this can be very intefesting. Such usual griefs."

"To me they are not usual." She could not imagine Christian, for whom acceptance was imperative, recounting his rebuffs, or acknowledging "my griefs." Even in the entrancement of the coffee-shop the threat came over her that Christian was in this the more infirm, the more defenceless; and that Angus Dance was fortified by reversals and by his refusal to dissimulate. She recalled his simple commitment to Rupert, how he had said, "I promise." Such fearlessness could not be required of Christian.

When she made contrasts with Christian it was not just the disloyalty but that Christian always seemed to gain.

Doctor Dance offered buns. "I had a grand time at your party. I should have called to say so."

Grace thought of the scuttling of the *Tirpitz*, and the chief's commemorative flowers, a soaked wreath on swirling waters. Lest we forget. "It seems so long ago."

"I've not seen you since."

It was the mingling of great and trivial that could not be misunderstood.

He went on, "Yet we are so close."

She fell silent, leaning back into colours and shadows of the room: not in fulfillment, which could hardly be, but in voluptuous calm, at peace. Her hand was outstretched on the table, the sleeve pushed up. It was the first time he had seen her inner arm. She knew it might be the only such passage between them, ever. If the usual griefs were coming to her at last, so was this unprecedented perfection.

Grace was seated at the piano. She turned a sheet of music, but did not play. Rupert came and stood beside her. "What is it?"

"It's Scarlatti."

He had meant, What's wrong.

Like a lover, he stood near enough to suggest she should embrace him. With her right arm she drew him against her side. Her left hand rested on the keys. She leaned her head to his upper arm. It was like an Edwardian photograph. She said, "I do love you, Rupey." This was the last child with whom she could get away with such a thing—and only then because his illness had given them an extension during which a lot might be overlooked. They both knew it. Emulating her mood, the boy became pensive, languid; and at the same time remained omnipotent.

She said again, "I do." To get him to say it back. She thought, So now it has come round: *I* am trying to draw strength from *them*. She thought the word "adulteress," and it was archaic as being stoned to death—a bigoted word, like Negress or Jewess or seamstress or poetress; but precise.

Her left hand sounded notes in the bass: sombre, separate, instructed. The room received them dispassionately. There was a click of her ring on ivory. She rocked the boy a little with her arm, and could feel the plaster armouring his X-rayed ribs. She took her hand from the piano and put both arms about him, her fingers locked over his side, her breast and brow turned to his body. This was less like a photograph.

He said, "What's up, Mum?" Moving his imprisoned arm, he put his own hand to the treble and struck a discordant series of keys, stressing and repeating vehement high notes. She released him, but he jarred a few last perplexed, excited sounds. And stood, still touching her, swayed between childhood and sensuality.

Christian came in with papers in his hand. "What's this, a duet?"

The boy sauntered off and switched on the telly. The news flickered over jagged devastations—Beirut or Belfast, the Bronx or Bombay.

Christian said, "Grace, I must speak to you."

Rupert yelled, "It's a programme on Pompeii."

Grace sat with Christian on a sofa that was rarely used because of the velvet. He told her, "Something momentous has occurred."

In her mind, Grace Thrale swooned.

"I have been given Africa."

He might have been Alexander, or Antony. The younger Scipio. Grace stared whitely, and he added, "South of the Sahara."

She was looking through such tears as would never rise for Angus Dance, who could not need, or evoke, pity for impercipience or self-exposure. She wept for Christian, insulated in the nonconducting vainglory of his days, and might then have told him all, out of sheer fidelity to the meaning of things. She said, "My darling."

"There's nothing in the world to cry about." Christian touched her face, pleased. "I can assure you." Perfect Grace. He unrolled the departmental chart in his hand. A small box at the top of the page littered into larger boxes underneath, fathering endless enclosures of self-esteem. He pointed—here, and here. "Talbot-Sims will only be Acting. But for me it's the real thing." As he leaned to show the pedigree, there was a sparse, greying place on top of his sandy head. He said, "My youth was against me," brushing a speck from the flawless page. "But in the end they waived seniority." The chart started to curl at the edges, struggling to rescroll. "It will make a whopping difference in the pension."

Grace wondered if their severance from each other's thoughts and purposes had at any time appeared so conclusive to him; if ever she herself had so grossly disregarded. She wondered whether, during summer separations, or the time she went to Guernsey, he had perhaps loved, or slept with—the one need not preclude the other—someone else. It was hard to imagine him sufficiently headstrong for it, now he did not have the self-reliance to read a book. If he had loved another woman, Grace, of all people, would understand it. Magnanimity shaped a sad and vast perspective. Or it was merely a plea for leniency in her own case.

Christian put his arm around her, stooping from heights where officials waved seniority. "I'm afraid we'll have to call off the Costa Brava. But when I've got things in hand I'll take you somewhere quiet." His mind ranged, like the news, over ravaged nations, seeking a possibility. All was pandemonium—Portugal, Palestine, Tibet: called off, one after one. Elation weirdly faltered in his throat, as on a sob; but recklessly resumed: "So you brought me luck, telling the old bastard off about his joke."

Angus Dance came into the brick passage as the rain began. He started to run; at the same moment that Grace Thrale, entering from the opposite end, ran too, under the rain.

Had it been possible to observe their meeting from above or alongside, like a sequence on film, they would have been seen at first precipitate, heads lowered against weather; then slowed in realization; and finally arrested. The arrestation being itself some peak of impetus, a consummation. They were then facing, about a yard apart, and rain was falling on Dance's hair and, like gauze, on Grace's coat of calamine blue. Ignored, the heavy rain was a cosmic attestation, more conclusive than an embrace.

Anyone seeing them would have said lovers.

Rain was silvering Dance's eyelids. He had taken hold of himself by the coat lapel. His expression was disarmed, pure with crisis. "This is what I meant about being close."

"Yes."

"Shall we get to shelter?" As if they had not already got to shelter.

Sloshing along the narrow tunnel, he took her arm at last. By not embracing they had earned some such indulgence. They then stood under an awning at the exit of a supermarket; and he said, proving her more right than she had ever been about anything, "You know that I love you." It was the response she had not been able to compel from her own child.

She would not even brush the water from her hair or

coat; and perhaps need never consider her appearance again. After moments during which the rain continued and they were nudged by shopping bags, she said, "It makes me happy." She thought she would tell the simple truth, now that she was indomitable. Opposite, there was the new hotel that took groups. Dance said, "It would be a place to talk."

"We can cross when it lets up." Her self-possession surprised, as in the tea shop.

He hesitated; and decided. "Yes. I'll have to telephone about the appointments."

She did not urge him to keep them. Nor did he ask if she was due in the Crescent. When the sky lightened, they crossed.

As they came into the hotel, the man at the desk put down the phone, saying "Christ." A heap of baggage—suitcases, golf bags, holdalls in nylon plaid—was piled by the foot of the stairs. In the lounge, which was one floor up, they might already have been at an airport, waiting to depart. Pylons of the building were thinly encased in plastic wood, with little counters around them for ashtrays and drinks. The sofas were hard and bright, yet far from cheerful. Slack curtains were tawdry with metallic threads, and on one wall there was a tessellated decoration of a cornucopia greenly disgorging.

As they entered, a group of women in pantsuits got up to leave. An old man with an airline bag said, near tears, "But they only had it in beige."

Grace Thrale sat by a window, and Angus Dance went to telephone. Had it not been for him, how easily she might have fitted in here. The enclosure, nearly empty, enjoined subservience—was blank with the wrath, bewilderment, and touching faith of its usual aggregations. It was no use now trying this on Grace, who scarcely saw and was past condescending. With detachment that was another face of passion, she wondered in what circumstances she would leave this place and if she would ever go home. Abandoned by her, the house in the Crescent was worse than derelict, the life in it extinct: the roast attaining room temperature on the kitchen counter, an unfinished note to Caro announcing Christian's promotion, a rock album that was a surprise for Hugh; and *Within the Tides* unopened on the bedside table. All suspended, silent, enigmatical—slight things that might have dressed the cabins of the *Mary Celeste* or embellished a programme on Pompeii: trifles made portentous by rejection.

She got up and spread the two damp coats on a nearby seat, to deter. She stood at a concrete embrasure looking at the rain, and knew he had come back.

He sat beside her on hard red plastic and said, "There's nothing to be afraid of." He touched his fingers to hers, as once at the hospital. "I am going away." You could see the colour ebbing down through clear, lit levels of his skin. "I have been offered a position at Leeds."

She sat with the air of supremacy, the triumphant bearing summoned for a different outcome. When she did not speak, he went on, "You must not think I would ever try to damage your life." Her life, which she stood ready to relinquish: whose emblems she had been coolly dispersing, as she might have picked off the dead heads of flowers.

He said, "As if I would seek to injure you."

As if she would not have gone up with him to a room in this place and made love, if he had wished it.

He was making an honest woman of her. She deserved no credit from the beneficiaries, having already thrown them over. Love would be concealed, like unworthiness, from them, from him. When she had coveted his standards, she had naïvely imagined them compatible with her passion. It was another self-revelation—that she should have assumed virtue could be had so quickly, and by such an easy access as love. It was hard to tell, in all this, where her innocence left off and guilt began.

Scrutinizing Angus Dance's drained face and darkened eyes, his mouth not quite controlled, Grace Thrale was a navigator who seeks land in a horizon deceitful with vapours. Eventually she asked, repeating her long lesson, "Is this a promotion?"

"An advancement, yes."

Such conquerors, with their spoils, their cities and continents—Leeds, Africa. Advancing, progressing, all on the move: a means of motion. Only Grace was stationary, becalmed.

"In that way, also, it's necessary. I can't go on doing the present job forever."

Only Grace might go on doing forever. Might look up Leeds in the phone book, like Dorset. Realization was a low, protracted keening in her soul. Here at last was her own shipwreck—a foundering beyond her parents' capsized ferry. She might have howled, but said instead what she had heard in plays: "Of course there would have been no future to this."

Colour came back on his cheeks like blood into contusions. He got up quickly and, as if they were in a private room, stood by the concrete window. Then leaned against a column, facing her, his arms spread along the ridge meant for ashtrays, his durable body making a better architecture, a telamon. "A man should have past and present as well as future." He moved his hand emphatically, and a dish of peanuts spilled in silence. It was a gesture that laid waste, as though a fragment of the column disintegrated. "Do you not think I see it constantly, the dying who've not lived? It is what we are being, not what we are to be. Rather, they are the same thing."

"I know that." Even her children were already staked on the future—their aptitudes for science or languages, what did they want to be, to be; they had never been sincerely asked what they would be now. She said, "Even those who have truly lived will die. It is hard to say which is the greater irony." Such discoveries were owed to him. She rose to his occasion, and no doubt would soon sink back, incurious.

He said, "I am near thirty-four years of age, and live with too much vacancy." She saw his rectitude existing in a cleared space like his parents' uncluttered house. He told her, "You cannot imagine—well, I do not mean that unkindly. But you, with your completeness—love, children, beauty, troops of friends—how would you understand such formlessness as mine? How would you know solitude, or despair?"

They were matters she had glimpsed in a mirror. She felt his view of her existence settling on her like an ornate, enfeebling garment; closing on her like a trap. She leaned back on the unyielding sofa, and he stood confronting. It was an allegorical contrast—sacred and profane love: her rapture offered like profanity. To assert, or retrieve, she said, "Yet there has been nothing lovelier in my life than the times we sat together at the hospital and looked at the photographs."

He came back to the sofa and replaced his hand on hers —a contact as essential and external as the print of fingers on X-rays. "It was like Paolo and Francesca."

She would have to look it up when she got home. But stared at his hand on hers and thought, without mockery, Scarcely Latin lovers.

He said, "It's true we could not have stood the lies."

The first lie was Grace drawing off her dress, her head shrouded in black, her muffled voice saying, *"Scharnhorst."* She said, "In my married life I never so much as exchanged an unchaste kiss, until with you on my birthday."

He smiled. Perfect, sheltered Grace. "There is so little laughter in illicit love. Whatever the theme, there must always be the sensation of laughing at someone else's expense."

Grace had last laughed with Christian over Sir Manfred's joke. She said, "I am serious." The kiss, the lie, the laughter—nothing would be serious again by that measurement. "I am serious," she said, as he smiled from his greater experience and lesser insight; from his contrasting virtue, since she was the one willing to do harm. He looked in her face with the wrong solicitude. Grace would not be called upon to testify. She remembered how, on tumultuous Corsica, her head had been turned away.

"In a new place," she supposed, "you will get over this."

"I still dream about a girl I knew when I was eighteen." He would not conform with her platitudes, he would not perceive her truth. He would dream of Grace, in Leeds. He said, "Memories cool to different temperatures at different speeds." He glanced about, at the figured rug and tinselled curtains, the column splintered into peanuts, the drab cornucopia: "What an awful place." And his condemnation was the prelude to farewell.

Grace Thrale said, "It is the world."

"I've said many things to you in thought, but they were never hopeless as this. Nor did they take place in any material world." He then corrected himself. "Of course there has been desire," dismissing this extravagance. His accent intruded, and he allowed time for speech to recover itself, mastering language like tears. "What I mean is, in thoughts one keeps a reserve of hope, in spite of everything. You cannot say good-bye in imagination. That is something you can only do in actuality, in the flesh. Even desire has less to do with the flesh than good-bye."

His face had never appeared less contemporary. Was one of those early photographs, individual with suffering and conscience.

"So I am to lose you." She might have been farewelling a guest: Dored it, dored it. Dored you.

He said, "I cannot do any more," and withdrew his re-fractive touch and passed his hand through his bright hair as in some ordinary bafflement. He got up again and took his coat from the chair, and stood over her. All these ac-tions, being performed very rapidly, reminded that he was expert in contending with pain. "I'll drop you. I'm taking a taxi." His reversion to daily phrases was deathly. It was ultimate proof that men were strong, or weak.

They stood up facing, as if opposed. And onlookers were relieved to see them normal.

"I'll stay on here a few minutes." She could not con-template the taxi in which he resolutely would not embrace her. She clasped her hands before her in the composed gesture with which she sometimes enfolded desperation. Raising her head to his departure, she was a wayside child who salutes a speeding car on a country road.

When Grace came down into the street, the rain had stopped and the darkness arrived. Men and women were coming from their work, exhausted or exhilarated, all pale. And the wet road shone with headlamps, brighter than the clear black sky with stars. Engines, voices, footsteps, and a transistor or two created their geophysical tremor of a world in motion. This show of resumption urged her, gra-tuitously, towards the victors—to Jeremy, whose eye needed bathing with boric acid, and Hugh's bent for mathe-matics, and Rupert's unexpected interest in Yeats, and Christian's saying "This is the best lamb in years." All of that must riot in triumph over her, as she would find out soon enough. They would laugh last, with the innocent, appalling laughter of their rightful claim and licit love.

With these prospects and impressions, Grace Marian Thrale, forty-three years old, stood silent in a hotel doorway in her worn blue coat and looked at the cars and the stars, with the roar of existence in her ears. And like any great poet or tragic sovereign of antiquity, cried on her Creator and wondered how long she must remain on such an earth.

34

Paul Ivory was writing to his mother:

My dear Monica,

It would be a great pity if you were to sell the Barbados place without a clear idea of settling elsewhere. Boring it may be, I don't doubt it, but all the world is now a costly shambles ruled by the tax laws. Frankly, I don't see you in Ireland, nor do I think you would be amused by their latest rerun of the Battle of the Boyne.

My play continues to prosper, though the notices were exclusively poor. It must mean the nation has taken me to its heart. Perhaps it is this boa-constrictor embrace that prevents me getting on with new work. I fritter away a lot of time at present, and have even been to the zoo—though that in fact was because Felix hopes to make a film there, and wants me to finance it. I suppose I shall—everyone else's son is making a film, why not mine?

The only other thing I recall doing lately was a party at Manfred Mills's new house. Victoria Square always was a hard little place, and now there is a concrete ellipse in the middle of it, like a prehistoric mound or as if some immovable monstrosity had been cemented over out of decency. Tertia would not come, I took Felix. Manfred's son—Felix's age but dreadfully earnest, with a Blue for cross-country running —met us on the stairs and said with determination "You must enjoy yourselves." Of such, I always imagine, is the Kingdom of Heaven. Upstairs, an odd mixture—too many suburbanites discussing trains, and a flock of civil servants who hung around Manfred, obsequious and expectant, like queers around a rich old widow. Pliant to his every opinion. In other words, a thoroughly conventional crowd—except for a pianist so shy he could only meet celebrities, an R.C. priest who was actually unmarried, and a Soviet dancer who had not yet defected. Manfred, for the occasion, had had his sideburns frizzed and hung himself with chains. Madeline had wisely contracted pneumonia and never appeared.

Among the permaflex officials was Christian Thrale, now a caricature of a bureaucrat. With him, everything is a palace bulletin. When I asked after his wife, who used to be rather pleasant, he said with pointed delicacy, "Grace is unwell today." I cannot describe the pomposity. He had come with his sister-in-law—a woman I once knew well, now some years widowed and not seen in ages. She was here briefly from New York, staying with the Thrales. Still handsome—in contrast at least to the assemblage of commuters and tax inspectors—though teetering precariously on the verge of distinction, a pitfall women cannot be sufficiently warned against. As a girl, she already displayed this dangerous tendency.

The encounter moved me to a page or two today. I should like to do something with it, though not just another round-up party in the Proustian manner. Not only has that vein been worked to death but I'm not yet venerable enough for the last volume of Proust. Nor, of course, was Proust. He wasn't much older than I when he wrote that party. He fudged it. He was good at the future as well as the past.

I think you're wise to accept the Washington invitation, since we may shortly have a new government and someone else's relatives installed at the embassy. If you do get to the USA as planned, you might send me any press notices you see on the film of *Act of God*, which will be opening about that time. My agent holds them until they're all in, and I can't rely on friends to send them unless they are highly unfavourable.

Felix asks that I thank you for the birthday cheque. You must forgive him for not writing himself, and indulge him as you do.

Your loving son

Caro said, "Paul Ivory was at a party I went to this week." She was lunching with Ted Tice.

"Paul must be showing through a bit by now."

"He looks amazingly the same."

"I daresay he has a portrait of himself festering in a cupboard."

Caro thought how Paul had stayed smooth, his smile now rare and less intense. He was sparing himself, like an ageing dancer; and reserved the right to be, on occasion, the one who was bored.

She said, "His son was there. Very tall, very thin." An emaciated cavalier: long fair drooping hair, an elegance of nose and brow, a refinement of structure. Eyes more truly blank than Tertia's. Perhaps simple, in a selfish way; but breeding can look deceptively like intelligence. Wearing a white lawn blouse embroidered in coloured flowers, with cuffs of frilled lace; the shirt belled over jeans snug as a saltimbanque's. His feet were bare. You might have said, What beauty. Instead, Caro introduced herself. Monosyllables were planted like bollards, closing every avenue. The boy had not forgotten what to say: he had chosen a part with no lines. He was cool and, except for the wrists, unruffled. One talked as if to a child, "What's your name, where do you go to school?" His name was Felix, and he was to go somewhere—no doubt Oxford, or doubtless Cambridge—in the autumn. When someone else came up he disappeared instantly, having somehow stuck it out till then. A woman said, "I just know he's going to be a surgeon, he has those wonderful fingers with curved tips."

Caro had not noticed that the boy had Paul's hands. When Paul came over to her she looked at his fingertips, the evidence of love. Paul said, "Let's move away from that priest and his ecumenical smirking."

In the restaurant, Ted Tice was watching Caro's lowered eyelids: the tragedy is not that love doesn't last. The tragedy is the love that lasts.

A platter of breaded fish was brought, and divided between them. Caroline Vail had not foreseen that she could ever meet Paul Ivory without emotion. In place of agitation there had been a sense of the long accident of life, and of Paul's claim on her memory till death.

Ted Tice said, "Watch out for bones." He asked, "How's Josie?" He sometimes liked, with Caro, to make domestic inquiries that fixed him as her familiar. And had struggled a lifetime to achieve this much intimacy at least.

Josie, who had travelled to Sweden with a tariffs congress and remained there, was to have a baby. Caro said, "I'm going to see her there in September, after the baby's born." She said, "I wish—" and paused on the obvious. She did greatly wish; though unable to imagine Adam with his grandchild.

She bore her loss with as much composure as the world could reasonably, or otherwise, expect of her. But in private would still make clumsy appeals, to God or to the dead, and disfigure remembrance with salt tears; while Adam, in her thought, remained always calm. She told Ted Tice, "Memory is more than one bargains for. I mean, if it goes on like this, this sense of past, past, past, that can turn even the happiest memories to griefs."

Her appearance, and the impetuous manner of saying "Past, past," were so at odds with sad words that Ted nearly smiled. "Caro, we're not old enough for this repining."

"Paul said the other evening that I was on the verge of distinguished old age."

"I suppose it riled him, your being beautiful."

Ted watched Caro take a fishbone from her mouth. On her wrist, a big heavy watch that must have been Adam Vail's. Her lifted wrist, and her husband there on her pulse keeping track of her time.

I have no happiest memories of her, yet the hours with her have been the best.

Caro said, "And then one distorts memory to one's own advantage, from vanity or remorse. I do anyway. Not you —you were born truthful, and have also been trained in the truth." She thought of his work vaguely as ever, imagining a great deal of silence and exactitude.

"Even through a telescope, some people see what they choose to see. Just as they do with the unassisted eye." He said, "Nothing supplies the truth except the will for it."

Looking away as if ashamed. I cannot so much as say I've been true to her; she has never required that form of truth from me.

Caro was wiping her fingers and thinking that it might be childlessness that drove you back on the past. On the other hand, it was hard to envisage the future in Paul Ivory's son. She asked Ted, "Do you have a picture of your children?"

Ted brought out his wallet. He showed a photograph of two adolescent girls and a small boy, standing with their mother. The women fair and somewhat serious, the dark boy convulsed with laughter.

Caro said, of the children, "We were never as young as that." She held the photograph carefully by its edges. "Your wife is very lovely."

"She is entirely lovable." They had long since ceased to marvel, politely, that Caro and Margaret had never met. When Caro handed back the picture, Ted looked at it some moments. "My son is the image of my own brother at that age."

Caro had forgotten Ted Tice's brother, who existed only as a streak in Ted's eye. "What does your brother do?"

"He wanted to be a farmer, and managed to put himself through agricultural college. For some years now has been farming in a profit-sharing arrangement in Yorkshire. He works terribly hard, but also contributes to farming journals and has written a respected treatise on voles. He has a taciturn wife, who works as hard as he, and a pretty daughter."

(At the party, Paul Ivory had said to Caro, "My brother has run off with a little shopgirl." And Caro in reply: "I too have been a shopgirl. We are not necessarily diminutive."

Paul always aroused some sarcasm. Ted's associations had a candid health.)

"So you've both done what you wished."

"In one sense." Ted was looking at the photograph, in which his son held an ungainly dog. "The puppy is called Phobos. Fathered by Mars." He put it away, drew out a creased snapshot, black-and-white, and showed it to her. He was curious to see how she would turn this aside.

Against a segment of garden at Peverel, there was the

image of a girl in profile, black hair hanging loose, one hand raised. Caroline Vail held the picture in her palm. A slight shiver on her expression might have been awe, or the suppression of tears. She said, "I don't remember that dress."

She gave back the photograph. So she had been that person. Around the room the fantasy of existence extended to everything—to forks and table-legs and the striped collar of a shirt, and to the soft prickling of plush banquette against her calves.

Ted would have been sorry to make her cry, though having tried so hard for it.

He said, "When you come through in September, will you let me know?"

"I promise."

"You won't go back on it?" Like a child.

"Of course not. I love to see you."

A short flight of steps led up to the street. Ted watched the sway of scarlet coat at Caro's knees as she went up. Saw too her shoes that were shiny as black glass, and thought that he had never seen her feet bare.

It was now well into the afternoon. Caro was taking the Underground. Ted went to the ticket booth with her. "Good-bye." They kissed. He watched her red coat pass the barrier, move with the Down escalator, gliding, diminishing, descending: a rush-hour Eurydice. At the last moment she looked back, knowing he would be there.

35

On a hot morning of that early summer, Mrs. Vail was sitting in a doctor's office opposite her own house. She read aloud from a chart. Her dark eyes were darkened and dilated. The doctor said, "I will give you a prescription."

"For eyedrops?"

"For glasses."

She stared.

The doctor had white hair, a sour breath. "Things catch up with you. You were always the one, weren't you, who could read the name on the boat, or the announcement on the billboard? You could decipher the fine print. Well, things catch up with you. Nature doesn't like exceptions."

"We're not here solely to appease Nature."

"She takes it out on exceptions. And all of a sudden, too. Us ordinary folks can tell more or less how things are likely to go on with us." The doctor handed her a slip and pushed away his prescription pad. Three months later he was to die in a plane crash on his way to an ophthalmologists' congress at Rome.

Out in the hot street, Caro's eyes smarted. She fumbled for a handkerchief, in a handbag worthy of Dora. The ledge of the curb baffled her vision. And a man coming from a doctor's office next door spoke her name.

"That you should be here."

It was like Paul, on a strange continent, to be surprised at Caro's presence on her own street.

"Is it Paul?" As if truly blind.

He watched while she blotted tears from eyes larger and

324

darker than remembered. He said, "My son has leukemia." Tears streamed from his own eyes without inducement.

She stood with a finger at her chin, her eyes closed. Shock affected her like languor. "What a nightmare."

"It's real enough. Though I've tried for a month now to wake from it." They stood, not noticing street or weather. People passed, and stared as they had always done. The city lumbered about them, soiled and exhausted.

Paul told her how the disease had been discovered. He had brought Felix to New York because there was a doctor, a hospital, a new treatment. Tertia would arrive after the Fourth of July.

Caro put her hand to her burning hair. "Can you come home with me?—I live across the street."

It was Caro, now, who had the key. Turning it in the complex lock she said, "Nobody's home. I'm staying in town over the holiday, to work."

The entrance was cooled. Surfaces were bare. On a table there was a handwritten list: "Newspaper, laundry, Gristede's." In the living-room, curtains silently swelled and slackened over an air conditioner. One chair, a sofa, and a glass table were free of dust covers.

Paul said, "Do you have anything to drink?" He had never interested himself in her circumstances, and could therefore resume as if they had parted yesterday, requiring no account of intervening life.

She felt it too: a resumption. Or a culmination.

Paul took off his jacket and dropped it on a chair. He walked about the shrouded room while Caro fetched a bottle and glasses. Distortions of her vision made it almost impossible to pour. Paul threw himself on the sofa and put his hand to his eyes, fingers upturned, white-shirted arm in air: ungainly for the first time—leg ricked up, elbow askew: a fractured modern mechanism it would be easier to replace than repair.

When he took his hand from his face, Caro gave him the cold glass. He said, "The treatment is drastic. He's suffering most immediately from that."

"I remember his beauty."

"With these new drugs, there is some hope."

She sat in her chair. "Where there's hope there is suspense."

"The time," he said. "The time that doesn't pass." He put his glass on the floor beside the sofa, where it formed a circle of condensation. His hand dangled beside it. "And this can go on and on and on. And I must hope that it does so."

After Adam Vail's death, Caro had repeatedly asked the time of day, and found it scarcely changed.

"Does he know everything?"

"Yes, and at present is more resentful than afraid." Paul said, "In some ways Felix is like Tertia."

Caro began to see Paul more clearly: his skin hot with sleeplessness, flushed yet grey; his reddened blue eyes and cobalt eyelids; the slight disorder of collar and tie. It was bizarre that a man with his preoccupation should shave and dress and walk the streets in conventional decency, and that humanity should expect it of him. She took his glass and refilled it. "I'll bring something to eat."

"No. Don't go." As if it had been his house rather than hers. He reached for her wrist, not touching it but joggling the tumbler in her hand. No contact in the gesture, merely the wish to detain. "If I hadn't met you I'd have got through today. It's being able to speak that breaks one up. Or down."

"What can I do?"

"Nothing. Stay here. In a little while I must go uptown to a friend of Felix's who's putting photographs in order— slides of a trip they made together. We thought he could enjoy seeing them, he can't concentrate to read."

"Is this his girlfriend?"

Paul said, "Felix is homosexual."

Caro sat, with Paul extended to her scrutiny. As never when he had lain at her side.

He said, "It's as if one had never known trouble, until this."

He had reached fifty, but had not got away with it. She said, "There is the terrible ignorance, looking back. Not knowing this was in store."

Paul said, "The rage—at fate, at God. Not merely being helpless, but in someone's—something's—power. The doctors and nurses with authority to tell you the worst, or lie to you. With authority to make mistakes. I've always detested any sense of power over me."

He sat up, lit a cigarette and let it burn in his fingers. An onlooker might have wondered whether Paul remembered who Caro was.

"Could I come tomorrow?"

"I'll be here all weekend, working."

"Working?"

"On a translation, from Spanish."

"Oh—yes—I saw you were doing that." That he had not asked about herself, her life, her loss, gave reality, in an atmosphere of dream. It made a fact of Paul's presence—material as statistics might have been, or talk of money. He said, "Is this an ashtray?" and put out his cigarette. "Till tomorrow then."

Caro let him out. She closed the door on the stifling day, and wondered if he would ever come back. She took the coloured plate into the kitchen and rinsed it at the sink, in a smell of wet nicotine.

In the night she came down from her bedroom to look at crumpled cushions and ice melted in a tumbler. She went to the kitchen and saw the plate from Palermo. Years before she had sought evidence of her own presence in this house. Now Paul's very existence must be proved here. When the sun rose, Caroline Vail looked out from the top of the house at a sky of iron.

A heavy newspaper was delivered, a note from Una, a letter from Ireland.

Caro opened the door on a gust of heat.

"You supposed I wouldn't come." Punctual as an actor, he appeared to re-create the rehearsed scene of yesterday. He took off his jacket and sat on the sofa. His shirt was damp on his chest and between the shoulder-blades, making his body leaner, more visible.

"Where are you staying?" A hotel might vouch for Paul Ivory's existence.

"At the St. Regis."

She brought sandwiches on a plate, and a glass of whisky. Paul did not encourage kindness: he had some greater service to ask of her. He said that Felix had slept and was not in pain. Tertia had telephoned from London. Paul said, "His skin, his teeth, his hair. His hair lifts off in handfuls, like thatch." Paul held the glass in both hands and said, "His beautiful hair."

After a time he said, "It perhaps surprises you I should care this much for anyone."

It was not love that was new in him, but responsibility.

Words embellished a state of waiting. In sallow light, Paul's face was a mask of the most delicate and supple leather, or of lemon-coloured silk: features drained not so much by inward feeling as by outward show. Public appearances and innumerable photographs had exhausted the store of verisimilitude, leaving just this. Each exploitation had drawn off its portion, until only a film of expression remained.

He said, "What's become terrible is not the guilt, which I scarcely feel, even now. But the sense of retribution."

She thought he meant, because of her. He was looking at her in the half-light that showed only a chair, a form. She might have been a crone, or Helen of Troy. She said, "Many people might feel that. It's implicit in the very question, Why me? The sense of being singled out for such punishment."

"You know it's nothing usual like that." Paul could still create complicity. "But I have never been sure how much you knew."

He put down his glass, and waited. At last Caro said, "What have you come to tell me?"

Paul sat on the sofa, his hands lightly clasped between his knees. He would now speak with the voice, natural and so nearly beautiful, that he reserved for truth. In this voice, he said, "I let a man die."

He kept his eyes on Caroline Vail's face. It was her glance that fell, into darkness.

"I was twenty-five years old. It was just before you and I met, that summer at Peverel." He might have been making conversation. "I say I let him die, but in fact I killed him. I thought you possibly knew." It was this he had come to say.

"I saw—I knew there was something—" She would have added, "of the kind," but murder has no kindred.

"From things you said, figures of speech, sometimes your look, I supposed you knew. Though you could not possibly know all of it." Paul's eyes were alive in the kidskin mask with new, exposed prominence, as though lashes and brows had singed away in his stare. The woman was looking back at him with a moral effort. "You may remember"—the conventional phrases struck absurdity: there should be a separate language for havoc. "At Peverel there was an old couple who used to help with dinners, serve and clear away, that sort of thing."

Caro said, "They were hired for Grace's wedding. And were there the night, the night the Thrales celebrated your engagement to Tertia."

"They were called Mullion. They used to come to the castle as extra help when there were weekend parties. They had a grandson who sometimes pitched in—to bring the cars around, take people to the station, fetch and carry. That's how I met him, the grandson, at the castle, a couple of years before I knew you. I went out in the garden after dinner, and he was hanging about." Paul made the grimace, unremembered in many years, of tightening his eyelids. "I should say, I had seen him in the garden and for that reason went out. His name was Victor."

I see you at night, I look down and see you in the garden alone.

"His name was Victor Locker. The Mullions' daughter had married back into the same seamy side of London life her parents had been trying to deny all their lives. She married a brute called Godfrey Locker with a big blunt head and tiny little eyes, sharp teeth, like the profile of a whale; and she had—or developed—a temperament to match his own. I don't know what he really did, he was one of those who get along with odd jobs but always have something shady on the back burner. He'd been on the docks and at Smithfield, and he'd driven a van for a while. There were four children, and they all got hell. The father's name, as I said, was Godfrey, and they didn't call him Dad, they called him God. That is the truth."

"Was this where your play began—*Friend of Caesar?*"

"Yes. After I took up with Victor, I used to go there, go home with him. They lived at Kennington, in a scene of devastation. Victor used to say his father's profession was interior devastator. The children were terrified of the father, of his hands and his boots and his savage grin. The mother was a cow and a shrew and a drunk. Victor was the eldest—he was sixteen when I met him—though there had been a girl still older who had the sense to run away and disappear. And that's where I spent my free time after I took up with Victor, with the Lockers at Kennington." Paul said, "I mean, of course, that Victor was my lover."

"Yes."

"The father was careful with me. He had his plans and didn't want to scare me off. Watched me with his serrated grin, as if to say, You'll get yours. The grandparents, the Mullions, weren't much themselves, but a good cut above Godfrey Locker. They wanted to do something for the boy, Victor. All they could think up was cutting him in on the odd jobs at country houses—which at least got him out of Kennington occasionally, but was leading to other trouble because he started to pinch things and to think about doing an inside job with a gang of his peers. Then there were the opportunities on the side with me and my kind." Paul drank, and wiped his mouth roughly in an evocation of Godfrey Locker. "You did realize that, didn't you? About me?"

"Yes."

"My father was the first to see it. He was the first, with his deathbed quotation. Can we shut that machine off for a bit?"

Caro got up and switched off the air conditioner. She opened the window, holding the curtain aside. The street was empty, the litter fixed on its surface as if forever; the trees were living things that sensed a storm.

"As time goes on one gives oneself away, often deliberately. You can usually tell us, for instance, by our mockery of homosexuals." Paul almost smiled. He watched her return to the chair, sit down. "You take it coolly."

"What else is there to do?"

"By which you mean you've used up all the emotion you had for me." Paul said this with no sign of regret, the acknowledgment leading at once to egotism. "It is terrible that even telling you this, talking this way, scarcely shifts my mind from Felix. By now these things don't greatly matter." A perplexed animal movement of the head. "Through those weekend meetings at the castle Victor got a job, if you can call it that, driving and doing odds and ends for a bachelor with a country place near Marlborough. Between Marlborough and Avebury. He was a set designer, very fashionable then. His name was Howard. You get the picture. He had a flat in London and spent weekends in the country. And, for the brief period during which Victor struck me as essential, I went down there too, at weekends, and stayed at a seedy hotel nearby, hanging about waiting for Victor's time off. I never knew if Victor's employer was aware he was sharing him or not. There was no believing what Victor told you in that or any other line."

"You stayed at that inn. Where we went together."

In very different circumstances, I assure you.

"Yes."

There had been his satisfaction, then, in deceiving Tertia at the moment of betrothal. Caro, then, had been the one in the know. Now there was her ignorance of the greater, inner deception: that Paul had possessed her in the place—the room, the bed—of his lover. Her ignorance of his deepest pleasure.

I always had a taste for the play within the play.

"Nor did I ever know if Godfrey Locker and his son blackmailed the decorator. When they started on me it was in a small way. I was already giving Victor money of course, and this just seemed a bit more. A familiar enough story; and my only indication of youthful innocence, you might say, was to fall into it. Or it was self-confidence—I was used to winning, and to the idea that *I* was using *them*. When it began to build up, I could still manage the money, but I could see where it was leading. Victor had got hold of a magazine at his employer's flat and caught on I had a success coming—there was an interview about preparations for the first play, and a photograph of me with Tertia. On the one hand, there was all that, and on the other there was the smash-up, the Lockers, blackmail, scandal, the possibility of a prison sentence. The more I got what I wanted from the world, the greater the power of the Lockers." Paul said, "Until now, I never spent such hours and days as those."

Caro had stood in a freezing kitchen and wished to die.

"It seemed incredible I couldn't get the better of them with the weapons I had—superior intelligence, good connections. Victor had—not intelligence, but a quickness. The children of brutes develop that early, trying to keep one step ahead of horror. He was clever, for instance, about my play—knew exactly what was wanted when I needed help with speech or responses. There were no ideas in him, just this astuteness. But he put an immoderate value on his intelligence, because of the set he'd come from. Offspring of brutes have that in common with the children of affluence—they have no context for assessing their limitations.

"Well— Then something happened in my favour. Godfrey Locker was driving a lorry again for a spell, and he was in a smash on the Great North Road. He broke an arm and a hip, and a head injury kept him in a coma nearly a week. I'd skipped a weekend or two down at Marlborough—at Avebury—but now I went down on the Friday, thinking I might get Victor to settle for a sum while his father was out of the running. In the evening, when he had time off to eat, he came over to the pub as usual, but I met him out on the road. I was nervous by then about the Lockers' methods and I thought they might be setting up evidence with the landlord—who by his looks could've been part of the Locker dynasty himself. We sat in the car and Victor laughed, as they say, in my face at the idea he'd let me off the hook. 'You're in my future. A fortune-teller told me.' He was great on fortune-tellers. 'You're my pension plan,' he said, and leaned back grinning. I'd taken him up for his looks, and now he only reminded me of his father."

"What were his looks?"

"Fair, light eyes. It was convenient—people took us for brothers as long as he didn't open his mouth. As I say, that night, to me, he looked like his father. He leaned back and laughed—'I'm on a winning streak,' he said, 'now that God's on the blink.' He was nearly hysterical with excitement—rapture—over the old man's accident, which was a legitimate, if incomplete, satisfaction to the entire family.

"We arranged to meet in the morning at a place on the river where we'd sometimes gone when Victor had to be up all night. Victor would be up late driving home from some party, then he'd put the car away and walk down to meet me, without sleeping, after the sun was up. He would cross a bridge downstream, and walk back to meet me. There was a bend of the river where we used to go, just below a road, with an overhang of trees. The river was so narrow there, hardly a creek, and from the road above you wouldn't know it existed, let alone that there was the shelf of bank under the willows. Even Victor liked it." Paul said, with his prominent stare, "I say, even Victor liked it, because he was afraid of water, and felt safe that there was almost no river there—a trickle over stones, and swaths of bent reeds. He was afraid because he couldn't swim, like most of the poor of his generation, but out of pride he pretended that a fortune-teller at a funfair had told him he'd die by drowning.

"I found this out—the fear of water—because I'd once taken him to the Riviera for a few days, thinking he'd be pleased. Instead, there was this terror of the sea, and the humiliation of having to admit he couldn't swim."

Heat, sand, the sea. Lemon groves, vineyards, white walls.

"After I'd seen him that night, I went back to the inn. I only slept towards dawn, and when I woke it was already past the time for me to meet him at the river. When I got there I left the car at a curve of the road, as I'd always done, and walked the last stretch. I climbed down the bank, and found Victor under the trees, asleep. He'd been up all night, and he slept like the dead at any time." Paul said, "He looked beautiful again to me then, and I wished he would die.

"I stood awhile beside him, wishing he'd never wake up. I had no idea of injuring him, I just wished him to cease existing while he was still beautiful and hadn't been caught. And as I stood there a man came past on the other side of the stream, a few yards away. No one had ever come by there before, there was no access and no path, just a narrow swatch of grass beside the river-bed. He paused under the trees and looked at us, at me. I've said I'd no thought then of harming Victor, but he saw enough on my face to make him pause."

Paul waited for Caro to speak. When she was silent, he resumed. "We looked at each other across the few yards of stones and water, and I gave him a nod and smile. I was used to convincing people by my appearance, and I hated him for not being taken in. He saw at any rate that Victor was only sleeping—he openly watched to establish that—and after a minute he walked on upstream. What else could he do? His passing unnerved me, though, and I began to be

afraid of Victor's waking up and looking like his father
again. There was something awful about the brilliant morning and my looking on, wakeful, at his sleep. And after a
while, the apprehension of his waking, and of the transfor-
mation, got too much for me, and I went away and left
him sleeping like the dead."

Another movement of Paul's head, the turning aside
with which a patient might bear the probing of a wound.

"When I got near the top of the bank, there was a
policeman in uniform about to come down. I had some confused flash of an idea that the man passing had alerted the
police, and I was ready to deny whatever I had not in any
case done. He looked like a stage policeman—ageless, decent, responsible. Before I could say a word he started in
to tell me that they were clearing people off that stretch of
the river in order to flood it. There was a great storm
coming in from the West, and they were expecting a dike
to break a quarter of a mile upstream from where we
stood. A farmer had dammed up a tributary stream to
make a pond the year before, and it wasn't holding. They'd
brought a pair of engineers to open it under control before
the deluge came on, so it wouldn't flood the village farther
down. This was the only spot, where we stood, at which
they expected a rush of high water—it being so narrow
there. 'She'll fill up right here,' he said, 'but the rest'll be
child's play.' He had a colleague stationed farther downstream, and they were putting barriers on the road. 'Nobody else down there,' he said, 'was there.' I didn't even
have to say No. He took a good look over the edge, up
and downstream, and of course the only thing he couldn't
see was Victor.

"He said, 'We've orders to get clear of this section. But
if you'll come back up the road a bit you can be in at the
kill.'

"All the way up the road I was thinking, What if he
wakes? I had only what you might call practical thoughts,
no other realization, no hesitation. Then I thought, I can
say I never got down to the bank. If Victor calls out, turns
up, he can't know I was there. It was as if I'd forgotten the
passer-by. So I made conversation with the constable and
he at least was charmed. When we got up the rise to where
I'd left the car, there was an exchange of signals, and a

police car went slowly down the road to confirm it was clear. After some minutes, a small explosion, some smoke among the trees, and soon the sound of the water. It was over so quickly, in a moment—at first a flow, then gushing, and then, just as they had said, the rising of a crest at the narrow squeeze of the river, where it passed from our sight. The crest there reached to the top of the willows, and afterwards the trees hung down in the stream like wet hair, so that everything below was visible, even the little ledge where Victor had slept. And where now there was nothing to be seen."

At the window the gauze curtain filled and soared, released in a natural sway. A high wind was blowing before the storm. This was nothing more than an attempt to give the occasion its due. Paul went on speaking. In any pause the gale could be heard, and, far off, long rolls of thunder.

"Speech and behaviour came wtih unearthly ease. I was seeing and hearing myself, looking on at the event. While Victor was dying in the Kennet. We had to wait for the other constable to come back up the road with the police car. It seemed a long time—perhaps it was twenty minutes—but when the car appeared there was nothing new to report and the two men stood and talked idly in the road, waiting for an all-clear from the engineers. Finally there was a whistle, someone walked down towards us with a green flag, and a car or two came through. I'd already decided to return to the inn and go through an hour or so of seeming to wait, just in case. In case. My constable was heading that way, so I gave him a lift. All cheerful as could be. When we got up near the site of the exploded dike we stopped so he could have a word with the men there. And someone said, 'There's a chap been stuck here because of all this, and needs a lift to the station.' And it was the walker from the river." Paul said, "By then, most of an hour had gone by.

"He came over to the car, and he saw it was me. He knew nothing. Yet saw it in me, on me. He stood by the car, and saw into me. I felt his sight in me, and I feel it yet." Paul's hand across his eyes. "That was the only moment when the police—the two policemen—hesitated. For a second they felt something was wrong, and of course it was him they suspected, not me. They both glanced at him, fixing his appearance in their minds. Then it was over, the man got in the back seat and we drove on, my constable chattering all the way. They say it takes three to make a joke—one to tell it, one to understand it, and one to miss it. Perhaps it's that way with many things. That's how it was in the car—me, and him; and the policeman oblivious.

"The reaction was beginning to get me, the effort to drive was colossal. My hands. One said to oneself that one must do it—as if it were duty, or heroism. The man in the car had been on a walking tour of the West Country. He was beginning work again that day. He'd stopped off there to see Avebury Circle, God damn him to hell, and now he had to catch his train. He'd left his luggage at the station. All this came out because the constable questioned him a bit, sensing something uneasy in that car and not knowing why."

Paul said, "I got back to the inn," and drank. In his glass, as he held it, the barometer remained at steady.

Caro saw, after so many years, the unclean counter, the bleary bottles, the landlord. The room. The bed. The blood shed twice.

"When I was at the inn, the storm came on. That afternoon I was back in London, driving through the worst rain I've ever seen. Nothing came out about Victor until evening. His body must have been washed under the bridge downstream, and somehow got trapped there. When the storm hit, it carried the bridge away and the body was found in the debris. So it was never connected to the flooding farther up the river. His employer, the man Howard, didn't wake till the storm came on, and had no idea what time Victor went out. There were only the two of them in the house, and Howard had been sleeping off a binge. It was assumed Victor had been on the bridge when it gave way in the storm—it was a place where he often crossed, on the way to shop in the village or to go to a garage. At the inn they might've linked him to me, but the last thing the landlord there would have wanted was to invite the police into his affairs. Godfrey Locker was still in hospital with massive concussion—he stayed there for weeks, and when he did get out he was facing a manslaughter charge. He never got right again after the accident, and within two years he was dead. That part I learned later on, bit by bit, from the Mullions."

Paul said, "It couldn't have gone better if God had planned it." He put his glass on the floor. "Except for the one man. Who would see it in the papers but could be sure of nothing." He got up and went to the table, poured himself another drink. "Except that he was sure." He looked Caro over, weighing her response as if it was her very body. "Many people—most people, perhaps—have done something shady, even criminal, but they still genuinely live within society. What I'm telling you is a different order. After that, one's life within society is an imposture." Paul sat again, holding his glass. "And that, to me, was fascinating, even thrilling."

Sometimes the curtains parted, exposing a dark rapid sky. The room was now nearly lightless.

"There was the terror of course, the horror even. But there was also elation—a sense of deceiving, and thus controlling, all mankind, of defying natural laws. A state of being strengthened, omnipotent, some mad analogy with what heroes must feel who've risked their lives to defy the state, and survived. All the mysteries had ranged themselves on my side. I lived with superfluous energies then—I began to rework my play and, with this reality in me, it was far better. It was then too I determined to marry Tertia. We didn't pretend love. She knew my duality of tastes. Each of us had something the other wanted—she wanted to retain social advantages but to break out of the mausoleum into something more amusing or bizarre, or perhaps into a new world that would give full rein to her capacity for boredom. And I wanted not just access to, but a safe place within, the fortress of rank. And you see, we both wanted everything several ways."

"Have you— Does Tertia know?"

"No. But one of the attractions of Tertia, for me, was that, if I had told her, she would not have been surprised. It would have been about what she expected." Paul leaned back, tapped a cushion over and over with his fingertips. "Sometimes I could hardly be sure I hadn't told her—she was so entirely convinced of the worst in me."

Perhaps they know the worst about each other: that can be a bond.

"After Victor's death I wanted more than ever to secure myself in the castle. It was a safeguard, the last place anyone would look for a suspect. In the castle, believe me, they look after their own. It was enough to have seen the way the police fixed on the wrong chap, that morning in my car—the way their eyes lit on the one that looked and spoke the part, and had nothing but his innocence to back him." Paul ceased tapping, and stared at Caro. "But you must have heard some of that at least, from him."

"From him?"

"From Tice."

Water was beating, pouring on the windows. Caro said aloud, "Oh God." She heard her voice cry out above the storm, "God. God."

"It was Tice on the bank. Of course it was Tice. You knew it was Tice." An accusation.

"Oh no."

"He must have told you. He had every incentive to tell you." Paul might have suspected some trick.

Caro pressed her hands together. "No."

Feeling streamed through the room like the high wind, like a banner. The woman was still, but it was as if she writhed.

"That was the first change in the luck. The only one, then. Driving down to Peverel that day, weeks later, when it was all behind me, and finding Tice there. The first sign that God's sense of humour might extend to me too. Tice standing by the car glaring at me with that cut-up eye, the whole scene re-enacted. I knew I should refer to it right off, our seeing one another at the river, if I was to put it over on him. And I could not. He waited and, because I couldn't mention it, was doubly certain. Christ Almighty, how I hated being in that house with him, sleeping under the same roof. Sharing a bathroom with my nemesis. Everything else had gone right but this one item, which showed there were other factors I couldn't control." Paul looked at Caro's pressed hands. "Then there was you."

He got up and closed the window against the rain. His rising and walking created a new stage. There was alarm for what he would next violate.

Caroline Vail felt an almost physical barrier to recognizing the role of Ted Tice. She, who had spoken to Paul of ignorance, must assess the ignorance in which she had passed passionate years of life. All pride and presumption, the exaltation of her own beliefs, the wish to be humane, the struggle to do well, were reduced to this: a middle-aged woman wringing her hands and calling on God.

She had wanted knowledge, but not to know this. Knowledge had become a fearful current in which a man might drown.

Paul Ivory was handling the curtain, stretching his arm to the unfamiliar window.

Caro had a revulsion to the presence of Paul in Adam Vail's house.

Recrossing the room, Paul said, "Well?"

"I am thinking how Adam would have hated this."

"I understood he went in for sinners. Or was it only out-laws?" Even now, in Paul, a flick of self.

"He condemned all forms of violence." A prim epitaph for a defunct clergyman, when in fact the feelings roused in her were animal: these chairs and tables withdrew from Paul, as did the furniture of this woman's memory. Paul had become everything shoddy, derelict; the torn kite unstuck from the sky. He could reduce, reduce, until there was nothing but the equipment of a dubious inn.

And this man's very possessions, for her, had once been radiant.

Paul sat. Drummed with fingers that were stalks or stems: evidence of love. A few months past, in Victoria Square, Caro's eyes had lingered on these hands. She had played, that evening, at being an old woman, knowing, complacent, reconciled. All her beneficent vanity now shrivelled to this.

She said, "Was it for revenge, then, on Ted—that you took up with me?"

"There was that in it, naturally. That I should carry you off while he stood once more impotently watching. Jealousy is in any case an expression of impotence, and his was compounded by the other frustration. There was the vengeance for his having shown up again in that fated way. And a turning of tables on Tertia, too, who had taken to parading her lovers in my face. Just then there was a chap in the Guards who used to spend weekends at the castle, he's dead now, dead long since. There was risk in both these things—in maddening Tice and antagonizing Tertia. And I liked the risk."

"Yes."

"You remember that. Experience was insipid without some risk or deception. With you, that changed. Because I had never expected that degree of attachment, to man or woman. That you could arouse it gave you influence, and created one more reason to throw you over that afternoon when Tertia found us in bed—when I could see my entire construction falling apart."

It was hard to see how Godfrey Locker could have been more brutal.

"That afternoon when we drove off, when we left you at the window, Tertia made me stop the car in the road. We went into the fields and she made me take her there on the ground. Setting her seal on me."

So each of them had gone, that day, from one partner to another. A chap in the Guards, he's dead now, dead long since.

"After that, I regained control. I worked on my play and it went well. Because of the heightened state I was in, every day was a revelation in what I could handle—I never worked so fast again, or so well." Paul remained interesting to himself. "They're right to keep parroting that it's my best play, I never had so much feeling to put into anything else. I wanted to fix the Lockers in the world's mind. I know it sounds grotesque, but I wanted the play to be a memorial to—"

He was about to say "Felix."

Quick gesture of erasure. "A monument to Victor. I hadn't loved him, or anybody, then, but I began to see him clearly—poor little rat that never had a chance. He didn't haunt me, and the experience itself was receding, as was the scratched eye of Ted Tice. Victor had died painlessly, without waking, as I'd wished it. Unless you began to wonder about the gushing and roaring, and the choking terror. The only haunting was done, once in a while, by Godfrey Locker. I never lost the fear of him, even after the Mullions told me he was dead. Sometimes even now I half-believe he's still alive, and have to calculate that he'd be ninety. He's one of those who can't die. Like Hitler.

"So it all went right. I knew the play was good, and there was the public success and money and the castle. When you turned up again, I was astonished how I wanted you, because I'd felt no lack. I thought it would soon wear out, but it worked the other way. Sometimes I couldn't stand to be away from you, everything else was insufficient. After the first year I began to wonder about divorcing Tertia and living with you. That brought its own reaction, since there was your remoteness from the underside of my nature. In that respect your love was disabling, as if you were forcing me to feel shame. When I had other strength, through work or some winning streak, I wanted to use it against you, to show I could withdraw, because otherwise I foresaw I would tell you everything. I'd tell you about Victor's death and put not only my safety but my very nature in your hands."

Lightning was a mad grin in the room, thunder a shudder over all the earth.

"Once again, something happened. One night you told me about Tice's crime, and it took him out of my life at a stroke, because now he could never raise the question of Victor without exposing himself. If his own secret came out, who'd ever employ him again, in his line of work? I wasn't such a fool as to think he'd kept quiet about me out of fear. One thing about vice is that it gives you a nose —and an eye and an ear—for virtue. How could I work if I'd only had my own character to go by? The very fact that there was a complex morality in it from Tice's point of view was a further guarantee of security." Paul paused, recovering the narrative from which he had digressed. He said, "You loved me enough, then, to accept anything I'd done, even murder."

"Yes."

"But I knew, since you'd told Tice's story, you'd ultimately tell mine. If I told you about Victor, one day you'd love someone else enough to confide in him."

"So I was doubly punished for that." If it had not been for the incontrovertible fact of Adam Vail, her life might decompose, obscenely, in her mind's eye.

"It was an entirely female thing to do. A timely warning. By then Tertia had caught on to your continued presence in my life, which displeased her most particularly. The length of the association, also, no doubt suggested I might leave her. She wanted the child, to set her stamp on me once more. I was glad enough to have it resolved, in a way—because I knew I couldn't go through with it: love, revelation, metamorphosis." He said this last word sardonically, but meant it. "I'd also taken up again with a boy, in a desultory way, part of the move away from you. The boy was called Valentine—his mother had been a fan of silent movies. He was passed on to me by an actor who appeared in my first two plays. That's how I came by him—a fox-faced little thing called Valentine."

"I remember him." A bubbling radiator, and the boy eating grapes.

"God knows where he is now."

I was glad enough to have it resolved. God knows where he is now. Caro's crossed bare legs were slipping off one another in a confluence of sweat and skin lotion and the dankness created by the storm. Sweat ran, breath rose and fell. In a cotton dress, the animal flutter of a heart.

"It is tempting, now, to plead my youth. But in any case I'm not pleading. And the capacity for excitement in such an experience was not something I expected, even then, to outgrow."

There were those who enlisted Death on their side, as stimulus or instrument: Paul, Dora, Charlotte Vail.

"The compulsion to tell was something quite arbitrary, alien, that came on me with Felix's trouble. That is something you can't foretell—that a state of mind will overtake you like an event. The confessory mood has an urgency not necessarily related to repentance—it may be a wish to implicate others. Ideally, one should confess to one's worst enemy, I suppose, since only he can truly give absolution. That would be Tice, in the present case." Paul said, "Otherwise, there is the sense of being weakened. Just as I felt empowered by Victor's death, the act of imparting it, now, to you, is a loss of strength, indecent as the crime." There was this overwhelming self in Paul, that his very sins were impressive to him. At that moment he felt nothing for Caro, who had received his necessary admission as she had once received his love, making no use of the authority it gave.

Paul said, "What I can't believe is that Tice never spoke

of it to you. Seeing you turn to me—and with that weapon to his hand. It's inconceivable. Anyone else would have told."

"Yes. No." Adam Vail might not.

"As it is, his silence makes him supreme. Silence tends to do that anyway, and this is an extreme case. A dated nobility"—Paul could still surprise with the precision of a word—"you might read of but can't believe in. I'd forgotten it was supposed to exist."

It was Tice on the bank, of course it was Tice. Caro could not assimilate Ted's role, or a terror of it. A dreaded circumstance, still to be resolved, on which the mind could scarcely bear to touch. Yet what could injure Edmund Tice, who was now supreme?

Unless it was herself she feared for. Knowledge had not finished with her yet.

"Barely credible," Paul said. "The self-command."

"Which leads to sovereign power."

He looked with some curiosity. "His ascendancy has come twenty years too late." He got up, took his jacket from the chair. "By now his own offence is very like virtue. That happens to any humane action, if you wait long enough. My trespasses, on the other hand, are only compounded with time and concealment." Speaking of himself at length had revived Paul's conviction of an importance from which Ted Tice must not detract. Exhausting his theme, he renewed his energies.

Until this day they might have imagined that, left alone in a room, they would embrace out of fateful continuity, as in a play, or fall in with some other dramatic suggestion. But such imitations had become unthinkable; and no truth would rise, in words, that had not already been outdone. Deprived of inarticulate possibilities—of weeping, or making love—neither knew how to conclude.

Drawing on his jacket, Paul was suggesting they reclaim their social selves. "You're to be in England in September?" His tone was ready to disavow what had taken place. His stare would dissolve the listening woman in the chair.

"On my way to Sweden."

"As of now," he said, "I cannot see ahead." He doubted he would wish to see Caro again in all his life. "You'll be staying with your sister?" It was remarkable how he could recover and clothe himself, in a jacket and normality, even now.

Caro saw him to the door. Following the storm, a sickly warmth; a humid sun pearling a film of gasoline on the steaming street. Rain-water swirled in sluggish gutters, re-depositing rubbish. As much as might be hoped for on a day when none could look for cleansing or refreshment, and in a place that seemed, itself, a sullen challenge to the elements.

"Caro, good-bye."

Paul took the subway at Seventy-seventh Street. In the train the hot air was substantial, the stench tangible. Streaked and scrawled, the walls gave way to rubber floor-ing that had been intermittently savaged. Shaped seats of a defaced plastic, hard as iron, confronted one another in long penitential rows. Underfoot, cigarette butts, smeared wrappings, the sports page crumpled on the rictus of a wealthy athlete. A beer can rolled from side to rocking side, the train careening, shrieking, racketing. Unable to reach a strap, Paul was supported on the denim flanks of three unsmiling girls. At the level of his eyes there were ranged the coloured imperatives of advertising: "Come to Where the Flavor Is," "Give to the College of Your Choice."

Everyone is thinking, a bit of danger. One of these sullen, standing men might present his own imperatives, Give me the bag, the wallet, the watch. Everyone has a bad com-plexion, acne, a rash; or a worn, unsupple skin, as if they had been down here too long. Pouches of bad air below the eyes. In this place, as in any hell, none has the advan-tage: briefcases give neither pathos nor immunity; a jewelled ornament is a target.

At Eighty-sixth Street, a withered woman in red flowers pushed aboard with surprising force. The doors closed, but the train remained stationary: an endurance test during which no one so much as sighed. A boy and girl, Puerto Rican, clung to a stained pole and shifted gum to kiss. Into the foul air, a loudspeaker gave out sound that was a shower of molten sparks from a blow torch. When the train started up, there was no murmur of surprise or relief.

These might have been the founders of a new race that disdained expression and was indifferent to cruelty or compassion, or their own dis-ease. If, here among them, Paul fell dead on the dirty floor, he would be no more than an obstacle to the exit. Similarly, no value was attached to his remaining, though sickened, on his feet.

A boy with frizzed head, like a small tree, got up from his seat: his arm a branch that reached, through interlacing limbs, to touch Paul's shoulder.

"Have a seat, Pop." This boy, being mortal, grinned around the car. He could not help his better nature, or his worse. And had not ceased to crack a double-jointed thumb.

Paul slid into place. Aware of an unaccountable exception, but incapable of thanks.

In her house, Caroline Vail was opening the letter, in purple ink and an unfamiliar hand, from Ireland.

"Without wishing to disturb your peaceful existence, I feel you will want to know of Dora's trouble, or plight. . . ."

36

Grace said, "She loses the sense of time."

Grace and Caro were driving, in Grace's little car, to visit Charmian Thrale. Christian had had his way, and his mother was in a place, for old people, called Oak Dene, or Forest Manor, or Park View.

"One moment she remembers the boys' birthdays, everything. The next, she imagines Chris and I are newly married." The car turned in between brick gateposts. "They say it's circulation."

Parched grass was dying, in the dry, exceptional September.

The directress of the institution was something more than capable. Tall, grey, reticent, she maintained a sensible distance and would not accept Caroline Vail's affinity, even by a glance. If you once got into that, there'd be no end to it. Caro was a sister again, walking with Grace down a tiled corridor: they were two women doing womanly things. It was a relief, occasionally, to appear conventional, blameless; even to the cool eye of a grey headmistress—in this case, of a finishing school.

These two had walked by the salt sea after school. Now it was mortality that expanded, an immensity, at their side.

Grace said, "You'd think they'd find some way to disguise that disinfectant."

Charmian Thrale was in a section reserved for ambulatory residents. The floor matron was brittle, corseted, a wooden barque enclosed in an iron hull. She said it meant everything to have visitors. They were shown to a tiny bedroom where Charmian sat in a chintz chair, hands extended on arm-rests. Her hair was white and scant, her huge eyes scarcely blue; her body fleshless, a mere coat-hanger for cotton sleeves and shoulders, the neck a wire hook for the dandelion head.

The window gave onto a vegetable patch tended by the active inmates. There was a hard, ugly plant in a pot on the inside sill. The mirrored door of a wardrobe hung open. On the bedside table, a wedding photograph of Grace and Christian. Beside bottles of pills, there was a small stick, tipped with soiled cotton, of the kind used to clean out ears. On the bed, a pair of gold-rimmed spectacles lay beside a book.

Grace kissed her mother-in-law, and said, "Here's Caro." There was the temptation to raise one's voice. "Caro's on her way to Sweden, to see her stepdaughter."

Charmian Thrale said, "I loved my stepmother dearly. It is cruel that stepmothers should be stigmatized."

Grace said, "The same goes for mothers-in-law." And the old woman touched her cheek with a variegated hand.

The matron shouted, "Been making ourselves pretty." Charmian looked with polite amusement, or terrible cynicism. Her curved cotton back touched the chair. She would never, herself, have chosen a dress of conflicting colours. Her face had been powdered by somebody, even rouged. In the wardrobe mirror Caro and Grace were reflected— smiling, still blessed. Now get you to my lady's chamber and tell her, let her paint an inch thick, to this favour she must come. Make her laugh at that.

"She must see her telly show at eleven, she's quite set on it." The matron beamed. Charmian Thrale was an intractable infant who had at last taken an encouraging turn.

The old woman said with calm lucidity, "It's a programme on a poet, Rex Ivory. I met him several times, and Sefton knew him well."

"Think of that." The matron could not recall who was Poet Laureate now that John Masefield had passed away.

When the matron went out Charmian Thrale said, "When you are old, you are presumed to be a sage or an imbecile. Nothing is permitted in between."

Caro said, "Life is all a bit like that."

Helped to her feet, Charmian Thrale was a fragile construction that might crumple, ashes whose tended flicker must not ignite for fear of finality. Grace and Caro supported her into the corridor. Through an open door an ancient voice, high-pitched, cried out, "No, please, oh, no." In a wheelchair a man like driftwood put his fingertips together and reedily sang:

> *"Two German officers crossed the Rhine,*
> *Parlay-voo,*
> *To kiss the women and drink the wine,*
> *Parlay-voo."*

In an inner room, where empty chairs sat in judgment, a television set was in a frenzy. Grace expertly turned a dial. Bars of colour moved horizontally, voices snapped on and off. An announcer in a toupée grinned and gave the time. Coloured dots scampered. To the music of Delius, a sweet countryside was revealed in tropical shades; and off-screen a voice said, reverentially, "Derbyshire."

A young man with a glottal stop felt that the programme about to be shown had particular interest in view of the current Rex Ivory revival. A trained solemnity, together with horn-rimmed glasses, suggested special courses in cultural presentation. Photographs were reproduced on the screen—a purple baby, a schoolboy, a youth in military uniform, a middle-aged wraith in a cardigan; and close up, the title page of a book. Viewers would recall that a copy of this slim volume dated 1915 and inscribed by the author had recently fetched a high sum at auction.

With perfect self-possession, Charmian Thrale laughed.

On screen, a plump man with white sideburns was introduced as the godfather of the Rex Ivory boom. On sabbatical from the United States, Professor Wadding was enjoying the deserved success of his brilliant critical biography, a copy of which was now held up to public view: *Abnegation as Statement: Symbol and Sacrament in the Achievement of Rex Ivory*. Already a modern classic. Doctor Wadding had suspended his groundbreaking work on the Lake Poets so that Rex Ivory might benefit from critical elucidation.

Professor Wadding explained that he had by no means set Wordsworth aside: "Have no fear of that." But recalled that, during his visit to Britain in 1946, he had met and interviewed Rex Ivory. He had written to the poet on an impulse, and received a most gracious answer inviting him to Derbyshire. "To think now," he said, "that I hesitated."

"Cold feet, Doctor Wadding?"

Professor Wadding explained that the expression "cold feet" derived from the occasion on which the Emperor Henry IV stood waiting in the snow at Canossa for Pope Gregory VII, in 1077. In his own case, hesitation had been due, rather, to doubts over the injection of the personal factor into the critical-creative dialogue.

"And you have never wavered, Doctor Wadding, in your critical assessment?"

Grace said, "They keep calling him Doctor."

Charmian Thrale said, "Like Doctor Goebbels."

Professor Wadding maintained that Rex Ivory had given cognitive meaning to an ethics of renunciation. He would classify Rex Ivory as aristocratic, patrician, prestigious, and arguably the most major poet of his generation.

Caro said, "His suit can't really be that colour."

Wadding's spectacles glinted. "My task, as I see it, is to adumbrate the sources of his entelechy."

A publisher was introduced, and described as the most painful moment of his entire professional career a postwar Saturday morning on which his firm had discovered that paper was lacking for an intended edition of *The Half-Reap'd Field*. "It is not too much to say that, as a firm, we were heartbroken." Thankfully, they now had the privilege of bringing out Doctor Wadding's brilliant work.

A boy wearing a band round his forehead recounted Rex Ivory's rise as a poet of the antiwar movement. He felt that Rex's message to the young might be summarized as, "Keep the Faith, Baby."

That phrase, Professor Wadding explained, was an invocation of the Christ Child. He would be interested to know what contemporary role might be assigned to a poet such as Wordsworth.

The boy shrugged. "To me, he's a name on a sweatshirt." He said, "Rex comes on like he's laid-back. He's a very laid-back guy. And this I like."

The speakers looked out at the unseen audience to gauge the effects of their calculations.

"As if," said Grace, "they are watching us, rather than we them."

Footage was replayed of the BBC's postwar interview in the Dukeries—the Sealyhams and flowered borders, a dim library, Rex Ivory's thin face, sparse hair, pale lashes. His elevated fingertips pressing tobacco in a pipe, eyes blinking at each tap: a synchronized toy. After the fictitious colours of the introduction, the black and white looked like truth.

Caro said, "Sepia would be even better."

The old film flickered, blinking like the poet. Ivory had a light, meticulous voice from another century. Though responding politely, volunteered no information. The first influence he recalled was a leather-bound copy of *Sohrab and Rustum,* given him by a beloved aunt for his seventh birthday: "I can still recite the entire work—by heart, as the fine saying goes."

The questioner hastily interposed, "So had it not been for the accident of your aunt's generosity—"

"Generosity is not something that happens by accident."

The interviewer smiled, but hoped to get even. "Our most eminent critic has said that only the literature that changes society will last. I take it you reject that view?"

"As to lasting," said Rex Ivory, "that is any man's guess."

"Of course. But the critic in question has maintained that our century is uniquely receptive to the moral persuasion of literature. And has charged you with a failure, as he puts it, to perceive this as an obligation."

Ivory's pale lashes drooped. He might have been asleep, or in some predicament. At last he said, "I was in the trenches, you see. And he was not."

Colour flowed back like violence. Doctor Wadding interjected, "I believe I can elucidate here." Grace turned off the sound and said, "Surely they will bring Paul into it."

Mrs. Thrale remarked, "Paul Ivory's son has been very ill."

"Christian heard he is holding his own amazingly."

At that moment, Paul was introduced. Grace restored the sound. Paul's appearance was now beginning to separate, like an unwholesome substance. Eyes, mouth, and expression were no longer quite complementary: a composite portrait of a suspect or fugitive. Thinner, older, no less charming, he did these public things with greatest ease.

"My father was a pure spirit, an innocent. He had old-fashioned virtues—self-sacrifice, self-effacement, charity, civility. Fidelity to unfashionable ideals. I am not like that myself, but I had—and have—enormous respect for him and for his work."

Caro, too, might have been sleeping. The jar of Marmite on the table. We're hungry enough here, too.

Adam Vail had said, "They will put the great mysteries to service."

Paul gracefully turned aside an allusion to his own work: "After all, we're here to celebrate my father." Invited to assess Rex Ivory's literary standing, he was both open and judicious: "Perhaps he was not a great poet. But he was a true poet."

Charmian Thrale looked at the screen with extreme politeness. On the reappearance of Professor Wadding, she asked that it be extinguished.

Helped back to her room, she sat in the flowered chair. She said, "Rex was the only one left alive. It was the others who looked dead." And closed her eyes.

Christian was standing in the hallway when Grace and Caro returned. He was surprised to think that of these two women, who were both beautiful, one was his wife.

"Ready for tea," he said, "by the look of you."

Grace went to the kitchen, and could be heard filling the kettle. Caro stood in the hall. She had a bright scarf on her head, peacock colours, and put up her hand to draw it off. Below her lifted arm, the soft dress clung; and Christian, thinking of a cat's supple side, could imagine placing his hand there.

"Well, Caro, you keep yourself trim. I must say."

So I'm at the stage of You keep yourself trim. She was loosening the silk scarf.

"What colour would you call it, that dress?"

"Burnt Sienna."

"Haven't heard that one since I was a nipper with a paintbox." Christian, like his father before him, had taken certain expressions in protective custody.

Caro completed the gesture with the scarf. Her heavy hair tumbled about her shoulders. There was scarcely any grey. Christian wondered, Is it dyed? There was a novel—

the name would come to him—in which a youthful love, encountered in age, revealed her white hair. The idea that Caro's hair might now be dyed shocked Christian, as it seemed to him, no less. He stared.

Caro said, "It is natural, as yet."

She went into the living-room and, walking to the empty fireplace, leaned an elbow on the mantel. An oval mirror Grace had bought at Bath reproduced her fatigue. Make her laugh at that.

The kettle shrieked in the kitchen, and was silenced. These days one was always switching on or off.

Christian fell into a chair, which gave an upholstered sigh.

Grace came in with tea on a tray. There were small sandwiches, a cake. The three of them sat—Caro and Christian facing each other, and Grace between. There was warm light at the windows and in the bronze of Caro's dress.

"Well, this is very comfy." Christian approved the domestic scene as a reliable substitute for happiness. The women said, of his mother, what he would wish to hear; and he responded, "This place is first-rate. Absolutely first-rate."

Caro said, "Your mother has great fortitude." The obituary phrase consigned Charmian Thrale to the earth: After a long life borne with much fortitude.

When Grace described the television programme, Christian said, "Good Lord, Rex Ivory. He gave me *The Golden Treasury* when I turned ten. National monument now, is he?—Could I have a sandwich?—Well, that does make me feel old."

Grace handed a plate.

"What's in them?"

"Watercress."

"A wee bit fibrous for me, I'm afraid."

"The others are fish-paste."

Christian helped himself. "Good old fish-paste." He brushed at crumbs. "I've still got it somewhere, *The Golden Treasury*." When Grace got up to fetch hot water, he said, "I'll take my second cup in the study."

He went into the adjoining room, where weekend work lay on his desk. There was always something new from

Africa. Through open double doors the two women saw, or watched, him unfold a newspaper and stretch himself in an easy chair.

From her place on the sofa, Caro looked on while Grace took Christian his tea. Grace's chin was no longer quite defined, nor her waist. Beneath the clasp of a necklace, her nape was slightly humped. Caro was seeing her sister more tenderly than she had ever done: childhood closeness had always seemed suspended, as though it might resume. In childhood memories, Grace was always kind. Caro thought it rare that a child should be kind.

The dichotomy between them might have stood for more: they had exercised so little influence on each other's lives, and exchanged few confidences. It was not even clear now, as formerly, that Grace was satisfied with chintz and china—with Christian saying "A wee bit fibrous," or hoisting his trousers at evening and announcing, "Must get my eight hours." It was not quite certain Grace had remained a spectator. Those who had seen her as Caro's alter ego might have missed the point.

Grace had presumably passed through an experience that could only be love; or had some inward revelation. Paul Ivory had said, "A state of mind can overtake you like an event."

In Caroline Vail's own life and thought, Ted Tice had become supreme. Consciousness of Ted Tice was the event that pervaded her waking and sleeping life. His greatest strength had been his secret; his very truth enclosed his mystery.

Caro had been dwelling on memory, and on possibilities remote as memories. For the first time, had dreams in which she and Ted met as lovers, in a vivid, unfamiliar land. She would lie awake and think how little, even of kindness, she had ever given him; would remember light, flat, callous words, worthy of Paul Ivory. Ted had shown her her own image, and she had said, "I don't recall that dress."

She thought how she could go to him, and yet would not. She imagined her arrival, his happiness. His streaked eye, his joy.

She pictured Margaret Tice in her golden beauty. Caro looked into her own mirror, clothed or naked, aware of pathos. Aware of women before her who had done the same. Her body was a dress, now for years unworn, unshown; unknown.

She knew his illusion might fall away. Yet it was terrible that she might go to him, and would not.

Caro had walked in the streets and thought about Ted Tice. She had sat to her work and feared to die without seeing him again. One day she had written on the page where she was working: "If he came now, I would do whatever he asked."

If Ted were to die, the world would be a room where no one looked at her.

She had no more control over these fantasies than she had had over the bodily changes of adolescence. She tried to see how it had come about, and only knew she had been seeking some extreme. That extreme might be the force, pure and terrible, of a man's attested strength of will. It was as if Ted Tice had created this event in her through the cosmic power of love.

She was helpless to change, though not to act.

Caro said to Grace, "I'm considering a trip to Australia."

"Any particular reason?"

"I find I remember it more these days. That seems to create a reason to go there." She said, "Would you come with me?"

Grace asked, "For a few weeks, would it be?"

They were speaking in lowered voices. Christian, if he heard the sound, would assume they were discussing ailments and be reassured by their subjection.

Caro said, "I'd like to see what I was incapable of seeing then." Of all she had been blind to, at least that much might be retrieved.

Grace relived, in an instant, certain summer nights—walking through a dark house, every door and window wide for air. An entire city turned, expectant, towards the sea. She said, "To see the Pacific again."

"Do you remember, when we were little, Mother would sit out in a cane chair on the lawn at dusk, while we played?" Caro was stroking, as if maternally, the sleeve of her own bronze dress. "There was a trellis of climbing roses, a row of hollyhocks, the lemon tree, and the swing.

Mother would sit out on summer evenings in a garden chair, and watch us." She meant, Watch over us.

Grace said, "That was Dora."

Grace got up and went into the next room. She asked Christian, "Did you call me?"

"I was only yawning."

As she turned away, he said, "You can take the paper, there's nothing in it."

Several times, in the mornings or evenings, Grace had put aside what she was doing and turned to her husband. She had left the dishes in the sink and gone upstairs to find him. Once he was using his electric razor, and could not hear her; another time, his Water-Pik.

Christian was glad to be rid of the newspaper, in which there was a letter, on treaties, signed simply "Elphinstone." For Elphinstone, who had received a peerage in the honours list of a departing prime minister, now wrote frequently on public matters. At the time of the peerage, Christian had swallowed his pride and telephoned to congratulate. Greeted kindly enough by Mrs.—or Lady—E., he had heard a background voice say, "For God's sake don't put me on."

Christian told Grace, "I can't get excited because Elphinstone slept with somebody at Downing Street."

Grace returned to the living-room carrying the newspaper. She sat on the sofa at Caro's side. "I meant to show you this."

There was a photograph of scientists leaving a government conference. Flanked by politicians, Ted Tice looked straight ahead. He had the private, civilized face one sees on the interpreter between two grimacing heads of state.

"You see that he'll be in Sweden while you're there." Grace read out that Professor Tice would present a paper on the controversial theme. Grace had an advantage here, having learned, from her sons, about black holes, red shift, the Big Bang. "I daresay you knew."

"I haven't called Ted this time."

Grace watched while Caro handled the tassel of a cushion. She said, "So much happens in your life."

"It happens only to me. Your life has meaning for others." Caro had never seen Grace shrug before. She went on, "How can a life be motiveless when others depend on it?"

Grace smiled. "Abnegation as statement." Neither of them had forgotten the nursing home, the television screen; how Charmian Thrale had said, "They are already dead," of those who had lost track of their own absurdity. Grace suddenly asked, "Did you love Paul Ivory?"

"Yes."

"I suppose it ended badly."

"Yes."

"You must have been very unhappy."

"I died; and Adam resurrected me." Intending to say this lightly, Caro gave in to deadly earnest. They were throwing caution to the winds, as their only outlet for violent feeling.

"I saw you once in the street together. The way you kept apart, not to be seen touching." Grace said, "I wish I'd known. Or helped. But you did not—could not depend on me for your stability."

"What help, for that matter, was I to you?" ·

"Oh—by then I was presumed stabilized." Same smile, neither bitter nor complacent.

Caro said, "Can I help you now?"

"No."

They sat, inclined towards each other, and exchanged some pain for a tragedy not exclusively theirs. Grace got up and went to the piano, as to a haven. Then turned and looked at Caro. "At first, there is something you expect of life. Later, there is what life expects of you. By the time you realize these are the same, it can be too late for expectations." What we are being, not what we are to be. They are the same thing.

Caro said, "I don't know that suspense ever ends." The suspense of life itself, then the expectation of death. Valda had once said, "There's the waiting." By suspense, women meant the desire to love, be loved: great expectations. "Even small expectations are part of the larger uncertainty —waiting for an arrival, a phone call, a letter."

Grace said, "A letter is the worst."

Grace stood by the piano, facing Caro. Had she turned away, Caro would have got up to embrace her, would have said, "Darling," like a lover. As it was, they remained in place, looking at one another.

Grace said, "Is there someone, now, whom you love?" When Caro did not answer, she went on, "Because you seem more handsome to me now than you ever were."

"I was remembering," Caro said, "that you were generous even as a child." Not something that occurs by accident.

Grace stood by the piano, listening.

Caro said, "If Ted calls." The corners of her lips were not quite civilized. It seemed she might not speak again. High feeling was ultrasonic, audible. "If Ted Tice rings up, I don't want him to know I'll be in Sweden. Or to see him there."

Grace had not foreseen her sister could develop such a mouth. But was thinking of the letter—instant, full, unflawed by delay—that could never now arrive. Or of the letter paid by particular suffering—a slow, inward bleeding of hope and humiliation—that likewise could not exist. There might be eventual word, by then unawaited, noncommittal; a fleeting touch on the wound. Meantime, she had learned to shrug.

Grace had discovered that men prefer not to go through with things. When the opposite occurred, it made history: Something you'll remember always.

She said, "Women have to go through with things. Birth, for instance, or hopeless love. Men can evade forever."

There were exceptions—Ted Tice, or her own son. It would be dreadful if Rupert were to lay down his life, as Ted had done. Dreadful, and not unlikely.

Light came through long windows, there was a scent from stock in a vase. Two women were silent, one seated, one standing. While a man slept, like a baby, in an adjoining room.

37

He asked at the desk. She had gone out. The hotel lobby
was overwarm with a noon of endless summer, and flamed
up here and there in lit vitrines displaying silver jewellery
and curved objects in glass or wood. Ted sat down in a
leather chair, holding but not reading a magazine: a detective commanding the approaches. Couples on their way
to elevators glanced at this angular, watchful man; at
his high forehead and blemished eye.

A heavy tourist in American seersucker stumbled short-
sightedly on Ted Tice's feet. A woman came out of a
phone booth, smiling. A slim boy was pulled past by two
leashed poodles.

Ted went back to the desk, wrote a message, wrote her
name. The concierge remarked on the exceptional weather,
regretting the drought. Ted said, "In London this morning
it was raining."

The concierge had seen this man's lean face in a newspaper, in connection with a university ceremony. The reference to drought was his polite, encoded tribute. Later
that week he was to tell his family, "He was in the hotel on
Tuesday. Large as life."

Edmund Tice was approaching the peak of his career.

Ted went outside on the quay and looked at the harbour: the small ships, the Finland boat, a row of ferries
offering excursions on lakes or canals. Large sky, clear
light. He could not properly recall Caro's appearance,
having too much remembered it. He stood at the edge of
the waterfront, passing the last moments of thirty years.

Yesterday Grace had said on the phone, "So little time
is left to tell the truth."

He stood in the sun, bleaching like all north Europe. The Swedish earth was blowing like fine sand: a world passing on the wind, seeping away, pulverizing. In the countryside, birches were leaning to the ground, dying in shallow soil. Only the sea stayed sceptical, an arctic blue: the same salt and tarry smells, the scavenging gulls.

It was said the drought would alter topography forever. This was untrue: the earth would reassert itself within a year.

When he returned to the hotel, Caro was at the desk asking for her key. Holding out her hand to receive his message.

He stood at a little distance, watching this dark stranger. Who would turn and be fully known at last.

He was handing her into the boat, which was open, with rows of wooden seats, like a small bus. All varnished inside, and the varnish sticky with salt and sun. Scarcely a dozen passengers, but twice that number of circular life-belts painted with the name of the boat, the umlaut picked out in red.

Caro said, "Though you wouldn't drown in a canal."

"It's the sea, really. A waterway of the sea." There was a sign, in three languages: the ferry made a tour of the canals twice daily, as long as the weather lasted.

She had said, "Let's go out." Had walked out on the quay where there were no enclosing walls, no doors, curtains, or beds. She had stood exposed in the sunlight and said, "We can take the boat." They boarded a ship that would not turn back at their bidding. These were her last decisions. Setting this boat in motion, she became inactive.

She sat on a slatted bench and tied a scarf on her hair, the same bright scarf that Christian had admired one week ago. At her side Ted Tice was watching her movements which seemed, even to her, to have special accuracy and meaning: gestures in dream. It was she who filled his eyes, and not the sea.

A man in uniform threw his cigarette in the ocean, and spat. With that signal, the engines started up. There was white churning of water, and a barefoot boy released the rope by which they had all been tethered. At the very last, a pair of tourists ran up with a child and were taken aboard with some clamour—shouts, leaps, gasps, and a bit of clanking. An English family, the man girlish, the woman like a man, the child a cherub: choosing places in the sun, they were pink, self-conscious, but laughing for this rightful outcome to their moment of urgency and rescue. At the outset, a happy ending.

The boat sailed, leaving behind a palace, an opera house, a museum, a fortress; bridges, turrets, prisons, spires. A city fully equipped. Activity ceased to be interruption, and made part of the flow. They were moving in the light of a past or other world. The scene, too, in its humane dimensions, was experienced, discoloured, flawed, lacking the modern gloss. Or it was they who lacked the modern retina that gives precision to old scenes and makes them, like the coloured reproductions of great paintings, sharper, brighter, less resplendent than their originals.

The ferry rocked in the wash of a small steamer. The child squealed in delight at this new emergency, having learned that all dangers are surmounted. Ted and Caro were flung against each other, and did not part.

He said, "I was thinking, before you came, that I hardly knew what you look like. I'd lost the image with picturing it." He had stood in the hotel lobby, and she had turned: a look greater than recognition.

Caro said, "I have never been so glad to see any human face." Staring now at the grooves and shadows of his face with great curiosity, as one consciousness might seek another in the moment before death or battle: the crisis of existence so closely shared, indivisible. The self supreme, yet helpless.

The boat was slowly turning into a passage of the sea, calm and narrow, where ivy covered a low embankment and trees sloped towards water. Gliding by, they could see smooth lawns among the trees, and square white houses. Fair men and women walked in dry gardens and looked at the boat, shading their eyes. A youth sat in a cane chair, holding an open book. Caro took off her watch—her own watch, a woman's watch on a small gold strip. Laying it on her lap, she reached her fingers down to the water. Ted took up the watch. It was a way of holding her, the little circlet warm as if alive.

When she withdrew her hand from the sea, he dried it and held it in his own.

"Until now I never touched you."

"No."

Ted Tice said, "Will you say you love me?"

"With all my heart."

The man looked at the trees lolling in white water. These trees were in his eyes, in streaks, in tears. "It is hard to imagine any stroke that could take that from me."

She said, "My dear."

"My dear." He was trying her endearment on his tongue, an act of love.."I was never with you on the water before." Making the elements bear witness.

He put his hand to her hair, and the scarf slithered back. When the colours fell from her head, it seemed some resilience left her. Having been serene, obedient, she now grew solemn and obscure. He could see her pondering, in a moment, the coming hours and years that were closed to her, unknowable. Only he could know, having prepared for this always. He had been so long creating this moment that it could not be new to either of them.

In the gliding boat he was watching brightness slip away. He said, "Trust me." He proposed his love to her as wisdom, even genius. As if he knew, and she did not.

The passengers saw the Royal Canal, as they had wished to do, but also saw these two who represented love. Pale woman, with her dark hair blown. A man's tender arm along the back of the seat, his other hand clasping hers. The sweetness that all longed for night and day. Some tragedy might be idly guessed at—loss or illness. She had the luminosity of those about to die.

They were passing close to shore where an old ship lay in drydock, a wooden vessel raised, after centuries, from the ocean floor: figurehead, decks, sterncastle. Built of oak and pine, named for a king; carried to the bottom by her bronze overload of cannon; grappled back to earth as a plaything. The child stood on a seat to look, and was told the story of planks and sea-chests, pewter dishes and coins of gold or silver marked with a crown. And was confirmed once more in a belief of survival.

The boat sailed through a broader waterway. Caro told

Paul Ivory's story. It was as Paul had said: One day you will love someone else and tell my story.

Years ago, sitting on a wall, she herself had assured a callow boy, Things come round so strangely.

She asked him, "Have you ever met again the German you helped in the war?" It was the first time she had referred to this.

"Many times."

"And have never identified yourself?"

"No. Nor of course has he recognized me—even with this eye." Ted said, "He is so confident, alert, assertive, and I observe him from our common, unshared secret. Like God. It gives authority I would not forgo. In spite of all his wakefulness, he sleeps, and I watch him."

"Was this what you felt towards me, then, with Paul?"

"I never had, or wished for, power over you. That isn't true, of course. I wanted the greatest power of all. But not advantage, or authority."

"I've been thinking, these past weeks, of the summer when we met. I remember whole days, whole conversations. Or am inventing them."

"Sefton Thrale, the telescope." The past that Ted Tice, for a lifetime, had inhabited alone. They were trying to discover what had led to this, and never would. They were briefly innocent as any pair of lovers. "Now they are speaking of telescopes of many metres, and of platforms in space."

"It might be a way of discarding the earth, out of pique."

"Because we couldn't make it work, you mean?"

"Because it was too good and great for us."

The ferry was beginning to turn, in order to take them back. It made a wide, gradual arc, the slow water fanning in its wake. They had taken long to come out, but would return quickly. Once the curve was completed there was the nervous change, the engines stronger and louder. The passengers, too, had had enough of loving-kindness, and were overheated besides. The child ran rashly from side to side of the boat, as if he would tip it up, and called out in a precise little voice insistent questions about the bottom of the sea.

"Josie will be waiting at the hotel." It was again as if

Caro went out a door and boarded a boat. She asked, "How far must you go?"

"About eighty kilometres. They're sending a car to fetch me." That evening and the following day, a university was to celebrate Ted Tice's achievement. "I have to speak there tomorrow afternoon. Then they all go on, these people, to Rome and Sicily, where there is a conference." He said, "I will do what you choose, and go wherever you are."

Caro watched the child. Josie's baby, held that day in her arms, would presently stride about a deck and have questions no one could answer. She did not look at Ted but at the child and at the world to which they were returning.

"They would manage without me," he said, "if I died." He did not mean the conference, but the world. "Why not if I live?"

She did not know whether strength would be to accept or deny.

Ted said, "I'm afraid to leave you, to lose you." He looked down her profile, as once when they had sat in a country bus. Same line of coarse hair, deeper hollows of dark eyes. In a summer dress, her breast was the realization of desire. "You won't run away. When I call you in the morning, you'll be there."

Don't die, don't disappear.

"Yes."

"In any case I'd find you."

The windows of her room gave on the water. Women through curtains of coarse linen, the early light was tinted, rose as the flesh that webs a finger or circles an ear.

For the last time, Caroline Vail lay in a bed alone.

"Have you slept?"

She was lying back on pillows, holding the telephone. "I kept waking, to think of this. To think of you."

"It's new for me, to imagine that."

In their speech they were already joined.

Ted said, "I haven't slept."

The curtain had a design of scrolled tendrils and flowers like stars. From the quay below, exhaust of an early bus, the whistle from a boat, the wheeling, heeling cries of seabirds. Dim light illuminated a woman in bed.

He said, "I am happier than I have ever been."

She could see herself in a mirror, turned on her side. Slight groove between the breasts, hair streaking a pillow. Pale silk, white shoulders, everything one's heart could desire.

She loved and desired herself, as if she were Edmund Tice. As if this were a self from which she too must part forever.

He said, "I am happier than I have ever been."

"That might be enough. That is fullfilment." Where the mirrored door of a wardrobe hung open, she saw herself reflected. She said, "Some of that will last."

"If you left, I'd find you." He asked, "With this possibility, shall I live out my time like others, wondering and withering and numbering my dead? Congratulating myself on my close escape from life?" He said, "I will soon be with you."

When she got up she held aside the curtain, and looked at the street and the harbour. She thought how she had been a child beside the sea, and then a woman in high rooms like rooms in dreams, and tangled gardens. She thought of continents and cities, men and women, words, the beloved. Josie's child. As if she listed every graceful moment of her life, to offer in extenuation.

"I said I'd find you"

In the airport, a total absence of morning, climate, and substance. There was white light, thin air, and a sign that said "Departures."

"I'd have been gone, but for the strike." She was leaning on the check-in counter. She put her hand in his. "There's a strike at the other end."

"I thank God and the trade-union movement."

"Modern love."

In front of them a man was saying, "You will find I am listed VIP."

A uniformed girl moved her pencil down a row of names. "Are you VIP first, second, or third category?"

"You will discover I am not an unimportant person."

Caro was next in line. Ted Tice prevented a porter from taking her baggage. "Come away from here and talk to me."

They sat in plastic chairs. There was a sign that said "Passengers in Transit." Ted touched her face. "In one hour there's a flight for Rome." He made it so simple, words of one syllable. "If you take it, I'll join you there by evening." He was swift, unhurried, indestructible. "I'll stay and give my talk this afternoon. With the charter plane I can be in Rome this evening."

"Ted." She began to cry like a child. "Ted, what can change for us?"

"Something has changed."

Like a child, she stopped crying from curiosity or dread. "I have telephoned Margaret. I've told her."

It was as when, on the boat, brightness fell from her hair. She said, "The misery," and leaned against his arm. She left off weeping, in deference to another's tears. As if told of a battle, joined far off, in which many must die.

Ted was exercising great kindness: she must be helped through this. Despite himself, his strength blazed like rejoicing. It was hard to believe so much misfortune must attach to it. He had his arm round her, his hand resting on her breast. He thought how she had been proud and decided, and would be again. And that she was here leaning and weeping, and loving him best.

They were natural and supernatural, in that blank place, like amorous figures from mythology.

When she sat up, she wiped her eyes and said, "My love."

He stroked back her hair. He said, "I'll go and get the ticket," and his own mouth trembled on prosaic words. He took out paper and a pencil, and wrote the name of a hotel in Rome. They exchanged the name, and already saw the south.

Beyond the departure gate there was an arrangement like a door frame where passengers were searched—for gold, perhaps, or guns. Handbags were set on a moving counter, and slid out through a little chute.

Caro remembered the barrier where she had last said good-bye to Edmund Tice. She had stood with a crowd on a shifting stair and raised her hand, and he had watched her go. There was an earlier farewell, when he had told her, "I will accept any terms," and she had stood remote, not knowing it for a rehearsal.

The passengers passed through the disembodied doorway, one by one. There was a woman in pink linen: "Does this machine spoil pearls?"

They became competitive as to what might be spoiled: "Will it affect my pacemaker?" "What about radiation?" At the little chute, a man in tweeds leaped to save a tumbling carton.

"Got the crown jewels in there?"

"It's a rather lovely tea-service, actually."

They were claiming, clutching, harbouring: departure was doing this. There was one man, heavy, pale, familiar, who wore American seersucker and used a leather bag as a battering ram. He did not greet Caro, and might have been myopic. This was the doctor from New York who had proposed she wear glasses.

Paul that day in the hot street saying, "Caro?" Paul in her own doorway saying, "Caro, good-bye."

She could recall farewells on ocean liners. The lunch on board, which Dora did not enjoy. Streamers, handkerchiefs, the world before a war. The great shape passing through the Heads on its leisurely way to heaven.

"Your flight," they said. All the while she was looking back, in case Ted should be there. "Your flight is boarding."

On the plane she was shown to a seat by the window. Beyond the runway you could see a grove of spruces, dark, reclusive, genuine. On the airfield the technicians were gesturing with hands and flags. Their blond hair and blue clothes were blown in the slipstream. They wore devices to shield their ears from the roar.

The roar could be seen, reverberating on blue overalls, surging into the spruces. Within the cabin, nothing could be heard. Only, as the plane rose from the ground, a long hiss of air—like the intake of humanity's breath when a work of ages shrivels in an instant; or the great gasp of hull and ocean as a ship goes down.

ABOUT THE AUTHOR

SHIRLEY HAZZARD has written five other books: four works of fiction *(Cliffs of Fall, The Evening of the Holiday, People in Glass Houses,* and *The Bay of Noon);* and *Defeat of an Ideal,* a study of the United Nations, where she worked for some years. Many of her short stories have been published in *The New Yorker;* her work has received, among other recognition, a First Prize in the O. Henry Short Story awards.

Shirley Hazzard was born in Australia. She now lives in New York with her husband, Francis Steegmuller.